2015

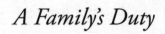

A Family's Duty

By Maggie Bennett

The Carpenter's Children
A Family's Duty

A Family's Duty

MAGGIE BENNETT

Allison & Busby Limited
12 Fitzroy Mews
London W1T 6DW
www.allisonandbusby.com

First published in Great Britain by Allison & Busby in 2013.

Copyright © 2013 by MAGGIE BENNETT

A CIP catalogue record for this book is available from
the British Library.

First Edition

ISBN 978-0-7490-1378-3

Typeset in 11/16 pt Sabon by
Allison & Busby Ltd.

To my dear grandson,
George Kirill Bees

CHAPTER ONE

1938

Sir Cedric Neville preferred to cover the four miles between Everham Magistrates' Courts and Hassett Manor on horseback, rather than take the infrequent train service. It was a perfect day in May, but Neville's thoughts were not on the verdant Hampshire countryside all around him. He had seen half a dozen cases that morning, and heard pleas of guilty from the drunk and disorderly, petty thieves and a couple of women whose public fight had resulted in a black eye for one and a split lip for the other. He had judged them to be about equally matched, and had cautioned them both for their 'disgraceful behaviour'. Both had children under school age, and he therefore let them go with a warning of a fine if they came before him again. A drunken tramp had been fined five shillings, and another allowed to go free with a caution, because Neville could seldom punish a war veteran, having served in France himself. Where the man had a wife and children who suffered because of his drinking, Neville gave him a severe reprimand and ordered him to pay one shilling; persistent offenders got a short prison sentence. Neville was conscious of his own inadequacy as a magistrate, because he always thought he should do something to help the poor devils, and would if he had the time and the wherewithal. He had been so much more fortunate than any of them, for he had married Isabel Storey, a war widow with two children, now in her early forties, who was well known in the adjoining villages of North Camp and South Camp; he often thought that she did more good than he did.

He found her about to leave for the Rectory when he reached the manor, to attend the Ladies' Hour held there every Wednesday by the curate's wife, Mrs Kennard.

'Rebecca's at the stables today, so I hope Miss Pearson will be there to play the piano for us,' Isabel said. 'Otherwise I shall have to give them the note to start on.'

'Well, don't start too high or too low,' he said with an affectionate grin. 'Can't you ask Philip Saville to play for you? The council offices are closed on Wednesday afternoons, and I passed him on the Everham Road, coming home. I could go back to the cottage in the pony-trap to bring him back if you like. His aunt hasn't got a telephone.'

'Do you think he'd mind?' asked Isabel doubtfully. 'All of us old ladies, I mean – hardly an incentive to the poor man!'

''Course he wouldn't mind, it would do him good.' Cedric laughed. 'And *you're* not old! – though it would be nice if you could introduce him to a suitable unmarried lady. What about that girl who works at Thomas and Gibson's, the one with the old dragon of a mother. What's their name . . . ?'

'Poor Miss Pearson? I was going to ask her to play for

us, only she gets flustered if she doesn't know the tune – and she's so painfully shy.'

'There you are then – introduce her to Saville and let them play duets to entertain the ladies!'

'You do say some silly things, Cedric! They'd both be so embarrassed that they'd never come again.' Isabel accepted that her husband was a tease, but she cared about the feelings of those who did not share his brand of humour. 'Go on then, get out the pony-trap and go and ask Mr Saville if he'll play for us. I'll come with you as far as the Rectory.'

'Aye, aye, captain.'

Thomas and Gibson's haberdashery had stood on the main street of North Camp well before the turn of the century, long after Mrs Thomas and her sister Miss Gibson had passed on. It had changed hands twice, but had kept the ladies' names engraved on the glass of two bay windows facing the street. The present manager Mr Richardson liked the shop's cosily old-fashioned yet respectful air, reflecting over fifty years of good customer service. Young Mr John Richardson would take over his father's business in the course of time, and meanwhile worked as a floor manager at Page's, the big department store in Everham, four miles away but not as distant since the 'Spur' had been built – a cul-de-sac railway branch line that joined North Camp to Everham on the Southern Railway from London to Southampton. A disabled war veteran acted as ticket seller and collector, and waved the flag when the three-carriage train steamed back to Everham.

Wednesday was early closing day, and Miss Pearson tidied the glass-topped counter with its yard-long brass tape measure inserted; she put away the ribbons, buttons and zip fasteners, and the sharp scissors used for cutting lengths of material.

'Are you ready to leave, Miss Pearson?' called Richardson from his office at the back. 'Two letters to post on your way!'

'Right, Mr Richardson,' she answered, clearing away the tea tray, emptying the pot, and rinsing the leaves down the drain. She took down her felt hat and long jacket from the hook in the passage, and pulled on her gloves. Mrs Pearson, her mother, insisted that she wore a vest and liberty bodice until the end of May.

Freedom! The church bell chimed for one o'clock and Miss Pearson set out to walk towards the meadows beside the Blackwater river, where she sat down under a tree to eat her packed lunch; it consisted only of two cheese sandwiches, but she knew there would be some of Mrs Kennard's home-baked cakes and biscuits at the Rectory. Her spirits lifted; for the next hour she could enjoy the rural scene, the fresh new foliage on the trees, the sunlight on the water; and she could indulge her secret thoughts in solitude, reliving the moment when young Mr Richardson had breezed into the shop yesterday and commented on her hair, swept up into a bunch on the top of her head and secured by hair pins which tended to loosen and fall out. He had bent down and picked up a stray pin.

'Why don't you take them all out, Valerie, and let that pretty hair fall down over your shoulders?' he had teased, and as always she had been unable to think of a suitably witty rejoinder. He had called her Valerie, and she longed to call him John, but that wouldn't have been right; her mother would be horrified at such forwardness – so he had smiled and passed on into his father's office. Whatever must he think of her stupid shyness? Thank heaven he could not read her thoughts, and here by the Blackwater she could indulge in day-dreams where the two of them held long, intelligent conversations, and he would reach for her hand and look deep into her brown eyes with a love that reflected her own.

At the Rectory Mrs Kennard, wearing a voluminous smock, was preparing for the Ladies' Hour. Lady Neville had already arrived, but without Miss Rebecca Neville. There would be Miss Rudge who taught at St Peter's Church of England Primary School which closed on Wednesday afternoons, Councillor Mrs Tomlinson, Mrs Lupton the doctor's wife, Miss Pearson and sometimes Mrs Pearson, and two young mothers who lived next-door to each other and took turns at attending, the one at home looking after the other's child as well as her own. The curate's wife had tried unsuccessfully to provide a crèche for the children, but the rector and Mrs Allingham who had lived here for over thirty years and considered it theirs, had flatly forbidden it because of the noise and general disturbance which would shatter the peace of the six-bedroomed Rectory.

'It would be no more disturbing than our chatter and singing,' Joan Kennard now confided to Lady Isabel. 'And when the baby comes—'

Isabel had smiled and shrugged in sympathy. 'I'd gladly offer Hassett Manor for the meetings, only it's such a long way out of North Camp for the older ladies to walk,' she said. 'In any case, you have every right to hold the Ladies' Hour here – it's your home now, as much as the Allinghams. You need to put your foot down, Joan, politely but firmly. Would you like *me* to speak to Mrs Allingham?'

'Thank you, Lady – er, Neville, but—'

(If only I were just plain Mrs Neville, thought Isabel.)

'—but it might cause bad feeling between them and us.' Joan Kennard lowered her voice. 'There's tension between Alan and the Reverend Allingham as it is, and I don't want the old . . . the rector to start complaining about the Ladies' Hour. It's such a good way to get to know the women of the parish and their families.'

'Yes, I find it helpful, too,' said Isabel, who privately thought the Allinghams envious of the Kennards' popularity. 'Ah, there's Miss Pearson coming up the drive, and – oh, it's Grace – Mrs Nuttall – on her bicycle.' She laughed. 'We must get them *all* cycling, it's going to be the fashion of the future!' This was a joke, of course, as not many of the women had bicycles, and to pedal along showing their legs was generally considered rather fast.

Grace Nuttall dismounted, nodded to her sister and took her cycle round to the back of the Rectory. 'I've just been recommending it to Miss Pearson,' she said. 'She could halve the time it takes to get from her mother's house to Thomas and Gibson's.'

Valerie coloured and shook her head, muttering that she had never possessed a bicycle, and knowing that her mother would never approve of her making such an exhibition of herself. Isabel Neville shook her head at her sister, for she knew of Mrs Pearson's domestic tyranny; having lost her son in the war, and her husband in the influenza epidemic that followed it, she had clung to her unmarried daughter with what she thought was devotion. Herself a war widow, Isabel had seen this situation played out over and over again; the loss of a whole generation of men had left a generation of single women whose duty – even their privilege, some thought – was to care for their ageing parents.

'If only we could introduce her to some nice young man,' Isabel had said in a low voice to Joan Kennard, remembering her husband's words. 'There are so many sweet souls who'd have been happy wives and mothers if it hadn't been for that – that – *wicked* war! Now they have to care for an older generation while they themselves grow old. It's so unfair.'

Mrs Kennard nodded. They all knew that Lady Isabel had lost her first husband, an Anglican vicar of an East End parish who'd survived the war only to die a broken and cynical man at the end of it. Sir Cedric Neville, her second husband, had also served in the war among the first men of the tank corps; now, in addition to running his estate, he gave his services as a councillor and magistrate, and was active in the British Legion on behalf of war veterans and their families.

'Where's Miss Rebecca, then?' the ladies asked.

'She can't come this afternoon, unfortunately – she's at the riding stables,' said her ladyship. 'But Cedric has gone to ask Philip Saville if he can play the piano for us. Ah, yes, there they are now, in the pony-trap.'

'We're all very grateful to you, Philip,' she said as Mr Saville came in, and Mrs Kennard echoed her words. The ladies murmured their appreciation, and their eyes softened, for here was another victim of the Great War, and worthy of their consideration. Once the golden-haired boy of North Camp, the son of the previous incumbent of St Peter's, Philip had excelled at tennis and cricket, and his dazzling good looks had stirred the heart of many a young girl who dreamt of him choosing her as his wife. When he had enlisted early in 1915, half of North Camp came out to cheer and wave farewell as he boarded the train at Everham. The Reverend Mr Saville and Mrs Saville hid their fears beneath smiles of pride, though as the war had gone on and casualty lists grew longer, they shared their anxiety with many of their parishioners who were comforted by their example.

When the telegram had arrived at the Rectory, it was said that Mrs Saville had fainted. When her husband opened it, he read that Philip had been wounded, and was in a hospital in northern France. It was five months later, in September 1917, that Mr and Mrs Saville had been summoned to London to collect their son from Charing Cross Hospital, where he had been taken on arrival from the crowded ambulance train that had carried the latest wounded up from Southampton. They had brought him home to the Rectory, and the people of North Camp eagerly looked forward to greeting their golden boy in church again; but it was almost Christmas before they caught sight of a thin, one-legged cripple walking unsteadily on crutches, his blue eyes sunk into bony orbits, having looked upon unspeakable horrors. When he opened his mouth he gave a deep, rattling cough, the result of inhaling poison gas. Words of congratulation froze on the lips of those who recognised Philip Saville, now an object of silent pity.

That had been twenty years ago. The Reverend Saville had retired and moved with his wife to another Hampshire village, but Philip had wanted to stay at North Camp, a clerk in the council offices in Everham, and lodging with his mother's sister, his Aunt Enid, in her cottage on the Everham Road. He had not followed his father into the Church, but instead had studied music and now played the organ at St Peter's. He had been fitted with an artificial left leg made of wood, but walked stiffly with a stick, as it had no movable knee joint. His spirits had sunk when Sir Cedric Neville came to ask him to play for the Ladies' Hour, but he could not refuse the polite request, which now earned him the embarrassing approval of the ladies. Grace Nuttall was the only one disappointed at Miss Neville's absence, and regretted making the effort to attend today, but she hid her feelings as best she could.

Mr Saville seemed to know every tune requested of him, both sacred and secular, and accompanied them on the piano with verve and versatility. The Ladies' Hour opened as usual with a hymn, and this week the choice had been 'To Be a Pilgrim'; then Mrs Kennard introduced their speaker, a plump, bosomy lady wearing an enormous hat, who spoke emotionally about the work done by the Royal Society for the Prevention of Cruelty to Animals.

'Picture an unhappy horse in a field, whose tail has been cruelly cut short, so that the poor creature can't swish away the flies that torment it on a day like today,' she said, 'or a pathetic pet dog kept tied up to a post in a garden, without water at hand, and unable to run up and down the path; this is what breaks my heart, dear ladies. I've brought copies with me of our magazine, *Animal Ways*, which I'll gladly distribute among you at the end of my talk, and I'm sure you will want to make a small donation to our very good cause.'

When all the magazines had been bought up (Lady Isabel bought the last half dozen and put a generous donation in the collecting box), the lady stood up with tears in her eyes. 'God bless you all, dear ladies! Any friend of animals is a friend of mine!'

When she finally sat down, Mrs Kennard called upon Miss

Rudge to sing a solo, 'Sweet Lass of Richmond Hill', and a young mother, whose toddler had been left in the charge of her friend and neighbour, rose to read a poem about a pet cat by a Mr Christopher Smart. Then refreshments were served, cups of tea were handed round, along with the delicious home-baked cake and shortbread biscuits for which Mrs Kennard was renowned.

Councillor Mrs Tomlinson, a widow in her seventies, observed with quiet satisfaction the curate's wife and the lady of the manor, who presided each week over this social occasion designed to bring the women of the parish together. She listened to the accounts of domestic comings and goings among them, and the gossip, mostly unmalicious, over the cups and tea-plates. She joined in the thanks for Mrs Kennard's hospitality when that lady ought really to be resting, in her condition, and wondered what the poetry reader would have thought if she'd known that poor Christopher Smart had been incarcerated in a lunatic asylum when he wrote his touching poem in the mid-eighteenth century.

She also kept to herself the anxiety she felt as storm clouds gathered over Europe. Widow of a brigadier killed in the Great War, she heard worrying news from her son in the diplomatic service, now resident in Vienna, and fervently hoped that the recent Anglo-Italian agreement would guarantee that Benito Mussolini would be a firm ally in the event of another war, which heaven forbid. He was in a good position to stand up against this maniac German Chancellor, Adolf Hitler, now seriously persecuting European Jews. She gathered that Mussolini was more of a dictator than a premier, as indeed was Hitler and his Fascists, but he had done a great deal to revive Italy's prosperity since the dark days of the war; oh, surely, *surely*, thought Mrs Tomlinson, there could not possibly be a return to those dark days again!

The Ladies' Hour, which quite often went on for an hour and a half or longer, ended with the singing of 'All Things Bright and Beautiful', but Lady Neville stayed on a little longer to talk with Philip Saville.

'I'm glad to have the chance of a word with you, Philip,' she said pleasantly, as if an idea had just struck her, though she had in fact been turning it over in her mind all the afternoon. 'How is Miss Temple these days? It's some time since I've seen her, and I really should call on her. Is she well?'

'Thank you. My aunt keeps reasonably well, but the rheumatism is still troublesome,' he answered with cool politeness.

'Then thank heaven she's got you there to do the man's jobs, bringing in the coal and digging the gard—' Isabel checked herself, remembering his disability.

He shrugged. 'We are mutually obliged to each other. Aunt Enid is a very good cook, and sees that I always have a clean shirt to put on.' A faint trace of a smile hovered over his face for a moment, and Isabel saw her opportunity to put a suggestion to him.

'The Reverends Allingham and Kennard are very appreciative of your services as church organist,' she said, 'and your playing this afternoon was quite brilliant – and tactful,' she added in a low tone, 'for the skilful accompanist must be able to cover up the singers' mistakes and get them back to the right key! You must have a library of tunes in your head.'

He gave the slightest of nods, and she hoped he didn't think her patronising. It was time to come to the point.

'One of the grooms at the Manor has twin boys, fine little

fellows, now seven years old, and always singing in perfect tune, though they've never learnt music. Miss Rudge at St Peter's Primary School has recommended that they learn the piano, and I asked them to come with their mother to see how they fared with our piano in the drawing room at Hassett Manor. I tell you, Philip, it was a revelation to see and hear those little boys play simple nursery rhyme tunes, entirely by ear, as they've had no lessons, nor is there a piano in their home. It occurred to me today, listening to your expertise, that you could give Charlie and Joe lessons if a suitable time could be arranged. What about Saturdays, or evenings after five o'clock, at the Manor?'

Philip Saville looked dubious. 'I can't walk very far without pain in my non-existent leg, and I haven't actually *taught* music before, nor have I had much experience with children. I'm sure you could find somebody more suitable to teach them – a lady, preferably.'

Isabel noticed that he had not addressed her as *Lady*, neither did he show the deference to her social standing such as she received from the ladies at the Rectory. She found his attitude quite refreshing, for she would rather have been plain Mrs Neville. Daughter of a North Camp carpenter, she had married an eager young curate sent to assist Philip's father, and moved with her husband to his London parish. After his tragic death she had returned to North Camp with her baby son Paul and a baby girl she had adopted from a desperate single mother. Now married to Sir Cedric Neville of Hassett Manor, Isabel had never forgotten her origins, and was embarrassed at being addressed as Lady Neville and referred to as her Ladyship by North Camp people she saw as her equals, especially in front of her sister, Grace.

She now spoke as an equal to Philip Saville. 'I hope you'll be prepared to give it a try, Philip, and see how you get on. I will send the pony-trap to fetch you over to the Manor and take you back, and of course I would pay you, say . . .' And she named an amount well in excess of the usual payment for music lessons.

Philip showed no sign of being impressed by her bounty. 'If I were to meet these boys and assess their skill for myself, then we might come to a decision whether or not it would be worth your while,' he said, and she had no choice but to accept. It was agreed that he would attend at Hassett Manor on the following Friday evening at five thirty.

She thanked him and said she would take him home in the pony-trap. It would be a pleasure to meet Miss Temple again and commiserate with her over her rheumatism.

The Tradesmen's Arms had stood in the main street of North Camp before the turn of the century, and was a meeting place for the older men of the village, a refuge from domestic turmoils and the behaviour of the younger generation, the grown-up children of men like carpenter Tom Munday and house painter Eddie Cooper, widowers in their seventies, who still obliged friends with their expertise. They could well remember the Great War that had sacrificed a generation, and for what cause? It had not ended in victory but in an armistice.

'Nobody who never lived through *that* can ever imagine what it was like,' said Tom Munday, setting down his glass.

Eddie agreed. 'Nor the arrangements that had to be made for the girls left behind with babies inside 'em, like my Mary, after Dick Yeomans was killed,' he said in a low tone, so as not to be heard by other patrons of the bar room.

'It turned out all right, though, when Sidney Goddard took her over, *and* the farm – by Jove, that was a stroke of luck for everybody concerned,' replied Tom. 'Mary and Sid have been happy with a nice little family, and the Yeomanses—' he hesitated.

'And the Yeomanses have got their son's child, our little Dora, even if she's called Goddard,' said Eddie with the reminiscent smile of one long resigned to a situation that had caused emotions to run high at the time. 'And your Isabel's done better than all of 'em, marrying into the Nevilles and taking Storey's son with her, as well as the girl she adopted – look how well *she's* turned out.'

Tom Munday took another long draught from his glass, and Eddie went on. 'It's a shame she hasn't been able to give Neville a kid of his own.'

'Cedric looks upon Paul and Rebecca as his own, and he's been a good father to them – couldn't ask for a better,' said Tom firmly. 'Nor could I ask for better grandchildren.' He set down his glass with a gesture of finality. 'Another?'

'Thanks, don't mind if I do,' said Eddie, sensing that it was time to change the subject. Unlike Tom who had remained a widower, he had married again, and Annie had given him a son, Freddie, now living up north, married with kids of his own. No doubt *there* about the paternity! He smiled to himself, and then sighed, for Annie had died of cervical cancer only two years ago.

'How's Ernest getting on these days?' he asked. '*There's* one who's done well after going to hell and back.'

'Yes, but he's settled down well with Aaron's sister, Devora, and Miriam and David are lovely children,' answered Tom. 'Old Pascoe looked upon him as the son he lost.' He paused for a moment, and then went on, 'It's as well, I reckon, that they're over here and not over there, in Elberfeld, with Aaron's brother and his family. I don't care for the sound of what's going on in Germany these days. This fellow Hitler is very anti-Semitic, and needs watching – if he rises to power, heaven help the Jews.'

'I shouldn't worry, old chap. This Hitler makes a lot of noise, but so does an empty drum. Good God, Tom, we couldn't – we surely *couldn't* – go through anything like that bloody war again!'

'As I say, I'm not sorry the Everham Mundays are safely out of the fellow's reach,' Tom said gravely. 'They say he's out to rule over every country in Europe, and stockpiling weapons as well as training a bigger army than any of 'em.'

'I think you're underestimating the opposition he'll come up against,' said Eddie. 'Our Prime Minister has got the measure of him, and we've signed that agreement with Mussolini and his Eye-ties, so *he'll* have a fair-sized army, too. And don't forget the Empire – they'd be more than a match for a raving loony like Hitler.'

Tom sighed and finished his beer. Perhaps Eddie was right. He'd better be, because a Europe under a German dictator was too terrible to contemplate.

CHAPTER TWO

1938

Dora Goddard had a spring in her step as she walked the half mile between Yeomans' Farm and the sports pavilion, swinging her racquet. She knew how well her white outfit showed off her trim figure: a short-sleeved blouse and matching skirt with pleats all the way round, that flared out as she moved around the court. The North Camp hard tennis courts had space for three games to be played at once; it was conveniently close to the cricket ground with its pavilion, so the North Camp team, under their captain Rob Nuttall, could mix freely with the mostly female tennis players, an arrangement appreciated by all.

Billy Yeomans had not been ready to accompany Dora when she set out. He was the surviving son of his widowed mother, his elder brother Dick having fallen in the Great War at about the time of Billy's birth, and Billy considered himself the head of the Yeomans family and heir to the farm. He had lately taken to sprucing himself up when he came in from the milking shed, changing his underwear and washing his feet as well as his face and hands before shaving and slicking his hair back with Brylcreem. A young lady was responsible for this new fastidiousness, and today he had brought her home to meet his mother. Pam Barker seemed a nice enough girl, a giggling trainee hairdresser with no experience of life on the land. 'She'll need to get her hands dirty before he takes her on,' Mrs Yeomans had said, though she had no serious objection to the girl, and thought that at twenty-six it was high time that Billy settled down, whether with Pam or another.

When he was ready to leave, Billy took Pam's arm and steered her towards the lane that Dora had taken, towards the sports pavilion. He was partly dressed for cricket in a white shirt and his best grey trousers, just as Pam was partly dressed for tennis in a light cotton print dress with white plimsolls and ankle socks. Her racquet was newly bought.

They found Dora playing a knockabout with Barbara Seabrook from the butcher's, practising their forehand and backhand drives.

'Both got their eyes looking out for a chap to come along,' said Billy, and Pam giggled.

Rob Nuttall and his son Jack were out on the adjoining cricket field with two or three local lads, including Robin Seabrook, the butcher's son. They were joined by Billy, leaving Pam standing at the side of the court, forlornly holding her racquet and hoping that somebody else would arrive to play. She did not have to wait long; Howard and Lester Allingham from the Rectory sauntered down the lane, and as soon as Barbara Seabrook saw them she put down her racquet and made a bee line for the brothers. Howard, the elder, was a pleasant young man destined for the church, and Lester, good-looking and self-assured, was said to be interested in aviation. Barbara, plump and pretty, looked up at him with big, china-blue eyes.

'Care for a game, Lester? I'm sure that – er – that nice girl over there will lend you her racquet,' she said, nodding towards Pam Barker whose eyes were on Billy, practising bowling in the cricket field.

She's got a cheek, thought Dora, throwing herself at him like that, but Pam was only too pleased to lend him her racquet and hurry over to the cricket field to gaze adoringly at Billy's rather erratic bowling. When Lester and Barbara commenced playing, shouting and laughing as they dashed from one side of the court to the other, Dora, seething inwardly, tried to appear unconcerned, and flashed a smile at Howard who came over and introduced himself. Dora asked him which he liked best, tennis or cricket; he said he really hadn't a preference, but congratulated her on her own skill at tennis. When he told her he was soon to start at theological college, she smiled and told him she was attending Everham Commercial College to learn office skills, and perhaps, who knows, she teased, she might one day be his secretary.

'I think I'd like that,' he said shyly, and thought how pretty she was, her face flushed and her hair tousled from exercise. They laughed together, and Dora remembered that there might be a couple of old tennis racquets stored in the cricket pavilion. She ran to find out, and returned in triumph waving one in a circle above her head.

'Right, now we shall see who's best!' she said, and, although he protested that he was out of practise, she insisted that they went onto the second court, starting with a knockabout 'for you to loosen up,' she said with a smile, giving herself every opportunity to jump and twist, returning the ball and showing the pleats of the white skirt swirling around her knees. Howard was enchanted, and Dora thought him worth encouraging over the summer months, in the absence of any serious competition.

Meanwhile Barbara and Lester had stopped for a rest on one of the bench seats at the side of the court. He casually flung his arm across the back of the bench.

'I see you're an expert at the game,' he said admiringly.

'Oh, yes, I suppose that's why you won,' she answered, looking away from him, conscious of his arm behind her back. 'You've had more tennis practise!'

'Who said anything about tennis?' he murmured, and she looked round, meeting his humorous dark eyes, and for once not knowing how best to answer.

'That's meant as a compliment,' he grinned, 'though I'll apologise if you want me to.'

Barbara Seabrook blushed but managed a little smile. He was certainly better looking than his brother, she thought.

'If I'm forgiven, perhaps I can make amends,' he continued. 'That amazing cartoon film, *Snow White and the Seven Dwarfs*, is going to be shown at the Embassy in a couple of weeks' time; would you like me to take you to see it?'

Barbara's mouth opened. 'What, really? Do you mean that place behind the builders' yard off Everham High Street?'

'No, no, that's the old flea-pit. They've got this new place now, the Embassy Cinema. It hasn't long been open, but it's the big attraction, and they say the film took America by storm – incredibly good. So shall we go and see it for ourselves – Barbara?'

'Well, yes, seeing that you've asked me, and thank you,' she replied carefully, while her heart thumped and she tried to stop herself from showing her delight. Now she would be the envy of every girl in North Camp, and Lester was certainly a charmer, even if he *was* the son of that old bore the Reverend Allingham!

The stable yard at Hassett Manor dated from the days of coaches and carriages; now there was Sir Cedric's Daimler and the useful little pony-trap. Perrin the groom was as proud of the horses as if they were his own, and nodded to Rebecca as she stroked the nose of her grey palfrey, Sunbeam.

'Seems we've got visitors today, Miss Rebecca.' She turned to see Paul and his friend from Cambridge, who was spending some of the summer vacation at the Manor. The Perrin twins were clamouring to ride Sunbeam.

'Wait a minute, boys,' said Rebecca. 'Let Mr Bannister see her. She's a beauty, isn't she, Geoffrey?' she said, with a smile at Paul's friend, and of course he agreed, and patted the necks of the two fine stallions, Mercury and Playboy, on which he and Paul had ridden earlier in the day, to the annoyance of Rebecca who would have come with them if she had known of their plan.

'We'll go for a gallop tomorrow morning, Becky,' said Paul, and she nodded.

'That will be fun, won't it, my pretty Sunbeam? You're more than a match for those great big fellows!'

The mare nuzzled her neck, and the twins jumped up and down, begging for a ride.

'You'd better let them, Perrin, or we'll never have any

peace,' said Paul good-humouredly, at which they roared, 'Look, Mr Saville, we're going to ride Sunbeam!'

They turned to see that Philip Saville had come into the stable yard, leaning on his walking-stick to counteract the absence of a knee joint in his artificial leg. He nodded to Paul and Bannister, and half smiled at Rebecca.

'The boys insisted that I come to see the horses,' he explained.

'You're welcome, Saville,' said Paul. 'Meet Geoffrey Bannister, the son of the Right Honourable John Bannister, MP, who's staying with us for part of the vacation – and Geoffrey, meet Philip Saville, veteran of the Great War, and music tutor to these two rapscallions!'

Geoffrey leant forward to shake Saville's hand.

'He's making a jolly good job of it, too,' Paul went on. 'The Perrin boys'll end up as famous concert pianists, I have every hope!'

Bannister was a little surprised that a musician should be teaching the groom's children, and Paul guessed what he was thinking.

'All due to Mother; she persuaded Saville against his better judgement! She must have seen – or rather heard how good he was, and snapped him up – not that he was very keen at first, were you, Saville?'

'Lady Isabel is most kind, and the boys are amazingly quick to learn. I'm most obliged to her,' said Savillle, a little awkwardly.

'And so am I, Mr Saville; she's a great lady,' added Perrin in a low tone, for he had never been asked to contribute money for the lessons.

When Perrin and Rebecca led Sunbeam away towards the

paddock with the delighted boys seated on her back, Paul asked Philip Saville to come with them back to the Manor.

'If we're lucky, Mrs Tanner will give us tea in the garden,' he said. 'Come on, Philip, don't be shy – she'll put out more scones if you come with us.'

They slowed their pace for him to keep up with them, and sure enough, a light folding table had been set out before the open casement windows, with a checked tablecloth on which Mrs Tanner placed a tray of tea and home-made scones warm from the oven. She smiled at Paul, nodded to Saville, and looked Bannister up and down before leaving them.

'That was a very suspicious look she gave me!' remarked Bannister. 'Who is she, exactly?'

'Sally Tanner served at the vicarage in Bethnal Green where my mother was wife to the vicar there, my father,' said Paul. 'He went out as an army chaplain, and *his* father, a retired clergyman, came to take his place.' Paul hesitated, looking back on a time that was seldom spoken of. 'Sally Tanner had lost her husband in the war, and Mother took her in as a sort of housekeeper. She helped look after me as a baby, and practically looks on me as her own, and Becky as well; she saw Mother through my father's death, which was pretty tragic, really – he'd lost his faith and wasn't easy to – but this isn't much of a subject, so have another scone! And you, Philip? Butter? More tea?'

Sally Tanner wiped her hands on her apron and went to Lady Isabel's study, next to her husband's but half the size. Isabel looked up from her writing desk and smiled.

'Have the boys had their tea, Sally?'

'Of course they have, Isabel, along with poor Mr Saville. I took a good look at that Mr Bannister, and, though it's a bit

early to say, his face favours him, and he gets a thumbs up.'
She illustrated her words with a thumbs up sign.

'Well, that's a relief,' teased Isabel, 'though you really
ought not to subject our guests to these examinations, Sally!
It could be very embarrassing if they ever suspected. I hope
you didn't give Mr Saville the same scrutiny.'

''Course I didn't – stands to reason *he'd* get a thumbs
down, what with being a one-legged cripple twice her age!'

'Oh, *Sally!*' Isabel shook her head in disapproval, but
could not hide her smile. In fact her friend's judgement was
usually right in matters of relationships.

Rebecca's eyes sparkled with exhilaration as she rode
Sunbeam at a gallop, digging her thighs into the mare's flanks,
and bouncing up and down on the saddle as they covered the
stretch of heathland that rose above North and South Camp.
The clear, cold light of early morning was for her the best part
of the day, before the August sun rose above the Hampshire
fields and woodlands. Ahead of her two companions, she rode
down into the Blackwater valley, across the old pack-horse
bridge, returning by the water meadows. With flushed face
and windblown hair, she dismounted and patted Sunbeam's
heaving shoulders as she awaited Paul and Geoffrey who were
following on. Geoffrey Bannister was unstinting in his praise.

'Well done!' he cried, panting from the exertion of the
last gallop up from the meadows. 'That was magnificent,
Rebecca, a lesson in horsemanship – don't you agree, Paul?'

'Quite good,' said Paul with a grin. 'Coming along quite
nicely, I'd say.' He dodged her fist, privately amused at his
friend's raptures; it looked as if a romantic liaison was on
the cards.

'Don't let her lead you astray, dear boy,' he chuckled, but Geoffrey scarcely heard. Still breathing rapidly from the cross-county gallop with his eyes fixed upon the girl's back, he was coming to believe that she was his ideal of womanly perfection: a girl he could love.

Enid Temple raised a questioning eyebrow. 'Are you all right, Philip? Were you held up at the Manor?'

'I'm fine, Aunt Enid. It was due to the boys – they made me go with them to the stables, to show off the Hassett Manor horses and watch them ride Miss Neville's mare. They're a pair of scamps, but Paul Storey's very good with them, and they got their wish. And then, well, Paul asked me to join him and his university friend for tea in the garden.'

'Good,' said his aunt, pleased though rather surprised that he had let himself be drawn into everyday life at Hassett Manor. The piano lessons for Charlie and Joe Perrin were turning out to be a blessing, she thought; there had been a definite brightening of her nephew's rather lonely life since he had taken up Lady Neville's suggestion.

'And was Lady Neville there?' she enquired. 'And Miss Rebecca?'

'Miss Neville was there, but not her mother; I think she was in her office. We were served tea by a lady called Mrs Tanner, and Paul was telling his friend about her history.'

'Ah, yes, Sally Tanner, she's devoted to the family, and knew Lady Isabel when she was Mrs Storey,' said Enid with a sigh. 'I remember Mark Storey's determination to marry Isabel Munday, although she was only sixteen. Of course, your parents were in the thick of it, and my sister was very sorry for him. He had to wait another two years, but he got her in the end and took her off to that rough East End parish just as the war broke out.'

Philip Saville remembered it well, and the involvement of his father, the Reverend Mr Saville. And he also remembered Isabel when she was sweet Miss Munday, the carpenter's daughter, and how all the fellows had envied Mark Storey.

'But the marriage ended in tragedy,' Enid continued. 'Poor Mr Storey was never the same after going through all that—' Enid quickly checked herself, and glanced at her nephew, for the same could be said about him. Philip never spoke of his experiences of trench warfare, the horrors he had looked upon, images that still remained with him and haunted his dreams.

'It's all right, Aunt Enid, don't worry,' he said quietly. 'There were hundreds of thousands of us, those who were killed and those who came back with their ghosts.'

Enid had no answer, and he went on, 'Like Isabel's brother Ernest who slogged through Passchendaele with that friend of his, Aaron Pascoe.'

'Yes, Ernest was a conscientious objector at the start of the war, but changed his mind when Aaron enlisted,' she recalled. 'After Aaron got badly wounded and died, Ernest was taken prisoner, which probably saved his life.' She paused, remembering the events of twenty years earlier. 'Then he took over Aaron's place in the family firm, and married Aaron's sister as soon as she was old enough.'

'They've been happy, haven't they, with their children?' asked Philip.

'Yes, it seems so, though we don't see much of Ernest and Devora these days, living in Everham,' said his aunt, and kept her next thoughts to herself. If only Philip had been

31

blessed with a Devora to marry, he might have recovered and become an active member of the community instead of the semi-recluse he was now, playing the organ at St Peter's and refusing all invitations from well-meaning parishioners. Ernest Munday was now senior partner in the firm of Munday and Pascoe, chartered accountants, formerly Pascoe and Munday. Of course, the family were not Christians, but Jews, and Ernest had converted to Judaism. Enid Temple wondered what his mother, the late wife of Tom Munday, would have said about her son's choice.

But now Enid Temple, sister-in-law of an Anglican clergyman and leftover spinster from the Great War, found that her views had broadened: did it really matter?

It was the eve of Bannister's departure, and Sir Cedric led Paul and Geoffrey out onto the terrace with their postprandial coffee and brandy; Geoffrey longed to spend these last few hours with Rebecca who had gone with her mother and Mrs Tanner to the drawing room for what Cedric affectionately termed their 'petticoat council,' much to Rebecca's resentment.

'As if women weren't able to appreciate the superior wisdom of men's minds!'

On this particular evening, however, both husband and wife wanted to do a little discreet 'sounding out' – 'testing the water' as Cedric put it to Isabel. Geoffrey Bannister had stayed at Hassett Manor for ten days, and had made a good impression on his hosts. In addition to riding, playing tennis on the Manor court, driving the Daimler down through verdant farmland for a picnic on the downs, their guest had assisted with fruit-picking in the orchard, and the less attractive, back-breaking labour of lifting potatoes. Cedric commented on 'Farmer Bannister' as they sat in the August twilight, darkening into the warm velvet of a late summer night.

'You may tell your parents that we have all enjoyed your company, and hope they will spare you to visit us again soon – perhaps in the Christmas vacation?'

Young Bannister acknowledged the compliments with what he hoped was a modest smile. 'Thank you, Sir Cedric, I've enjoyed every minute here, and look forward to visiting again,' he said, wondering if the father and son would hear the unspoken words – his admiration for Miss Neville. The smiles and understanding nods of Sir Cedric and Paul were reassuring, allowing him at least to hope for a closer relationship with her in due course.

But there was something else that Cedric thought should be mentioned.

'Your father's at the centre of government, Geoffrey; how does he view these events in Europe? It seems as if this German Chancellor has got his eye on countries in eastern Europe, and possibly more. How great a threat does Mr Bannister think he is?'

'Father believes he needs watching, sir, but he isn't really concerned. If Hitler ever thought of marching his troops into Czechoslovakia, the opposition to him is formidable – Great Britain and France, Italy and the Low Countries – *and* we've got the might of the Empire behind us, that should be enough to warn him off.'

Paul interposed. 'What does your father think of the Prime Minister?'

'What – Mr Chamberlain?'

'Yes, Mr *Neville* Chamberlain.' Paul smiled as he emphasised the name.

'With that name he *must* be a good man!' quipped Geoffrey, though he knew that his father, like many others in the House, had serious reservations about the Prime Minister's ability to deal with a megalomaniac dictator.

Paul laughed, but Sir Cedric looked grave. 'We must hope so, we must fervently hope so,' he said, adding with uncharacteristic emotion, 'my dear boys,' which surprised them; he then deliberately steered the conversation away from politics.

In the drawing room, Lady Isabel asked her daughter outright how she felt about Paul's university friend.

'I like him well enough, Mother, and enjoyed his company, but it's much too early to talk about anything serious,' answered Rebecca, and smiled as she noticed Sally Tanner's approving nod. 'And he'll have to get his degree before he can start courting!'

'But you like him,' prompted her mother.

'To be honest, I'd like to have a bit more life of my own before I think about marrying *anybody*!'

'What a wise girl,' murmured Sally Tanner.

Later that evening, as Isabel and Sally talked together over their night drinks, they returned to the subject.

'We've heard how Rebecca feels about marriage, but there's something else that would have to be told to any prospective husband,' said Isabel. 'Before an engagement could be announced, he would have to be told that we adopted her.'

'Don't tell him yet,' said Sally Tanner. 'The penny'll drop sooner or later, when he works out that Paul and Becky are both twenty-one, with birthdays only six months apart!'

* * *

When Valerie Pearson saw Lady Neville and Miss Neville coming to Thomas and Gibson's she stood smartly to attention, and replied to the Lady's 'Good morning, Miss Pearson' with a 'Good morning' to each of them, adding, 'How may I help you?'

'We're looking for some trimmimgs for lingerie,' Lady Neville told her, and Valerie quickly opened some drawers behind the counter and put out the contents for the ladies to see.

'Oh, what exquisite lace!' cried Rebecca. 'Just right for edging round your knickers!'

'Rebecca! What will Miss Pearson think?' chided her mother, though she smiled, and as she fingered the lace, casually asked, 'How is your mother, Miss Pearson? I didn't see her in church on Sunday morning.'

'She – she's fairly well,' stammered Valerie, and on hearing this reply, Isabel Neville added kindly, 'Please excuse us, Miss Pearson, perhaps we're *all* a little on edge. I mean this German Chancellor Adolf or whatever his name is – he may be a source of amusement to some people, but for us who lived through the Great War, the very thought of going through all that again – ugh!'

Valerie Pearson watched the two women, the mother and daughter so at ease with each other, able to agree or disagree without rancour or rebuke, so different from the tension between herself and her own mother. She recalled the fear in Mrs Pearson's pale blue eyes as she listened to the news on the wireless last night about the continuing unrest in Europe.

'If that Hitler man ever turns on *us*, like the Kaiser in the Great War, it would be another war, and B – O – M – B – S day and night,' she had said, spelling out the dreaded word as if there were children present, for to her Valerie was still a delicate child to be protected; she was unable to see that their roles were becoming reversed.

Suddenly Valerie made up her mind to ask Lady Neville a question, encouraged by that lady's reference to the German Chancellor.

'Lady Neville – please, Lady Neville, will you give me your opinion about – about the subject you just mentioned: the trouble in Germany, this man Hitler? My mother is so nervous. She went all through the Great War, you see, and lost my father and brother, and she thinks that if it were to happen all over again – I'm sorry, Lady Neville, but Mother and I would – we're wondering what Sir Cedric thinks. If you wouldn't mind—' Valerie's pale face flushed, and her voice stammered to a stop.

Together mother and daughter raised their heads in surprise and concern.

'My dear Miss Pearson, what a pity about your poor dear mother!' Lady Neville's voice was full of sympathy, for she too had gone all through the Great War and lost her husband, though she made no reference to this. 'Please, my dear, let me reassure you and your mother, because in fact Sir Cedric hopes that this Hitler can be kept in check, and on the whole he's optimistic. Last month we had Mr Geoffrey Bannister, the MP's son, to stay with us, and his father is of the same opinion. We can only hope and pray that they are right. Please try not to worry, my dear.'

'Oh, Miss Pearson, what a shame!' exclaimed Rebecca. 'Just tell your poor mother that my father thinks old Adolf Hitler is like a balloon full of hot air, and as soon as other leaders stand up and prick him, he'll go down like one! And tell her too that she's lucky to have you for a daughter. I wouldn't be as patient with *my* mother!'

'No, I'm sure you wouldn't,' said that lady with an amused smile at Valerie, and having chosen and paid for their trimmings, the ladies thanked her and left.

As soon as they were out of earshot, they shook their heads at what they had heard.

'That *poor* girl, Mother! What a life she leads with that tiresome old woman – she must be thankful to get away to Thomas and Gibson's, though old Richardson isn't exactly brimming over with gaiety – oh, the poor lamb!'

'Ah, Becky, suppose *we* were like those two, wouldn't it be just too awful for words?' said her mother with feeling. 'And Mrs Pearson isn't that old, she must be in her fifties.'

'Yes, it would be dire – but at least you've given them something to cheer them up a bit,' said Rebecca, striving to be hopeful.

Her mother made no answer, being not entirely convinced that their optimism was well-founded. She suddenly thought of her brother Ernest and the Jewish family into which he had married. She wondered if their father, Tom Munday, had heard from him, and would have called on him today if she had been alone, but, having Rebecca with her, she avoided meeting Grace Nuttall at close quarters. She decided to call her brother on the telephone.

On that same afternoon Ernest and Devora Munday made a surprise call on his father at 47 Rectory Road, the house Ernest had grown up in with his sisters Isabel and Grace. Their mother had died shortly after the end of the war, without living to see her son's return from being a prisoner of war in

Germany. Tom, being now in his seventies, was happy to live with Grace and his son-in-law Rob Nuttall who had been his apprentice and had taken over the carpentry business. Their son Jack was already apprenticed to his father, and their daughter Doreen still lived at home, a quiet, shy girl of sixteen who helped with the housework.

'Good to see you, Ernest,' said his father. 'We've been wondering how you are.' He kissed Devora and noticed with dismay how pale she looked, her eyes full of anxiety.

'It's Devora's brother Jonathan, Dad,' said Ernest without preamble. 'He and his family live out in Elberfeld, as you know, and Devora's making herself ill, worrying over this anti-Semitism in Germany.'

'Yes, my people are being persecuted by this madman Hitler!' Devora cut in. 'They are being turned out of schools and colleges, their businesses are boycotted, and it gets worse by the week. I want Jonathan to bring his family over here to live with us.'

'And I have willingly agreed,' said Ernest, 'but Jonathan and Ella won't leave their home. You can't blame them, it's their money and possessions, their business, friends, the children's schools – everything that makes up their life. Devora wants to go out there and speak to Jonathan face to face, but I've had to forbid it, Dad. All this unrest may blow over in another year.'

'How can you say that?' cried Devora. 'That madman's assembling a huge army under his Fascist National Party, and they must be training for a purpose. What would my brother Aaron have said?'

Ernest closed his eyes at the memory of the friend he had loved more than life. Devora knew and understood, and had always known. Even now when making love to her he would sometimes cry out, 'Aaron, my love – oh, Aaron, my love!'

Devora burst into tears. 'You *know* Aaron would have saved our brother at all costs! Oh, Tom, please persuade my husband, *please*, I beg of you!'

'Hush, Devora, you can't ask that,' said Ernest. 'It's Jonathan's decision, and only he can decide.'

Tom Munday endeavoured to stay calm. Grace had come into the room, drawn by the noisy exchanges, and he winked at her and whispered, 'Make some tea!'

Aloud he said carefully, 'Give Jonathan a bit more time. Let the Pascoes go on working hard, show themselves to be good German citizens, and no menace to the state. I honestly believe that Germany has got more sense than to follow a madman. Devora, my dear, you must be patient for a while longer; as Ernest says, it's Jonathan's decision to make, to leave everything behind and bring his wife and young Jonny and Ayesha away from the only life they know.'

Ernest nodded gratefully, but Devora remained stubbornly unconvinced. Grace brought in a tray of tea, and could add nothing to what her father had said. She had always thought it a pity that Ernest had married into a Jewish family and taken on their religion.

But Tom's heart ached for his son, and hoped that he had given the right advice; he felt unable to be of any real use in a crisis like this.

CHAPTER THREE

1938–1939

It was Friday, the last day of September, and the Reverend and Mrs Allingham were listening intently to the wireless, and the news of Prime Minister Chamberlain's enormous efforts to speak face to face with Chancellor Adolf Hitler, and the twelve-hour conference that had taken place at Munich between the two leaders. Mr Chamberlain had obtained what he had striven for – an Anglo-German agreement signed by the leaders, assuring them that Germany would not invade eastern Europe. And Mr Chamberlain had that day arrived at Heston Aerodrome to be greeted by huge, cheering throngs as he waved the precious document. Later, said the newsreader, he had appeared on the balcony at Buckingham Palace with the King and Queen. Mr and Mrs Allingham almost wept for joy at Chamberlain's words, 'There has come back from Germany to Downing Street peace with honour: I believe it is peace in our time.'

'Thanks be to God!' said Roland Allingham with emotion. 'What a great Prime Minister we have, a man of peace who will go to any lengths to preserve peace in our nation!'

In the Kennards' living room downstairs, Joan was trying to comfort baby Josie, born at the end of June, and inclined to cry in the evenings and early mornings. Alan was out visiting a bereaved family, and Joan had offered the breast again to the baby, and checked that her nappy was dry.

'Oh, Josie my little girl, what's the matter? Are you still hungry? Haven't I got enough milk for you? Should I try you with some watered-down cow's milk with some sugar? Have you got a tummy-ache? – is it the colic? – oh, darling, if only you could tell me!' she sighed, rubbing the baby's back. Then she heard footsteps descending the stairs.

'Oh, heavens, she's come to complain about the noise!' she said to the baby. 'If only your daddy were here to talk to her – but I'll have to manage without him.'

'Mrs Kennard! Mrs Kennard!' Mrs Allingham almost shouted, bursting into the room without knocking. 'Haven't you been listening to the news on the wireless?'

Flustered at the intrusion, Joan Kennard stood up, holding Josie against her shoulder and continuing to pat her back to shift the wind from her little tummy, though the crying went on without a break. Joan turned a flushed face to her visitor.

'I'm sorry, Mrs Allingham, I'm trying to quieten her, but she just won't settle,' she apologised, close to tears.

'Didn't you hear what I just said, Mrs Kennard?' The rector's wife raised her voice above the din. 'I'm surprised you're not listening to the news.'

'I beg your pardon, Mrs Allingham, I didn't quite hear—'

'For heaven's sake, Mrs Kennard, put that child down and pay attention!'

For answer, Joan held her crying baby even closer against her enlarged breasts while Mrs Allingham shouted her news.

'Mr Chamberlain has returned from meeting with Herr Hitler with a declaration of peace! Everybody's cheering our wonderful Prime Minister. It's "peace in our time", he says – we're safe from the threat of war. Could there be any better news?'

'Oh – yes, I see,' faltered Joan. 'It's wonderful, isn't it? I'll tell Alan when he comes in. He's out at present – there's been a death – and I don't know what time he'll be back.'

But Mrs Allingham had returned to her husband, having lost patience with the curate's wife's stupidity.

Dora Goddard was both tired and bored with the tensions at Yeomans' Farm. Her parents seemed to talk of nothing else but the changes that were coming and would affect their lives. Ever since Billy had married Pam Barker at the beginning of the month (and not before time, as was being whispered), he had been asserting his ownership of the farm, his status being above that of Sidney Goddard, a son-in-law. He had offered the lease of the Bailiff's Cottage to Sid, and to make him second-in-charge, while Billy would manage the farm and Pam the farmhouse in place of Mary Goddard who had conscientiously ruled the kitchen ever since her marriage to Sid.

The Bailiff's Cottage had been empty for some time, and was a small, old-fashioned building with no hot running water and one cold tap in the kitchen, an outdoor lavatory and no heating other than open fires and an ancient range oven. Sidney and Mary were horrified at the prospect, and Billy's widowed mother had urged her son to carry on as they were for a year or two; Sidney had become a skilful all-rounder farmer, and Mrs Pam Yeomans had a lot more to learn before assuming to take over Mary's area of expertise. And besides, there was the event expected in March, when Pam would be thankful for Mary's help.

This evening Sid and Mary, Billy and Pam, with old Mrs Yeomans, were in the kitchen, talking it over yet again, and Dora had come out to breathe the evening air and get away from them. She could not get on with the new Mrs Yeomans, and the prospect of Bailiff's Cottage was too awful for words.

Suddenly she heard hurrying footsteps in the lane: who could be visiting? When Howard Allingham came into view and saw her, he broke into a run, and, when he reached her, to her amazement he encircled her in his arms.

'Come for a walk with me, Dora, I must talk with you!' he panted. 'Such news!' Dora was startled, even a little alarmed by this uncharacteristic behaviour, but preferring to walk with him rather than listen to the endless griping over Bailiff's Cottage, they walked a little way down the lane, his left arm around her.

'Dear little Dora, haven't you heard the news? Surely your parents must have heard about Mr Chamberlain's peace mission – mine are celebrating with champagne!'

'No, Mum and Dad do nothing but talk about Billy and Pam turning us out into Bailiff's Cottage,' she replied. 'I don't think they've had the wireless on much lately.'

She began to tell him about the family problems, but he cut her short.

'But Dora, my sweet girl, haven't you *heard*? Mr Chamberlain has come back from Germany with a peace agreement! Don't you understand what that means?'

Without giving her time to answer, he went on, 'It means there's not going to be a war, and we can all breathe again. Oh, my dear, I can tell you now, I couldn't before – if this country had gone to war I'd have had to join one of the armed services – but now I won't have to, and oh, my Dora, can't you see what a difference this makes to me?'

'But Howard, you've never said anything about this before,' said Dora, puzzled by his disjointed speech, and conscious of his arm still holding her tightly round her waist. He had kissed her a couple of times this summer, but had not grabbed hold of her with such urgency as this. Could he possibly have been drinking, she wondered, seeing that his parents were celebrating with champagne?

'You see, I've kept my fears to myself, and didn't want to tell you or anybody of my – my fear of what might happen, but – oh, Dora, now I won't have to bear that awful burden any longer. It's "Peace in our time", Dora, so kiss me – let me kiss you! – oh, God be thanked!'

She obediently held up her face and he kissed her passionately as never before, then held her close against him, murmuring brokenly in her ear, 'I've been so afraid, Dora, God knows I've been so afraid. But it's going to be all right now.'

Instinctively she started to push him away, and when she broke free, there were tears on her face. *His* tears. She hardly knew how to reply; of course she liked him, but had never

44

been in love with him, and this sudden need for her was alarming.

'I'm happy for you if *you're* happy, Howard,' she said, trying to speak lightly. 'I hadn't, er, realised how important this is, about Mr Chamberlain going to see that Hitler man, but if it's good news, well – of course I'm pleased.'

Which was the moment when Howard Allingham realised that he had expected too much of Dora Goddard, and while his relief at Chamberlain's successful mission was enormous, his behaviour towards her this evening now appeared to be ridiculous, even bizarre. He began to feel embarrassed.

'Dora, I apologise for – for this display of – you must think I'm losing my mind,' he said. 'It's just that I've grown so fond of you, as you must have realised, and now that the awful threat of war has been taken away, I – er – I suppose I overreacted in this way. Perhaps we can walk a little further, it's a fine evening.'

But Dora was taking no chances. She smiled and turned down the corners of her mouth apologetically.

'Actually, Howard, I'd better be getting back. I think my mother needs some support – it's not been a good time for her or any of us. So I'll say goodnight now.'

She held out her hand for him to shake, and he raised it to his lips.

'Goodnight, Howard. I expect I'll see you again in church on Sunday.'

'Yes, the place will probably be packed with people giving thanks. Goodnight, Dora, and I'm sorry for all that – display. I'm truly sorry. Please forgive me.'

'All right, Howard, it's – er – all right,' she said, adding what she assumed he'd want to hear, 'Nobody will know about it, because I won't tell anybody. Goodnight, then.'

'Goodnight, Dora,' he said, adding under his breath, 'you sweet, beautiful girl.'

The Pearsons, Mrs and Miss, had also listened to Mr Chamberlain on the wireless, and Mrs Pearson clapped her hands.

'Peace in our time, Valerie, thanks to God's intervention through our wonderful Prime Minister! "Peace with honour!" Our country's freedom is saved, thanks to him. We shall go to church on Sunday morning, and give thanks from our hearts.'

'It's wonderful news, Mother,' said her daughter, thankful to see her mother so happy and confident in the future again. Unable to put these thoughts into words, she went over to the old lady as she sat on her armchair, and gave her a hug – whereupon Mrs Pearson tearfully returned the embrace, a gesture uncharacteristic of either of them.

On the Saturday morning at Thomas and Gibson's, Valerie shared the smiles of customers who had only one topic of conversation, and Mr Richardson beamed and said that the shop would shut at midday, to mark the triumphant conclusion of the Munich conference. She thought she would take her usual walk in the meadows by the river, but decided she owed it to her mother to share the afternoon with her; they could have something special for tea, and she would call at Seabrook's on the way home.

She had just made up her mind to get tinned salmon, which her mother preferred to the fresh fish, when suddenly everything in her life was changed. It happened at a quarter to eleven, while she had her back to the door, sorting out some embroidery silks in one of the shallow drawers behind the counter. Mr John Richardson strode into the shop, full of geniality towards the world, and to Miss Valerie Pearson in particular.

'Valerie! What are you doing here? You ought to be out dancing in the street, like some of our staff at Page's! Peace in our time, Valerie!'

And before she could answer, he leapt over the counter and seized her round the waist, carried her into the main space of the shop, and proceeded to spin her round him twice. She had to hold on to his shoulders as her feet left the floor, a shoe flew off, and she closed her eyes – for surely this must be a dream!

But it was no dream. When he let her feet touch the floor again, he thrust her backwards over his left arm as if she had been an oversized rag doll. His face leant over her and found her lips: what followed was something Valerie had sometimes dreamt of, but never like this – nothing so intoxicating as *this*. He kissed her fervently, deeply, his mouth covering hers and demanding a response. Was it for a moment or a minute or more? Valerie could hardly tell; his right hand ruffled her hair, pulling out pins that scattered on the floor, leaving it hanging in loose tresses over her shoulders.

'I've been wanting to do that for so long,' he murmured.

When he allowed her to stand upright again, she felt giddy and leant her head against his chest.

'Little Valerie,' he whispered, with a deep, quiet chuckle. 'Dear little Valerie.'

'John,' she whispered back. 'Oh, John.'

They stood there together in the middle of the shop for

what seemed ages to Valerie, until he gently set her free, sitting her down on the chair reserved for customers. He went into his father's office, and she heard the two of them talking about the news.

And time, which never stands still, continued to pass, and the earth kept on turning.

As had been predicted, St Peter's was full to overflowing that Sunday morning, and 'Now Thank We All Our God' rang out from every throat, guided by Philip Saville's all-stops-out accompaniment on the organ. The Reverend Allingham gave humble and hearty thanks on behalf of the congregation for deliverance from the danger of war, and in his sermon openly rebuked those persons who had expressed doubts about the outcome of Mr Chamberlain's untiring efforts to secure peace in Europe; such dismal sentiments had no place in Great Britain, he said, reigned over by a new King and Queen whose benign rule stretched across the world, the mighty British Empire. The Amens rose up, a solid block of sound echoing to the vaulted roof of the ancient church.

Valerie Pearson sang the hymns and responses with a fervour that surprised her mother, though the old lady was gratified at her daughter's ardent patriotism. Sir Cedric and Lady Neville also responded to the prevailing euphoria, as did Councillor Mrs Tomlinson, whatever her inward reservations. Some of the older parishioners who remembered the Great War that had ended twenty years ago exchanged meaningful looks of shared sadness, whereas some of the youngsters, Lester Allingham and Jack Nuttall, exchanged silent wry commiserations as their chance of an exciting new adventure had apparently been scuttled.

When Dora Goddard saw Howard Allingham looking in her direction, she quickly looked away. Their former easy friendship had ended with the encounter on Friday evening, for she had no wish for the kind of emotional attachment that he seemed to want from her. On his part, Howard cursed his foolishness, for what had been said could not be unsaid, and while he joined in the general thanksgiving, he was unable to suppress a nagging unease which he could not precisely identify.

The service ended with the National Anthem, and the congregation trooped out as Philip played the 'Trumpet Voluntary'.

On the Monday after that memorable weekend, Councillor Mrs Tomlinson was at the council offices in Everham, sharing mid-morning coffee with Sir Cedric Neville. When he asked her how she felt about the news, she put her head on one side like a thoughtful old bird.

'I wish I felt as reassured as the Prime Minister, poor man,' she said after consideration. 'If ever there was a peace-lover and a peace-maker, a man of principle, an English gentleman, that's Mr Neville Chamberlain. And that's why I'm worried, Cedric. Is he the right man to deal with a cynical megalomaniac like this strutting dictator? And if Hitler *does* march his troops over the Czech border, who is there to stop him?'

Cedric was silent, having no answer to give, while Mrs Tomlinson waited. Suddenly he wanted to argue against her, reprimand her for 'spreading alarm and despondency' – the old military charge came back to mind – refuse to listen to her, scold her, stand her in the corner.

But he had no words to contradict her.

* * *

'Adolf bloody Hitler hasn't even waited a week.'

The high-backed bench seat in the Tradesmen's Arms had been moved from its summer position below the window to its winter place near to the log fire. Several of the regulars were in, and a young couple, when Tom Munday sat down beside Eddie Cooper, already halfway into a pint of bitter.

Voices around the bar all spoke on one subject.

'Less than a week after Chamberlain came back, and he's marched into Czecho-czecho-whatever' – 'yeah, but it's a long way from 'ere, I'd just let 'em get on with it' – 'they say he's got his eye on *us* an' all' – 'who says so?' – 'don't believe every rumour you hear' – 'and the way he treats the Jews' – 'yeah, but they're Jews, ain't they? I don't trust 'em'.

'Doesn't sound so good,' said Tom heavily. 'Grace and Rob are hoping it won't come to anything. Their Jack's eighteen and says he wants to go into the Royal Air Force.'

'Got no sense at all, have they?' said Eddie. 'Twenty years since the last lot, and these young idiots are looking for another scrap.' He took another drink from his glass, and wiped his mouth. 'I say, look at Don Juan over at the bar there, talking to that little minx from Seabrook's. Who is he?'

'He's the younger o' the two boys from the Rectory. Wonder if mum and dad know where he is this evening.'

'More to the point, do the Seabrooks know where *she* is,' said Eddie. 'Look at him, thinks he's Clark Gable, and that's the third port and lemon she's knocked back. She'd better watch her step, I reckon, or she'll end up like—' He stopped speaking and shrugged.

He means like his Mary, thought Tom. Poor Mary Cooper, married off in haste to Sidney Goddard, and now being elbowed out by that lout Billy Yeomans since he'd got himself a wife.

'Your young granddaughter, Tom, now there's a nice girl. Must be about the same age as that one over there, but behaves herself better.'

'Oh, ah, Doreen's a homebody, helps Grace in the house, no trouble at all.' Tom gave an imperceptible sigh.

There was a burst of laughter from the young couple who then took their leave, letting in a chill October wind through the open door.

'Not a care in the world, eh?' said Eddie.

'No, it's only parents who worry,' muttered Tom, 'and them with Jewish relatives out there,' adding under his breath what he'd heard at the bar when he came in, 'He didn't even wait a week, the lying bugger.'

The Reverend Alan Kennard preached on the following Sunday, and his sermon was in chilling contrast to the rector's at the previous Morning Worship.

'We must indeed still pray for a true and lasting peace, but we must prepare ourselves for war,' he said to gasps of surprise. 'The German Chancellor has gone back on his word not to invade eastern European countries, and our hearts go out to the people of Czechoslovakia at this time. We trust that Almighty God will protect them from the invading enemy, especially those of the Jewish race. We have to face the truth of their persecution, because we cannot afford to ignore it.'

There was an uncomfortable stirring among the congregation, and the Reverend Allingham's face registered furious disapproval at this contradiction of his own sermon, so full of thanksgiving and hope for the future. The Reverend Alan Kennard would be severely reprimanded at the earliest opportunity.

At Hassett Manor the curate's words were the chief topic of conversation, and Cedric experienced a sensation close to relief at Alan Kennard's recognition of the dangers that might lie ahead. Facing the truth, however unpalatable, was better than living in a fool's paradise. Some Members of Parliament evidently thought so too, accusing Chamberlain of 'selling out to the Fascists,' and the First Lord of the Admiralty had resigned.

Any doubts that still remained about the intentions of Herr Hitler were shattered by the news of a savage all-night attack on the Jewish community all over Germany; so many windows were smashed, including shop fronts, that the Germans themselves jokingly referred to it as *Kristillnacht* because of all the broken glass that littered the streets afterwards. Ernest and Devora Munday now expected Jonathan and Ella Pascoe to leave Germany with their children forthwith, but to their utter dismay, Jonathan refused to flee. Things weren't so bad in a semi-rural area like Elberfeld as in the big towns and cities, he said, so Devora was left to fret and her husband to lose patience with the Pascoes in the face of such terrible danger.

At Yeomans' Farm that Christmas Dora had come to a decision. Billy sneezed and streamed with a cold, two farm hands were talking of going to join the territorials, and Sidney worked from dawn to dusk, seven days a week. Old Mrs Yeomans said she could no longer keep the farm accounts due to failing eyesight, and asked Dora if she could take over the record keeping, which Dora saw was in a chaotic state. She therefore went to Billy and said she would give up commercial college to become farm secretary and book-keeper, and give some assistance on the farm. He grudgingly accepted, even agreeing to pay her a minimum wage.

'But Dora, you *can't* give up your training,' Mary Goddard protested, but Dora's mind was made up.

'I'm not going to see you and Dad working yourselves into the ground,' she said, 'and you won't hear any more about Bailiff's Cottage from now on. Even *he's* got to admit that the Yeomanses can't manage without the Goddards!'

Even so, Christmas dinner was a subdued affair, with Billy coughing loudly and Pam complaining of continuous backache at six and a half months into pregnancy.

'Without us, Mum, they'd have had no Christmas fare at all,' said Dora grimly.

Valerie Pearson had saved up to buy John Richardson a gold tie-pin and matching cufflinks, and shyly presented the little wrapped parcel to him on the day before Christmas Eve when he breezed into Thomas and Gibson's to see his father. He kissed her on the cheek and said he was overwhelmed by such generosity, but that it was very naughty of her. In his father's office, he grimaced and said he'd have to rush out to buy a box of chocolates for her.

'I hope you haven't been playing fast and loose with that girl,' said his father with a frown. 'She's not a giggling young miss, but a respectable young woman of twenty-seven, a conscientious worker, and I wouldn't like to see her upset. What have you been up to – flirting? Kissing her?'

'Only the once, on the "peace in our time" weekend, Dad, when everybody was a bit over-the-moon, and – er, I'd been celebrating the peace treaty at Page's before I came over. She didn't make any objection, though of course it didn't mean anything, and hasn't happened again – only little pecks on the cheek when I pass through the shop, really quite innocent.'

'It would only be innocent if you intended to follow it through,' said Mr Richardson firmly. 'Are you genuinely fond of Miss Pearson? You could do worse.'

'Oh, no, Dad, she's a sweet little thing, but such a mouse! And two years older than I am – and lives with that old dragon of a mother – oh, no, it was never intended to be serious.'

'Well, show her some respect, then, and as I say, you could fare a lot worse. Otherwise don't let the poor girl get any wrong ideas about your intentions.'

'No, of course not, Dad,' said John sheepishly, because he knew by the unconcealed adoration in her eyes that she already had.

March brought an increase at Yeomans' Farm; but when Tom Munday sat down beside Eddie Cooper, his old friend irritably cut short his congratulations.

'Properly worn out, my Mary was, after two nights on the trot without sleep, at the beck and call of Billy's wife who's been having backache since before Christmas. She started the proper pains on Tuesday evening, and Billy went to fetch Nurse Howie, who came and said it was early as yet, and she ought to try to get some sleep, then went home again. Old Mrs Yeomans sat with her until about midnight, and then Mary heard a crash and a scream – went into the room to find the old lady nodding, young Mrs Yeomans on the floor, and the chamber pot overturned. My Mary took over, but the silly woman wouldn't settle, kept saying the baby was coming – but when Nurse Howie came back at around ten on Wednesday morning, she said there hadn't been much change, but the bowel needed emptying, and she gave her an enema – that's a pint of soapy water up the back end.'

'Oh, heck!' Tom sympathised, trying to keep a straight face. 'And did it work?'

'It did. There was stuff all over the bed and on the carpet. Nurse Howie cleared off, and Mary and Dora had it all to clear up. Dora sent her mother off to rest while she took over, and all the time young Mrs Yeomans was hollering that the baby was coming.'

'And was it?' asked Tom.

'Yeah, twelve hours later, after another night of it. Nurse Howie came back that evening, and Sid told her he'd take Billy downstairs for a drink, while my Mary and Dora spent the night waiting on young Mrs Yeomans and the midwife. Dora refused to go to bed while her mother stayed up – and around four o'clock Nurse Howie asked her to telephone for Dr Lupton. He came and said he'd have to use forceps to get it out; they were like a bloody great pair of tongs, Dora said, and Nurse Howie sprayed chloroform onto a square of cotton wool over the woman's nose and mouth. Lupton pulled it out just after six – a huge great thing, ten pounds on the kitchen scales. Mary made tea and toast for everybody again, and Dora went downstairs to tell Billy it was born – only he was so drunk he couldn't get out of the armchair. The mother fell fast asleep and didn't wake up till midday, and the baby hollered until Dora fetched the bottle and teat, and gave it cow's milk watered down and warmed up. They're calling it Samuel.'

By which Tom Munday assumed that the child was a boy.

'Well, thank God for that, Eddie,' he said, adding musingly, 'Thank God it didn't happen with bombs falling all around.'

'D'you really think it'll come to that, then?' Eddie clung to the belief that peace would yet prevail.

'Well, they're talking about digging air raid shelters, and getting the kids out of the towns before it happens.'

'For God's sake, Tom, we *can't* let that tinpot dictator drag us into *war*, surely?'

'That tinpot dictator has entered Prague. Whatever he says, Czechoslovakia is an occupied country, and he's rounding up the Jews there for God only knows what fate.'

'The bastard.'

For a moment Eddie Cooper's account of baby Samuel's birth was set aside while the two old friends contemplated an unthinkable future.

'Oh, Mother, here's something to take our minds off this ghastly war talk!' Rebecca Neville exclaimed over the weekly *Everham News*. 'Guess what's on at the Embassy all next week – the film of *Wuthering Heights,* with somebody called Laurence Olivier and that exquisite actress Merle Oberon – we just can't miss it. When are you free? Would Sally like to come?'

'Is there a matinee performance?' asked Lady Isabel, looking up from her correspondence.

'Wednesday.'

'That's the Ladies' Hour, so won't do.'

'Let's go Wednesday evening, then.'

Lady Isabel took off her reading glasses. 'Look, Becky, I don't really want to go, it can't possibly be as good as the book. What a pity Geoffrey Bannister isn't staying with us.'

'Oh, Mother! I'll have to go with somebody else, but who? Dora Goddard will have a male escort – I know, I'll ask that poor girl in Thomas and Gibson's, Miss Pearson. It would do her good to get away from her mother – I'll pop into the shop tomorrow and ask her, and won't take no for an answer. I'll take the old girl some flowers to sweeten her up!'

At Yeomans' Farm the new arrival was still bawling, as Dora wearily remarked, 'Listen, Mum, I'm taking you out on Wednesday, and Pam can jolly well take care of her baby for a change.'

'Oh, but—'

'No, I insist. We'll look around Page's and have tea at that little café by the station – and then we'll go to the Embassy Cinema and see this film that everybody's talking about. It'll do you good to dress up and put some of my lipstick on – and scent!'

Mary Goddard could not resist her daughter's orders, and was both pleased and touched.

'I'll wear that flower-patterned dress with the frilly front,' she said, 'and treat myself to a shampoo and set. Oh, I'm really looking forward to it!'

It was Dora who answered the knock on the farmhouse door on Tuesday. Howard Allingham stood there, looking apprehensive but determined.

'Oh – Dora,' he said with a shy smile, 'I'm glad you've come to the door, as it's you I want to see.'

'Hallo, Howard, how are you?' she answered in some surprise. 'I thought you'd gone to – er – theological college.'

'Not yet, but perhaps September if the – if the news – but I've come to ask if you'd like to come to the cinema in Everham tomorrow, to see this film of *Wuthering Heights*.'

'Ah, yes, it's supposed to be very good,' she said, her mind working quickly. Should she just decline politely without giving a reason – or could she accept in a friendly way, without encouraging him to hope for more than friendship? Yes! She *did* know of a way.

'That's very kind of you, Howard, and as it happens, I'm going to see it tomorrow with my mother who's been overworking and deserves a break. Would you care to join us?'

Howard's face was a study. He had been half-expecting a refusal, but was not prepared for this alternative. He decided that it would be better than nothing, so he forced a smile.

'That would be very nice, Dora, as long as Mrs Goddard doesn't mind.'

'Not at all, Howard, she'd be delighted. What time shall we meet?'

A queue had formed outside the Embassy cinema, and Rebecca and Valerie joined it.

'Oh, Valerie, look, there's that nice Allingham boy over there – he looks as if he's waiting for somebody. I wonder who she is?'

Valerie did not answer. Her eyes were elsewhere, and her heart had leapt as she caught sight of John Richardson looking quite the man-about-town in a light grey summer suit and shoes that were almost sandals but not quite. He was not alone; there was a smart young woman at his side, giving a tinkling laugh at something he'd said. Valerie abruptly looked away; she still dreamt that one day, at some future time, he would return her love. And now here he was with another girl. She mustn't look.

'Look, there's Howard, Mother, standing by the door,' said Dora, waving to him. His eyes brightened at the sight of her, though he politely greeted Mrs Goddard first.

'We must join the queue, Howard.'

'No, Dora, we don't need to, I've got three tickets, and we can go straight in,' he said, offering his arm to her mother and acknowledging their thanks with a smile, refusing payment. I did right to agree to this, he thought, conscious of Mrs Goddard's welcoming approval, and was further rewarded when they took their seats and Dora sat down between him and her mother.

'Dora! If you'd told me earlier that you were meeting young Mr Allingham, I wouldn't have come,' Mary whispered.

'Which is why I didn't tell you, Mother,' Dora whispered back.

During the interval when the lights went up, giving the enraptured audience a brief respite from the lovers' torrid passion, Valerie Pearson imagined herself as Merle Oberon, adored by brooding, black-browed Laurence Olivier, looking a little bit like John Richardson. Suddenly these thoughts were interrupted.

'Why, hello, Valerie! I didn't realise *you* were here!'

(Heavens above, it can't be John Richardson, but it *is*.)

'Hello, er, John,' she said with a shy smile, hoping that the dim light would hide her blushes. Rebecca looked from one to the other in surprise.

'Valerie! You've never said anything to me about a gentleman friend!' she teased.

'Yes, er, at Thomas and Gibsons, he's Mr Richardson's son,' faltered Valerie.

'And *I* didn't know that Valerie had such a charming friend,' he said. 'Aren't you going to introduce me? By the way, this is Miss Morcom from Page's lingerie department.' Miss Morcom nodded coolly to the two ladies.

'Yes, er, this is my friend from—' Valerie hesitated, and Rebecca laughed.

'I'm your friend Rebecca Neville from Hassett Manor, in case you've forgotten,' she said, gently teasing poor, tongue-tied Valerie. 'Very pleased to make your acquaintance, John – and Miss Morcom. Isn't the film marvellous? Look, the lights are going down – you must get back to your seats so as not to miss any of it. Perhaps we can arrange to meet again some time.'

John agreed enthusiastically, though Miss Morcom was unsmiling. She had been anticipating an evening to remember – but not if he was going to fall for this tall, elegant creature called Rebecca.

The second half of the film was even more tempestuous than the first, but when it ended, there was still the Gaumont British News to see, introduced by the familiar tune and the town crier ringing his bell. The audience was suddenly gripped by the shaky black and white newsreel film footage showing a long, winding trail of Jewish refugees – men, women and children, some with horse-drawn wagons, others with hand-carts or on foot, fleeing with their possessions from German invaders. Then there were pictures of the signing of the treaty between Herr Hitler and a broadly beaming Signor Mussolini, a 'pact of steel' between two Fascist dictators. The loss of Italy as a potential ally was a severe blow, and Howard Allingham confided to Dora and her mother that Mr Chamberlain's 'peace in our time' was now being called 'appeasement.' Privately he surmised that theological college would be replaced by military service, and he prayed for the strength and courage to face whatever the future held.

On a warm summer evening in the Tradesmen's Arms Eddie Cooper waited for his old friend. In the bar the talk was all of air raid shelters being dug, gas masks being issued, and conscription of young single men to swell the numbers of the armed forces. That would apply to Tom's grandson Paul Storey, thought Eddie, and the two sons of the Rectory; his own grandson Jack Nuttall would be nineteen this year, as would the Seabrook boy.

Tom Munday strode in, his face jubilant. 'Ernest's brother-in-law and his family are coming over at last, Eddie! They've had a letter from him, saying to expect them any day now. The reason for the delay was because they were expecting another child, and now it's born, a son, and they've called him Benjamin. So we'll have a baby in the house – and Devora's dancing for joy. Eddie, old friend, they've seen sense, thank God!'

They ordered a couple of pints to celebrate.

A week later in the Munday's house in Everham there was sudden urgency. A brief official letter had arrived, telling Mr and Mrs Munday to meet a midday train at Liverpool Street Station on the following day, instructing them to wear large labels with their names on. The Pascoes must be coming! They hardly slept that night, and set off early in the morning; from Everham they travelled to Waterloo Station, then by the underground railway to Liverpool Street, where they were amongst a crowd of others wearing labels. Officials scurried around with clipboards, getting ready to team up the arrivals with their families and friends.

The train, when it arrived two hours late, was full of children – sad, weary, bewildered children aged from five to early teens. Officials went amongst them, calling out names.

'Pascoe! Jonathan and Ayesha Pascoe!' called a woman's voice, followed by, 'Munday! Is Munday here?'

Fifteen-year-old Jonathan and his sister Ayesha, eleven, were brought forward to meet their aunt and uncle. They appeared exhausted, and Ayesha was crying. They spoke in German, of which Ernest and Devora knew only a little.

The inevitable question: 'Where are your father and mother?'

'They've gone to – to a kind of camp,' Jonny told them in his hesitant schoolboy's English. 'We were walking with them and many neighbours on a long road – and a man came up and took me and Ayesha away from them, and said we must go on a train.'

'And Mummy and Daddy told us to go with him!' sobbed Ayesha in German that Ernest and Devora tried to follow. 'Mummy was holding our baby Benjamin, and crying, but they told us to go with the man, and said *Goodbye!*'

'Oh, my God, you poor dear children,' Ernest muttered under his breath as he and Devora put their arms around the brother and sister, trying to comfort them while fearing that there was no comfort to give. An official passed by the group, still trying to match children with whoever had come to meet them.

'You're lucky,' he told them. 'This is the last train on the *Kindertransport* – the last ones out!'

And when they realised that their nephew and niece

had been saved by a humanitarian scheme to rescue Jewish children – and that their parents and newly born brother had been taken away to whatever awaited Jews under Hitler's rule – Ernest and Devora Munday knew for certain that war would be soon. They had no need to hear Mr Chamberlain's sorrowful announcement on the third day of September.

And Clarence Tomlinson had nobody to meet him when he abruptly left his post in the Diplomatic Service and fled from Vienna, home to his mother in England.

CHAPTER FOUR

1939

Tom Munday sat in the rocking chair that Grace and Rob had given him on his 70th birthday; it was by the window in the living room, and the view of his vegetable garden was the same as it had been last week and last year, and yet everything was now changed. In the mild September sunshine his thoughts were sombre; the newspaper with its shrieking headlines had fallen to the floor, and his granddaughter Doreen was idly dusting the sideboard that was her mother's pride, handed down from the grandmother she had never known. She picked up the *Daily Mail* and handed it to Tom.

'Is there really going to be a war, Granddad?'

'Yes, my dear, the war has started already, though it hasn't made much difference to North Camp as yet,' he said with a smile. 'There's no need for you to worry yourself about it, though – we don't know how long it will take.'

'But they've dug an air raid shelter, Granddad!' she said

eagerly. 'It's the other side of the green, in case we all have to go down in it to escape from the bombs!'

'I don't think that's very likely, dear,' he answered, straining his ears to hear what Grace and Rob were saying in the kitchen. Grace's voice was raised, and Tom could guess only too well what they were talking about.

'There's no "of course" about it, Rob,' Grace was saying, and Tom could hear the fear in his daughter's voice. 'They couldn't call up Jack, he's far too useful to us here, I mean he'll run the business when he takes over from you, just as you took it over from Dad. Which is why we've never been able to move away from North Camp,' she added in an undertone.

'I doubt there'll be so many jobs now that this war's started,' said her husband doubtfully. 'And as for the call-up, they're mobilising the reserves and territorials first, and your nephew Paul at Hassett Manor is likely to be called on first.'

'Oh, yes, Hassett Manor, I dare say Isabel will make a great song and dance about *him*,' she said bitterly. 'The likes of Paul Storey and his university pal – *they'll* be safely closeted in Oxford while the North Camp lads like our Jack get called up. It's not fair!'

Her voice had steadily risen, and Tom Munday got up from his chair, frowning.

'You stay here, Doreen, and finish your dusting while I have a word with Mum and Dad.' He closed the door behind him, and went into the kitchen.

'Hush, keep your voices down,' he told them. 'You don't want Doreen hearing that sort of talk. It's too early to start worrying about the call-up. Just think about Ernest and Devora, losing her brother and sister-in-law to these Nazis, and poor Jonny and Ayesha being rushed out of Germany without parents or possessions, landing on their aunt and uncle without a penny to their name, and not even able to speak English. I hope you'll find time to go over to Everham and see them, Grace. Isabel's been over with Rebecca.'

Too late he realised that the last sentence had been unwise. Grace was furious.

'Oh, yes, of course, her ladyship of Hassett Manor would be *sure* to go over there in the Hassett car – or maybe riding their horses? – loaded with home produce from their farm, taking the children out shopping for clothes – and showing off her beautiful, clever daughter. I can't compete, can I, with my poor, simple Doreen.'

'Be quiet, Grace,' said her father sharply. 'Such talk isn't worthy of you.'

Rob put his arm around her. 'How many times have I told you not to dwell on it, Gracie –it's all a long time ago, and people don't know, so the less said about it, the better.'

'Oh, for God's sake, everybody in North Camp knows, you can't keep a secret like *that*, especially when the people concerned live scarcely a mile apart!' she retorted.

Tom spoke again, very gently. 'Both those girls are my granddaughters, remember, and I don't see half as much of Becky as I do of our Doreen, and I prefer it that way. Doreen needs me – needs *us*, all of us, more than her cousin. Everybody likes her, she's so sweet and loving, and she'll never give you any kind of trouble. Little angel.'

Tom's voice trembled as he said the two last words, and Grace fell silent. Rob looked gratefully at his father-in-law, for the two men had long shared a mutual, instinctive protection of the mother and the daughter.

For Doreen Nuttall had been a 'blue baby', slow to breathe, and had grown up to be slow to learn. Her parents had removed her from school early, and her grandfather had taught her the alphabet and the basics of reading and writing. A pretty girl with a sweet face, her preferred occupation was to help her mother at the household tasks of sweeping and dusting, washing and ironing, preparing vegetables and gracing the table with her artless smiles.

'Miss Neville! Good morning to you – we're both up with the lark!'

Rebecca reined in Sunbeam, and looked down at the young man who had hailed her. His good looks were vaguely familiar, but his name evaded her.

'Good morning,' she replied, slightly raising her eyebrows in a question.

'Richardson – John Richardson, don't you remember? We met at the Embassy cinema when everybody was going to see *Wuthering Heights*. You were with your friend Miss Pearson, and she introduced us!'

'Ah, yes, of course.' Rebecca nodded. 'It seems so long ago now, after all that has happened since.'

'Yes.' He stood beside Sunbeam and looked up at her rider as if he had more to say. Rebecca wondered if she should dismount; they were on a bridle bath that led back to Hassett Manor. She had been out for an early ride, and a chill October mist still lingered over the ploughed fields; it now occurred to her that Mr Richardson was walking out early, and that he might have a reason for being here. His next words answered her.

'It's because of all that's happened since, Miss Neville –

I'd better be truthful, and confess that I've been hoping to meet you again.' He did not say that he had been hanging around in the vicinity of Hassett Manor on a number of mornings. 'As you say, being at war has changed all our circumstances, which is why I – well, I've thrown aside convention and decided to speak to you again before – well, there is a possibility that I may be conscripted.'

Rebecca gave a little gasp, and saw how intently he was regarding her. She climbed down from Sunbeam, and held the reins loosely. 'Ah, well now, Mr Richardson—'

'Please call me John – Rebecca.'

'Forgive me for asking, Mr – John – but is it certain that you'll be called up?' she asked. 'My brother hasn't received any information as yet, perhaps because he's an undergraduate at Oxford – though they expect to have their studies interrupted if it becomes necessary for them to join the armed forces. Have *you* received call-up papers?'

'I expect to receive them any day now, Rebecca, and before I do – would you – will you come with me to see another film that's going the rounds – *The Wizard of Oz*?'

'Isn't that a film for children?' she asked with a smile, trying to adjust her mind to this unexpected admirer.

'Yes, but it's for adults too, and all in this new technicolour, with amazing special effects, or so I've heard.' He was close to her, and she could breathe in the clean, soapy smell of his skin, and she blushed. This young man was expecting to be conscripted into the army, navy or air force, and here he was, practically begging her to go out with him. His manners were impeccable, and there seemed no reason to refuse; but . . .

'But if you'd rather not see the film, we could perhaps go

for a walk, or for lunch somewhere,' he added with respectful persistence.

'Thank you, I'd like to see the film,' she told him, and his eyes brightened.

'Thank *you*, Rebecca, that makes me very happy,' he said, eagerly taking hold of her free hand. 'Let me know when you'd like to go – one evening next week? Have you any idea where we could meet?'

'You could call for me at Hassett Manor,' she replied, letting him hold her hand, though she was taken aback when he raised it to his lips and kissed the fingers.

John Richardson could hardly believe his luck: to call at Hassett Manor would mean meeting Sir Cedric and Lady Isabel Neville, and here was his chance to make an impression on them, for surely she could have no other fellow in mind if she had accepted his invitation so readily. He watched as she remounted Sunbeam, and greatly daring, blew her a kiss as she rode away.

As for Rebecca, her thoughts were in a whirl, but she was not sorry she had accepted his unconventional invitation. And he was certainly good-looking.

At the Rectory there was both consternation and bewilderment. Roland Allingham had become even more hostile to his curate whose gloomy predictions had proved to be all too true. Joan Kennard was indignant on her husband's behalf.

'The way he speaks about you is downright insulting, Alan,' she said after a Sunday morning service when the congregation were leaving and commenting on the war. Mrs Pearson was worried because her daily newspaper was forecasting food rationing because of German submarines attacking merchant ships bringing vital food from overseas.

'Scaremongering, Mrs Pearson,' the Reverend Mr Allingham had told her, 'and to spread such alarming rumours is unpatriotic and will only play into the enemy's hands. Don't be disheartened by this kind of talk.'

'But Mr Kennard said at Evensong last week that—'

'I'm afraid Mr Kennard says a great deal of things that would be better left unsaid, Mrs Pearson, and I shall have to speak to him about it again. In the meantime let us all show our native British spirit, trust in God, be filled with hope and confidence – and don't be misled by the likes of Mr Kennard!'

'How *dare* he!' Joan muttered as she took a roast leg of lamb out of the oven. 'It's blinkered fools like *him* who should be disregarded, not realists like you!'

'Hush, Joan my love. Remember the Allinghams have two sons of an age to be called up for military service. Allingham probably dares not think about what might happen. We have no such sword hanging over our heads.'

Joan was not to be so easily calmed. 'Howard's supposed to going to Bible college, and the younger one's a trouble-maker. The Seabrooks have forbidden their daughter to go out with him, or so I've heard. *Their* son Robin might have to go, so they've got worry enough, without Barbara giving them more.'

'If that's true, there's no surer way of encouraging them to meet secretly,' Alan replied mildly, sharpening the carving knife.

'You're too kind to the Allinghams,' Joan said, lifting Josie into her high chair and tying on her bib.

Alan looked fondly on his two 'girlies', as he called them, his pretty young wife and fourteen-month-old daughter. As a clergyman he was not required to fight for his country, but he could volunteer as a chaplain to the Forces if he wished.

But that was something he did not share with Joan or anybody else.

In the Munday household in Everham, the two young newcomers were proving unable to forget the experience of being torn from their parents' side and sent on a terrifying journey that had ended in the home of this kind but unknown aunt and uncle who spoke a different language. Miriam Munday was ordered by her parents to be especially kind to her cousin Ayesha, and help her to mingle with the other children at Everham Council School. Though Ayesha was a year older, she was allowed to sit beside Miriam in class, so as to pick up English at her own speed. It was a slow process, for Ayesha pined for the life she had left behind at Eberfeld; at night she would dream she was back home again with her mother and father, only to wake up suddenly, screaming with terror and frightening Miriam who shared a room with her. Jonathan Pascoe, known as Jonny, was two years older than David, and his efforts to be brave were noted by his uncle Ernest with mixed admiration and pity. The boy was readier to learn English than his sister, and the Mundays engaged a tutor for him, letting him pass on his knowledge to Ayesha, with benefit to them both. Every so often the newspapers had to be hidden from the children when they reported Nazi cruelty to the Jews, and their banishment to sinister camps.

At home the news was bad enough: the sinking of the battleship *Royal Oak* in her home base at Scapa Flow brought the war before the nation in a way that overseas events did not. The *Royal Oak* and her crew had been torpedoed by a German submarine, a U-boat, and these enemy vessels were to become dreaded by Royal and Merchant Navies alike throughout the course of the war. Posters went up in towns and villages all over the country, warning that spies could be anywhere, and that careless talk about positions of ships could cost lives.

At Hassett Manor Cedric and Isabel were discussing the personable young man who had come to call for Rebecca to take her out.

'It's a great pity young Bannister isn't here, he'd soon see the fellow off,' said Cedric. 'Cheeky young upstart – a floor manager in a department store, if you please!'

Isabel shook her head. 'If he gets called up to serve in the armed forces, he'll be as good a conscript as any other,' she said quietly, and Cedric knew she was remembering her own origins as Isabel Munday, the carpenter's elder daughter.

'As you say, my love, danger is a great leveller,' he replied. 'And our young Don Juan will soon be put to the test. Another quarter of a million men are to be conscripted before Christmas, and I'll be going over to the recruitment board at Guildford.'

'Guildford? Why not Everham?'

'Because I'm not known there, so won't have to face boys who recognise me.'

She was silent, but he knew her thoughts. 'Paul and Geoffrey will be interviewed at the university,' he said gently. 'And if they pass their medical, they'll most likely be sent on an officer's training course, Sandhurst probably, being Oxford undergraduates.'

She nodded. 'And we shall ask Geoffrey to come and stay with us before they go.'

'We most certainly will, my love,' he said, smiling to hide his own misgivings about the destiny of the two young men.

When Isabel passed on this information to Sally Tanner, she also confided that she would take Geoffrey Bannister aside and tell him that Rebecca had been adopted at the end of the Great War, when so many desperate single mothers had been forced to give up their misconceived babies.

'And it won't make a ha'porth o' difference to him,' Sally replied.

Lester Allingham was incredulous, not to say dismayed, to discover that Barbara Seabrook was not willing to meet him clandestinely after her parents' prohibition. She had been so deliciously flirtatious on their outings over the past few months, actually encouraging him to take liberties with his hands on her delightful curves, and though he had not yet managed to explore below her waist, he was confident that he would reach his desired objective before the year was out – or before he received his call-up papers. He enjoyed a challenge, and had so far found most girls manageable, so he was taken aback when Barbara, who was old Seabrook's daughter and had all of her father's charm towards his customers, but also his hard head, had refused to give away more than was wise. While defying her parents, Barbara had not been deaf to her mother's warnings, and did not care to be labelled as *fast* among her friends. She was also aware of Lester's reputation, but when he told her he was called to serve his country in the Royal Air Force, her resolve wavered, and she might have agreed to one more meeting in the woods above the Blackwater valley; but because he could not hide his annoyance towards her and her parents – and the looks her brother Robin cast in his direction – he lost his chance, and his pride suffered a severe blow.

Thomas and Gibson's ordered a dozen bales of heavy black material and a hundred reels of black cotton for the women of North Camp to make black-out curtains for every home. Mrs Joan Kennard invited every member of the Ladies' Hour to bring her sewing with her, and while listening to the song, recitations and speaker of the week, their hands were not idle. Mrs Kennard's treadle sewing machine was put at the disposal of any lady who could use it, and those without one took lessons from the knowledgeable. There was silent sympathy for Lady Neville whose son Paul had gone to train as an officer, and Mrs Kennard began and ended every meeting with a prayer for all families with a son conscripted or volunteered into the armed forces. Her husband the Reverend Alan Kennard was the speaker one Wednesday afternoon in November, and although he could offer no guarantee that the conscripts would be protected from danger, his words were comforting. Councillor Mrs Tomlinson thought that some of the ladies would resent being offered comfort from a man, who, however kind and wise, had not got a son away defending his country.

At least one conscript was able to pour out his fears to Alan Kennard, and that was Howard Allingham, unable to confide in his father. Howard's hands trembled as he took a cup of tea from Mrs Kennard who then left the study, and Alan listened to the rector's son's catalogue of woe, one of his problems being that he could not talk to his father, either about warfare or his unreturned love for Dora Goddard: his regret that he had declared himself to her in the delirious but mistaken belief that there would be no war.

'I felt liberated by Mr Chamberlain's acceptance of Hitler's promise, sir, and therefore able to tell her how I felt – to grab hold of her and kiss her without first making sure that my feelings were returned. I made such a *fool* of myself, sir, I cringe to recall it now, the look on her face, the way she drew back from me, almost as if she were afraid – and now that I have definitely to join the army, I can't ask her to write to me – or to – to pray, sir. I have nowhere to turn, just when I need her most.' The last words ended on a sob in his throat, and Alan Kennard put a hand on his shoulder.

'Let's stop saying *sir*, or I'll start calling you sonny. My name's Alan, and I feel for you, Howard, and honoured that you feel able to confide in me.'

'My father would be so upset if he knew, but he'd never understand,' muttered Howard.

'Of course he wouldn't, he's of an older generation, but he doesn't think any the less of you for that.' Alan smiled but inwardly seethed against Allingham for making himself so unapproachable to this earnest young man. 'Don't blame yourself too much over Miss Goddard – she's a sweet girl but very young as yet to know the ways of the world. Just behave normally towards her when you meet, as if nothing had been said, and who knows, she might learn to think more of you, especially as you're going to be a soldier – very popular nowadays!'

'I can't ask her to write to me now, though.'

'Perhaps not, but there's nothing to stop you sending a postcard now and again – as long as you don't say where you're stationed or where you're to be posted! She'll come to appreciate you in time – in fact we're *all* going to change our views on a lot of things before this war's over – and God alone knows and understands how you feel, Howard. Do you pray? Can you speak to Him?'

'Not as I once did, I'm afraid. I get doubts.'

'As we all do. As St Paul did. *I* shall pray for you, and hope you'll pray for me in my dealings with your father!'

He laughed wryly, and Howard looked at him in surprise before he too laughed.

'How's Lester, by the way?' asked Alan.

'He's joined the Royal Air Force, and thinks it's all a great lark.'

'Good for him! Hard on your parents, though, to have both of you marching off to war. They'll be doubly proud – it'll be half a crown to speak to the Reverend Allingham!'

They stood up, and Howard said seriously, 'I'm tremendously grateful to you, Alan.'

'My pleasure. We'll keep this little chat between ourselves, then,' said the curate, adding with a wink, 'Don't forget – "Careless talk costs lives!"'

'We're gonna hang out the washing on the Siegfried line,
Have you any dirty washing, mother dear?'

The old Everham Hippodrome was packed for the matinee performance of *Dick Whittington and his Cat*, with Dick himself leading the audience in a roof-raising rendition of the song that jeered at the Germans' line of advance into France and Belgium. Rebecca Neville joined in, encouraging the six children to sing up. David and Miriam Munday were doing their best, though Jonny and Ayesha Pascoe had not as yet learnt enough English, and in any case Ayesha looked alarmed at the noise; the twins Charlie and Joe Perrin were happily bawling their heads off, and Rebecca smiled apologetically towards Devora. This pre-Christmas visit to the pantomime was her treat for them all, and for Devora who looked tired but returned her smile and shrugged.

'It's going to be a long struggle, Rebecca,' she had said earlier. 'Ernest and I are a poor substitute for the mother and father they've lost and might never see again. We probably give them more time and attention than we give to our own – no, I mustn't say that, they're *all* our own now, for always.'

'You're doing wonderful work, Devora,' said Rebecca seriously, knowing the story of Jonny and Ayesha, whisked out of Germany just in time to escape the fate of their parents.

'Where do you find your strength – from your church? – oh, no, I mean your faith,' she said quickly, remembering that the family had to travel a fair distance to the nearest synagogue.

Devora eyed her thoughtfully before replying, 'We do it for Aaron, my brother and Ernest's dearest friend, in fact they were closer than brothers. He was the love of Ernest's life, and Ernest would never have married any other woman but me, Aaron's sister. And we'll both persist with gaining the trust of Jonny and Ayesha, however long it takes, for the sake of their parents and their uncle Aaron.'

Rebecca nodded, knowing that her grandfather, Tom Munday, had once said that it was perhaps for the best that Aaron had not returned from the Great War with Ernest, but had died of his wounds in France.

But now the curtain was about to fall on Dick Whittington and his faithful Cat, as big as himself; the lights went up

77

enough for the audience to stumble towards the exits, and into the deep darkness of the black-out.

'It's been a lovely treat for us all, Rebecca,' said Devora gratefully, as the children held on to her and to each other. 'Safe journey home!'

'Come on, you two, let's all keep together,' Rebecca ordered the Perrin boys, but after walking a few yards she bumped into a man who immediately offered her his arm.

'I'm so sorry – are you all right?' asked John Richardson, and then exclaimed, 'Rebecca! Is it really you?'

'Oh, John, that was my fault,' she apologised. 'I've got two young men here, we've been to the pantomime, and now we're on our way to the station to get the train to North Camp, and then walk to Hassett Manor.'

'Good! Then I'll come with you,' he said, having waited for her to emerge from the Hippodrome with her charges, and then deliberately collided with her. 'No, I absolutely insist, you're not walking all the way from the station to Hassett Manor on your own.'

Faced with such insistence, Rebecca could only accept gratefully, but kept hold of Charlie and Joe. 'They're the sons of our groom Perrin, so they'll be coming all the way with me.' The darkness hid his expression of disappointment, but Rebecca was pleased to have the two young boys with her; it would prevent any romantic talk on the way, and she suspected, rightly, that Richardson was going to declare himself before leaving for army service; he had received his call-up papers, and she was not sure how she would answer, for she was not ready to commit herself to any man. The twins had saved her, and although John Richardson muttered under his breath while they bawled for the tenth time, 'We're gonna hang out the washing on the Siegfried line!' on the train journey to North Camp, he had to endure it without complaint. Off the train, Rebecca insisted that they held her hands, one each side of her, along the dark lanes to Hassett Manor while Richardson had to walk apart from them, hiding his frustration.

At the Manor Rebecca found Perrin waiting as arranged, and the boys duly thanked her for the treat, as did their father. Her mother came to the door and eagerly welcomed her in, saying that there was a surprise visitor for her in the dining room. She hardly noticed Richardson behind her daughter.

'You'll never guess – Paul's friend – on embarkation leave,' she began, but Geoffrey Bannister could not wait for a guessing game. He came out into the hall, and went straight up to Rebecca. They looked directly into each other's eyes, and then, without a word, as if by mutual consent, they drew together in an embrace, and he whispered in her ear, kissing her cold cheek. Sir Cedric Neville came to join his wife, and raised his eyebrows at the scene.

Rebecca drew herself away from Bannister, and awkwardly indicated Richardson who was standing transfixed at the sight of this man who was clearly no stranger here.

'Mr Richardson has kindly brought me all the way back from Everham, and I'm sure we've got some refreshment for him, Mother,' she said.

'Of course we have,' said Isabel, always the perfect hostess. 'Actually we were about to sit down to dinner, and you're very welcome to join us, John.'

After removing their coats and visiting the bathroom, the five of them sat down, waited on by Mrs Tanner. A delicious fish pie was served with carrots and greens from the Manor garden, followed by stewed plums, also home-grown, with custard.

'Great news about the *Graf Spee*,' said Cedric. 'That must have been a sight to behold, scuttling herself at the mouth of the river Plate surrounded by British ships. The captain must have decided to sink the battleship with all on board, rather than be boarded and the crew taken prisoners.'

'It's a fit payback for the *Royal Oak*,' said Geoffrey, 'but it brings it home to us that we're at war and it'll be worse before it gets better.'

'You sound just like father,' said Rebecca, but they all knew it to be true; Paul Storey had gone on an officer's training course, and Geoffrey Bannister had completed his; he was going to join the British Expeditionary Force in France, and had come to North Camp to take leave of Rebecca. Arriving at the Manor while she was away at the pantomime, Lady Neville had taken him aside and told him that Rebecca had been adopted at the end of the war, and brought up as the Nevilles' own daughter. And as Sally Tanner had predicted, it made no difference to his love.

'And what of you, Mr Richardson?' asked Lady Neville pleasantly. 'Have you had your billet-doux from the War Office?'

'Yes. I have to report at Aldershot straight after Christmas,' he replied, and, glancing at his watch, said that he had better be off; he thanked them for their hospitality, and nodded towards Rebecca.

'I'm glad I was able to see you home, Rebecca, and the two boys.'

'Thank you very much for your kindness, John,' she said with a smile, and rising from her chair, she saw him to the door and shook his hand warmly. For truth to tell, she was feeling a little guilty about him.

* * *

It had been a dark Christmas in every way. The Reverend Roland Allingham preached a solemn sermon on Christmas morning, exhorting the congregation to put their trust in God, and pray for the safety of the men from North Camp called to active service, and for their families, that they be granted strength and courage to bear their burdens of anxiety for their sons. Everyone in church that morning knew that the Allinghams' two sons had been conscripted, Howard to the British Expeditionary Force and Lester to the Royal Air Force, which disarmed criticism of their rector.

Mrs Joan Kennard sat cuddling Josie on her lap, and wished she could draw closer to Mrs Allingham who had dismissed Joan's words of sympathy.

'Both our sons are patriotic, and put their country first, above all other considerations,' she said loftily. 'They saw their duty, and did not hesitate.'

'Have either of them got a sweetheart?' asked Joan with a smile, and Mrs Allingham rounded on her.

'Certainly not. Howard's not ready to make any serious commitment, and would let us know at once if he found a girl who was likely to be a suitable clergy wife. And Lester, thank heaven, has given up that brazen creature, what's-her-name, the butcher's daughter. She's been pursuing him shamelessly all through the summer, but he's at last seen through her and sent her packing!'

That was not what the curate's wife had heard, but she nodded understandingly and said how well the brothers looked in their uniforms.

'They won't be short of lady followers, that's for sure!' Joan said unwisely, which infuriated Mrs Allingham.

'What a vulgar expression, Mrs Kennard! I hope that

you never talk like that in front of your daughter. Some of the words your husband uses are highly unsuitable for the pulpit, and you should not copy him, but rather set him an example!'

Acting on her husband's admonition to treat the Allinghams with compassion at this testing time, Joan simply lowered her head in apology, and thought how Alan would laugh when she told him.

The Pearsons, mother and daughter, had spent a quiet Christmas, enlivened by church in the morning, and the King's speech on the wireless when, struggling to overcome a lifelong stammer, he had given the nation an inspiring quotation:

'I said to the man who stood at the gate of the year, "Give me a light, that I may tread safely into the unknown." And he replied, "Go out into the darkness, and put your hand into the Hand of God. That shall be to you better than light, and safer than a known way."'

Mrs Pearson stood for the playing of the National Anthem, and Valerie did likewise.

'What a great, noble man we have for our King!' she said. 'It was surely God's will that brought him to the throne when his elder brother made such a fool of himself over that American woman. *She* did us a favour!'

Valerie felt so wretched that she looked forward to returning to Thomas and Gibson's after the holiday. Mr Richardson had informed her that his son was to leave for Everham and from there to Aldershot on Thursday the twenty-eighth of December, and that he would therefore be in late that morning, after seeing off his son at nine-forty.

'Why don't you come to the station with me, Miss

Pearson?' he asked. 'We could close the shop until midday, and go to that place by the dairy that serves coffee.'

Valerie was flustered. She had bought a pocket-sized, leather-bound New Testament that she was going to ask Mr Richardson to pass on to his son. But this unexpected invitation meant that she could give it to him herself, if . . .

'But – but won't Miss Neville be there to see him off?'

'No, she's chucked him over for another soldier,' he said briefly, giving no indication of whether he was pleased or sorry.

'Oh – oh, I didn't know,' faltered Valerie. This might mean that she *could* say goodbye to John and give him the book.

'Look, Valerie, this will be a difficult parting,' said Mr Richardson bluntly. 'We don't know when he'll be coming back, and if you were there it would ease the tension a bit.'

She shook her head. John would not consider her a substitute for Rebecca Neville, and what would she say when she gave him the book? She thanked her employer for his offer, but politely refused it.

'I'll be in the shop at nine o'clock as usual, Mr Richardson, and I'll have a nice cup of tea ready for you when you come in.'

He shrugged. 'As you wish, Valerie. I'll let you have the keys to open up. Not likely to be many customers. What an end to the year.'

Valerie made no reply. Her spirits had never felt so low.

Thursday dawned, with a dull sky and a dampness in the air that seemed to penetrate through to Valerie's bones. She let herself into the shop and pushed up the blinds, glancing at the wall clock. Five minutes to nine, and John and his father would be getting ready to leave. She took off her coat, shivering slightly, and opened her handbag where the book lay wrapped in tissue paper.

Nine-fifteen, nine-twenty, no customers. Nine-thirty.

She came to a decision. Throwing on her coat, picking up her handbag and locking the door behind her, she ran along the high street and down to the station approach. The train was in, and a few passengers were getting in or out. The Richardsons, father and son, stood on the narrow platform. The sound of her running footsteps made them look up.

'Good Lord, it's Miss Pearson, she's changed her mind,' said the father. 'Come on, my dear, he's just going!'

'Wait!' she panted, running up to them and holding out the book to John. 'It's for you, a New Testament to put – to put in the pocket of your uniform.'

He took the book and glanced at his father, then back to her. And then he put his hands on her shoulders and kissed her, first on one cheek and then the other. It was more like a brother's kiss than a lover's, still nevertheless it was a kiss.

'Thank you, Valerie. I'll keep it with me.' He turned to his father, and they shook hands. 'So this is goodbye, Dad, until we meet again.'

The guard blew the whistle, and a cloud of steam arose. John boarded the train, closed the door and pulled down the sash of the door window, from which he looked out at them. 'Goodbye, son.'

'God bless you, John!' she said, managing a smile. Not until the train pulled out for its return journey on the spur, and disappeared round a corner, did she shed tears, shaking her head in apology to John's father. He took her arm.

'Come on, Valerie. No sense in standing around here.'

CHAPTER FIVE

1940

It was the departure of 'the boys' that finally woke North Camp into realisation that Great Britain was truly at war, and her sons facing danger from a powerful enemy. Eddie Cooper's prediction of a short, sharp struggle, over within a year or less, had given way to Tom Munday's forecast of a much longer conflict against a nation which for a decade had been building a fleet of ships and aircraft, while training an ever-growing army to serve the Third Reich, the Nazi dictatorship of a man whose very name they hailed when speaking of him – '*Heil, Hitler!*' He had become an icon to the German people, to be followed with unquestioned loyalty, but in Britain he was an irreverent joke, lampooned in songs like 'We're Gonna Hang Out the Washing on the Siegfried Line!' – though in that dark winter he became less comical and more menacing. The British Expeditionary Force was suffering losses; false hopes were turning to fear.

Tom Munday's grandson Jack Nuttall had eagerly received his call-up papers and gone to train as a fighter pilot in the Royal Air Force, as had Lester Allingham, and the shadow that hung over the Rectory and 47 Rectory Road grew darker. Grace Nuttall seldom smiled – she had little appetite and lost weight; at night her sleep was troubled, and neither her husband or father could give her much comfort, being worried themselves. Doreen was bewildered by the tensions in the air, her mother's closed face, her father's gloomy silence. Only her grandfather was willing to listen to her, and encourage her to take pride in her brother's courage, his determination to go and fight for his country.

'And Jack *will* come home again when the war's over, won't he, Granddad?'

'Yes, Doreen dear, though it may take a long time,' he replied carefully, moved by the trust in her eyes, and trying not to show the pity he felt for her. 'Our Jack's a brave lad, and we'll have to say our prayers at night, to ask the Lord to keep him safe and bring him home again. And you'll have to be *especially* good for your mum and dad while your brother's away!'

Poor Doreen promised to be kind to her parents, and not to forget to say her prayers.

At the Rectory the Reverend and Mrs Allingham were finding it difficult to comfort each other; her constant anxiety made her irritable, and when he remonstrated with her, she told him to leave her alone, as if he did not share her fears for Howard and Lester. Alan and Joan Kennard tried to be as accommodating as possible, in deference to the older couple's burden, but Mrs Allingham showed no interest in little Josie, now toddling towards the rector's wife with a pretty smile.

'That child needs to be kept in her place, Mrs Kennard, or she'll be thinking she can wander upstairs and disturb the rector. Please make sure that she stays with you at all times.'

When Joan tried to show sympathy and offer to do shopping or to run any other errand, she was met with a dismissive frown, and overheard the lady say to her husband, 'It's all very well for *her* – she's got her child safe at home with her.'

Alan met with slightly more encouragement from the rector when he offered to take weekday services and help out with parish visiting.

'We must just give thanks for our blessings, Joan darling,' he told his wife with a wry grin, 'and "count it all joy" as St James advises,' though even as they both chuckled, they felt guilty because of those very blessings.

Grim news came in of merchant ships being torpedoed by the dreaded German submarines, the U-boats, with loss of crews and cargoes. Adolf Hitler was reported to declare that all shipping was at the mercy of his U-boats, and the losses led inevitably to food shortages. Under the newly formed Ministry of Food, the first rationing began early in the New Year. Lady Neville, now a member of the Women's Voluntary Service, joined Councillor Mrs Tomlinson and other WVS members at long tables in St Peter's church hall, to distribute the already printed ration books to every adult and child in North and South Camp and the surrounding rural area. Each had to be signed for, and the weekly allowances of butter, bacon and ham explained; each person would need to be registered with a named butcher and grocer which left them little choice, the one butcher being Mr Seabrook and the one grocer old Mr Cleveley, assisted by his daughter. Joan Kennard offered to accompany Mrs Allingham to the church hall to collect her two ration books, but was refused.

'We always get our bacon directly from Yeomans' Farm,' the lady said crossly. 'I have no intention of going to beg from that Seabrook man.'

When Joan gently explained that more foods would soon have to be rationed, items like tea, coffee and sugar, Mrs Allingham replied that she would go into Everham for them.

'I'm not going to be told which shops I must use,' she said. 'And what does your child need with a ration book?'

'She's entitled to extra milk,' replied Joan patiently, 'and at the Welfare Clinic she gets cod liver oil and orange juice.'

'That's more than *I* ever got at that age. There's too much fuss being made about children at a time like this. What about the elderly?'

Joan pretended not to hear, but that evening the Reverend Allingham got a detailed account of his wife's grievances.

'We must look upon these inconveniences as a test of our faith, Agnes,' he said, but got only a dubious sniff for answer. Mrs Allingham's faith had been badly shaken when her sons had gone to war, and she lived only for news of them.

On a bleak Wednesday morning in February there had been few customers at Thomas and Gibson's, and the inactivity had depressed Valerie's spirits even further, emphasising her feeling of uselessness at this time, and her secret disappointment at having had only one postcard from John Richardson, showing a picture of snow-capped Ben Nevis and saying that army square-bashing was very different from Page's department store. His father had received a letter that gave no information about his whereabouts for security reasons, nor what was happening, nor whether or not he was to be posted overseas. He had asked for his kind regards to be passed on to Miss Pearson, and that was all. Valerie imagined him slogging through army manoeuvres and learning about modern warfare, while here *she* was, uselessly stuck in a shop, selling bolts of stout black cloth and sewing cotton for making black-out curtains. But what could she do? She couldn't type or act as a telephone operator, she couldn't ride a bicycle, let alone drive a vehicle. It was no wonder that John Richardson preferred the vivacious Rebecca Neville to a timid, mousey creature like herself, she thought, and besides, her mother would never let her go to do war work.

'You'd better do some shopping when you leave work today, Valerie, before you go to the Ladies' Hour,' Mrs Pearson had told her that morning. 'Buy up what tea and sugar you can from Cleveley's, because they say they'll soon be on ration. I shan't be coming to the Rectory this afternoon, Dr Stringer says I need to rest more.'

Valerie looked forward to Wednesday afternoons, even though the talk was mostly about the war and the news, or lack of it, from the men in the armed services at home and abroad. Mrs Kennard had said they should now call themselves the North Camp Knitting Circle, as the ladies were now all knitting balaclavas, gloves and socks for the forces, using thick grey wool yarn supplied by Lady Neville as one of her many duties in the Women's Voluntary Service. They all knew that her son was an officer in the army, but she hid her anxiety under a smile, nodding to Mr Saville to play something bright and cheerful on this dull afternoon. One of the ladies had suggested 'Whistle While You Work' from the film about Snow White, and another had asked for 'There'll Always Be An England'; Lady Neville said they would sing both, exchanging a smile with Philip Saville who obediently obliged at the piano. He seemed happier these days, as if he actually enjoyed the discomforts of war; Valerie would have liked to ask him if his Aunt Enid listened to that awful Lord Haw-Haw on the wireless, with his Oxford English accent broadcasting from Germany, mocking Mr Chamberlain's efforts. Mrs Pearson insisted on turning on the wireless when Haw-Haw came on with his 'Gairmany calling, Gairmany calling,' followed by his eerie knowledge about which English town hall clock was five minutes slow, and where the air raid shelters were placed in another town, and how ineffectual they would be in a serious air raid.

Mrs Pearson listened to what he had to say, and then loudly contradicted him, point by point, as if he could hear her. If I have to listen to that man one more time, thought Valerie, I shall scream, *'Turn him off! For God's sake turn the bugger off!'*

And the next thing she knew was that she was lying on the floor with Lady Neville and Mrs Kennard on each side of her, holding her hands and soothing her with 'Sssh, sssh, dear, sssh, sssh,' and somebody was handing her a handkerchief.

Heavens, what a disaster, she must have *shouted the words out loud*, and now she could not stop crying.

Lady Neville was helping her to her feet. 'Come with me, Valerie, come this way,' she said, and taking her arm she led her out of the room and into Alan Kennard's study.

'Sit down, dear, there's a cup of tea coming for you soon.

Now, would you like to tell me what's the matter? Are you not well?'

Valerie wiped her eyes and nose. 'I'm sorry, Lady Neville, I'm not ill—'

'Please call me Isabel, and tell me what's the matter, Valerie.'

'I feel so *useless*, while other people are busy with war work, like yourself, Lady – Isabel,' she faltered, 'and my mother listens to that horrible man, and I can't *bear* it!' The tears began again, and Isabel took her hand, somewhat alarmed at hearing this.

'Hush, Valerie, don't upset yourself. *What* horrible man? You can tell me in strictest confidence, you know.'

'That Lord Haw-Haw, she always listens to him and answers him back,' said poor Valerie, thinking what a silly goose she must seem. Isabel laughed with relief.

'Oh, *him*! That traitor to his country, he'll come to no good end, and isn't worth worrying about! I think you've got yourself thoroughly run down, my dear, but is there anything else that's troubling you? Some friendship, perhaps?'

Valerie could not speak of her unrequited love for John Richardson, so shook her head. Isabel Neville felt deeply sorry for the girl, dominated by her mother and with nobody to confide in. She must be handled gently.

'Listen, my dear, would you like to do some local war work? There are lots of things you can do as a voluntary worker, if only for a few hours a week. Come and see me next Monday morning at St Peter's church hall, where the Women's Voluntary Service has its North Camp headquarters. We could talk things over, and find something to suit you. Do you like children? There's a nursery at Everham for under-fives, poor little mites whose mothers work at the munitions factory. Come and have a talk with me, and we'll work out a trial plan for you, how many hours you can give and so on. How does that sound to you?'

Valerie gave a watery smile. 'It's very kind of you, Lady, er, Isabel, but my mother would never agree to anything like that. She's elderly, you see, and needs me to do the shopping and everything. Besides, I've got my work at Thomas and Gibson's.'

'I would like to have a word with Mrs Pearson, and with Mr Richardson. I'm sure he could find a part-time replacement for you – an older woman, perhaps.' Isabel paused and looked very thoughtful. 'Because you see, Valerie, you're quite right – you *are* needed for the war effort, and you're too valuable to waste your potential as you are doing.' (And heading towards a nervous breakdown, she added in her head.) 'I believe it would be good for Mrs Pearson to do the local shopping, and a lot more besides. Leave it to me – don't say anything to her, and I'll persuade her. Come on, let's see you smile again!'

Even after a cup of tea and a slice of Mrs Kennard's fruit cake, Valerie felt unable to face the ladies again, but Isabel Neville did not want her to go home alone.

'Just wait here until we finish, Valerie, and then somebody will walk with you. I know, I'll ask Philip to see you home – he's going your way, and he'd be glad to.'

'Oh, no, I don't want to put Mr Saville to any trouble,' protested Valerie, but she was overruled. Mr Saville readily agreed, because it was Isabel Neville who asked him, and he could refuse her nothing. Even so, he felt sorry for the quiet girl who walked at his side, and having witnessed the scene at the Rectory, he could not help comparing her life with his; due to different circumstances, they shared the same inner emptiness, he concluded bleakly.

'Thank God it's nearly spring again,' Dora Goddard said to the pigs, her Wellington boots ankle-deep in the pig manure she was raking out of the sties and shovelling onto a wheelbarrow. Her charges were busy at the trough of swill, made up from kitchen waste and cooked mangolds and turnips mixed with oats. The newly delivered sow and her twelve new piglets needed special attention, and were kept in a separate pen where she was fed on offal cooked in milk and water. Dora yawned, having been up for two hours in the night, summoned by Billy who was having trouble with delivering a calf. The cow had lain for several hours, lowing with painful contractions; only the calf's forelegs were visible, but after some strategic traction, the head at last emerged, followed by the rest of the body.

'Bugger it!' said Billy. 'After all that effort, it's a bloody bull calf, when we need milkers. Should be ready for slaughtering come September. Anyway, let's get it sucking.'

'Can't the poor old girl have a rest for an hour or two?' asked Dora, patting the sweating animal, now lying exhausted on her bed of straw in the lantern-lit byre.

''Course not, the sooner it sucks the better – it's just thin, watery stuff at first, but get it sucking, and the proper milk'll come in. Come on, let's get cleared up – I need to get back to my bed. Sidney can deliver the next one.'

Dora did not reply, but seethed inwardly. Billy had taken advantage of her as a member of the family, and while her father and mother worked as hard as they had always done,

Billy lorded it over them since his elevation to husband and father, and reminded them of his ownership of the farm and their secondary place in the scheme of things. They got no help from Pam whose time was all taken up with baby Samuel, now a year old and toddling all over the farmhouse.

'I've had enough of it, Mum,' declared Dora when she came in for breakfast on this misty March morning. She pulled off her boots in the scullery, and washed her hands under cold water at the sink. 'I'm sick and tired of the way he treats us, and as for that silly little giggling Pam who never does a hand's turn in the house, I could slap her!'

Her mother sighed in sympathy, and could not disagree, but Dora had made up her mind. 'He's nothing but a slave-driver, and I'm getting out of this place,' she said.

'Oh, *no*!' Mary protested. 'Your dad and I would miss you so much – you're our one comfort now. And where on earth would you go?'

'Don't know yet, but somewhere I can work for Britain rather than Billy,' her daughter replied. 'I'll go to the Labour Exchange in Everham, and offer my services.'

'Do think about it, dear, and have a word with your dad,' said Mary with a sigh, but Dora had nothing more to say. A thought had crossed her mind, and not for the first time, that Howard Allingham was somewhere in France, a soldier fighting in defence of his country. Poor Howard – she could not return his love, but now wondered if she should have pretended a little, and given him some consolation as he went out to face danger and possible death. She could not forget his face on that Sunday morning after church when he had said goodbye to neighbours and friends in North Camp. Everybody had wanted to shake his hand,

and Lady Neville and Mrs Kennard had kissed him. He had held out his hand to her, and she had shaken it, but there was no kiss, not even the briefest peck on his cheek; she had looked into his eyes, and quickly lowered her gaze.

I should have kissed him, she now accused herself.

However bad the news of war, spring had returned to earth again, bringing a green mist of early foliage on the trees, and the orchards were sweet with pink and white blossom. A tall, fine-featured young woman stood at the door of St Peter's church hall, waiting for two friends to join her – and there they were, smiling in anticipation as well as a degree of apprehension.

'Come along, girls,' she said. 'Let's go in and offer ourselves up!'

Dora Goddard grinned, and Valerie Pearson was thankful for Rebecca Neville's offer to accompany them before the recruitment board run by the Women's Voluntary Service. Inside the hall, all was bustle and activity; long trestle tables were set out with senior members of the WVS interviewing female applicants of all ages and sizes. There was a queue, but Rebecca led Valerie to the table where Lady Neville sat, and pushed her forward.

'You're next to see her, Valerie, so take a few deep breaths and get ready to answer her simple questions,' she whispered with a distinctly unladylike wink, then returned to Dora who was waiting for the next vacant chair.

'Good morning, Miss Pearson!' said Isabel Neville pleasantly. 'How very nice to see you, and isn't it a beautiful morning! I've been thinking about you a lot since I spoke to your mother, and we both agree that The Limes Nursery at Everham would be very glad to have you as a part-time assistant. Have you thought about that?'

'Yes, Lady Neville,' replied Valerie who had been astounded at the change in her mother's attitude since her ladyship's visit, when a 'discussion' had taken place, though it had actually been shameless flattery on the part of Isabel Neville to persuade the lady that this had been her own idea. First she had remarked that a girl as sensitive as Valerie could not possibly work in a munitions factory, but that there were other openings, such as working as a part-time nursing assistant on the wards of Everham Hospital, or helping to care for children placed at The Limes while their mothers worked on munitions.

'She'd learn First Aid and basic nursing skills,' said cunning Isabel, not mentioning the changing of nappies and wiping runny noses. 'Just two days a week would be most helpful, and I've spoken to Mr Richardson at Thomas and Gibson's. He's willing to take on a young girl just out of school to replace Valerie when she's not there. I am sure that you can spare her, Mrs Pearson – in fact that would count as your own war effort.'

Seeing Valerie now sitting before her, it seemed that her diplomacy had worked.

'So, Valerie, shall we go for a trial period? You'll be given a special pass to use on the bus to Everham and back, though it would be a very good idea to learn to ride a bicycle. How do you feel about this?'

Valerie spoke up and said she would try to do her very best. She shook Isabel's hand with mixed emotions, but also with determination to succeed at the Limes; what would John Richardson say when he heard about this? Shy, timid little Valerie caring for children!

Dora Goddard sat down in front of Councillor Mrs Tomlinson who was now wearing the grey-green uniform of the service, and the silver and red badge with the letters WVS under the King's crown, for Her Majesty the Queen was their new President.

'Good morning, Mrs Tomlinson,' Dora said politely.

'Good morning, Miss Goddard,' came the formal reply. 'Well, at least we know where *your* talents lie – a farmer's daughter through and through, so I wonder you don't consider staying on at Yeomans' Farm.'

How much shall I tell, Dora had wondered before attending the recruitment drive at the church hall instead of the Labour Exchange at Everham.

'No, Mrs Tomlinson, I need to get away from the farm, though I shall be sorry to leave my parents,' she replied. 'I've lived there all my life, and want to see more of the world.'

Mrs Tomlinson nodded. 'Ah, I understand – and so the obvious place for you would be the Women's Land Army, and a posting away from North Camp – am I right?'

'Well, no, not exactly, Mrs Tomlinson. I'd like to have a change from farm work for a while.'

'Oh? What had you in mind?'

'I'd like to join the army, Mrs Tomlinson – the Auxiliary Territorial Service, and to go wherever I'm sent.'

'Well, to join any of the women's services you'd have to apply directly to the relevant headquarters in London, and they would interview you and you'd need to pass a medical examination. I see that you're now twenty-two, and if that's what you really want to do, there shouldn't be any difficulty. In fact I can just picture you in your khaki uniform, changing a tyre on an army jeep! Good luck, Dora, and let me know how you get on.'

'Thank you so much, Mrs Tomlinson.' Dora held out her hand with such a radiant smile that the Councillor wondered why she was so keen to leave home.

Rebecca next took her place facing Mrs Tomlinson who greeted her warmly but with some surprise.

'Good morning, Rebecca. I'd have thought that you'd discussed your plans with your parents.'

'I have indeed, Mrs Tomlinson, and I've made a decision,' answered Rebecca with a smile. 'But I haven't come to waste your time. My parents particularly want me to speak with you and hear your opinion.'

'Certainly!' replied the councillor. 'I'll be happy to give it. I can see you driving an ambulance, sending messages by wireless telegraphy and all sorts of essential duties.' She leant forward and lowered her voice as she continued, 'We'll be needing all the women with your skills for the services. The war isn't going at all well, with Hitler invading Norway and Denmark, and no good reports of the expeditionary force in France.'

Rebecca knew that Sir Cedric was of the same mind. 'But it's excellent news that we've got Mr Churchill as Prime Minister,' she said with conviction.

'I agree, but my heart goes out to poor Mr Chamberlain who must be broken-hearted, and from what I hear, he's a very sick man,' Mrs Tomlinson said with a shake of her head. 'But now we must talk about *you* and how best to use your talents, Miss Neville!'

'I'd like to be a land girl.'

'Really?' The lady was clearly surprised. 'I'd have thought you'd go for something more in touch with people, like one of the women's auxiliary services of the army, navy or air

force – you'd soon be promoted to officer status, I'm sure.'
She frowned slightly. 'Do you really think you'd enjoy winter
on the land – having to rise on a bitterly cold morning to
milk the cows, and mucking out after them?'

'I've always got on well with horses, Mrs Tomlinson, so I
think I could manage a herd of cows!' smiled Rebecca.

'And digging up turnips in frozen ground?' persisted Mrs
Tomlinson.

'I think I could do as well as poor Tess of the d'Urbervilles,
yes!'

'And there's the isolation to consider, you being such an
outgoing person – are your parents really in agreement?'

'They understand the reason for my choice, Mrs
Tomlinson.' It was Rebecca's turn to lower her voice. 'Half
our merchant ships bringing food from America and Canada
are being sunk by the U-boats, and the longer this war
continues, we're going to have to grow our own grain and
feed ourselves or face serious food shortages. The Land Army
is going to be a vital service, just as much as the others, and
I would like to become a regional organiser, which means I
must get at least six months' experience at the grass roots,
as it were.'

Mrs Tomlinson nodded. 'Yes, I think I follow you. And
where would you start?'

'Well, there are a couple of farms in this area, such as
Yeomans' – they're going to be short of hands, with two men
left to join the army, and – er – Miss Goddard leaving.'

Councillor Mrs Tomlinson considered for a moment, and
then said slowly, 'If you went there you'd be near at hand
for your mother who's in constant anxiety over your brother
Paul. Well, if she and your father agree, I'd better agree as

well – though I must give you a piece of advice, Rebecca. Don't go there as an employee. Wear the Women's Land Army uniform and be paid by the service, not by the farmer. Do you understand what I'm saying?'

'I understand very well, Mrs Tomlinson, and I have no intention of being intimidated by Billy Yeomans. I'm not a member of his family, you see.'

'Good! Then I wish you the best of luck,' said Mrs Tomlinson, adding privately in her head, *and the same to Billy Yeomans.*

The Ladies' Hour had ended, and Isabel Neville had listened to the somewhat embarrassed sympathy of its members. Grace Nuttall had not attended for some time, and Isabel thought what a pity it was, both of them having a son in the armed forces, yet as sisters they could not share their anxiety with each other. While Grace moped at home, Isabel kept herself busy with WVS duties, and at times felt utterly worn out. She leant back on the now vacant sofa, and closed her eyes. She was roused by a tentative male voice.

'Lady Neville – Lady Neville, may I have a word?'

'Philip!' she said, sitting up at once. 'I'm sorry, I was dozing off. Thank you for your playing once again – and for the lessons to the Perrin boys. Was there something you wanted to talk over?'

'Not really, Lady Neville, and I'm very sorry to disturb you,' he said awkwardly. 'May I say that you and Sir Cedric are often on my mind, daily in fact – and your son Paul in my prayers. I admire the wonderful example you set us all.'

'Oh, Philip, how good of you – but I'm no more deserving

than countless others with sons away. These are dark days for all of us, but thank you, I—'

And to his consternation she put a hand to her face and began to cry quietly.

He sat down beside her. 'My dear Lady Neville—' he began helplessly.

'Oh, do call me Isabel, all my friends do,' she said, sniffing away tears and trying to compose herself. 'I'm sorry, Philip, please excuse me.'

He took a large white handkerchief from a pocket, and handed it to her, not knowing whether to go or stay.

'Please – Isabel, it's I who am sorry, for causing you distress. Please forgive me.'

'You were in the last war, Philip, as my first husband was. He came through it, but he was changed. He was no longer a clergyman, and died in the influenza epidemic afterwards. Paul is his son, and I dread that he—' She paused for a moment, and then continued, 'If it were you, Philip, going to fight in France—'

'If it were me, I wouldn't go!' he burst out. 'I couldn't! Not through all that hell again. I'd drown myself in the Blackwater first, rather than face those guns – oh, I'm sorry, I'm sorry, I beg your pardon, Lady Neville, oh, my God!' He hid his face in his hands, and this time it was Isabel who offered sympathy.

'It's all right, Philip, I understand, don't worry. I prefer it when people speak the truth.' She wiped her eyes and stood up, holding out her hand. 'Perhaps we've both benefitted by showing our true feelings, and we must pray for each other, Philip.'

She leant forward and kissed him on the cheek. 'God bless you.'

He left the manor in a dream. Hitler had invaded the Low Countries, and Belgium and Holland had surrendered to the Nazis; France looked likely to be next to fall, followed by almost certain invasion of Great Britain – but *she had kissed him*, and something deep in his heart, long considered dead and forgotten, was stirring back to life, awakened after more than twenty years of suppression.

In his office Mr Richardson heard the ping of the shop door-bell as a customer entered. Would little Miss Nuttall be able to cope with this one better than the last two, when he'd had to go into the shop himself? It was nearly eleven o'clock and very quiet, which was just as well, because Miss Nuttall was struggling with her first job; it was all right if they only wanted a reel of cotton or elastic; it was when they needed advice on the best kind of material to buy for making summer dresses, or suitable matching buttons for a lady's cardigan or a baby's matinee coat. Mr Richardson kept his door open, and silently listened.

'Good morning, Miss Pears – oh, my word, it's Miss Nuttall! *You're* lucky, Doreen – you've got yourself a nice, easy job here at Thomas and Gibson's!'

'Yes, madam, thank you. Good morning – and how may I serve you?' recited Doreen as she had been taught by her employer and predecessor.

'Goodness me, we *are* formal these days, aren't we? Actually I'm looking for curtain netting for my downstairs windows. Those horrid black curtains have to be drawn at night, but at least we can look better in sunlight. What have you got?'

'The rolls of curtain material are over there on that shelf, madam. Shall I bring them over to the counter?'

'Well, yes, of course.'

Mr Richardson heard the sound of footsteps, and silence as the customer cast a sharp eye over the expanse of lace-edged curtain netting spread out over the counter.

'I don't think we've got it in any other colour but white,' said Doreen with a nervous smile, and Mr Richardson, silently sitting in his office, winced. He had recognised Mrs Seabrook the butcher's wife by her voice, and knew that she would spread the news all over North Camp that Richardson had got that poor, backward Nuttall girl in the shop to replace the Pearson girl, but that it was clearly a well-meant mistake.

Everybody was listening to the news: it was as if the whole nation was holding its breath. The Tradesmen's Arms had a wireless set that the publican had placed on the bar counter, now tuned in to the six o'clock news on a warm summer evening, and apart from the newsreader's voice the patrons stood immobile and silent, straining to hear every word. They heard the same as had been heard that morning: the British Expeditionary Force was fighting a rearguard action in northern France, and French families were fleeing before the advancing German hordes.

'This is all because of Belgium caving in,' said a man's voice at the bar. 'It made a gap in the British and French front line, so the buggers've come pouring through.'

'You can bet our boys will give as good as they get,' remarked Tom Munday.

'Yeah, but they can't get any further back than the sea, and then watch out! They'll be surrounded by the Jerries like rats in a trap.'

'Hey, we don't want that sort o' talk,' Eddie Cooper called out. 'They'll fight to the last ditch, our boys will!'

There was silence. Nobody wanted to talk about what would follow after such a calamity.

At the Rectory Agnes Allingham listened constantly to the news, which gave her small comfort and no reassurance.

'Don't lose hope, my dear,' said her husband. 'The latest news said that the enemy had suffered heavy losses.'

'That won't help my Howard, lying wounded and dying on some beach!'

'Agnes, my love, we must place them *all* in God's hands, and not imagine things we can't know.' Roland Allingham was showing more patience than at any other time in his life, and tried to pray for the safe return of his son Howard; Lester was still in training to fly an aircraft. The rector reminded himself that he must pray for the other sons of other parents, and shivered at the thought of having to visit the bereaved; he might not be able to console them because of his own fear.

It was haymaking time at Yeoman's Farm, and all hands were needed in the field; the weather had been kind so far, but Billy Yeomans said that rain was on the way, and that they were already late due to the absence of the two farmhands who had gone to the war, and Dora who had let them all down by clearing off to join the ATS, of all the stupid ideas. He reserved judgement on the Neville girl and her posh accent, though so far she seemed to be earning her keep. She had spent the last two days hand-hoeing the mangolds, swedes and turnips grown as winter feed for the cows, and now followed his tractor with a rake, with Sidney Goddard behind her to fork the cut grass into haycocks.

Rebecca's face and arms were tanned, and she had exchanged the Women's Land Army breeches and aertex shirt for shorts and a sleeveless cotton blouse. Working from dawn to dusk, her mind was also exercised; her brother Paul Storey, Geoffrey Bannister and John Richardson were all with the British Expeditionary Force, and just before his departure Geoffrey had declared his love for her, and Richardson had written a letter so full of praise and admiration that a proposal was clearly planned on his return. How would she receive it? Whose safe return did she most long for?

She straightened her back and brushed the wisps of hay from her clothes and hair; she had dust in her nose, mouth and ears, and she itched all over. She exchanged a grin with Sidney, plodding along behind her: what a decent sort he was! His wife Mary would soon be here with cheese and pickle sandwiches, new ripened tomatoes and the welcome flasks of tea.

And there she was, coming across the field, accompanied by Pam and little Sam. Sidney and Rebecca gave a cheer, and Billy halted the cutting for half an hour's rest and refreshment. The two women brought the latest news.

'It's hell let loose across the Channel,' Pam reported. 'We've just heard it on the wireless – they say if you stand on the south coast you can hear the bombing and see the smoke on the other side!'

'Oh, my God.' Rebecca paled beneath her tan.

'But they're sending out boats to rescue as many as they can,' said Mary with a frown at Pam. 'So there'll be a fair number saved.'

'Yeah, but they reckon they can only save a few hundred, out of all the thousands,' added Pam, smiling at Sam who was happily rolling in the cut hay.

'Be quiet!' Mary Goddard said sharply. 'You haven't got any thought for those who – for those who have chaps out there.' She turned to Rebecca. 'There you are, dear, a nice swig o' tea to keep your spirits up. They're bringing back as many as they can.'

But Rebecca had dropped her rake and stared at Mary. 'My brother – my brother Paul – oh, I must go to my mother. I must go to her.'

'Of course you must, dear,' said Mary. 'Just have a drink first, and then go.'

'And who's going to take her place?' demanded Billy.

'I'll send somebody up from the manor,' Rebecca gasped, wanting only to get home and share her mother's anguish. Hot and dusty as she was, she broke into a run.

'And meanwhile, what about Pam doing a turn with the rake?' asked Mary suddenly. 'It's time *she* did some work on this farm.'

'*And* to give you a hand in the house,' added Sidney, who usually never complained.

Pam flushed darkly, and called for her husband to stand up for her, but Billy Yeomans too had been shocked at the news of the terrible massacre on the beaches of France. He recalled how he had lost his elder brother over there in the trenches of the Great War, his brother Dick who had been killed at the time of his own birth. He frowned, shook his head at Pam, and bit into a thick cheese sandwich.

CHAPTER SIX

1940

Four days into June, the truth about the evacuation of British troops from the beaches of northern France, known as Operation Dynamo, was becoming clearer. The latest news on the wireless was that the last survivors were arriving on English soil, exhausted and filthy, some wounded, but all full of praise for their rescuers, the skippers of boats great and small, from naval destroyers to lifeboats, fishing boats, river cruisers and pleasure boats, all pressed into service at the request of the War Office and hastily made ready to sail. This motley fleet had crossed the Channel to pick up survivors from Dunkirk beach, crossed back and unloaded their human cargo on the beaches of southern England, then set sail again to pick up more. Overhead German Junkers were strafing the beach and the crowd of boats in Dunkirk harbour as they arrived and left. The nation heard with incredulity that far from rescuing a few hundred troops, more than three hundred and sixty thousand had been saved.

At Hassett Manor, Lady Neville waited with the faithful Sally Tanner at her side; they heard that the survivors were being put on trains to take them home or to their barracks or to hospital. The news came through that Howard Allingham had returned home, as had John Richardson. Of Lieutenants Storey and Bannister there was no word.

Rebecca had been warmly received on her arrival back at the Manor, but after one night spent at home, her mother had sent her back to Yeomans' Farm.

'Your first duty is to give all the help and time that you can to the necessary work of haymaking, Becky,' Isabel said. 'It's your service to your country. I'll telephone the farm immediately if there is any news.' She spoke in the tightly controlled voice that was meant to give an impression of calmness, though Cedric was not deceived; he longed to break down the barrier that she had erected around herself to ward off questions and expressions of sympathy. He felt her silence as a rebuke, a refusal to accept any consolation from a man who could not share her fear for the son of her first husband; Sally Tanner seemed to be closer to her than he, having shared her life at the time of Paul's birth and ever since.

On the following morning the news was that Operation Dynamo was nearing an end; there had been hundreds of deaths, including crews of the rescue boats; when Isabel again telephoned the Bannisters at their Berkshire home, there was no news; they too were waiting, their hopes fading by the hour.

John Richardson made an early visit to Hassett Manor, though his father advised him to wait a day or two, as there had been no news of Lady Neville's son.

'But I must see Miss Neville, to let her see that I've returned in one piece,' John said impatiently, being anxious to see her before her university admirer turned up. 'Don't worry, I'll tread warily until there's news of her brother.'

But there had been no news, and the Manor was silent, shrouded with dread. There seemed to be nobody about but Sally Tanner who informed him in no uncertain terms that Lady Neville was resting and not seeing any visitors.

'I'm very sorry to hear that, Mrs Tanner,' he said with due respect. 'May I enquire about Miss Neville? Is she at home, by any chance?'

'No, she isn't, she's working dawn to dusk as a land girl,' Sally said curtly.

'Really?' He was genuinely surprised. 'May I ask where?'

'No, you may not. I'm not here to give out family matters to all and sundry, so I'll wish you good-day.'

Seething with indignation at this set-back – that fellow Bannister would have had a different reply, he guessed – he went back to North Camp to call at Thomas and Gibson's, where poor little tongue-tired Valerie Pearson would surely greet him with shining eyes. But again he was disappointed, for her place had been taken by a very young girl who rattled out a greeting as she had been taught.

'Good afternoon, sir, how may I be of service?'

He frowned, shook his head and walked out. Why on earth hadn't his father told him about the change of assistant?

'I shall return to my work with the Women's Voluntary Service tomorrow,' Isabel announced at breakfast. 'And today's Wednesday, so there will be the Ladies' Hour at the Rectory, and I must be there.'

'Oh, *no*, my dear, nobody will expect you to go,'

remonstrated Cedric. 'There's really no need to face—' He hesitated, and she finished the sentence.

'To face other women whose sons have come back to them, and those who have *not*,' she replied stonily. 'We bereaved mothers need each other.'

Joan Kennard made an effort to appear calm as usual when Lady Neville appeared at the door, asking if she might have a word with young Mr Allingham before the meeting.

Howard came at once, and was led by Mrs Kennard into her husband's study where Isabel Neville awaited him, clasping her hands tightly together. She motioned him to sit down at the curate's desk; he looked pale and had lost weight.

'You'll have guessed why I've asked to speak with you, Mr Allingham,' she said. 'Thanks be to God that you've returned safely – and have you any news of Lieutenant Storey? Had you seen him at all lately?'

Howard Allingham wished with all his heart that he had positive news for her, but he shook his head. 'No, Lady Neville, I did not see him, but neither did I see him among the – the dead or badly injured. It was difficult to recognise anybody in the confusion.'

He closed his eyes briefly as he remembered the noise of gunfire, the dead bodies and parts of bodies that had to be trodden underfoot as the surviving men made their way into the water and towards the waiting boats.

'I'm deeply sorry, Lady Neville, that I have no news for you.'

'Or of Lieutenant Bannister?'

He shook his head.

'It must have been hell for you all.'

He shrugged at the memory of the stench of death, the groans of the fallen.

'Thank you, Mr Allingham,' she said, rising. 'Your parents must be rejoicing. Please convey my compliments to them. And now I must return to the ladies. Good afternoon.' 'Lady Neville.' He made a brief bow.

Mrs Kennard had told the members of the Ladies' Knitting Circle to avoid the subject of Operation Dynamo, and to treat Lady Neville with their usual respectful friendliness, not alluding to the war as she gave out the thick grey yarn for them to knit for the forces, and collected the finished items, the gloves, scarves, balaclava helmets and sea-boot stockings for which there was a particular demand, she told them. Philip Saville provided a discreet musical background to their conversations, choosing Brahms' Lullaby and Solveig's Song from *Peer Gynt*; as he played he imagined the notes rising up like prayers for this brave woman who was keeping her emotions under iron self-control.

A telephone rang in Alan Kennard's study, and the room fell silent as Mrs Kennard rose to answer it. Philip changed his choice of music to the old American song 'Shenandoah', playing it quietly and slowly.

The ladies looked up as Mrs Kennard returned from the study, holding the door open.

'It's a call for you, Lady Neville. Sir Cedric is asking to speak with you.' She gestured towards the open door, and Isabel rose with hope and fear in her eyes. The ladies silently awaited for her return, while Philip continued to play 'Shenandoah', giving it a special poignancy and tenderness. Mrs Kennard put a finger to her lips, and rose quickly when Isabel Neville came back into the room, white-faced and shaking. They all held their breath.

'My son's in hospital at Southampton,' she whispered.

'He's alive and – and coming home!' She almost fell into Joan Kennard's arms as the flood tide of repressed emotion broke through her self-control, and she sobbed out her joy, her relief and thankfulness. There were sympathetic tears in the room as Philip continued to play, turning the melancholy old song into a hymn of rejoicing in which some of the ladies spontaneously joined.

> 'Oh Shenandoah, I long to hear you,
> Away, you rolling river!
> Oh, Shenandoah, I long to hear you,
> Away, I'm bound away –
> 'Cross the wide Missouri!'

Somehow the quaint, unexplained words fitted the occasion, and stayed in every woman's memory of that summer afternoon.

Rebecca was called to the farm telephone to be told the news.

'He got left behind with Geoffrey Bannister who walked miles with a machine-gun bullet embedded in his right foot,' her mother explained in a voice that shook. 'They finally got picked up two days later by a lifeboat that crossed the Channel and eventually they were taken to Southampton General Hospital. Geoffrey's foot was septic, and he was feverish and delirious, and Paul waited until his parents arrived, and then telephoned us. Oh, Rebecca, he's coming home to us! He's coming *home*!'

'Thank God, Mother. And do we know anything more about Geoffrey?'

'Paul says he's very ill with blood-poisoning, and may

have to lose that foot, so we can only wait and hope. I don't know if you'll want to visit him, Becky, or whether—'

'Thank you, Mother. I'll visit on Sunday when I get the day off.'

It was potty time, and Valerie braced herself as a row of two- and three-year-olds were seated on the white enamel pots provided for their use after mealtimes. Some sat down obediently, used to toilet training, but others loudly protested and struggled. Nurse King would stand no nonsense, and ordered Miss Pearson to hold down Georgie Tonks firmly until he did his job, as the process was called at The Limes.

'We need to save nappies, Miss Pearson! And it's a disgrace that boy isn't yet trained at three years old!'

Valerie hated potty time, and tried to whisper placating words to the naughty boy, telling him that if he did a wee-wee or poo-poo in the potty, he would be allowed to go outside and play on the lawn of The Limes in the sunshine. Apart from Nurse King who was in charge of staff and children alike, the assistants addressed each other as Miss or Mrs So-and-So, while the children had to say 'Auntie' followed by their Christian names. Auntie Valerie was the oldest and the least experienced, relying on Nurse King's sharp tongue to instruct her, and copying the other assistants.

The Limes had been a large and imposing family residence in the early years of the century, the home of an Everham general practitioner; it had now been taken over by the Red Cross as a centre for the training of Red Cross nursing assistants who learnt First Aid and basic nursing skills in the event of an air raid, when The Limes would become a rest centre for the injured and homeless. At the present time most of the ground floor was being used as a crèche for under-five children whose mothers worked at the munitions factory a mile out of Everham. The children were mainly from the poorer classes, though a few doughty housewives from the residential area worked as factory supervisors, and their children tended to be better fed, better dressed and better behaved than the sometimes malodorous products of the council estate. Valerie Pearson felt as if she had been pushed in at the deep end of child care, and would hardly have survived a week of Nurse King's tongue and the strict routine of mealtimes, potty times and playtimes if she had not been determined to justify Lady Neville's efforts on her behalf, and picturing John Richardson's surprise – and admiration? – when he heard of this change in her life. She'd heard that he had been with the survivors from Dunkirk, but so far he had sent no word to her.

Mary Goddard was surprised to see the curate's wife on the doorstep, all smiles.

'Mrs Goddard! It seems a long time since we last met. May I have a word with you? It's all good news, I promise!'

'Well, yes, all right – come in, Mrs – er – Kennard.' Mary stood aside and showed her visitor into the old-fashioned farmhouse parlour, indicating an armchair. She sat herself down on a sagging sofa with antimacassars over the back and arms, hoping that she was not going to be invited to join the Ladies' Circle.

'We hear that your Dora has gone to join the ATS, Mrs Goddard,' said Joan Kennard, privately shocked to see how Mary had aged. 'Am I allowed to ask where she's stationed, or is it all hush-hush?'

'She went to the reception centre at Lynchford for the first

114

two weeks, with a dozen other girls who had to sleep in a long hut with not much hot water for washing,' Mary said dully. 'They had to drill and collect their khaki uniforms, and sign for their own knife, fork, spoon and mug to take to the canteen, and wash them up afterwards.'

'Mercy on us, what a change for those girls,' marvelled Mrs Kennard. 'And I expect you miss her very much, don't you?'

'Yes, we do, Mrs Kennard,' said Mary with a sigh. 'Now she's been sent to a Maintenance Unit, they call it, near Gloucester, to train in electrics and wireless.'

'Good for her – and isn't it a miracle that so many of our men were rescued from Dunkirk!' Joan went on eagerly. 'Lady Neville's son Paul finally reached these shores with a badly injured friend, otherwise the news has been better than expected. The rector's son, Howard Allingham, has made it home, you must tell your Dora; they had many a game of tennis on the North Camp courts this time last year, so she'll be glad to hear he got away.'

Alan Kennard had instructed his wife to pass on this piece of information, which was the real purpose of her visit. 'Dora must be missed on the farm, too,' she added.

'Yes, but Lady Neville's daughter has come here as a land girl, and according to Sidney she's as good as a man – but there's no pleasing Billy Yeomans.'

Joan Kennard smiled. 'If I know Rebecca Neville, she can stand up to Billy! Well, I'll be on my way. Do let Dora know about the boys – and you know you'd be welcome to join our Wednesday afternoon circle at any time.'

'Thanks, Mrs Kennard. Good of you to call.'

* * *

'Auntie Vally! Auntie Vally!' howled naughty little Georgie Tonks, running up to Valerie with outstretched arms, wanting to be picked up. Nurse King was not in sight, so Valerie lifted him in her arms and tried to find out what was the matter. Straying into the strictly forbidden territory of the flower garden, he had tripped over an inverted flower pot and fallen headlong into a prickly rose-bush. He knew he would get no sympathy from Nurse King, so turned to Auntie Vally who comforted him as well as she could; she carried him indoors to the washroom and gently dabbed moist cotton-wool over his scratches, smiling and telling him he would soon be better. He calmed down and put his arms around her neck, pressing his dirty face, wet with tears and runny nose, against hers.

'I loves 'oo, Auntie Vally,' he told her.

Which made Valerie Pearson wonder what it must feel like to be a mother.

'Got a late pass tonight, Dora, so let's get the bus into Gloucester and see *Gone With The Wind*! They say Clark Gable's kisses set your knickers on fire!'

'No fear, Gwen – when I get a midnight pass, I don't spend it sitting in a cinema swooning over a film star, I go dancing! There's a dance on at the NAAFI canteen on Friday, and Pip – that's Sergeant Seagrave who's giving me driving lessons – has asked if I'll go with him.'

Gwen sighed. 'I don't know how you do it, Dora, you're a real *femme fatale*. People would never guess you were a farmer's daughter up from the country!'

'That's 'cause I've got a lot to catch up on,' chuckled her friend. They sat on a wooden bench by the Maintenance Unit at Inchcombe, enjoying a lunch break in the June sunshine. The Royal Engineers occupied the barracks to one side of the MU, and the ATS were lodged in the hutted camp on the other; both male and female staff were employed in the MU workrooms, and Dora was one of six girls training in the Electrical and Wireless Technology section, for which they had to wear thick navy overalls. She found the work challenging but fascinating, and was becoming quite adept at dismantling, cleaning and servicing the generators; her lecture notebooks with their complicated diagrams had actually been remarked on favourably by the Warrant Officer in charge.

'Look out, there's our NCO coming this way, we'd better salute,' warned Gwen, and both girls stood, to receive a sour look from the uniformed lady who did not return the salute.

'I never know when you should or shouldn't,' said Gwen. 'It's if they're in uniform and so are you, salute – but if one or other is in civvies, I suppose it's salute if in doubt!'

'Not necessarily,' replied Dora with a rueful grin. 'What about Shirley Corbett when she stretched herself out on that grassy bank behind the huts, took off her cap, undid her buttons, and dozed off – and woke up with a start to see this WO glaring down at her! Poor old Shirley sat up and saluted, which made things worse, and she ended up on a charge of "wilful neglect toward the King's uniform" and got six evenings in a row of cookhouse duty, which is no joke – you have to scour those heavy pans with food baked onto them, it's as hot as hell, and you're up to your ankles in cockroaches and the pong of the bins of pig swill—'

'Stop, stop!' said her friend with a shudder. 'Whatever would our families say if they could hear all this? My mother would have a fit.'

'So would mine – whoops, it's time we got back to our beautiful shed – come on!'

Back at work, Dora smiled to herself. Joining up was the best move she had ever made. The tyranny of Billy Yeomans and the irritation of his wife were forgotten in this new environment of hard but interesting work, the camaraderie of her colleagues, the jokes and the laughter – and the prospect of going to a dance on Friday evening with Pip Seagrave, whose kisses might not be like Clark Gable's, but at least he was real and not a shadow on a screen.

These thoughts recalled to her mind the letter she had received from Mum yesterday. Rebecca Neville was more than a match for the farmer by the sound of things; and there was the news that most of the North Camp boys had got back safely from Dunkirk, including Howard Allingham. Poor Howard. Ought she to write to him and say she was glad about his escape? In the end she decided not to run the risk of raising his hopes, and simply asked her mother to convey her good wishes.

With the fall of France, Prime Minister Mr Churchill reminded his countrymen that Britain now stood alone against the might of the Third Reich. Families gathered around their wireless sets to hear the man who on his accession to office had promised them nothing but 'blood, toil, tears and sweat'. Now with an invasion looming, he sternly told them to brace themselves to do their duty. As if his words addressed every listener personally, he promised that the British would defend their island, fighting on the landing-grounds, in the streets, the fields and the hills. 'We will never surrender,' he said solemnly.

Listening to this man, Mrs Pearson lost her fear of Lord Haw-Haw. Even now that Valerie worked every day at the Everham crèche, her mother had discovered that she was not old, only in her fifties and able to do the shopping and set a meal on the table each evening when Valerie returned at around six, tired but on the whole satisfied with her day's work.

One evening when they had just finished supper, they heard a ring at the doorbell, followed by the sound of footsteps going round the house to the open kitchen door. The visitor walked in uninvited and Valerie's heart missed a beat: he was Corporal John Richardson in his uniform!

'Ladies!' He made a low, theatrical bow before them. 'My belated greetings to you both! My father foolishly omitted to tell me of the change at the shop, and how you'd gone off on your war effort, Miss Pearson. Something about a kids' nursery, he said.'

Valerie blushed, and her heart beat fast. 'Yes,' she said hesitantly, 'I help to look after young children whose mothers are working at the munitions factory.'

'And *I* keep house while she's away, so that's *my* war effort,' said Mrs Pearson. There was a short pause, and Valerie added shyly, 'We were very thankful that you got away safely from Dunkirk, John.'

'Yes, it was fairly horrendous, treading on the bodies of your comrades to get to the boats, so as to be saved for another go at the Jerries,' he replied with a grim smile meant to impress them. 'And before I get whisked away again, Valerie, I've come to ask if you'd like to see *Gone With The Wind* at the Everham Embassy. Are you free on Saturday evening?'

'Oh, er, well, yes, thank you,' stammered Valerie, unsure

whether this was real or a dream. 'That would be very nice.' She glanced at her mother who simply shrugged and asked Mr Richardson if he would like a cup of tea. Valerie thankfully got up and went to put the kettle on; it gave her a chance to compose herself and reflect on his sudden interest in her. He had been home for over a week, yet had not contacted her until now. Had he already been to see Rebecca who had refused his invitation? Yet what did it matter, he was asking *her* now, and she was happy to be his second or even third choice.

Especially as he was soon to return to the front, and might not return . . .

It had been Lady Neville's idea that Paul, Geoffrey's proven friend, should drive Rebecca to Southampton and accompany her to the bedside. She also telephoned the Bannisters at their Shaftesbury home to tell them that Paul and Rebecca were intending to visit that Sunday.

They found Geoffrey in a single private room, having had a below-knee amputation of his right leg two days before; he was conscious but not completely aware of what had happened to him, and had no memory of that last journey from France. John Bannister, MP, and his wife were already there, looking pale and strained.

'It was too far gone, and they were afraid that gangrene might set in,' Mr Bannister told them quietly. 'They say he could go either way now. He's had a blood transfusion, and that's a sugar and salt solution now running into a vein in his arm.' He looked at Rebecca. 'He's been saying your name, so he'll be glad to see you, Miss Neville. I must beg you not to – to disappoint him in any way.'

Rebecca nodded. She knew that she was expected to show only love and hopefulness to this young man whose life hung in the balance – and who, if he lived, would have to face life with only one leg. The war was over for Geoffrey Bannister.

She leant over the bed, her face close to his; his eyes were closed.

'Hello, Geoffrey,' she said quietly while his parents and her brother watched. He opened his eyes and saw her.

'Rebecca.'

'Yes, I'm Rebecca, and I've come to see you, Geoffrey,' she whispered.

'Rebecca, my love.' The words were only just audible. His mother gave a gasp, and put her hand to her face.

'Rebecca, my love,' he repeated. 'I'm ready to die now.'

'Good God, dearest Geoffrey, my boy, you're not dying!' Mrs Bannister cried out, and her husband put his arm around her shoulders and led her out of the room, soothing her into quietness, though she continued to weep silently. A nurse appeared with a syringe in a dish, and said she was about to give the patient a pain-relieving injection. He winced briefly as the needle entered his upper arm, and Rebecca held his hand.

'Rebecca, my love – is it really you?' he whispered in some agitation. 'Kiss me.'

She leant over and kissed his cheek and forehead.

'Kiss me, Rebecca.'

She kissed him lightly on the lips, and he closed his eyes, drifting into sleep as the morphia took effect.

Paul touched her arm. 'We'd better go now, Becky. He looks more peaceful.'

* * *

On that same Sunday afternoon a couple sauntered down to the Blackwater, their arms entwined.

'I couldn't go back to the base without seeing you again, Babs,' he said, kissing her. She gave him a radiant smile. 'And I wouldn't have let you go, no matter what Mum and Dad said.'

They stopped to embrace, then continued to walk slowly on until they were hidden behind the alders that grew down to the riverbank. He pulled her down beside him on the dry grass.

'Let me—'

She made no resistance as he pulled at her summery dress and with increasing urgency thrust a hand up between her thighs.

'You're the sweetest girl, Babs, let me make you happy,' he said thickly, and she shivered in eager response, kissing his mouth and helping him to reveal her naked breasts. He kissed her nipples, first one and then the other, drawing them into his mouth. She gave a sharp gasp at the unfamiliar sensation on her tender flesh, and in the next moment he had climbed on top of her, and she felt his hand seeking an entrance; he did not need to ask her – she quickly removed her underwear and spread her legs for him. He thrust his hard erection inside her, and reached a climax almost immediately; she cried out at the stab of pain, for in spite of her reputation as a flirt, Barbara Seabrook was a virgin.

'God, I've needed that ever since—' he groaned with satisfaction. 'By God!'

She lay passively beneath him as his panting subsided, scarcely able to believe what had happened, which was that Lester Allingham had possessed her, and she had freely consented. Now she was his and he was hers, before he returned to his air base.

Tom Munday and Eddie Cooper avoided each other's eyes. They were easily the oldest among the men who had turned up on this summer evening at the cricket pavilion for the first meeting of the North Camp Local Defence Volunteers.

Seabrook the butcher had put himself forward as unchallenged leader. 'We're here in answer to the Prime Minister's call to all of us, whatever age or occupation, to be prepared to defend our island,' he said, to be answered by eager nods. 'We haven't got a uniform as yet, but armbands and forage caps will be issued soon. We must each imagine that a German invasion has taken place – and that could happen at any time. With so many of our young men away in the armed forces, it's up to us, their fathers, to fight here at home.' He lowered his voice to add, 'My own son Robin has gone to join the Royal Navy, and it's up to us old stagers to back our boys up, right?'

He had spoken for them all, and Tom and Eddie exchanged a glance and a nod.

Each volunteer gave his name, address and whatever skills he could contribute. Weapons ranged from rifles of the Great War to pitchforks and pickaxes to face the foe. Any overture on the part of the German invaders to seek their cooperation was to be repulsed, and in true Churchillian style Seabrook thundered that any talk of defeat, any spreading of 'alarm and despondency' should be publicly rebuked.

'We're sworn to serve our King and country to victory, at the cost of their own lives if need be,' he told them, and echoed the Prime Minister's vow that '*We shall never surrender*.'

And if the Local Defence Volunteers were something of a joke among their communities at first – 'the Long-Toothed Volunteers' – their numbers increased nationwide, and by the winter of that dangerous year they were properly kitted out with standard issue army uniforms and renamed the Home Guard.

But much was to happen before then.

'But Mother, how can I go on saying what I don't mean and don't feel, just to placate him?' asked Rebecca. 'At some time he'll *have* to be told that I can't marry him out of pity.'

'Don't look too far ahead, Becky,' answered her mother. 'The poor boy may not recover, and in his present state he needs to believe that you return his love, so you must pretend, at least for the time being.'

'But I feel so *guilty*, Mother, seeing how his eyes light up when he opens them and sees me standing there. If only I could help him in some other way!'

Isabel looked thoughtful. 'Actually, there is one way you *might* help him – take Philip Saville with you when you next visit. His leg was amputated over twenty years ago, and so he knows how Geoffrey feels – and how he too might overcome the loss. The two have met here, when the Perrin boys took Philip down to the stables, and Paul and Geoffrey asked him to take tea with them on the terrace.'

'Oh, Philip would be much too shy and wouldn't know what to say – it would be too embarrassing for words, he'd never dream of visiting!'

'He just might if I were to ask him,' Isabel said with a little smile, and when Rebecca stared in surprise, added, 'Leave him to me!'

'Wasn't it wonderful?' enthused Valerie as she and John Richardson were walking home from North Camp station, having caught the last train from Everham. 'That American Civil War was a long time ago and a long way away, and yet – all those wounded soldiers crying in pain, and the wives and mothers dreading the news of their loved ones – it could be today.'

'Hardly to be compared with Dunkirk,' John replied with a short laugh. 'We were real men under bombardment, not actors as in the film.'

'Yes, but they were re-enacting what happened *then*, and war is war, wherever it is,' said Valerie, 'and anyway, it was a wonderful film.'

'I suppose you were swooning over Rhett Butler,' he teased.

'No, I didn't care for him at all, I much preferred Ashley Wilkes.'

He laughed at her seriousness. 'For my money, Scarlett O'Hara beat them both into cocked hats! So, little Valerie, you're doing your bit on the home front. I can just picture you with those kids at the nursery. Hitler must be scared stiff!'

'You can mock, but the children all have mothers working at the munitions factory, which they couldn't do without us,' Valerie pointed out, disappointed at his attitude. 'And I'm so grateful to Lady Neville, who got me the job and persuaded my mother to agree to it.'

'Lady Neville – ah, yes.' He wondered how much Valerie knew about Rebecca. 'Her son got out of Dunkirk, didn't he?'

'Yes, but only after most of the survivors had got away. He stayed back with a friend who'd been wounded, now in hospital at Southampton. His father's an MP, and Miss Neville goes to visit him when she gets a free day from work at Yeomans' Farm. She's a land girl.'

'Oh. That must be a big consolation to him.'

'I've heard he's very ill, and might not recover,' she said seriously.

'Let's hope for the best, then.'

His expression gave nothing away, and when they reached her home, she turned to face him on the doorstep. 'It was a wonderful film, John, and thank you for taking me.'

'My pleasure.' He put his arm around her waist, anticipating the further pleasure of a kiss. Willing and wanting to return it with equal warmth, she offered her lips – and drew back with a sharp gasp when he pushed his tongue between her teeth, and held her body close against the hardening beneath his trousers. Never in her dreams of John Richardson had she imagined anything as physical as this, and to her shocked surprise found herself repelled; she just wanted to say goodnight and get indoors.

'I'd like to ask you in for a cup of tea, John,' she said breathlessly, 'but Mother and I keep very early hours, you see. It's nearly ten o'clock, and—'

'It's all right, little Valerie, I understand,' he said, and kissing her lightly on her nose, disappointed by her silly shyness, but glad to be spared another encounter with the old trout.

* * *

126

Paul had returned to the war in Europe, and Rebecca and Philip Saville travelled down to Southampton by train; it was a weekday, because of Saville's duties at St Peter's on Sundays.

Trying to make conversation, she remarked that her mother appreciated his piano lessons to the Perrin boys, and his provision of music for the Ladies' Knitting Circle on Wednesdays.

As always, he glowed with admiration at the mention of Lady Isabel Neville.

'You and your brother are fortunate in having such a lady for your mother, Miss Neville. And I expect you take after her,' he said with shy sincerity that Rebecca found rather touching.

'It's kind of you to say so, Philip, and I hope I can live up to her example, but in fact she's not my birth mother. I was adopted, soon after my brother Paul was born.'

His jaw dropped in amazement. 'But – you look so much like her!' he exclaimed.

'She has been a good mother to me – I couldn't have had a better – and I'm very thankful indeed that she took me as her daughter – but yes, I was adopted.'

No more was said on the subject, but Philip pondered on the information, wondering what circumstances could have led to the adoption of a second child so soon after Isabel Neville had borne Paul, the child of her first marriage.

At the hospital, Geoffrey Bannister was improving. He was no longer feverish, and was strong enough to take a few steps with the aid of crutches. He seemed to welcome Saville, though privately thought him a poor advertisement for life as an amputee; and when Rebecca said she would take a walk around the ward to speak to other patients, he did not object; in fact he took advantage of a few minutes' time to talk to Saville alone.

'I've appreciated your visit, Philip,' he began. 'It's obvious that Rebecca brought you over to give me encouragement, but in fact I've got another use for you.'

'Yes, Geoffrey?' Philip wondered what on earth was coming.

'I don't need to tell you how much I care for her, and the dear girl says she cares for me in return. We're not officially engaged, but – both families expect us to be, as soon as I'm stomping around on a handmade leg.'

Philip was mystified. 'Go on.'

'The truth is that I don't intend to marry her or any other girl until I've got my life in order. Things are completely different now, and I'll have to look for another way to live out my life and still be of use. And that could be – a year? Two years? Five years? I don't intend to allow her to sacrifice her life to look after me, nor do I need pity. She must be free to do what she pleases in this ghastly war, and who knows, we may come together when it's all over, or she may find another lucky fellow. That's where you come in, Philip, to explain this to her, comfort her if necessary, and you may need to talk with her parents, though I shall write to them, and explain to mine. Understood?'

'My dear chap – are you really sure?' Philip was unable to miss the irony of the situation. Isabel Neville had asked him to accompany Rebecca on her visits to this man, not only because of the experience of amputation that they shared, but also to shield Rebecca from too close an intimacy, because, she had confided to him, *Rebecca was not in love.*

'Absolutely sure. You can choose the time and place to tell

her, if there is ever a right time for something like this. Only don't water it down at all, let her know that this is final, that I'm breaking off the unofficial engagement. Her mother will comfort her, if it comes as a very great shock.' He held out his hand. 'Thanks, Philip – sorry to land you with it, but there's no other way.' His mouth was set in a hard, straight line, and Philip was bereft of words as he shook hands. 'And another thing, Philip, get yourself a decent artificial leg with a proper knee joint, and throw that stick away. It's not too late for *you* to join the land of the living.'

When they left the hospital, before they reached the railway station, the news was on everybody's lips, all around them, being broadcast on the wireless ahead of the newspapers. There had been an air raid on London: bombs had been dropped, and people killed and injured. Suddenly the air raid shelters, the sandbags and wail of the air raid siren had become reality.

Britain was under attack from the air, and all other news became insignificant. Philip Saville never plucked up courage to give Geoffrey's message to Rebecca, but quietly told her mother that a letter from Bannister would arrive for her and Sir Cedric. He was overwhelmed by her thanks, and it was she who told Rebecca.

CHAPTER SEVEN

1940

Ernest Munday's thoughts were bleak as he cycled the four miles from Everham to North Camp on a sunny Sunday afternoon. It would have been perfect, he reflected, were it not for the ongoing invasion from the air, the wave upon wave of Messerschmitts flying over from a conquered Europe to the southern shores of England, to be met by the Royal Air Force, the young, newly trained men piloting Spitfires and Hurricanes which met machine-gunning with machine-gunning, so that aircraft from both sides went nose-diving down into the sea or hit the ground, where they usually burst into flames. People looked up from the streets of London or the green countryside of Kent, Essex and Sussex to see the 'dog-fights' overhead, holding their breath to see whether the aircraft with the swastika or the concentric circles on its wings would fall to earth. Or both.

Ernest was visiting his father and the family at 47 Rectory

Road, though Devora had hoped he would join her and the family on a picnic. A houseful of teenagers on their summer holidays was not easy to manage, especially now that Ayesha was getting asthmatic attacks quite frequently. These would have terrifying onsets, in which she gasped for breath and went blue in the face. She had been prescribed an inhalation contained in small glass ampoules which Ernest and Devora, now their only parents, had to break into handkerchiefs and hold the released vapour to her nose and mouth. Ernest was sorry to leave them, but had insisted that he pay a family visit to his father and the Nuttalls at a time when young Jack Nuttall was facing danger and death in the battle of the skies.

'Dad! How are you?' He clasped Tom's hand, noticing how pale and tired he looked. Young Doreen, not at work, greeted him eagerly.

'It gets very tense here, Ernest,' said his father in a low voice, 'with young Jack out there – or rather up there, facing those Messerschmitts. He's a rear gunner, hardly trained to fly, let alone engage in battles. Grace is taking it very badly, poor girl.'

'We all went to church this morning, Granddad, except for Mum,' said Doreen, 'and Mr Kennard prayed for our men in their aeroplanes, and specially mentioned our Jack and the rector's son. Did you go to church too?'

'No, Doreen, my family's Sabbath was yesterday,' he said with a smile. 'And as we haven't got a synagogue in Everham, we join with two or three other families to share the readings and a meal in the home of one of us. Where's Grace?'

'She's resting. Didn't have a very good night,' said Tom. 'And Rob's gone out to the LDVs – I mean the Home Guard, as they're called now – at the cricket field. It's hard on him, too, him being Jack's father.'

'Hello, Ernest, I thought I heard your voice,' said Grace, coming into the room. 'Are you on your own?'

'Yes, Gracie!' He got up to kiss her. 'I didn't think you'd want an invasion from my howling mob, the Mundays and the Pascoes!' Too late he regretted the word *invasion*, seeing that young Jack was among the RAF fighters resisting invasion from the air.

'How are the Pascoe children?' asked Tom.

'Not bad, really. Young Jonathan and David are like the ones in the Bible, just like brothers. Ayesha's not so well – she gets these asthma attacks that frighten us to death, and she still wakes up screaming in the night with bad dreams, which wakes us all up. Devora's very patient with her, but doesn't get thanked. I suppose Ayesha can't forget what happened to her own parents, and won't accept us taking their place.'

'Poor child,' sighed Tom, but Grace said curtly that it would be a lot worse for Ernest and Devora if their David was in the RAF at this time, and Ernest nodded and agreed.

'The rector's son Lester is in the same situation as your Jack,' he said gently. 'We pray for them all, these young heroes, in church and synagogue, and at home.'

Grace was not to be persuaded out of her chronic, corrosive anxiety, and scowled.

'*I* shan't set foot inside that church again until I see my son alive,' she snapped. 'Nor that Ladies' Circle or whatever she calls it now. She was calling round here the other day, that curate's wife, and I soon sent her on her way.'

'That was a pity, Grace,' said Ernest. 'It just doesn't sound like the Grace Munday I used to know – a little tomboy always up to mischief, but full of life and fun.'

'Oh, yes, I was a proper little goer,' she answered with a dangerous edge to her voice.

After a pause, Ernest took a large round pie-dish out of the leather bag he had carried on the back of the bicycle. 'Devora sends her love to you all, and has made you this apple pie from our own early apples.'

'Very kind of her – thank her from us,' said Tom, smiling.

'Strictly kosher, I suppose,' said Grace without smiling.

'How's our David getting on?' asked Tom. 'He must be – er – fourteen by now.'

'Fifteen this year,' said Ernest. 'Yes, he's a good lad, says he wants to come into the family firm later on, so Munday and Pascoe Accountants of Everham will go on!'

'Oh, very nice, what a comfort,' said Grace with bitter sarcasm. 'Here's my Rob can't get enough woodwork jobs to pay our way, and my poor Doreen doing her best to please the Lady de la Mucks who go to Thomas and Gibson's – but the Pascoes of Everham will never go short of anything; that's Jews for you!'

There was a stunned silence from the men, and Doreen looked anxiously from one to the other. Tom muttered, 'Grace, that's a wrong thing to say—' and then Ernest spoke quietly.

'You know that's not worthy of you, Grace, not the little sister I used to know. I accept that you're under an intolerable strain, and I pray every day that your brave boy will come through this hell. But if you're going to make insulting remarks about a persecuted race, I can't come here, or any of my family, which is hard on Dad and my niece Doreen.'

He paused, expecting some sort of half-apology, which he would have instantly accepted. But Grace, avoiding his eyes, left the room without another word, and Ernest took his leave soon after, commiserating with his father over their present troubles.

On reaching home again, he found that the family had not gone on a picnic after all because Ayesha had had another asthma attack, frightening them by stopping breathing while they watched her eyes staring blankly out of a livid blue face. Devora had broken one of the glass ampoules and held it to Ayesha's nose and mouth, after which her colour returned and she breathed normally but more rapidly than usual.

'I *know* it's because she's unhappy, Ernest, but I also know that she brings on these attacks deliberately at the most inconvenient times,' said Devora. 'It's only rarely that she has an attack at school. I think she gets a kind of satisfaction out of upsetting us all.'

'We must be patient, Devora, my love,' he said. 'People who are anxious and unhappy for whatever reason are to be pitied, and we have to make allowances for them.' He sighed heavily, thinking of Grace Nuttall. 'When you remember how Ayesha and Jonny were forcibly removed from their parents and baby brother, it practically moves *me* to tears. We have to go on doing our best, and not expecting thanks.'

By the end of August the Luftwaffe had lost more aircraft and men than had the RAF, and the Prime Minister had praised the 'Few' to whom the many owed so much. Lester Allingham had returned home a war hero, decorated with the Distinguished Flying Cross and bar, and more than one WAAF in love with him. Jack Nuttall was in the Queen Victoria Hospital at East Grinstead with burns on his face and hands.

* * *

Barbara Seabrook's joy at the homecoming of war hero Lester Allingham was such that her parents had to rejoice with her, and be prepared at last to receive him at their home. In the evening of the day of his arrival, Barbara walked up to the Rectory wearing a light-green sundress and white sandals; her heart fluttered at the thought of meeting the rector and his wife, and she hoped that Lester had prepared them to receive her as their soon-to-be daughter-in-law. She carried an invitation from her own parents for them to visit with Lester at their earliest opportunity, though she longed above all to be with him alone. She had something very important to tell him, and felt nervous but sure – fairly sure – that he would be happy to share her secret – their secret – and arrange for an early wedding, when they would have to face their relatives and the whole of North Camp. She felt sure she could count on their sympathy; he was after all a war hero, one of the 'Few' that Churchill had so openly praised. She held her head up high as she walked up to the Rectory door and rang the bell. It was answered by Mrs Kennard.

'Hello, Barbara! You look very nice! What can we do for you?'

'I've come to see Lester – and Mr and Mrs Allingham, if it's convenient,' she said with a smile. Joan Kennard hesitated for a brief moment, and then invited her in.

'They're all upstairs in their living room, Barbara. Shall I go up and tell them that you're here? They just might be having their celebration supper – it's such an exciting time!'

'No, Mrs Kennard, no need to announce me,' said Barbara with a confidence she showed in her happy smile, and without another word made for the staircase. The living room door was open, and conversation mingled with the clink of champagne glasses. She went in.

The Allinghams were indeed celebrating with friends of theirs, standing around in groups, and they all turned to look at her. Tall and handsomely attractive in his RAF uniform, Lester Allingham stood by a buffet table, holding hands with a pretty woman wearing the matching uniform of the Women's Auxiliary Air Force Service, a WAAF.

'Oh, er – hello, Barbara,' he said with a smile and a quick glance at his companion. 'I was, er – thinking of calling on you some time tomorrow, so many people to see – and this is Vicky, she's my good luck charm when I'm up in the air – Mother! Can you pass that plate of vol-au-vents to Barbara, please – and Dad, is there still some champagne?'

The look that Mrs Allingham gave Barbara was far from friendly, and she made no move to pass the vol-au-vents, though Roland Allingham picked up a bottle and glass, glancing briefly towards his wife.

'I have to do what I'm told, you see,' he said with a heavy attempt at humour. 'Champagne, Miss – er – or would you prefer sherry?'

Barbara stood rooted to the spot, unable to move or speak, and realised that she was going to be sick. She turned and raced down the stairs, her hand over her mouth, hoping to find the toilet before she threw up. She hadn't time to look for it, and had to use the kitchen sink, only just in time. Joan Kennard came to sympathise and offer water to clean her mouth when she finally stopped retching. 'Sit down for a while, dear,' she said, 'until you've recovered.'

Barbara shook her head, and not another word was said as she left the Rectory.

What on earth was she to do? Her period was now thirty-seven days overdue, and she could not tell a soul, least of all her mother – and to tell Lester now would be a disaster. What should she do, to where could she turn? She had heard whispers among girls, even as far back as schooldays, about how some girls 'got rid of it'. They spoke of knitting needles and crochet hooks being pushed up the vagina, or a face-flannel soaked in boiling water and thrust in as far as it would go. She'd also heard of the dangers, and how one girl had died in North Camp last year. She was desperate, almost at the point of bursting into tears and telling her mother all, especially when Mrs Seabrook asked about Lester, and was he coming to visit them? She simply shook her head, and no more questions were asked, though her mother looked at her anxiously and advised her to eat more.

Then she heard two women talking in low voices at the shop while waiting to be served with their meat ration by Mr Seabrook.

'Yes, she'd gone three weeks past the time they said she'd have it, and was as big as a house,' one said in a loud whisper. 'In the end the midwife gave her this huge great dose of castor oil to take.'

'Go on! And did she manage to swallow it without throwing it straight back?'

'Yes, she kept it down, and in the night she had this terrific clear out – couldn't get to the lav in time, but it did the trick, and the labour pains started that night – and she had a big baby girl by morning – weighed ten pounds.'

Mr Seabrook was now ready to serve them, and they stopped talking, but Barbara had heard enough. As soon as she could leave the shop, she went to the chemist's for a bottle of castor oil. It was worth a try, and she forced down as much of the thick oil that her stomach would tolerate.

She never forgot that night. She was seized by violent, agonising cramps, and had to stuff a handful of sheet into her mouth to stop her from crying out. She heaved herself out of bed and stumbled to the lavatory where she sat while her bowel discharged its contents, hard at first, then softer until it was pouring out copious evil-smelling liquid. Her head swam, and she felt herself falling.

She came to, and found herself lying awkwardly on the floor, still discharging uncontrollably from the bowel; the mess was all over the toilet seat, the floor and her nightdress. She groaned aloud, and tried to heave herself up to sit on the seat again.

And there it was, mixing with the bowel matter – *blood*! And more blood that trickled down her legs, definitely coming from the vagina. Her delayed period! Barbara burst into tears. Oh, thank you, God, thank you, thank you!

Hearing the sound, her mother left her bed and came to her daughter. Her mouth dropped open in horror at what she saw.

'*Barbara!* What's happening? Oh, what awful diarrhoea, whatever have you eaten? And your period's come on – oh, my poor girl, let me run you a bath and clear it all up!'

Her ordeal was over. And Barbara Seabrook never knew whether her period had been delayed by emotional anxiety, and brought on by the over-action of the bowel, or whether the violence had caused an early miscarriage.

She was never quite sure, only of one thing – that she would never take such a terrible risk again. Not ever.

* * *

Tom Munday's eyes were shadowed with anxiety when he spoke to Eddie Cooper in the Tradesmen's Arms, and indeed the whole of the public bar fell silent, trying to hear what he was telling his old friend.

'Came down in the Thames estuary, and the Messerschmitt who shot 'em got away. The pilot and the other man were killed straight away when it burst into flames, but our Jack by some miracle got clear of the plane and floated on the water; he doesn't remember much about how he was hauled onto a Thames barge and ended up in a hospital in Margate.'

Tom paused, and his hearers listened.

'As soon as they heard, of course, Rob and Grace went off to visit him. What they must have felt when they saw him . . . well, they *didn't* see him, not his face, it was covered over with wet cloths, and his hands were covered in wet bandages.'

He paused, and Eddie said softly. 'Poor boy. Poor Rob and Grace. Did they speak to a doctor at all?'

'The ward sister told them that he'd been visited by a surgeon who specialises in burns, and treats them in a new way that he's worked out. Only it means that Jack will have to be transferred to this man's hospital at East Grinstead, so it's not going to be quick or easy.'

'And – how did his mother react?'

'Well, needless to say, they both had to agree, and they're going down to the Queen Victoria hospital, as it's called, on Friday. Me and Rob, we say to Grace that at least the boy's still in the land of the living, and if this man's half as good as he's made out to be, then our Jack's in with a chance. And there'll be no more dicing with death in the RAF.'

* * *

The next family member to visit the Nuttalls was Isabel Neville, having heard of Jack's condition from her father. She went alone, taking early fruit and vegetables, and pots of her own home-grown and home-made blackcurrant jam. She met with even more hostility than her brother Ernest, for scarcely had Tom showed her into the parlour than Grace Nuttall stormed in after her.

'You can come round here with your garden produce, but don't imagine I'll ever forget what you did, my Lady Isabel! There's *your* son sound in body and mind, while *mine's* lost half his face burnt away, and a crazy old doctor carrying out experiments on him!'

'That's why I've come today, my poor sister, to try to give you a little comfort,' Isabel said steadily, having steeled herself for a rough rejection of her sympathy. 'Jack's injuries are not of my making, you know. He lives and therefore there's hope, Grace. Look, let me sit down here beside you, and—'

'No! *Never!* You took my little girl – you took her away, and never let me have her back – and now that she's grown into a beautiful woman, you take all the credit for her!'

Isabel turned to her father in near despair.

'That's not true, Grace, and you know it – and you know it, too, don't you, Dad?'

'I guessed it when Grace came home looking so poorly after having Becky,' said Tom sorrowfully. 'And when you married Cedric—'

'Yes, when she married Cedric!' Grace almost shrieked. '*That's* when you should've given me back my Becky! After all, you'd got a son and a rich husband, plus a manor house to live in, *Lady bloody Neville*! You never offered her back to her own mother, so don't come round

140

here weeping crocodile tears over my poor Jack, when you stole my daughter!' She spat, her face contorted with rage, and Isabel drew back, very pale. There was clearly no point in trying to reason with her sister. She picked up her bag and crossed the room to take her father's hand.

'Very well, Grace, if that's what you think of me, I'll leave now, and won't come back until I'm invited. Dad, you know you can come and visit me at the Manor whenever you like, and so can Doreen and Rob. And give my love and best wishes to Jack, tell him I look forward to seeing him again when he's out of hospital.'

'What do *you* care about my poor Jack?' barked Grace in fury. 'You've got Paul – oh, go away, go away!'

Isabel left the house she had been brought up in, and got into the pony-trap. Her thoughts were of Rebecca as a tiny baby, and what kind of a scene might erupt if Grace and Rebecca were to meet in North Camp. I shall have to tell my poor girl and warn her, she realised, though she shrank from the very idea.

Reaching home, she led the little pony to the stables, and then sought out Sally Tanner, her loyal friend and confidante.

'I was afraid something like this would happen one day, Isabel, and always hoped it wouldn't. It's going to be much more difficult now,' Sally sighed. 'I'll stay while you tell her, and comfort her as well as I can.' (*And you too, Isabel*, she thought to herself.)

'We won't bring her back from the farm – we'll wait until she next comes home, and then tell her together,' said Isabel, dreading the inevitable moment when she would have to ask her daughter to sit down and listen to something very important.

Sure enough, Rebecca was mystified, and felt suddenly

alarmed, as if she was being asked to hear unwelcome news. Paul? No, it was not about Paul. Then what?

'I've always told you that I adopted you from a desperate single girl whose fiancé had gone back to the fighting and been killed there, Becky, in that terrible war,' said her mother.

'Yes, Mother, I've always known that. And I'm very glad that you adopted me.'

'Well, now, Becky dear, certain things have happened that make it necessary for me to give you more information,' said Isabel, trying to speak steadily.

'What things, Mother? Tell me, for heaven's sake!'

Rebecca's voice rose, and Sally Tanner took hold of her hand. Isabel forced herself to continue. 'Your mother was – is – my sister Grace. Now don't upset yourself, please—'

For Rebecca had given a long, low moan, a cry from the heart, and buried her face in her hands. Sally put her arms around the girl, and made gentle shushing sounds.

'No, Mother, it's not true, it *can't* be true! Tell me it's a mistake!'

'I'm so sorry, Becky, but it is true. Listen. You were conceived shortly before your father had to leave Grace and go back to that war, that dreadful war, that carnage, that blood-bath – I lost my own husband because of it—' Isabel paused and put her hands to her face.

'Be brave, Isabel,' whispered Sally, and so she continued with the account of what had happened on that fatal, faraway day.

'Your father was a captain in a Hampshire regiment, and it must have been so terrible for Grace when she learnt that he was killed in battle, decorated posthumously for his courage and care for the men in his charge. And then to find herself expecting his baby—' Isabel's voice shook, but she composed herself and continued.

'It was all arranged that you were to be adopted at six weeks old, but on the very day that a woman official came to collect you, Grace – your mother – was in such a state of grief that I couldn't bear it, I feared she might harm herself, and I told the woman that *I* would take you and bring you up as my own, a sister for Paul. And that's what happened.'

'Yes, Becky, that's exactly what happened. I know, because I was there,' said Sally.

'Oh, Mother!' said Rebecca, weeping. 'I just can't take this in. I knew I was adopted, but you always said you took me from a desperate single girl who couldn't keep me.'

'And that was true, Becky, she couldn't. But I could, and I did.'

'Your mother's an angel, Becky,' said Sally.

'Oh, Sally!' Rebecca turned to this woman she had known all her life. 'Dear Sally Tanner, even *you've* been more of a mother to me than – than Mrs Nuttall is. I don't even *like* her, and I can *never* call her Mother. Not ever.'

'Hush, dear. She'll go on being your Aunt Grace,' said Isabel, 'and I'll go on being known as your Mother, though in fact I'm your Aunt Isabel.'

'Never,' said Rebecca. 'I'll *never* call you aunt. And why have you decided to tell me all this now?'

'My poor sister Grace is in a turmoil over her son Jack who has been severely injured when his plane came down. I believe that it has unhinged her, and I'm telling you not to go near her, dear. Keep away from Rectory Road. She's got this idea in her head that I should have handed you back to her when I married Cedric – your Dad – and she might completely lose her reason if she saw you now. Oh, Rebecca, my own dear, precious daughter!'

Tears were shed by all three of them, and then Sally bustled off to make tea. Rebecca was due back at the farm that evening, and she was thankful for the hard work that filled her busy days and gave her little time to ponder over what she had learnt. It explained her strong family resemblance to both her mother and aunt, and it also accounted for Grace Nuttall's cool, unsisterly behaviour over the years towards Lady Neville. Rebecca felt that she never wanted to set eyes on her again.

Grim news continued that autumn of relentless bombing of London. Thirty miles from London, the wailing of the air raid siren situated in Everham became a familiar, almost daily, sound, warning that enemy aircraft had crossed the Channel and could be anywhere overhead. Every morning people switched on their wireless sets to hear of the devastation that had taken place in the night: first the East End, the docks, power stations and gasworks were hit, and the homes close to them, then the terror spread to other parts of the capital, and they heard of air raid shelters that had suffered direct hits, so the people chose to sleep on the platforms of the Underground railway network while explosions took place above them.

'Just imagine it,' said Joan Kennard at a Wednesday gathering of the Knitting Circle. 'Imagine sleeping on that hard, cold platform amongst complete strangers – and what do they do about needing the lavatory?'

Isabel Neville shook her head. 'It puts all our troubles into perspective when we think of the courage of those Londoners.'

'And there's nothing we can do to help them, is there?' said one of the ladies.

144

But it turned out that there *was* vital help to be given by families in North Camp. Before the heavy air raids began, many evacuated children were brought back to London by their parents; now there was urgent need to re-evacuate them. Sir Cedric and Lady Neville opened Hassett Manor to a girl of seven and a boy of five from the East End. At the Rectory space was found for two little motherless boys, terrified of what they had seen and heard; Roland Allingham insisted to his wife that they should do this act of Christian charity, and Joan Kennard put the boys into Josie's room, returning her cot to the bedroom she shared with Alan. Billy Yeomans refused to take in any evacuees, as did the Nuttalls and Mrs Pearson, but after conferring with her nephew Philip, Miss Enid Temple agreed to take in a silent, underweight boy of ten called Nick Grant who seemed to have no relatives and at first shrank back warily from Philip, though when he realised that the quiet man was friendly and showed him how to play simple tunes on the piano, his fears were replaced by trust and a growing attachment which became mutual.

From Everham came news that the Mundays had opened their home to two young Jewish children from Whitechapel, Ruth and Sarah. 'We've got a full house, but Devora manages to keep us all usefully occupied,' reported Ernest.

The whole of North Camp tuned in to their wireless sets at teatime on an October day to hear a broadcast message from fourteen-year-old Princess Elizabeth, a message directed towards all the children who had been sent away from their parents to places of greater safety.

Miss Temple wiped her eyes when the princess, seated beside her younger sister, ended her speech with a heartfelt, 'Goodnight, and good luck to you all.'

'Excuse me, I'm sorry,' she apologised to Nick, who had listened with her, and his shy reply, 'Don't worry, Auntie Enid,' brought more embarrassing tears to her eyes.

More tears were shed at the news of the death of Mr Neville Chamberlain, aged seventy-one, remembered now for his 'peace in our time' speech after visiting Hitler.

'After all that good man did to try to save us from war,' wept Mrs Pearson, 'and then to die a broken man.' Tributes were paid to him from all levels, from his colleagues in government down to the patrons of the Tradesmen's Arms, where Tom Munday and Eddie Cooper agreed that 'Chamberlain was a gentleman, which made him no match for that lying old bugger Adolf Hitler.'

Soon after this the fury of the Luftwaffe turned from London to the centres of British industry: Birmingham, Sheffield, Manchester and Glasgow became the targets of the enemy's bombs, and on one dreadful night of destruction the beautiful medieval city of Coventry was virtually razed to the ground, over a thousand of its citizens killed, and its ancient cathedral left a blackened ruin. At 47 Rectory Road Tom Munday and his son-in-law reminded Grace Nuttall that her son was well out of the ongoing action, and could look ahead to recovery from his injuries, horrendous as they were.

'Things are going badly, Tom,' said Eddie from his chair by the small fire in the public bar. Tom nodded.

'Yes, they are,' he said. 'And the funny thing is that when we sat here a couple of years ago, and couldn't believe that there'd be another war, in fact we hardly dared think about it – but now that we're right in the thick of it, I don't dread the future any more – it's as if we're determined to see it through – take everything old Hitler can throw at us, because we know we're going to win in the end.'

'Yeah.' Eddie took a deep swig of bitter from his glass. 'Yeah, like old Churchill said, no surrender. Not us.'

In Ward Three of the Queen Victoria Hospital at East Grinstead, a historic market town in Sussex, young Jack Nuttall was experiencing the darkest night of his life. He lay in his bed, unable to help himself even to reach out for a glass of water with his burnt and bandaged hands. The skin graft to his face had sloughed off, and would have to be attempted again. It smelt unpleasant, and in the silence of the night Jack felt utter despair, for at twenty years of age his life and future had been taken away from him. He had to be fed and helped to use a urinal bottle; he dreaded a bowel movement when he had to be lifted onto a bed-pan, and found it easier to be led to the lavatory during the day. His one change of scene came when he was led to the tepid saline bath in which he could soak without bandages, and every few minutes he took a deep breath and lowered his head right under the water, easing the pain of his face. One day a week he was visited by his parents, which gave him no comfort, for his mother could not contain her distress at seeing him lying there unrecognisable, his face hidden by saline dressings that covered his lidless eyes. She always burst into tears and had to be led away by his apologetic father.

As he lay there in the silence broken by snores and mutterings of the other men, he gave a long-drawn-out groan which turned into a stream of obscenities.

'Bloody hell, fucking hell, bugger, bugger, bugger, bugger . . .'

The next thing he heard was a man's voice close by the bedside. 'Saying a little prayer for us, mate?'

Jack recognised the familiar tones of Smithy, an ex-patient of Ward Three, an early example of Archibald McIndoe's plastic surgery before the war. His nose and four fingers had been frost-bitten from climbing in the Alps, and although he had to lose his fingers, two from each hand, his nose had been reconstructed over a period of five operations. He now worked in the administration offices of the Queen Victoria Hospital, and as a voluntary visitor to Ward Three, where he would turn up unannounced at any hour of the day or night.

'Want a fag?' He lit a cigarette, took a draw of it, then put it in Jack's mouth through the space in his facial dressings for breathing and feeding. And then he took a chair and began to talk about his own experiences and those of others treated by McIndoe – the Boss, as he was referred to.

'You know, this is the right place to be, lad, because although it may take a long time and several operations, the Boss is a genius with his knife and tweezers. He'll do that graft again, and *again* if need be – you've got plenty of spare skin on your bum and thighs – and count yourself lucky you've still got your crown jewels intact – there's many a bloke who's had 'em fried. I tell you, Jack old son, in this place you can always find somebody worse off than yourself.' He gently removed the cigarette to shake off the ash, and replace it between Jack's lips, before going on talking, easily and unsentimentally.

And that was how Jack Nuttall started to return to the land of the living. It would be a long, hard journey, but in that dark hour he discovered new hope.

The bombing of Britain's towns and cities continued relentlessly, and the whole nation grieved for those killed, injured and made homeless. That Christmas, the second of the war, was shadowed by deepening austerities and worsening dangers facing the country at home and abroad. Listeners heard about the terrible night of the twenty-ninth of December, when incendiary bombs had rained down on London, creating an inferno that lit up the sky with fiery light that could be seen thirty miles away; people in North Camp stood on their doorsteps and watched in awe; it was being called by newsreaders the Second Great Fire of London, three hundred years after the first.

Abroad, trouble was brewing in North Africa, where British and Commonwealth troops were guarding Egypt and the Sudan from imminent invasion from the Italian army, which greatly outnumbered them. Paul Storey wrote to report that the food parcels from home had arrived, and Valerie Pearson received a postcard from John Richardson with a photograph of the Great Sphinx, telling her of the discomforts of life in the Western Desert, all itchy heat and flies. She sighed over it, reminding herself that he was thousands of miles away, not knowing when he would return, if ever. She also remembered her embarrassment when he'd taken her to see *Gone with the Wind*, and what had followed. Gone were the illusions she'd cherished that one day he would truly return her love, and sweetly enfold her in his arms, whispering of marriage and sharing a home together. Going with two friends from The Limes to see the film of *Rebecca* had been far more enjoyable – here again was Laurence Olivier with looks to dream about – imagining tender love-scenes, safely remote from overheated, heavily breathing intimacy.

CHAPTER EIGHT

1941

Daffodils were fluttering in the cold, blustery wind of an early April day, and Rebecca Neville, county representative of the Women's Land Army, thanked heaven that spring had come round again. The winter had seemed interminable, miserably cold indoors as well as out, food was becoming scarcer, and there was the constant worry about the men in the armed services, now being shipped abroad to North Africa in larger numbers; every day brought the fear of a telegram with the worst news. Seated at her desk at the Everham office, Rebecca had five applicants to interview; their numbers had been increasing since the recent compulsory registration of women over the age of twenty. She had to be careful to give them fair warning of the hardships as well as the good points of life on the land, especially in winter, and to help them consider the other auxiliary forces: the ATS in which Dora Goddard had discovered a new and exciting life, or the WAAFS who supported the men who were defending the country from invasion from the air, and increasingly going on raids over Berlin and Hamburg, giving the Germans a taste of the bombing; or the WRNS, the women who supported the navy, beset by the dreaded U-boats, the German submarines which sank so many ships of the merchant navy carrying food supplies, and their Royal Navy escorts.

Rebecca considered the applications of the five girls to be interviewed today. Two of them were from rural areas in Hampshire and Berkshire, so could be sent straight to farms, if possible to places of their choice, but firstly to where the need was greatest. Three town girls with little or no knowledge of rural life might benefit from a course of instruction at one of the WLA courses like the Cannington Farm Institute in Somerset; she hoped that its Nissen huts with concrete floors, hard beds and a slow combustion boiler to heat water would not put them off.

Having dealt with the new recruits, Rebecca got down to paperwork. She had to visit and inspect every farm in her area at least once a week, and prepare reports for the regional offices. There were usually complaints from the land girls or the farmers or both. The girls protested that the farmers' wives expected them to work indoors, especially in winter, after they had fed and cared for the livestock – the cows, sheep and pigs – while in summer they had to work up to twelve hours a day at haymaking and harvesting time. Rebecca usually found that a little give and take on both sides was needed, and in winter it was fair to give some help in the farmhouse, but that it should be limited to preparing food and washing-up, cleaning of pots and pans that had been used; there was to be no house cleaning, and certainly no emptying of chamber pots. 'We don't mind mucking-out the cow sheds or the pig sties, but we draw the line at mucking-out the pots,' one girl had complained. Some of them were homesick, especially those who came from stable family backgrounds, while others were only too pleased to get away from the demands of home life. Rebecca found it worthwhile to sit down and have a talk with unhappy girls, and sometimes she was able to transfer them to another farm or bring another land girl to share the placement.

Home life. Rebecca sighed, for they had their problems at Hassett Manor, which was no longer the haven of peace that it had once been. Their evacuees, a girl of seven and a boy of five, had dirty language and dirty habits. Sally Tanner had to bear the brunt of the chaos they caused, and Rebecca braced herself for another tirade of disapproval when she arrived at the Manor this afternoon. She boarded the train waiting on the North Camp spur line, and stepped into a carriage where two people were already seated.

'Miss Neville!' cried Philip Saville and Valerie Pearson in unison.

'Oh, what a nice surprise,' she said, putting on a smile, for she usually found conversation rather hard work when faced with either of these neighbours.

'How's life at The Limes, Valerie?' she enquired, and was surprised at how the girl's face lit up.

'It's very rewarding, Miss Neville,' came the reply. 'Some of the children are so sweet, so – so in need of care and attention. I shall always be grateful to your mother for digging me out of the rut I was in!'

Philip smiled. 'Yes, Miss Pearson, Lady Neville is a remarkable, er, lady. She has visited my aunt to check on our evacuee, Nick. He's ten years old, very silent and solemn at first, but now he's coming out of his shell, and we talk about what he's learnt at school, and all sorts of things.'

Rebecca was pleased at both of these reactions. The war had brought sorrow and suffering to so many families, but had proved to be not such a bad thing for these two; they positively bloomed.

'You've made a difference to Charlie and Joe Perrin, Philip,' she said. 'They're excellent young pianists! What about this little boy Nick – would he like to come over and meet the Perrin twins?'

'I'm sure he'd love to, Miss Neville,' Philip replied with a smile and a nod. 'I've given him a basic knowledge of the keyboard, but we haven't attempted any lessons as yet. The boy's had more than enough new impressions to take in, but yes, it's a very good idea, and most kind. Shall I bring him over to Hassett Manor when the next lesson's due?'

'Certainly, Philip – but be on your guard against the two tearaways we've got!'

'You mean the Perrin lads?'

'No, no, they're positively angelic compared to our evacuees,' she said wryly. 'Jimmy's five and Lily's seven, and so far we haven't made much progress with them. Heaven only knows how they were brought up!'

'Oh, how awful for poor Lady Neville!' said Philip in real dismay. 'She leads such a busy life with her voluntary service work – not to mention the anxiety over Paul—'

'Not to mention it,' said Rebecca firmly, as if to stop further talk on the subject.

There was a short silence, broken by Valerie. 'Is anybody going to see this film *Pinocchio* on at the Embassy all next week?' she asked. 'It's a full-length cartoon film, like *Snow White*, just right for children.'

The silence continued while Rebecca and Philip took this in, and then they both spoke at once.

'I could take Nick and the Perrin boys,' said Philip, just as Rebecca said, 'I could take Lily and Jimmy – we could go to a matinee on the Saturday.'

'Or on the Wednesday, when the children are off school,' said Philip. But Rebecca reminded him of the Ladies' Circle.

'Make it the Saturday, then,' she said, 'and what a very nice thought, Valerie! Would you like to come with us? We'll need your skills at child management, as you'll see when you meet Lily and Jimmy!'

And so it was settled – an outing to the cinema as a treat for the evacuees.

On her arrival home, Rebecca was faced with a highly indignant Sally Tanner, both her parents being out. Sally's biggest complaint was of the thieving from the kitchen as soon as her back was turned, and utter disregard for the trouble they caused.

'It's very difficult for you, I know, Sally – you get the worst of them, with my parents so often out,' Rebecca said placatingly. 'They've been brought up in a rough area, and don't know any better.'

'Rough area be blowed, they're just pig-ignorant!' stormed Sally. 'Them two, they do their business in corners of rooms, so no wonder the whole house smells to heaven. And their talk is so disgusting, I don't care to repeat it to you. They don't show any respect, they went upstairs into my bedroom, opened drawers, took out my underwear and *wee'd* on it, then put it back. They're always shouting and hollering – they're no better than animals, dirty little tykes!'

'Oh, that's awful, and I shall have to speak to them very firmly,' said Rebecca in dismay. 'Try not to upset yourself, Sally—'

But Sally was not to be soothed. 'I tell you what, Becky, if it wasn't for your poor mother, I wouldn't stand for it – I'd sling me hook and go back to Bethnal Green, bombs or no bombs!'

Seeing angry tears in Sally's eyes, Rebecca shook her head helplessly. Her mother had worries enough with Paul out in North Africa, and spent most of her time with the Women's Voluntary Service; Sir Cedric was also taken up with the training of the Territorials, in addition to his position as a Justice of the Peace and running the Manor Hassett estate with a depleted staff. Even so, Sally deserved to be treated better than this, and something would have to be done. Rebecca decided to have a serious talk with her mother.

While many families waited in dread for news from abroad, the atmosphere at 47 Rectory Road had lightened, for which Tom Munday was thankful, for it made Grace easier to live with. Her weekly visits with Rob to the Queen Victoria Hospital had raised her spirits, seeing Jack's slow but steady improvement, the success of the second attempt at a skin graft to his face, and the new eyelids which did not quite close, but allowed him at least to see a blurred vision of his surroundings. His face was recognisable to his mother and father, and he was able to acknowledge them. McIndoe had removed two blackened, stiffened fingers from his right hand, and he still had his thumbs, so was able to grip objects, to hold a knife and fork, a pencil, a cigarette – and to talk, not only to Rob and Grace, but to McIndoe and his surgical team, the nurses and the other patients in Ward Three, to whom he introduced his parents, quoting Smithy's words that there was always somebody worse off. He made an effort to cooperate with McIndoe as the reconstruction of his face and hands proceeded. Rob Nuttall was immensely proud of his son, and both he and Grace looked forward to the day when Jack would be able to come home, and Grace would be able to devote all her time to his comfort. And she need never again dread news of planes shot down or reported missing.

Other parents, other families of men in the Royal Air Force continued to fear for their sons. The Luftwaffe continued to bomb London and other provincial cities: centres of industry and shipbuilding. Liverpool, Belfast and Clydebank were battered, and in the south, Portsmouth and Southampton. Mary and Sidney Goddard received a shock when Dora wrote to tell them that she had accepted a transfer to London, to play a more active part in the war. A directive from the War Office recommended that the ATS should learn how to operate the huge searchlights used to spot and track enemy aircraft in the night sky. Caught in the crossed beams of two or three searchlights, the bombers became visible to the anti-aircraft gunners.

'Gwen and I are with a smashing bunch of girls,' she wrote. 'Every night we put on huge thick overcoats and boots, with tin hats on our heads, and we yell like fury when we catch a Jerry plane in a beam – it's like a game, and when one's brought down, it's such a thrill, we enjoy every minute. Look after yourselves, Mum and Dad, and don't let Bully Billy or Pregnant Pam get you down!'

Mary Goddard missed her daughter more than she could confide in Sidney, not wanting to worry him further, as he looked so tired, working six long days a week – seven if there was extra work to be done. Pam was expecting another baby, and Sam was crawling into every room and every kind of mischief. Sidney, did she but know it, worried in much the same way about her. Old Mrs Yeomans was unable to be of much assistance to Mary, and tried not to be a 'nuisance', as she put it, though her memory was failing, and she was unable to go up or downstairs without help, usually from Mary. The downstairs lavatory was outside, and in bad or wet weather Mary produced a chamber pot for the old lady, shutting the parlour door for privacy.

At least the food rationing did not affect farmers as much as the butchers who had to deal with their registered customers. The Yeomanses were not short of milk or eggs, and when Billy killed a pig he had pork enough to sell directly to favoured customers as well as to supply Seabrook's. Being no philanthropist, he charged high prices for his off-the-ration meat, and resentment grew among families on limited incomes against the better off such as the Nevilles of Hassett Manor who had an extra family of evacuees to feed.

'It isn't as if *we* ate more than our fair share, Mother,' said Rebecca. 'It's the children who help themselves from the pantry, and make Sally's life a misery—'

'I know, I know,' said Isabel wearily. 'The irony of it is that I spend quite a lot of my time helping families who have problems with evacuees. I've been inclined to leave ours to Sally to deal with.'

'Yes, and it's most unfair, Mother. *We* need to discipline Lily and Jimmy, Mother. I shall draw up a list of rules which must be obeyed, mealtimes and bedtimes, no wandering around the house and getting into mischief in the bedrooms. And I'm sorry, but you and Dad will have to do your share in training them, and where necessary, punishing them.'

'Oh, Becky, that sounds very hard!'

'No harder than it is for Sally – I'm more concerned about her than for them. Hasn't she *told* you about their dirty habits? No, because she doesn't want you to be bothered, when you're so often out on WVS work, and besides, there's the constant worry about Paul. No, Mother, we've *got* to be firmer, starting today – and by the way, I've got a sweetener for them. Philip Saville is taking the Perrin boys and his own evacuee, Nick, to see the film of *Pinocchio* next week, the Saturday matinee. And I'll join them with Lily and Jimmy. We've asked Valerie Pearson to come along with us because we'll need an extra helper.'

'That does sound like a very good idea!' Isabel nodded approvingly. 'Valerie has blossomed out remarkably since she started working at that Everham nursery.'

'All thanks to you, Mother, and the same can be said for Philip Saville. Right, now let's have some tea before I get down to a pile of paperwork – there's never enough time to do it in the office. And we've got another big problem coming up – literally hundreds of Italian prisoners of war coming to work on the land. They've been taken in the Western Desert, and don't sound to have put up much of a fight. It'll be up to local WLA representatives to place as many as we're given, and heaven knows how we shall communicate with them. Ah, well.'

When Sir Cedric heard about Rebecca's plans to get the two evacuees more usefully occupied, he brightened at once.

'My dear Isabel, why wasn't I told about this? I shall take

more part in dealing with these children – take them round
the estate with me, show them the horses, the chickens, and
get them interested in country life.'

When told of the new arrangement, Sally at first was
sceptical. 'Get 'em on muck-spreading,' she muttered.
'That'd be right up their street.'

Saturday dawned. Mrs Pearson was feeling rather neglected.
'I have to manage all through the week without any help,
but I don't expect you to disappear on a Saturday,' she
complained.

'I'm sorry, Mother, but Miss Neville asked me to help with
this outing to the cinema,' Valerie apologised, half inclined
to regret her acceptance of Miss Neville's offer. 'There are
five children going, three of them evacuees, and I, er, agreed
to go with her and Mr Saville.'

'And what has Mr Saville to do with evacuees?'

'He has one of them – I mean Miss Temple has taken a
ten-year-old boy, and there are two at Hassett Manor, a girl
and a boy, quite young.'

'That's not very wise of Enid Temple!' answered her
mother. 'I hope you don't make a habit of this sort of thing.'

Valerie made no reply, but as she did the shopping that
morning, she kept an eye on the time; she was to meet Mr
Saville and the boy, Nick, at North Camp station at one
o'clock, where Miss Neville would join them with the Perrin
twins, Charlie and Joe, now ten years old, and the little girl
and boy staying at Hassett Manor.

But Miss Neville was not there; Lady Neville met them
with the children and brought apologies from her daughter
who had a severe headache.

'Rebecca's very sorry, but she really needs to rest, Mr Saville – and Miss Pearson,' she said. 'I'm sure you two will be able to cope with the children. Here is the amount you will need for the cinema and train fares – no, I insist, you are doing such a good service for these children who don't get many treats. I hope you all enjoy the film – I've heard it's very good.'

Valerie smiled politely and said she hoped Miss Neville would soon recover. She noticed how Philip Saville blushed and stammered as he thanked the lady for the money.

The train arrived, and the excited children scrambled on board, settling in a compartment that already contained a well-dressed lady and gentleman.

'Oh, dear, it looks as if we're being invaded,' the lady murmured to her husband, and gave them a patronising smile. 'Are you off to somewhere nice?'

'Yeah, we're orf to the pictures,' said Lily, and raising her voice, began to sing:

'We're orf to see the Wizard, the wonderful Wizard of Oz!'

The rest, except for Nick, joined in with gusto.

'Because, because, because, because, because – because o' the wonderful fings he does!'

'We're going to see *Pinocchio*, actually,' said Valerie, and the lady looked pained.

'Whatever it is, they make enough noise about it!' she said. 'Can you quieten them down a little?'

'Er – I'm sorry, they're just a little excited, they don't get many treats, you see,' Valerie apologised, smiling at solemn-faced Nick and frowning at the Perrin twins who giggled and blamed Lily.

'It's 'er what's makin' all the noise, so tell 'er orf, not us!'

For answer Lily stuck out her tongue at them. 'Turnip 'eads!'

'Be quiet at once, children!' ordered Philip, his face flaming with embarrassment. 'People will think you're very rude.'

The Perrin twins hung their heads briefly, but Lily was defiant.

'Bet they're Jerry spies,' she muttered half under her breath, prompting her young brother to utter the rudest words he knew:

'Arse 'oles!'

This was too much for the lady, who got up and beckoned to her husband to do likewise. 'What disgusting behaviour! Come on, Charles, we'll go to another compartment, and get away from them.' Turning to Philip and with a glance at Valerie, she added, 'And you can be sure that I'll complain to the railway authorities. Children like yours are a menace to law-abiding passengers!'

As the couple swept out of the compartment, Lily shouted after them, 'Mrs Knicker Elastic! Spyin' for ol' 'Itler, that's what you are!'

Valerie and Philip looked at each other helplessly. Turning to the silent boy beside him Philip said quietly, 'I'm sorry about this, Nick.'

The boy shrugged. 'It's all right, Uncle Philip, I know plenty o' worse words than them.'

Valerie looked severely at the other four. 'One more rude word, and we'll take you home – you won't see *Pinocchio*. Do you understand?'

Silence descended on their compartment until they arrived at Everham.

'Miss Pearson, do you mind taking charge of Nick and er,

Lily,' asked Philip, 'and I'll take the twins and her brother. We'd better keep together.' Raising his voice, he added, 'And we'd better behave ourselves!'

They arrived at the cinema just as the doors were opening to let in the patrons who had been queuing outside. When Philip paid for the tickets, Lily and Jimmy demanded sweets, but being rationed, the only sweets available were a tube of wine-gums, and only one.

Reaching a row about halfway down, 'Uncle Philip' said that he and 'Auntie Valerie' should sit at each end of seven seats, with himself at the end, Jimmy at his side, then Nick, then Charlie and Joe, Lily and Valerie. He looked across at her with raised eyebrows, as if asking whether she was satisfied with the arrangement, and she nodded back; they exchanged wry smiles.

What a sensible girl she is, he thought, and willing to give up a Saturday afternoon for what he privately thought of as a penance. Then the lights went down and the curtains drew back to show the certificate for *Pinocchio*. The children joined in the happy screaming of others in the audience, and the film began.

It was Jimmy who first said he wanted to wee-wee, and Uncle Philip got up to accompany him to the men's lavatories. Then it was Lily's turn, and Auntie Valerie got up to take her to the Ladies, only to find that the girl did not really need it.

'I can't go, Auntie Valerie,' she said, pulling up her knickers, and Valerie, who by this time wanted to go herself, but didn't care to sit on the toilet seat in front of the little girl, and not inclined to leave her unattended, accompanied her back to their seats. Then it was Joe's turn, and Charlie's; people were shuffling and fidgeting impatiently at the to-ing

162

and fro-ing, and when Jimmy wanted to go again, Valerie took him to the Ladies this time, much to the annoyance of the others, having to draw up their knees to let the pair of them go past and then come back again.

'Right, that's enough,' said Philip, 'no more visits for anybody until the interval!' It meant that Valerie also had to wait for the interval, and leaving the children with Philip, she made her visit as quickly as she could. Each child was given the reward of a wine-gum.

'Now, I want you to be very, very good during the second half,' Philip told them, and caught Valerie's eye. Their faces simultaneously broke into smiles.

'D'ye think we make good parents, Miss Pearson?' he asked.

'You ain't our parents!' interposed Lily. 'My Dad could knock you out in one go!'

'Then I'm very thankful your Dad's not around,' Philip answered, followed by fidgetings and whisperings all around them.

'That family's very naughty, aren't they, Mama?' piped up a little voice two rows behind them.

'They won't keep quiet, and we can't hear Jiminy Cricket,' said another.

'Between them they've been to the lavatory thirteen times', said an older boy's voice, ending on a laugh in which the others joined.

'Now then, keep quiet yourselves,' said a lady's voice firmly, 'or the film will be spoilt for everybody.'

At that moment a message was flashed across the screen: *An air raid alert has been sounded.* A few people got up to leave, but the majority stayed to enjoy the rest of the story of the little wooden boy's adventures and the voice of his 'conscience', Jiminy Cricket. The children gaped at the screen, and Philip looked across at Valerie, just as she turned to look at him: they dared not speak across the five children, but he gave her a wink and she smiled back. Apart for a demand for another wine-gum, the rest of the film was shown without disturbance, either from toilet necessities or enemy action.

'*Hey diddle de dee! an actor's life for me!*' sang Lily, Jimmy and the Perrin twins, skipping along the street back to Everham station, having picked up the song from the film.

'Come on, Nick, we'd better catch up,' said Philip, and Valerie too increased her pace behind them.

'*Hey, diddle de dum, an actor's life is fun!*'

It was impossible to keep a straight face, and when Philip turned round to ask Valerie if they were going too fast for her, and added, 'I'd join in with them, only people would think I was drunk!' she laughed aloud, and he responded, as if he was seeing this shy, quiet girl for the first time.

The North Camp train was waiting on the spur line. 'Let's see if we can find an empty compartment this time,' he said, shepherding the children on board; but the train was filled with other families who had been to see *Pinocchio*, and they resigned themselves to a rowdy journey.

Lady Neville was waiting at the station with the pony-trap.

'I hope you've all been good,' she said with a smile, and Philip avoided her eyes in some confusion. Valerie was more forthcoming.

'We've *tried* to be good, Lady Isabel, but some of us were more good than others!'

Isabel laughed. 'Well, as long as you tried,' she said, pleased that her little white lie had worked, and Rebecca had been able to get on with a backlog of paperwork.

'I can squeeze Charlie, Joe, Lily and Jimmy into the trap,' she said. 'Philip, will you and Nick take Valerie home? It's a lovely evening.'

'Certainly we will,' said Philip, and the three of them set off for the Pearsons' cottage. 'You've been marvellous, Miss, er, Valerie, I don't think I would have survived without you,' he told her.

'It's all right, er, Philip, I think we both did very well, don't you? We'll be able to look back and laugh about it!'

And just as naughty Georgie Tonks at the nursery had made Valerie Pearson wonder how it would feel to be a mother, this afternoon's outing had made her imagine herself as a wife with a family. Better behaved, of course.

It was Devora Munday's idea to take the whole family to see the Saturday matinee of *Pinocchio*. There were six children now, with the addition of the two little girl evacuees, Ruth and Sarah. Jonny Pascoe was now a tall lad of sixteen, and had left school to help in the office of Munday and Pascoe; in another year's time he would be due for call-up, and Ernest banished the thought from his mind.

'Yes, it will be a treat for us all,' he agreed, 'especially for little Ruth and Sarah.'

All that week the children talked about Saturday in happy anticipation; Devora too looked forward to this family outing and the pleasure she and Ernest would get from the children's enjoyment.

Saturday dawned, and Devora prepared an early lunch,

to give them plenty of time to join the queue outside the Embassy Cinema.

And it was just as they sat down to eat that Ayesha began to wheeze and pant, her eyes stared as if in terror, and her nose and lips turned a purplish blue. She opened her mouth and gasped, but no words came out. It was a severe and therefore frightening asthmatic attack.

Ernest rose from his chair. 'You stay with her, Devora, and I'll fetch a phial.'

On a top shelf in a kitchen cupboard were the glass phials containing the instantly effective iodine compound with menthol and chloroform; he folded one of them in a large handkerchief, broke it and returned to hold the vapour to Ayesha's nose and mouth. Jonny was standing beside her, whispering reassurances, and Devora was serving the others with their lunch, her mouth set in a firm straight line.

Ayesha started to take breaths again, shallow at first, becoming deeper as the vapour took effect. 'Stay with me, Jonny,' she panted, 'don't leave me, please.' Jonny said he would stay with her, and told Ernest to go to the cinema with the others.

'I understand her, Dad, I'll be fine,' he said.

Ernest lifted Ayesha up in his arms and took her into the parlour where he laid her on the sofa, propping her up with cushions.

'I can't risk it, she might have another attack,' he told Jonny, 'and I'd only worry about her. I'm happy to stay, and you go to help your mother with the others.'

Jonny reluctantly agreed, and Devora had no choice; she hid her resentment as well as she could, and at the cinema she and Jonny were shown into a row of seats with her at one end and him at the other. The curtains drew back, the children cheered, and the film began.

While the younger children stared in wonder at the screen, Jonny and David's amused attention was taken up with the antics of a family two rows below them, not very well controlled by the couple who were presumably the parents. When the second part of the programme began, the parents had a brisk exchange with the children.

'That family's very naughty, aren't they, Mama?' said little Ruth.

'They won't keep quiet, and we can't hear Jiminy Cricket,' said Sarah.

'Between them they've been to the lavatory thirteen times,' said David amidst laughter, but Devora saw nothing to laugh about.

'Now then, keep quiet yourselves, or the film will be spoilt for everybody,' she said firmly, thankful that her own little brood was much better behaved; for as her husband was not with them, she did not recognise the other family in the dark.

As spring passed into summer, the sinking of food supply ships by the German U-boats became worse, and rationing had to be tightened up; every household felt the shortages, and those with sons in the Royal or Merchant Navy had the additional constant anxiety of the dangers their men faced. Then came a terrible blow, the loss of one of the country's largest battleships, the *HMS Hood*, sunk by the German battleship *Bismarck*, with the loss of 1,400 men. The *HMS Prince of Wales* was badly damaged in the same sea battle, but managed to escape under cover of a smokescreen. North Camp mourned with the rest of the nation at this disaster, and everybody's thoughts were with those who had lost men; it was a tremendous relief to hear that young Robin Seabrook was not among the dead, though his parents' fear for his life was felt by Mr Seabrook's customers.

'That *Bismarck's* supposed to be invincible,' Eddie Cooper said gloomily in the Trademen's Arms when the news had come through. 'It's heavily armoured, and torpedoes just bounce off the bloody thing.'

'There isn't a ship on the ocean that can't be sunk if it's blown up,' replied Tom Munday. 'And you can bet your life that the navy'll have one aim and object from now on – to sink the *Bismarck*.'

It was true. Less than a week later the great 'impregnable' battleship, relentlessly pursued by the *HMS Ark Royal* and three other battleships of the Royal Navy, and pounded by their armour-piercing shell from their heavy guns, was hopelessly crippled; overnight she was a flaming shambles, and the next morning sunk beneath the waves with all hands on board.

'Sweet revenge for *HMS Hood*!' The newsreaders gave out the glad tidings on the wireless, as did the newspaper headlines. It came at a moment when British towns and cities were being bombed by enemy aircraft day and night. In London thousands were killed or injured, and people wept in the streets at the sight of such devastation. Dora Goddard wrote home in jubilation to say that the ATS searchlights had helped to bring down several of the bombers. In the Tradesmen's Arms the patrons cheered and celebrated the end of the *Bismarck*, though North Camp gave a mixed reception to the other news, the arrival of fifty Italian soldiers taken prisoner in North Africa.

'While we're sitting here waiting for old Hitler to come over and invade us, if you ask me we've already been invaded,' was the verdict of one regular in the public bar. 'Wouldn't trust any o' them wops further than I could spit.'

There were noddings and head-shakings. 'I hear they're going to live in Nissen huts – not the last word in luxury, but better than the desert,' said Tom Munday.

'Poor buggers,' muttered Eddie Cooper, though whether he was referring to the Italian prisoners of war or to the crew of the *Bismarck* was not quite clear.

CHAPTER NINE

1941

'Wanna go 'ome! Wanna go 'ome! Wanna go *'ome!*'

'This is unendurable, and I shall go out of my mind if those children don't stop this awful noise. My husband can't write his sermons, and neither of us get any sleep!'

Mrs Allingham certainly looked strained and unwell, thought Joan Kennard. The two little brothers who had been taken in at the Rectory as evacuees had not settled at all well. Both the curate and his wife tried to divert them and gently persuade them to accept their change of circumstances, but the grieving children, Kenny, aged six and Danny, aged four, refused to be comforted.

'I've never seen more sad-looking children,' Joan told her husband. 'They won't eat, they both wet the bed, and Danny has to wear a big terry napkin in the day, that's why he often smells. He won't say when he wants to wee-wee, only "Wanna go 'ome", over and over again. Mrs Allingham complains, but *they* don't do a thing for the boys – they're praised for taking two evacuees, but I have all the care of them, and I don't get time to spend with Josie, and I'm expecting again, I don't get time to rest, and I'm *tired*!'

Alan was alerted by the sharpness of her tone, and tried to give the boys more attention, talking to them and taking them out in the sunshine as often as he could. The dreadful truth was that they were homeless and motherless after a bombing raid on London.

'We have to remember that both the Allinghams' sons are in the thick of the war, my love. And they're getting on in years.'

'But no easier to get on with,' replied his wife quickly. 'I've asked her to call me Joan, but she says she prefers to keep to titles – so I'll never call her Agnes. It's quite ridiculous.'

'Isabel Neville's got the same trouble with *her* two. They caused an uproar at *Pinocchio*,' said Alan with a wry grin. Joan was not amused.

'At least she can send them to St Peter's,' she replied. St Peter's Church of England Infants' School took North Camp children from five up to the age of ten, after which they went to the Council School at Everham until they left at fifteen.

'But why can't Kenny go to school at St Peter's?'

'Not without Danny who's only four. Just think of the hullaballoo if they were parted!'

'Oh, don't upset yourself, my love,' begged Alan, noticing how distressed she looked. 'Look, I'll have a word with Miss Stevenson, and ask her to take Danny as well as Kenny in the circumstances. I know she'll agree, and it will give you some time to spend with Josie.'

'At least the Allinghams don't complain about *her* any

more,' Mrs Kennard replied. 'She's turned into a little angel in their eyes. But when this next one arrives—'

The very next day the two little boys started to attend St Peter's School where the wail of 'I wanna go 'ome' became a joke to the other children. Mr Kennard told Miss Stevenson their sad story, adding that their future probably lay in a children's home. So she made no complaint, but gave of her time and patience, as Mrs Kennard did. But it was not easy.

That June the ladies' Wednesday meetings at the Rectory acquired a new name: the Make Do and Mend Circle. The rumours of clothes rationing had become a reality, and in addition to food ration books, there was now a book of sixty clothing coupons issued to each person.

'We shall have to go through our wardrobes and find whatever clothing we can alter or mend,' Lady Isabel told the Circle. 'A mother's old dresses may be let out or cut down into dresses for her daughter, and men's trousers used to make shorts for boys. Holes must be darned or patched, seams reinforced, and old knitted jumpers and cardigans unravelled and knitted up again into something new. The Women's Voluntary Service can now supply standard knitting wool to make men's, women's and children's garments as well as comforts for the Forces – though our men in the desert won't be wanting woollies.'

So children's jumpers, cardigans, vests, scarves, gloves and knitted hats were made and proudly passed round at meetings to show what could be done. Very soon after the first clothing coupons were issued a new brand of ladies' fashion was launched, the 'Utility' label on dresses, coats and other garments; it signified quality material with no frills or flounces, some of them designed by leaders of the fashion industry.

'Now we can *all* look like models!' said Isabel to her sceptical hearers.

In the Nuttall household there were more pressing matters than fashion. All was in upheaval, for Jack was being discharged home. He had been transferred from the Queen Victoria Hospital at East Grinstead to convalesce at Marchwood Park in Hampshire where there were workshops and instructors who taught McIndoe's ex-patients to make items to a very high standard, notably for aircraft navigation. Grace had been impatient for Jack to be sent home, but he had requested extra time at Marchwood Park to learn to use his remaining eight fingers to the best of his ability.

Tom Munday's heart fluttered with both anticipation and apprehension when the car drew up outside 47 Rectory Road, and his grandson got out. Rob and Grace accompanied Jack, but he refused assistance as he walked up the path ahead of them. Tom stood at the door, a hand on Doreen's shoulder; he had tried to prepare her for her brother's changed appearance, and told her to smile as she greeted him – but she clapped a hand to her face and gave a little cry of dismay, while Tom had to hide his own shocked pity behind a smile and a hearty 'Welcome home, lad!'

Yes, Jack was home again after all these months, back with his family and his own bed in his own room, and his mother was weeping for joy.

'Home at last, my son, my little boy, you're out of that

173

hospital, and I'll look after you, and I'll go to church again on Sunday, to give thanks!'

'That's right, Grace,' said his father. 'We'll all go.'

While Jack Nuttall tried to adjust himself to his new life as a veteran of the RAF at twenty-one, and Lady Isabel exhorted the women of North Camp to 'Make Do and Mend', there came news so unexpected that it was said to have surprised even Prime Minister Churchill. At midsummer Adolf Hitler broke the non-aggression pact he had signed with the Russian leader, Joseph Stalin, and immediately invaded that vast territory. German forces rapidly pushed deeply into Russia, while the German Luftwaffe bombed Moscow.

In the Tradesmen's Arms various conjectures were put forward as to what had prompted this move, but no satisfactory conclusion was reached.

'He's after their coalfields, I reckon,' said one.

'And whatever else he can grab after he's crushed the Russian people,' said another.

''E's orf 'is chump,' said a third.

'I'll tell you what,' said Eddie Cooper. 'It takes care of *us*. If he's using his army to invade Russia, he won't have many left to parachute over the Channel!'

Tom Munday nodded, his thoughts straying sorrowfully to his war-scarred grandson.

'Yes. Whatever his reason, the Russians are going to get what we were going to get, God help them!'

On this bright Sunday morning in July, Rebecca Neville noted that St Peter's church was packed. Families who would once have gone cycling, picnicking, playing tennis or cricket – or

174

just stayed at home gardening – now attended Divine Worship where prayers were said for their men in the armed forces. The Seabrooks were there as well as the regulars like Sir Cedric and Lady Neville, and Mrs Tomlinson with her son; and there were many more children; Rebecca had brought Lily and Jimmy, and Joan Kennard was accompanied by Kenny and Danny as well as little Josie. Miss Temple had brought young Nick, fascinated by the sight of Uncle Philip at the organ. Before the service began, Danny's wail of 'Wanna go 'ome!' assaulted the ears of the worshippers, and Joan wished he could go into the Sunday School in the church hall; however, that might drive away their excellent voluntary teacher, and could not be risked.

There was a slight disturbance at the west door, a murmur of voices as the Nuttall family arrived. Tom Munday entered with his granddaughter Doreen who looked as if she had been crying. He had his arm around her, and whispered, 'Be proud of your brother, my dear.'

Heads turned to look and smile at the returned hero, but Rebecca noticed the shock on many faces as they saw Jack's scars: the right eye drawn down at the corner, and without an eyebrow, and the mouth twisted into an unnatural grin. She felt a pang of pity for the young man and his family. My mother, she thought, my half-brother and sister. My grandfather. She glanced down at Lily and Jimmy, and realised that she would have to avoid their seeing the ravaged face – which meant avoiding close contact with him when the service ended.

Philip began to play the first few bars of the voluntary, and the congregation stood. The Reverend Mr Allingham conducted the service, and the Reverend Mr Kennard read the intercessions, praying for all the men of North Camp serving in the armed forces, and giving thanks for the return of Jack Nuttall.

At the end of the service, as the people filed out into the bright sunshine, Isabel Neville approached the Nuttalls to greet her nephew with a kiss. Rebecca felt that it was important for her to keep Lily and Jimmy away from Jack, in case they made some hurtful remark; but the only regrettable words she heard were from a woman leaving the church: 'I don't think it's right to let such an awful disfigurement be seen in public – I mean, it's so *grotesque*, enough to terrify a child!'

Rebecca had to control herself and refrain from rebuking the woman aloud, because that would draw attention to Jack's terrible scarring, which would indeed frighten some children; so while her mother exchanged smiles and greetings with her sister Grace and the family, Rebecca called firmly to her two charges.

'Come on, Lily, don't hang about. Come *here*!' Taking their hands she headed for the Hassett Manor road, for fear of what they might have said about her brother's – no, her half-brother's – face.

But Grace Nuttall had seen her hasty retreat.

Fifty Italian prisoners of war had been divided between three farms around North Camp. Billy Yeomans was unimpressed, and said so.

'They're no more use than them dopey land girls you sent us two months back,' he grumbled. 'Bone idle and cheeky with it, that Paolo and his mates.' He pronounced the name as Paulo, and although Miss Neville, the regional representative for the area, was inclined to agree that the Italians were work-shy, she would never admit as much to the surly farmer.

'They need some time to settle in,' she said. 'We must remember they're strangers in a strange land, and can't even speak the language.'

'I'd give 'em language, the lazy bastards,' he retorted. 'No wonder they was taken prisoner – they gave 'emselves up just to get out of the war while our poor chaps are slogging it out in the desert. They ought to be locked up in camps with barbed wire all round, instead of laying about in my fields and begging bread and sausages off my Pam – and living in an army camp with every comfort and convenience!'

Rebecca let him rattle on, though she doubted that there would be much comfort or convenience in an unheated Nissen hut when winter came. She told him that he would be sent another two land girls, but on condition that they were billeted in the farmhouse, strictly separate from the prisoners. He turned down the corners of his mouth.

'Eating us out o' house and home – makes me wonder if they're worth the trouble, what with the wife expecting, and an elderly mother to look after. All right, I'll try another two girls, but they'd better behave 'emselves!'

No mention of Sid and Mary Goddard, Rebecca noticed, the two people who probably worked the hardest at Yeomans' Farm, indoors and out.

'Very well,' she said briskly. 'Two girls will arrive at the beginning of next week, and I hope they'll be made welcome.'

She turned away, for she found it difficult to be civil to this man, and briefly called on Mary Goddard who as usual was in the farmhouse kitchen, and as usual looked tired.

'Thank you, I'm keeping pretty well, Miss Neville – it's my Sidney who could do with a rest,' she said. 'Billy's all talk, but it's Sid who does the donkey work, and I keep telling him he should see Dr Stringer.'

Rebecca sympathised, and felt sorry that two new land girls lodging in the house would give Mary yet more work.

'Make sure they help in the kitchen, and make their own beds, Mary. And I hear that you also have Italian prisoners calling at the back door.'

'Well, they're prisoners, aren't they? And at least they're cheerful,' said Mary with a little smile. 'They'll do anything my Sidney tells them.'

'Hm.' Rebecca heard the unspoken words: that Billy was a harsh boss, and Sidney a kindly one.

Before she left the farm, she walked down to the barley field, now waving tall and golden, almost ready to harvest. She found half a dozen Italians playing cards behind a thick bramble hedge.

'*Ciao!* Hard at work, I see,' she said with a frown as they scrambled to their feet.

'*Bon giorno, Signorina!*' said the young man called Paolo, whose scanty English made him the unofficial spokesman. 'Is beautiful day, yes? You come to inspect our hotel, yes? Such facilities!'

Rebecca did not smile. It had been embarrassing when they had first arrived, and she had found herself in unofficial charge of them, Billy Yeomans having refused, saying that he was far too busy.

'*Mi scusi, signorina, ma dobbiamo stare qui?*' they had demanded when taken to their quarters. '*Quando mangiamo? Dove dormiamo?*' It had been her reluctant duty to tell them that this hut was where they would both eat and sleep.

'*Dove il bagno?*' And she had to tell them that there was one bath and one lavatory at the end of the sleeping quarters. When they groaned she replied sternly that they were better off than British soldiers in German prison camps.

'*They* don't have time to play at cards and write letters when there's work to be done. Don't let Mr Yeomans find you here!'

'Ah, Signor Yeomans, a man of great compassion and generosity,' said Paolo, rolling his eyes heavenwards. 'But the Signora is kind,' he added, and the rest of them smiled and nodded. 'Always she find food for us when we have hunger!'

Rebecca realised that they were referring to Mrs Goddard. 'I hope you do not pester her at the kitchen door,' she said, disconcerted by a broad wink from Paolo's brother, Mario.

'Well, I have work to do,' she said, refusing to smile. 'So I shall bid you *bon giorno*.'

She turned on her heel and walked smartly back to the lane, waving to Sidney Goddard who was working in the pigsties. The men regarded her retreating back with admiration, and Mario's dark eyes gleamed.

'*Caspita! Che belleza!*' he murmured.

'*Adoro queste donne inglesi – sono cosi fiere, non trovi?*' another man said.

She could not hear the words they exchanged, but guessed they were far from respectful, and did not turn back. They were, after all, no responsibility of hers.

Life had been bad enough in Ward Three for Jack Nuttall, but as the weeks and months had gone by, surrounded by his fellow patients in 'McIndoe's Army' as they called themselves, and braced by Smithy's unsentimental philosophy, he had not fallen into the pit of despair, but had survived. His face and hands had healed, and his sight was now adequate, if not as good as it had been before the incident that had changed his life.

But now, returned to his home and family, a Battle of Britain hero at twenty-one, his hope seemed lost and his courage had deserted him. It was worse than anything he had experienced at the Queen Victoria Hospital, where the people of East Grinstead were accustomed to seeing damaged faces, and where he could go down to the pub with a couple of other chaps from Ward Three, to be greeted by the barman as regulars, like the patrons who invited them to join a card game or help solve a crossword puzzle – or just *talk* about anything and everything – the war, their families, pets, memories of schooldays – just to be treated as fellow human beings. In North Camp it was so different. People stared or looked away hastily, a young child out with its mother screamed in terror, and a woman fainted. He was a freak, a Frankenstein's monster to be feared by the ignorant and pitied by the more intelligent, and he did not know which was worse.

He had to be firm, even stern with his mother who wanted to take him out with her, show him off to friends and neighbours, restored to his loved ones. She seemed unable to see the extent of her beloved son's scars, though the rest of his family had to make an effort to see beyond them. Doreen would sit and talk to him for a while, but then would burst into tears and rush from the room. His grandfather forced a smile and tried to talk on everyday matters, but Jack could see that it was an effort, and could not avoid the deep pity in Tom's eyes.

Inevitably there was a violent altercation, like the erupting of a volcano.

'It's no *good*, Mum, I shan't ever set foot in that bloody church again!' he shouted at poor Grace Nuttall who had now set foot in St Peter's for the first time in months.

'But they'll get used to it, dear, I know they will,' she pleaded. 'Just wait and see.'

'Damn and blast their eyes, Mum, I couldn't give a fuck whether they get used to me or not! Can't you understand, *I* don't want to see *them*, the bastards!'

Grace winced at hearing these words from her good son. 'But Jack, my love, my own dearest boy—'

'Oh, shut up, woman. I wish I was back at East Grinstead.'

She was shocked beyond tears, and his father intervened.

'Tell you what, Jack, let's go into the workshop, take a look at some o' the jobs I've been doing lately,' he said. 'Repair jobs, mostly, but I've been amusing myself with a bit o' carving. Come on, just you and me, eh?'

And it was in the carpenter's workshop that Jack poured out his misery, and Rob listened. Both men gave way to tears, but, as Rob said, that didn't matter, there were only the two of them to see. Jack's nostalgia for Ward Three struck his father as crucial, and an idea came to him.

'How about asking this Smithy bloke to come and stay here for a weekend? He did you good at the Queen Victoria, and maybe he could do the same here.'

Jack raised his head, and wiped a tear from his cheek. He looked at his father with incredulity mixed with longing.

'I reckon he's about the only person who could, Dad, if anybody can. But d'you think he'd come?'

'Well, he's been – er – damaged himself, isn't he? And believe me, son, I'd make it worth his while!'

For the faint light of hope that he now saw in Jack's face, Rob Nuttall would have been willing to hand over every penny he possessed to this Smithy bloke, just to come to see his son.

'We'll write and ask him, get a letter posted off today,' he promised, and as the tension in the atmosphere subsided, he showed Jack the woodcarvings he had been making in recent weeks when there had been few demands on his carpentry skills: doll's house furniture, tables and chairs, a bed and a tiny rocking cradle.

'All from wood left over from repair jobs, Jack. Like to try your hand at it? Doreen takes them to Thomas and Gibson's, and Mr Richardson lets her sell them to customers. Maybe you'd like to try it, eh?'

As a qualified aeronautical engineer, Jack was not drawn to toy-making, being far more interested in the request made to Smithy, so was much relieved when a prompt reply arrived. Smithy agreed at once to come to North Camp for the following weekend, and said he needed no other payment than a donation to Ward Three at the Queen Victoria Hospital.

The news quickly spread around North Camp, and within twenty-four hours everybody knew that the rector's son Lester was home on sick leave from the RAF. Various rumours followed, one that he had a fractured spine, another that he only had cuts and bruises. His parents were very protective of him, and he was not seen out of doors, even in July.

Sharing the Rectory, Alan and Joan Kennard soon discovered that Lester had a fractured pelvis, but no spinal injury. He had to lie flat on a bed or settee, waited on hand and foot by his mother. When she came downstairs to tell Mrs Kennard that the children's noise was preventing her son from resting as he should, Joan's reaction was not entirely sympathetic. With barely two months to go before her confinement, she was in sole charge of Kenny and Danny who went unwillingly to St Peter's school, and Josie played alone in the garden, watched by her mother from the kitchen window.

'I can't keep such young children quiet for a whole day and night,' she said. 'I suggest you keep the door to Lester's room shut, and find something else for him to think about.'

Affronted at such rudeness, Mrs Allingham stalked off, but it soon became clear that young Lester's physical condition was matched by his mental attitude. He was restless, impatient and demanding; his mother was sent out to buy grapes and figs, only obtainable on the black market at a huge cost, and the rector quietly asked his curate to shop for Turkish cigars, whisky, two bottles of red wine and soda water. Alan Kennard agreed, while making it very clear to the wine merchant that these goods were for the Allinghams, not the Kennards.

When Lester fretfully asked for former North Camp friends to be invited to visit him, he was disappointed when they all seemed to be in the services. He then asked after Barbara Seabrook, and his mother reluctantly told him that she worked in her father's shop, whereupon he immediately asked her to go and invite Barbara to tea at the Rectory. Mrs Allingham was most unwilling, having always considered the girl common – a butcher's daughter who had shamelessly pursued her son.

'Once that young Miss gets over the threshold, she'll lead him astray in every way,' she told her husband. 'Most unsuitable for Lester, especially in his present weak state.'

'Mm,' replied the rector. 'I wonder what happened to that glamorous WAAF he brought home last time. No sign of *her*.'

But Lester was insistent on seeing the girl he'd seduced so easily, and demanded to be helped downstairs where he could lie on a settee padded with cushions. Alan Kennard was willing to assist him down the stairs, but refused to go on such a personal errand for him, which meant that Agnes Allingham, much against her better judgement, had to walk to the Seabrooks' shop, and inform Mrs Seabrook that Flight Lieutenant Allingham wished for her daughter to join him at tea. This interview took place in the Seabrooks' parlour, and when Barbara was sent for, she came straight from the shop, still wearing her striped apron as she told Mrs Allingham that she sent her best wishes to Mr Lester for a speedy recovery, but had no wish to see him again. Mrs Seabrook was surprised at this answer, though not truly sorry, and after Mrs Allingham had indignantly left, she asked her daughter the reason for the snub. The girl's face was flushed, and she had tears in her eyes, but she silently shook her head. Suddenly her mother remembered that night last September when she had found her daughter collapsed in the lavatory, and without any further words she guessed the reason for it, and wondered why she had been so blind. Barbara had not confided in her at the time or since, and she decided that she would say nothing now.

But it was not easy for Agnes Allingham to convey such a humiliating message to her son.

* * *

184

Miss Stevenson was having a hard time trying to control herself. Teaching at St Peter's Infant School had become a daily challenge to keep order among the evacuees. She kept telling herself that they were to be pitied, but she found it increasingly difficult to keep her temper, especially with Lily and Jimmy. Their impudence and foul language was being picked up by the other children, and Danny's constant wail of 'Wanna go 'ome!' tried her patience. If only he *could*, she thought, though it must be far worse for poor Mrs Kennard at the Rectory, getting near to her confinement in this hot weather; her ankles were swollen and she seemed to frown more often that she smiled. Reflecting on this, Miss Stevenson told herself she should not complain. But that pair from Hassett Manor would try the patience of a saint . . .

'Hey, you kids, d'you know why that Mrs Kennard's swole up like a balloon? She's got a baby in 'er belly!'

The other young children were intrigued, not having yet confronted human reproduction.

'An angel will come and hand her the baby,' said one little girl.

'No, it's not an angel. Dr Stringer'll bring it in his black bag,' said another.

'Gawd, don't you kids know *nothin'*? It's in 'er belly!' repeated Lily.

'How'll it get out, then?'

'Same 'ole as it went it, stupid!' grinned Lily. 'Mr Kennard put it in there when they was—'

'*Be quiet!* You will not say another word, you naughty girl!' cried Miss Stevenson, picturing the irate parents who would come to the school to complain about what their young children were being told. At the end of her patience, and fearing that she might break down and weep in front of them if she had to endure another minute, she dismissed the evacuees a quarter of an hour early. They needed no second bidding, and ran out into the sunshine, shouting, 'Wanna go 'ome!' amid shrieks of laughter.

Miss Stevenson sat at her desk, holding her aching head between her hands; the remaining children watched her in silence. She did not hear the curate's footsteps approaching.

'Miss Stevenson! Are you all right? Where are the evacuees?'

She raised her head. 'Mr Kennard, I'm so sorry, I sent them out early today. I – I couldn't stand them any longer.' Her voice trembled.

'Oh, poor Miss Stevenson, you should have let me know. You need more help now that the school's bursting at the seams – but where are Kenny and Danny? I don't hear the usual howl.'

'They've gone home, Mr Kennard, they've all gone.'

'But where are they? I haven't passed them on the road. Which way did they go? There's no sign of them.'

Unease turned to fear, and fear to panic. 'Good heavens, we must go and find them at once,' said Alan, picturing them lost and in danger of being run over.

Outside they found Nick Grant, about to go home to Miss Temple. Alan seized him.

'Where have the little ones gone, Nick? For God's sake, where?'

'They went that way, sir,' said the boy, the oldest child in the school at ten years. He pointed in the direction of Yeomans' Farm.

'Nick, stay with these children until their mothers come for them. Come on, Miss Stevenson, they could be playing with farm machinery, for all Billy Yeomans will care. Let's go down the Manor Road where we can see across the fields.'

He broke into a run, and she followed him, now thoroughly alarmed and blaming herself for dismissing the children. Alan stopped at a stile in the hedge, and looked across the field of barley. He beckoned the teacher to come to his side and look.

The children were staring at the shabby-looking men in dusty uniforms. Lily told the other three not to go too close and give themselves away by speaking too soon.

'They might be Jerry spies, so watch out,' she warned. 'They'll try to trap us into giving secrets away.'

'Ain't got no secrets to give 'em,' muttered Kenny, wishing they had not followed her from the school.

'Shut up, you,' said Lily, undecided what to do. Could they trust these blokes?

'Say something to 'em, Jimmy, see what they say.'

'Arse 'oles!' he obliged, and the children gasped.

'That's torn it, yer silly little bugger,' muttered his sister. 'Now we'll get into even more trouble.'

But the strange men seemed not to have taken offence at Jimmy's greeting. One of them came towards the children, his sun-browned face smiling, showing white teeth and a dimple in his cheek. They waited to hear what he would say.

'*Come ti chiamo, piccolino?*'

The children looked at each other in alarm: so they *were* Jerries, then, speaking in their own language.

'*Mi chiamo Stefano, e questo e il mio amico Mario.*'

'*Si, mi chiamo Mario,*' said his friend. '*Sono italiano.*'

The children stared. These men seemed too nice to be Jerries.

'You Mario?' asked Lily cautiously. Another man strolled up, who seemed to know a little English.

'*Mi chiamo Paolo,*' he said in a friendly way. 'He tell you his name, *piccolino*. Now you say you name also for us.'

'Jimmy.'

'*Ti chiami* Jimmy!' beamed Stefano. '*E tua sorella?*' he asked, looking at Lily, who still regarded these blokes with suspicion, but offered her name, 'Lily.'

'*Ciao*, Lily! And this little one?' he asked, looking at Kenny who stared and then burst into tears. Danny joined in. 'Wanna go 'ome!' he roared.

Suddenly the man called Stefano swept up both Kenny and Danny in his arms.

'*O carissimi bambini miei, siamo tutti cosi lontani da casa!*'

'Look, 'e's blubberin' as well!' said Jimmy in awe at such behaviour from a grown man. Stefano continued to hug the little boys to his chest, telling them not to cry.

'*Non piangere, bambini, non piangere,*' he said, while tears rolled down his own face.

And it was at this moment that the curate and the schoolteacher came upon the scene. They stood still and watched the dark-eyed Italian embracing the two little boys and speaking to them with emotion.

'Good heavens, it's those Italian prisoners of war!' cried Miss Stevenson. 'Kenny! Danny! Come to—'

But Alan Kennard gently held her back. 'Wait! I think he says they're all exiles, a long way from home. I don't think the children are in any danger.'

Paolo noticed them, and clearly expected to be reprimanded by this man.

'*Ciao, Signor, Signora,*' he said politely. 'Have no fear, we are friends.'

'*Si, ma saremo amici, e vero,*' said Stefano, putting the boys down and pointing them towards the English couple. '*Torna a trovarci domani!*'

Alan thanked them in halting Italian, but did not promise that the children would come again. Miss Stevenson thought this was the first time she had seen Danny actually smiling, and forgetting to say 'Wanna go 'ome!'

Strangers in a strange land, thought Alan Kennard as they walked back to the school.

If the evacuees disappeared again, at least they would know where to find them.

Smithy's visit to 47 Rectory Road had far-reaching consequences. Tom Munday saw his grandson turn from a bitter, disillusioned young man into one who, with regained self-respect, could see his way through life; in his own words, he rejoined the human race.

But it came at a heavy cost to Grace. Gone was her dream of supporting Jack with the loving care that only a mother can give; she felt herself rejected by him. When he told her that he that he was going back to the RAF, she could not believe it at first; even when she understood that it would not be as a flier but as a member of the vital ground staff that every airfield needs – a competent aeronautical engineer to repair and maintain the aircraft that carried his colleagues and friends into deadly danger; such work had to be of a very high standard, and he had lost two fingers.

'Their lives will be in his hands, Grace,' Tom Munday

reminded her, looking to his son-in-law for confirmation, 'and he won't be risking his.'

To some extent she was consoled by the change in Jack; from bitter resignation to anticipation towards a useful career. He even offered to accompany the family to church, and the second occasion proved much better than the first. He was less self-conscious, and chatted easily with the organist Philip Saville whose life had been blighted by the Great War, scarcely a quarter of a century ago, but who was now coming out of the reclusive shell with which he had shielded himself.

'You know, Jack, I've listened to you talking about your time in that hospital and the chaps you saw there – and that friend who said we can always look round and see somebody worse off . . . like these poor little evacuees.'

Even as he spoke, Nick came over, smiling. 'I say, Uncle Philip, d'ye know what Danny said to me this morning? Oh, sorry—' He stopped when he realised that the two men were deep in conversation. 'Good morning, Mr Nuttall.'

'Hello Nick,' said Jack. 'Don't leave us in suspense, tell us what the little chap said!'

'He said – excuse the pronunciation – "*Come ti chiami? Mi chiamo Danny!*"'

'Good heavens, did he really?' said Philip. 'He must have been talking to the prisoners at Yeomans' Farm!'

'Yes, that's what I thought,' said Nick. 'And then his brother came up and said, "Yeah, that's German!"'

In the laughter that followed, Jack quite forgot about his face, and smiled at Miss Temple when she came over to ask what was the joke; but before they could reply, Alan Kennard could be heard raising his voice urgently for somebody to look after the three children while he took his wife to Everham General Hospital. '*Now!*' he begged.

'Heavens, she's not due for another month!' cried the ladies. 'Won't the Allinghams take the boys and little Josie until Mr Kennard's back?'

It seemed that they couldn't, and there were no offers from the Nuttalls or the Pearsons; then Miss Temple spoke up.

'*I* can take them. Come on, Philip, let's go and tell our poor curate that we'll take the children – after all, I've got you and Nick to help me, haven't I?'

Mrs Kennard gave birth to another little girl, Elizabeth, weighing just over five pounds; she had the help of Miss Temple during the day while Philip was at work and Nick at school. Lady Neville would have sent Sally Tanner to help out, but her time was taken up with Lily and Jimmy, especially during the school summer holiday, and their behaviour was definitely improving. It was an open secret that Sally took them to see the prisoners-of-war at Yeomans' Farm, approaching the fields from the road to avoid the farmhouse; and, being Sally, she usually found little gifts of buns and biscuits for the children to offer them. In return, Stefano and Paolo carved spoons and simple toys from wood passed on to them from Rob Nuttall's workroom, at his father-in-law's suggestion.

The summer passed, and winter threatened to be cold and hard. Shortages of food were bad enough, but shortage of coal was even worse. When Mrs Pam Yeomans gave birth at home to a second boy, Derek, she demanded a fire in her bedroom, and Mrs Goddard found it very difficult to keep other rooms warm. She and Sidney spent their evenings in the kitchen, which retained some heat from the morning's cooking in the range oven.

'That awful Nissen hut must be perishing,' Rebecca said when November came in with cold winds shaking down the last of the leaves. St Peter's church was so cold that the congregation wore coats, scarves and gloves; Miss Stevenson was distressed when some of the children arrived at school with hands blue with cold, and chilblains; Lady Neville, who now took charge of the Wednesday afternoon Circle, asked the ladies to step up knitting children's clothing for their own local little ones.

A grey fog of depression settled over North Camp. The war news continued to be bad, and the Russians seemed to be fighting a losing battle against their German invaders. Air raids over Britain were less, but were just as devastating in their effects; RAF raids over Germany continued to take vengeance on the Luftwaffe for the Blitz, but the great munitions factories of the Ruhr were a long distance from the shores of the Channel, and well protected. And of course there was always the nagging anxiety for the young men in the armed forces: Howard Allingham, Paul Storey and John Richardson in North Africa, Lester Allingham who had returned to the RAF as a bomber pilot, and Robin Seabrook in the navy.

'It's going to be a cold Christmas this year, my love,' said Cedric Neville to Isabel.

'The Manor will be impossible to heat – winters are cold enough at the best of times, and we'll have to close some of the rooms and take weekday meals in the kitchen with Sally and the children – and Rebecca when she's here, of course.'

'I'm going to get a lot of people's backs up,' she told him thoughtfully. 'Rebecca says that life on Billy Yeomans' farm is utter misery in this weather, and I'm going to invite a few of the prisoners to take a meal with us – that'll please Lily and Jimmy! – and then we can invite others in rotation, say four or five at a time, and see how it goes.'

'Hm.' Cedric turned down the corners of his mouth. 'Be careful, Isabel, you're going to antagonise a lot of people, especially those who have got boys out there fighting.'

'Yes,' she replied. 'Boys like my Paul. And if Paul was ever a prisoner in an enemy country, I would bless the woman who gave him food.'

December came in and families prepared for a frugal Christmas and not much hope of better news, though it was said that Soviet forces were driving the German army back from the gates of Moscow as the Russian winter closed in.

'He's made the same mistake Napoleon did,' said Sir Cedric Neville, reading the latest newspaper report on the invasion of Russia. 'Poor devils, all of them. They've got it much worse than we have.'

But then on the seventh of December came unexpected news that reverberated around the world within hours.

'Quick, switch on your wireless sets!' neighbours and shopkeepers called to each other. 'There's been a huge raid by the Japanese on the American fleet – right out of the blue it was. They flew over and dropped bombs on the ships as they lay at anchor, somewhere called Pearl Harbor. It's terrible!'

In the Tradesmen's Arms that evening the regulars gathered

close together over the small fire and gave their various opinions.

'Who'd have thought it? I never knew there *was* a Japanese air force!' said one.

'Well, there most certainly *is*, mate. The little yellow bastards must've been planning it for ages, and caught the American Navy on the hop,' said another, shaking his head.

'Blimey, I bet old Churchill's bowled over!' said Eddie Cooper.

Tom Munday drew on his pipe and gave his own somewhat different opinion.

'The old man must be chortling to himself on the quiet,' he said. 'The Yanks have played low so far, and kept out of it. But now they'll have to come in, and it'll change the war.'

CHAPTER TEN

1942

The band struck up with 'Don't Fence Me In', a quickstep, and Doreen Nuttall feared that it would be too quick for her uncertain feet; up until now she had managed the waltz, with its *one*, two, three, *one*, two, three time, gazing down at her shoes instead of looking up into her partner's face – but this smiling GI guided her confidently, drawing her to his right side, then to his left, expertly whirling her round to the music. It was exhilarating, and Doreen blessed her friend Marjorie who had invited her to come to the Saturday evening dances at Everham Town Hall. Her mother had reluctantly consented, on condition that she came home with Marjorie immediately after the last dance, and Dad had seemed not to mind; in fact Rob Nuttall had his doubts about a dance organised by the GIs, the American soldiers who had made such an impact on North Camp with their friendly, outgoing attitude and generosity. They organised children's parties at their Everham base camp, introducing the young guests to ice cream and peanuts; children ran after them in the street, begging for candy, bars of chocolate and the mint-flavoured chewing gum they all seemed to carry in their pockets. And there were the Saturday dances, admission free to the girls living in and around Everham, including free American cigarettes; Marjorie showed Doreen the sheer nylon stockings she and other girls had been given by their GI partners.

'Getting paid for enjoying myself, Doreen! Ask your guy if he's got any.'

A guy was not an effigy to be burnt on a bonfire on Guy Fawkes' night, but simply meant a man, like a chap or bloke; and instead of saying a girl was sweet or charming, they called her a swell kid. To Doreen who spent her days serving cloth and sewing materials to the sometimes hard-to-please ladies of North Camp, a Saturday evening dance at Everham Town Hall was an undreamt-of treat, and she eagerly told her parents and grandfather that she'd never had such fun in her life before. Tom Munday listened indulgently, happy to see her smiling again, and her mother cautiously invited her to ask a soldier home to tea on a Sunday afternoon. So far she had been too shy to do so, but her partner on this warm June evening whose name was Gus Rohmer accepted gratefully, and at the end of the dance she and Marjorie and four other girls were driven home in a US army jeep. Doreen briefly forgot the miseries of the black-out, the shortages, the constant anxiety for sons and sweethearts far away fighting for King and country – and suffering such injuries as her brother Jack had sustained. At least *he* was safe now at an air base in Wiltshire, an aeronautical engineer serving the men of RAF Bomber Command, as well as if he had all ten fingers. His mother wished he could come home more often, but had to accept that he was virtually on call around the clock, using his talents as a non-combatant.

Tom Munday confided in Eddie Cooper that having met Gus Rohmer, he was not worried about Doreen's excitement over the dances.

'He's all right. Comes from Maine, a proper gentleman, good manners, good-humoured, you can tell he comes from a decent background. And it's nice to see our Doreen having a bit of fun.'

'Glad somebody's having fun,' muttered Eddie. 'Things aren't going at all well out there in the desert, by what little we hear.'

It was true. Field Marshal Rommel's tanks were continuing to drive the allies back, and the Japanese were claiming victory after victory in South Asia, culminating in their capture of Singapore before it had been completely evacuated of British civilians, including women and children.

'Wouldn't want anybody o' mine falling into the hands o' them little yellow bastards,' said Eddie, and nobody in the Tradesmen's Arms disagreed with him.

Rebecca Neville frowned and pushed back the hair from her forehead; she seldom bothered to wear the brown felt cowboy-style hat of her uniform. Hers was the unenviable task of sorting out problems between land girls and farmers, and she was expected to visit every member of the Land Army in her district at least once a month, to check that billets were satisfactory, whether wages were correctly paid, including overtime, how much leave was given, and dealing with such unforeseen situations as faced her now, a land girl who was found to be three to four months pregnant. She had named the farmer's son who denied all responsibility and said it must be an Italian prisoner of war. There was no man willing to marry the girl, and Rebecca not only had to arrange for her discharge from the Land Army, but also to visit her parents to see if they were willing to have their daughter home again. This was not part of Rebecca's official duties, but she felt that she needed to know what would happen to the girl, and to give what help she could.

Barbara's parents lived in Surbiton. Rebecca braced herself to face them, and rang their doorbell.

They took it badly. The father shook his fist in the air.

'If I ever lay hands on that farmer's son, I'll throttle the bugger, that I will! I'll go there and confront him, I'll have it all out in the open, I'll – I'll—'

Rebecca shook her head. 'We don't know for certain that he is the father,' she said. 'We'll just have to keep calm about this, and try to avoid upsetting Barbara too much while she's pregnant. After her confinement you can consult a solicitor about the matter.'

'I'll see a solicitor straight away, thank you, Madam!' he shouted. '*You're* supposed to look after these girls, and I'll make a complaint about you, too. You'll find yourself in hot water, you will!'

'You can call me what you like,' said Rebecca grimly. 'All I need to know from you is whether you'll take Barbara to live at home with you, because I'll have to let her know.'

'And suppose we won't?' he demanded.

'In that case she'd have to go to a Moral Welfare Home for mothers and babies.'

'Oh, *no!*' cried the wife. 'My poor girl, she can't go to one o' them places. I wouldn't have it!'

'Very well,' said Rebecca to the woman, ignoring the man. 'I'll go back and tell her that you'll have her back home with you. She'll be officially discharged from the Land Army next week. Good afternoon.'

She sighed as she got into the car she had on loan from headquarters. If it was a trial to deal with strangers' families, it was not much easier to deal with her own. Her mother lived in a constant state of fear for her son Paul, and the news of Rommel's inexorable advance struck further terror into her heart. Her husband and daughter tried in vain to comfort her, but to no avail. She had actually turned on Cedric and spoken harshly.

'I lost my husband because of that bloody Great War – and I'm going to lose his son in this one, I know it. Oh, my son, my son Paul, I shall never see him again. Don't try to talk to me, it doesn't help.'

Rebecca and the man she called Father looked at each other and shook their heads helplessly. Cedric tried not to feel irritated by Sally Tanner who frowned at them both over Isabel's bowed head, as if she understood and cared more about his wife than he did.

On the day that Valerie Pearson passed her thirtieth birthday, she scarcely noticed it. She was now Deputy Superintendent of The Limes Nursery, working under Nurse King and deputising for her when she was off duty. She was in charge of four young nursing assistants who worked in shifts, a middle-aged state registered nurse who would have been made deputy if she had worked full-time, a cook who also took care of the laundering, and Molly the cleaner who was called Mrs Mop after the charwoman in ITMA, the weekly comedy on the wireless that helped to keep the nation's spirits up.

Most of the children's mothers worked at the munitions factory that had formerly made furniture and now turned out shells for the army and navy. Those with young children were exempted from night shifts, but the day shifts were long, and The Limes opened at seven in the morning and closed at six o'clock, or until the last weary mother came to collect her tired child. When she was on the early shift, Valerie stayed overnight, in spite of her mother's protests. She found an ally in Enid Temple, who had learnt from her nephew Philip about the long hours that Valerie worked, and started visiting her mother while Nick was at school.

'We're *all* inconvenienced these days, Mrs Pearson,' she said firmly, 'and you must feel very proud of Valerie's vital contribution to the war effort. We must support our country in every way we can, and why don't you come along with me to the Make Do And Mend Circle at the Rectory on Wednesdays? It would do you good.'

When Mrs Pearson agreed to attend the next Circle, she found that Miss Temple was in charge that week, assisted by Councillor Tomlinson. Lady Neville was not there, and the curate's wife was having to deal with little Josie and the new baby Elizabeth; Kenny and Danny were at school until four, and would go to see Stefano Ghiberti before coming home. It was known that a few of the Italians had been invited to Hassett Manor for an occasional Sunday dinner, which they much appreciated, and North Camp residents had mellowed into an easy or at least a tolerant attitude towards them.

Stefano told the Nevilles that his father worked in the car industry, and he hoped eventually to follow in his footsteps.

When the Circle broke up and Philip Saville put down the lid of the piano, he quietly asked his aunt why Lady Neville was not there: was she ill?

'Not well at all, I'm afraid, Philip,' she answered gravely. 'Her son Paul is out there with the Eighth Army, and, er – well, enough said.'

When the doorbell rang, Rebecca went to answer, to save Sally from leaving Isabel's side.

She was faced with Philip Saville. 'Good afternoon, Miss Neville,' he said.

'Oh, yes, it's piano lessons today,' she remembered, frowning slightly. 'You're early, aren't you? The boys aren't here yet. Er, come in. I'll get you to wait in your usual room.'

As she ushered him past the door where her parents and Sally sat, she explained to them briefly, 'It's Mr Saville, come to give the boys their lesson. He'll wait for them.'

Her mother looked up. 'Philip?' she called sharply. 'Come in here, I'd like to see you.'

He was already ahead of Rebecca, holding out his hand to Isabel as if nobody else was present. Cedric stared in surprise.

'I'm glad to see you, Philip. Sit down.' She indicated the place beside her on the sofa; Sally sat on the other side. 'You were in that terrible war, and lost a leg. It changed you, just as my husband was changed by it.'

'I know,' he answered quietly, keeping hold of her hand. 'I remember Mark Storey when he was my father's curate, and you were Miss Munday. I was at your wedding.'

'Yes, you were a good-looking young man,' she said,

actually smiling at the memory. 'All the young ladies had their eyes on you, and half of North Camp came to see you off at the station when you went away in 1915. Oh, Philip, you and Mark were in that hell together!' She sobbed afresh, and he put his other hand over hers. Cedric watched in silence; he too had been through the Great War.

'Yes, Isabel, and I came out of it, and – and he didn't.' Philip's voice was barely a whisper.

'Oh, yes, he did, Philip, my husband came home, but he was changed. He wasn't the same man of God, and couldn't continue as a clergyman, though he'd served as an army chaplain. He was embittered, and openly said there was no God. He didn't believe, not after he'd knelt beside a young soldier who'd been blinded by a shell fragment, and was crying out to God until he choked on his own blood and died. It changed my Mark; he said he was an atheist after that. He wasn't the same man – he used to curse and swear, even in front of little Paul, and Becky, because I'd adopted her by then. He was . . . brutal when we . . . when we were . . . he'd been horribly injured and couldn't . . . I couldn't get near to him. He got a post as a teacher of English and Latin at a boys' preparatory school in Surrey, and a house went with it, so we moved there, and dear Sally got work as a cleaner in the school, and came with us. That was in 1919.'

She paused, and looked across at Sally who nodded to Philip in confirmation, and then continued, 'Poor Mark – he wasn't popular with the boys or the staff, and I worried in case he'd be dismissed, but then came the influenza epidemic. It spread to the school, and he fell victim to it, and died after only forty-eight hours. It was a merciful release, Philip, truly a *release*, though I'd prayed so earnestly that I'd be able to lead him back to the faith that had made him such a wonderful vicar in Bethnal Green. Before he died he was delirious, but said something to me: that he loved me – oh, Mark, my love! – and asked for forgiveness, and I trust that God heard him. I married Cedric, but I wasn't able to give him children, though Rebecca is a dear daughter to us both.' Again she paused, and Cedric murmured, 'Yes, my love, she is.'

'But my son Paul, oh, my son, *his* son, out there in the desert, oh, Philip!' Words deserted her, and she laid her head upon Philip's shoulder and sobbed. He whispered to her and stroked her hair while her husband and daughter looked on, deeply saddened by what they had heard, and Sally had tears in her eyes at the memories she had shared and now relived.

After a few minutes Isabel stopped crying and sat up, freeing herself from Philip's light embrace. She wiped her eyes and blew her nose.

'Thank you, Philip. I think I heard the boys coming in. You must be there for them.'

He rose, and turned to Sir Cedric Neville who held out his hand, which Philip shook, glancing back at Isabel.

'I'll be all right now, Philip,' she said. 'I must be patient and wait for news, like all the tens of thousands of other mothers who must wait.'

Cedric followed Philip out of the room. 'Thank you, Saville, you've helped her. She needed to remember some things I never knew.' He smiled, though it had not been easy for him to watch her being comforted by another, a man who had known her as a girl when she and Philip and Mark Storey had been young and full of hope, before the dark shadow of war had blighted their lives.

* * *

The departure of the GIs was sudden. Gus Rohmer told Doreen that they did not know their destination for security reasons: if the Germans knew where they were going, they would make due preparation to meet them there. There was a great deal of speculation: many believed that they would join the army in Europe, under General Eisenhower. Others would have welcomed a drafting to the Far East, to join their own countrymen in a desperate attempt to halt the Japanese. Gus was among the first to leave, and kissed Doreen goodbye, hoping that he would see her again 'when this show's over', as he put it. She was in floods of tears, and her friend Marjorie told her to cheer up.

'It doesn't have to mean that there'll be no more Saturday nights at Everham Town Hall, Doreen,' she said. 'There's still a few GIs waiting to be told where they're going. Come along and enjoy yourself!'

When Doreen went to the next dance a cheerful GI called Chuck, who said he was a 'buddy' of Gus's, came up to ask her for a dance, and had nylon stockings and Hershey chocolate bars to offer in return for a few goodnight kisses. Against her better judgement Doreen left the Town Hall with him, but soon decided that she wouldn't see him again. She felt that she had betrayed Gus, and was alarmed at the liberties that his buddy took, laughing at her hesitation.

'This is war, kid, and a guy has right to have a bit of a good time before he goes off to follow the flag.'

So she had let him kiss her, thrusting his tongue into her mouth and pulling up her dress.

At Yeomans' Farm the Italians were resigned to their fate for the duration of the war. Letters from home were scanty, as only a few of them got through. Envelopes marked 'Sweden' were usually from home, and the news was uniformly bad. Organisation by both national and local authorities was chaotic, and families left without breadwinners soon fell into poverty, added to which there was the constant fear of invasion. In September came terrible news of a ship carrying eighteen hundred Italian prisoners, torpedoed and sunk by a German U-boat, mistaken for a troopship, and there was no information about the names of the lost men.

On her latest visit to Yeomans' Farm Rebecca found the prisoners in a state of helpless grief and anger. She had by now learnt enough Italian to understand their feelings, though she felt she could do nothing to help. Except that Stefano was pleading with her . . .

'Signorina Neville, we have no church, no priest to hear our confessions or give us the Sacrament of the Body and Blood. How far is the Roman Catholic Church?'

Rebecca reproached herself for not attending to this matter earlier. The Reverend Alan Kennard had visited them, but he was no substitute for a Catholic priest, and got the impression that most of these men paid little regard to their religion anyway, but in their present affliction a great cloud of despair seemed to hang over them, and they needed the consolations of their church. A young man who looked scarcely twenty came forward and showed Rebecca a creased snapshot of an equally young woman.

'Ecco la mia promessa sposa. Si chiami Giovanna.'

'Your – er, your fiancée?' Rebecca said with a smile. 'What a very pretty girl!'

Paolo translated for her, and the young man sadly agreed. 'Si, e molto bella.' Tears came to his eyes. 'Sono triste senza di lei!'

'Yes, Guiseppe very sad without her, Signorina.'

At that moment Rebecca knew that she *must* find a way to solve this problem; she knew that there was a convent situated on the main London Road out of Everham, at least six miles from North Camp. It would be quite impossible for these men to get there, even if there was transport available, for they were prisoners and therefore enemies of Britain.

'Leave it with me, Stefano, and I may be able to arrange for a priest to visit you here.'

There were murmurs of appreciation as she left, determined to keep her promise.

The telephone directory yielded two numbers for the Convent of Our Lady of Pity: one for the church and one for the convent school. When Rebecca phoned the latter as soon as she got home, she was answered by the Mother Superior who told her there was no resident priest.

'Father Flanagan comes to us every day to take Masses in the church and visit the pupils in the classrooms,' she said. 'He's quite elderly and doesn't drive, so I don't know if he would be able to come over to – where did you say?'

'Yeomans' Farm, er, Mother,' said Rebecca, uncertain of the correct form of address. 'It's at North Camp, about six miles from you, the other side of Everham. The men are living at a prison camp there.'

'Are you a Catholic?' asked the nun cautiously, and Rebecca was tempted to ask what that had to do with anything, but she restrained herself, and replied, 'No, but these men are, and need the Sacraments of the church brought to them.'

'I'll pass the message on to Father Flanagan when he comes to celebrate the 10 a.m. Mass tomorrow, then.'

'May I ask for his telephone number?' asked Rebecca,

patient but persistent. 'If necessary I could come over and fetch him in my car.'

'I don't think I should disclose Father's telephone number to a stranger. Did you say these men were prisoners?'

'*Italian prisoners of war*, and I'm surprised they haven't been contacted by their church,' replied Rebecca impatiently. 'Who is the Bishop of your Diocese?'

'Oh, there's no need to bother the Bishop,' came the hasty reply. 'When Father arrives tomorrow, I'll ask him to telephone you if you'll give me your number.'

'Very well,' said Rebecca. 'I shall be here until eleven, and if I haven't heard from this elderly priest by then, I shall telephone you again, right?' She felt that she had made her point and intended to pursue it.

The next day the telephone rang well before ten o'clock, and in answer to her cool 'Hello, Hassett Manor', a cheerful Irish male voice greeted her.

'Good morning! Is that Miss Neville I'm hearing?'

'Yes. Are you Father Flanagan?'

'At your service, milady! And how sorry I am that your prisoners have been so overlooked. The Home Office doesn't always bother to keep the church informed of these things. Look, I'll send Father Orlando over – he's from Turin, so officially an enemy, but no language barrier. How would that suit you?'

'How soon?'

'This afternoon, if that's convenient. Did you say that this farm is near North Camp?'

'Oh, yes, *yes*, Father Flanagan!' Rebecca sighed with relief, picturing the faces of Paolo and his fellow internees when this Italian-speaking priest arrived with the Sacraments.

There was one more hurdle to be overcome. She went to inform Billy Yeomans, and as expected he was uncooperative.

'Bloody cheek! I won't open my farm to any holy Joe who hasn't even bothered to ask my permission. Lazy bastards, any excuse to stop working!'

'Yet I'm sure you'll allow this priest to visit these men and bring them the comfort of their church, Yeomans,' said Rebecca levelly. 'Better a clergyman than a police inspector coming to investigate black market dealings.' She turned her back on him and walked away, leaving him to ponder over the choice. Bitch, he thought. She's got me over a barrel!

The smiling eyes of the prisoners were ample reward for her efforts, especially when Stefano stepped forward, took hold of her hand and kissed it reverently.

'You are an angel, Signorina Neville.'

'No angel, Signor Ghiberti, only a friend.'

Three years into the war, there was a change of attitude towards it. At first there had been a sense of excitement and adventure, especially among the young. 'Ol' 'Itler' and his Nazi henchmen were going to be thoroughly walloped and the washing hung out on the Siegfried line, but those illusions had now been shattered; life was grimmer and harsher, food and fuel were becoming scarcer – and yet on the whole the people were defiant, grimly resolved to keep going until the very end.

'Let 'em bomb us all they like, we'll bomb 'em back, Tom,' said Eddie Cooper in the Tradesmen's Arms, 'that man won't ever break us.'

'Yeah, but it's our boys, isn't it,' returned Tom Munday. 'What with our ships being sunk by U-boats, and our men sweating it out in the desert, like my grandson Paul, the

Yanks out in the Far East, finding those little yellow bastards more cunning than they thought, and God help the prisoners, having to work for the Japs.'

To which Eddie had no answer, and there was a gloomy grunt of assent from the other regulars. September passed with no news, and then in late October word came through that General Montgomery had scored a triumph: Rommel's advance had been halted at last. In every home in North Camp people listened daily to their wireless sets, to hear that there had been a terrible battle at a place called El Alamein, and by November Rommel was said to be in full retreat from the Allies, who pursued him with their tanks and army lorries. There was unconcealed excitement in the voices of the newsreaders, and on Sunday the fifteenth of November the church bells rang out all over Great Britain, in celebration of the victory at El Alamein. Isabel Neville held her breath as the Monday went by, and the Tuesday, and then on the Wednesday morning a scribbled envelope marked 'Cairo' arrived at Hassett Manor; it was from Paul, a survivor of the battle, sending his love and hoping for a short leave at Christmas or early in the New Year.

Cedric Neville hugged his wife who was sobbing with thankfulness, then opened his arms to include Rebecca and Sally Tanner in a four-way embrace.

'How shall we celebrate?' he asked when at last they drew apart.

'I know what *I* shall do,' said Isabel, brushing the tears from her cheeks. 'I shall go to the Ladies' Make Do and Mend Circle at the Rectory this afternoon, and ask Philip Saville to play "Shenandoah"!'

* * *

The news about Paul Storey spread around North Camp in a few hours, but it was soon followed by news of a telegram received at the Rectory. Howard Allingham was among the thirteen and a half thousand men who had fallen at El Alamein. Mr Richardson's son John was another survivor.

'Alan, how can I possibly comfort a mother and father who have lost their child?' Joan Kennard asked her husband, and he could only reply that they must both be there for them.

'Make them one of your beef casseroles, my love, and a cake – whatever you can rustle up from the rations. I will wait before I speak, and pray with them if I'm allowed.'

When Grace Nuttall realised that Doreen was pregnant, about four months gone, she could not speak or cry; it was as if the calamity had paralysed all sense and feeling. When Jack had been daily risking his life in a Spitfire, firing at Messerschmitts who had fired back until his craft was hit and sent nose-diving into the Thames estuary, causing his face and hands to be hideously burnt, she had suffered daily and nightly anxiety for weeks. When he lay in the Queen Victoria Hospital undergoing several operations and gradually recovering the will to live, her anxiety turned to tentative hope until he was discharged home. His return to the RAF had saddened her, but she had come to accept the permanent change in his life, and that he now seemed to be reasonably content was a cause of thankfulness to her and Rob.

But what had happened to poor, innocent, pliable Doreen was a calamity that Grace tried not to believe at first. But Doreen's third missed period, combined with her wan appearance and refusal to eat breakfast, forced Grace take her to Dr Stringer's evening surgery. The junior partner, Dr Lupton, was seeing the patients this evening; he gently questioned tearful Doreen, and got her to lie down on his couch and put his hands on her tummy, feeling for a healthy swelling above the pubic bone. When he quietly told her mother his diagnosis, Grace had nearly fainted. Doreen's confession of how she had given in to Gus Rohmer's so-called 'buddy' seemed to exonerate Gus who had left North Camp before what had happened only once with a GI called Chuck who had by now also left.

Her husband and father had talked with Grace, telling her it was not the end of the world, and that many other girls had found themselves in a similar predicament.

'We've got to support our girl all the way through the next five months, and when she's had it, it can be put up for adoption,' said Rob, but Grace was unable to discuss the matter. It was not only that Doreen was expecting, but that Grace was being led back into memories suppressed for a quarter of a century; to a room near to Dolly's Music Hall off Piccadilly; of meetings arranged and money exchanged; of frightened young soldiers on the eve of their departure to the filthy trenches of northern France and Flanders; and of one man in particular, older than the others . . . she had thought it a nightmare buried in the past, but now the shadows arose and came back to her, whispering, accusing, tormenting. She knew in her heart that Rob was right, a sensible father who had dealt wisely with his injured son; and who now would deal as wisely with their daughter.

'We'll have to work out a plan,' he said. 'Either she stays at home, or goes to one of those Mother and Baby homes in another part of the country. She'd come back without the baby – that'd be put up for adoption – and then we could all forget about it.'

'*I* shan't ever forget it,' said Grace stonily, for the shadows of the past would never set her free.

* * *

It was the last Sunday of November. Paul had written again, and still hoped to get home leave in the New Year. Alan Kennard had taken over all the clerical duties at St Peter's, and his wife had cooked meals and run errands for the bereaved parents. Alan had prayed with Roland Allingham, but Agnes would not stay in the room. There was no God, she said, and spent hours staring out of a window that looked out over the garden and was safe from prying eyes. Alan Kennard was himself deeply saddened by the death of Howard, a young man who had chosen to confide in him rather than his own father. He wondered how Dora Goddard would take the news; by all accounts she was enjoying life in the ATS in London, where danger was an adventure.

The congregation filed into the pews for Morning Worship. Sir Cedric and Lady Neville were there with Rebecca and Mrs Tanner. There were those who gave thanks for their sons' preservation and those whose hearts were broken. At almost the last minute the rector arrived without his wife, and joined the choir in procession up the aisle, with Alan at the rear while Philip played a solemn voluntary. Alan smiled reassurance to the rector, and the sympathy of the congregation seemed almost palpable. Isabel Neville caught sight of her sister Grace with Rob, but Doreen and Tom Munday were absent. She made up her mind to go over and speak to them after the service – a gesture prompted by her own happiness.

As the people filed out of the west door, the clouds parted and weak winter sunshine came through, lighting their faces. Isabel whispered to her husband.

'I'm going to say hello to Grace and Rob. We've seen hardly anything of each other all this year, and now that we know that Paul's safe, I must offer an olive branch. You wait here – and you too, Rebecca. I won't be a minute.'

But the encounter lasted longer than a minute: it became a story associated with St Peter's for years to come.

'Grace, my dear! How nice to see you – and Rob too. You'll have heard my news, I expect, that Paul came through El Alamein alive, and hopes for home leave sometime in the New Year. How are Dad and Doreen? Sorry not to see them this morning. Are you—'

Isabel stopped at the sight of her sister's face: it was contorted with hatred.

'So, Lady Isabel, are you inviting me up to Hassett Manor to take tea with the daughter you stole from me? I've heard tales about her and those Italian prisoners. Don't you *dare* come patronising me with your—'

'Grace! Stop it! Stop it at once, behave yourself!' ordered Rob as heads turned at the sound of their voices. 'Your sister means no harm – she only wants you to be friends again, for goodness' sake!' He tried to pull Grace away as Isabel shrank back from the bitter words.

But somebody else heard them, and now came quickly to her mother's side.

'You dare to speak to my mother like that!' cried Rebecca. 'You're a wicked, jealous woman, not fit to tie up her shoelaces. And don't try telling me what I know already, that I'm your daughter that my mother adopted, because I'm just thankful that she *did*. I'm sorry for Doreen, with a mother like you. Come, Mother, let's go home.'

She took hold of Isabel's arm to lead her away, but it was that reference to Doreen which maddened Grace more than anything else. She spat at Rebecca and would have

213

physically attacked her if Ron had not held her back. Later it was said by those who saw her that she had been like a woman possessed by a demon.

'Oho, your ladyship, so fine, so posh, so much above the rest of us, gloating over my poor Doreen! Yes, you're right, you *are* my daughter, I gave birth to you – but do you know who your father was? No? Neither do I. I never knew his name, or any of their names, those poor, terrified boys being sent off to that hell in the trenches. A prostitute doesn't get told many names, but I remember your father, the last one I had – he was an officer, a Captain somebody or other, older than the rest. He blamed me for being what he needed, he slapped me across the mouth and called me a whore, hit me when he went inside me; I was covered in bruises – he was vile. So that's who *you* are, Rebecca bloody Neville: a bastard with a prostitute for a mother and a savage brute for a father. You're *nobody*. And now you'll come and gloat over my poor Doreen, damn you!'

At this point Rob took her arm and led her away forcibly. Her words turned to sobs as they passed under the lych-gate. Everybody saw. And heard.

At Hassett Manor Isabel and Sally comforted Rebecca as well as they could, though Isabel was visibly shaken.

'That was news to me, Becky – she told me that she'd been engaged to your father who'd died in the war, but not the circumstances. We must never repeat it, my dear – we must pretend we never heard it.'

'But Mother, everybody outside the church heard it – it's no secret now,' Rebecca pointed out. Cedric poured out a glass of sherry for them all.

'As a matter of fact, I had a good idea of what she was

doing in London,' he told them. 'I visited Dolly's Music Hall once with a friend, and we took a couple of the chorus girls out for a meal, nothing more – and she was one of them and recognised me. I told her to get in touch with her parents and you, which she did.'

'Yes, that was when she told me that her soldier friend had gone off to the war in France, and was killed there,' said Isabel. 'And then she realised that she was pregnant. I knew she'd been a chorus girl at a music hall, but not—' She stopped, unable to say the word they had heard.

'And what did she mean about gloating over Doreen?' asked Rebecca. 'I hardly ever see the girl. She wasn't at church this morning, and she usually comes with our Granddad.'

'Grace was completely off her head, and didn't know what she was saying,' said Cedric. 'You'll have to avoid her, though it's hard on Doreen and your father, Isabel.'

'She ought to be locked away,' said Rebecca. 'I'll never forgive the way she spoke to you, Mother.'

'Ssh, dear, she's to be pitied, and we mustn't hold any grudges against her. We won't do anything to embarrass Rob and Granddad and Doreen,' Isabel said quietly. 'And when we're ready we must forgive Grace. We've been so blessed by Paul's survival, and Jack Nuttall has suffered those terrible burns. We must pray for them all.'

Rebecca said nothing. She was thinking over what she had heard. She was the bastard child of a prostitute and a brute. What would the prisoners think if they knew?

CHAPTER ELEVEN

1943

It was time. Ernest and Devora Munday had to face saying goodbye to their nephew Jonathan Pascoe, as dear to them as a son, returning to the continent after fleeing from it as a Jewish child refugee four years ago. Now he was a British soldier in khaki uniform, and Ernest could not banish from his mind the thought that Jonny was going back to avenge the persecution of his race. The whole family, including little Ruth and Sarah, now schoolgirls, turned out to see him off at the station. They were joined by Isabel Neville who knew that the Munday household would be upset by Jonny's departure, and the grief of his sister Ayesha who went into frightening asthma attacks brought on by her fits of crying; Ayesha rejected all attempts by her uncle and aunt to console her, and Ernest feared that her brain had been permanently damaged by her terrible experience of being forcibly dragged away from her parents and baby brother.

'I'll take her under my wing while you say goodbye to Jonny,' said Isabel who knew how difficult this would be. Jonny looked pale but resolute, and kissed his aunt and sisters, briefly embraced his uncle and brother, and boarded the train. He hung out of the door window and gave a determined smile to them all, waving his hand as the train moved out, gathering speed until it disappeared from sight.

Isabel kept hold of Ayesha's hand, and walked a little apart from the others.

'Now, Ayesha, you're fifteen years old, and I know that you're going to help your aunt and uncle all you can. Remember that they're very sad, too, now that Jonny has gone to the war, like hundreds and thousands of other brave young men. Now, I want you to stop having asthma attacks.'

Ayesha eyed her aunt suspiciously. 'I can't help having asthma,' she said sulkily.

'Maybe not, but you can sometimes stop an attack from coming on. When you feel one starting, take slow, deep breaths like this.'

Ayesha stared as Isabel gave a demonstration as they walked along. After a few hesitations and a glance at her Aunt Devora, Ayesha saw that Aunt Isabel had to be obeyed, or there would be trouble. She obediently started taking deep breaths.

'That's right. In through your nose and out through your mouth, a long exhalation, nice and slowly, Ayesha. Good girl!'

Ernest and Devora, walking arm-in-arm, exchanged a look.

'What do you think is your sister's secret?' Devora whispered.

Isabel heard her, and without turning round, said, 'Perhaps you could come over and deal with Lily and Jimmy one day. Other people's children can react very differently!'

Back at the Mundays' home in Everham, Isabel was invited to stay to lunch. Devora's cooking, even on rations and according to strict Jewish prohibitions, was much commended.

'You look tired, Ernest,' said his sister.

'So do you,' he answered with a wry grimace. 'So do we all. This war seems to be getting nowhere. The Jerries go on bombing our towns to rubble, and we return the compliment. The Japs are on the rampage in Burma, teaching the GIs a lesson, and—'

'Wasn't it terrible about that girls' school in Catford that was bombed in broad daylight?' Isabel shuddered. 'Over thirty pupils and half the staff. It must have been a sight to make the angels weep.'

'But old Rommel copped it at El Alamein,' interrupted David, feeling that some positive thinking was required.

'Yes, but at what cost? All those lives,' said Isabel. 'My boy was spared, but the Allingham boy wasn't. If they had not got their other son, I think Mrs Allingham would lose her reason.'

'Talking of which,' said Ernest, 'is there any news yet of our poor niece Doreen?'

'Not yet,' answered Isabel in a low tone. 'I'm not quite sure when she's due. It can't be much fun in that Mother and Baby home in Berkshire, knowing it's going to be adopted in the end.'

'If she was a daughter of mine, I'd keep her at home and see it through with her.'

'So would I, but Rob had no choice. Grace is half out of her mind, and Doreen's better off out of harm's way. Dr Stringer has put Grace on these tablets, phenobarbitone they're called, and they make her sleepy. Dr Stringer says she might have to go into one of these – you know – mental asylums. I feel so sorry for Rob and Dad. I don't know whether they've told Jack, not that he can do anything.' Isabel sighed.

'Thanks for coming over, Isabel,' said her brother. 'It helps to have the support of the family. Are you – are you expecting to see Paul soon?'

'I really don't know, but at least we can exchange letters now. They're on what he calls "mopping-up operations", but he hopes it'll be before Easter. And needless to say, so do I.'

Isabel's patience was rewarded and her prayers answered at the end of February. Captain Storey and Sergeant Richardson suddenly appeared on their home doorsteps, on leave for seven days. They were thinner, and their tanned faces showed signs of the hardships they had endured after months of desert warfare; but they were alive and home!

Life had never been so good. Corporal Dora Goddard and her closely knit circle of friends in the ATS were positively enjoying the war. When not on duty at the searchlight station – an adventure in itself – they danced the night away in the most glamorous of venues, the Covent Garden Opera house, converted into a huge ballroom where servicemen and women could meet and spend an evening of escape from the war. There were not only the GIs but Canadians and West Indians, in addition to which there were Czech airmen and

Norwegian sailors, all of them courteous and eager to meet girls like Dora. A black GI was especially exotic as a dance partner, and Dora smiled and joked as she danced with a nimble Afro-American who turned her round in complicated twirls, swinging her off the floor and landing her safely back beside him. Air raids might be going on outside, and fearful accidents like the one at Bethnal Green underground station where pedestrians rushing for shelter were caught in an avalanche of bodies falling down the staircase on top of one another in a tragic domino effect, crushing and killing a hundred and eighty. And still the dancing and the laughter went on, as if the Opera House was somehow magically protected from the dark and dangerous world outside. Clasped in the arms of an admiring soldier, sailor or airman, Dora imagined herself dancing among the stars in the night sky, an ecstatic experience.

Until on a day in early spring when she was summoned to the Warrant Officer's desk.

Expecting some new order or a caution on a matter of discipline, she hurried to obey. The officer's face was serious but not stern.

'There's a telegram for you, Goddard,' she said, handing over the envelope. Dora gasped and tore it open. At first she could hardly take in the words: who was William Yeomans? Oh, of course – it was Billy – and she stared at his message.

Sudden death Sidney Goddard stop come home at once stop.

Sidney Goddard? *Dad?* Dear, kind, plodding Dad who did the lion's share of the work on Yeomans' Farm, never complaining nor appreciated? Dead? When? How?

'Is it bad news, Dora?' the officer asked gently, and when

told that it was the death of a parent, she immediately agreed that Dora must go home and take forty-eight hours of compassionate leave, beginning at once.

'And it can be extended if need be,' she said. 'I am very sorry that it is such sad news.'

Mary Goddard was sitting dejectedly in the kitchen, but quickly rose when Dora entered through the kitchen door. Mother and daughter clung together in a long embrace.

'Dora, my own dear girl,' Mary whispered.

'I've come as quickly as I could, Mum – just walked up from the station. How are you?'

'I just can't take it in, Dora, it was so sudden. He was all right when he went upstairs last night, though tired out as usual, after a day in the piggeries with a farrowing sow – seventeen piglets she had, and he said he'd have to get up around two o'clock to see how she was doing, with only ten teats for seventeen piglets. When I went up he was fast asleep, but when I woke at around six, he was laying just in the same position, but something was wrong, and I said to him – oh, Dora, he was dead!' She sobbed as she clung to her daughter as if she was drowning, and Dora led her gently back to the basket chair she usually sat in.

'All right, Mum, all right, I'll put the kettle on,' she said.

'I never said goodbye to him – he just passed away in his sleep,' wept Mary. 'He was tired out, and he'd been like that for months, but he wouldn't go see Dr Stringer. I blame myself for not being firmer with him. Billy phoned Dr Stringer who came and said his heart had given out. Billy said he'd telephone your base, then my dad, but my dad hasn't come. At least Pam came down and got breakfast – there was some ham already cooked, and she fried half a dozen eggs. Oh, Dora, he was so good, he never complained, I couldn't have had a better husband, no matter who – and a father to you!' She wept afresh, and Dora was conscience-stricken. *She* should have noticed Dad's tiredness, *she* should have taken him to the doctor. As she was making tea, little Samuel came running into the kitchen. 'I want a biscuit, Mary!' he demanded.

'Now, Sammy, you know that's not the proper way to ask for anything,' replied Mary in a tone that sounded as if this was a regular request. 'What do you say first?'

'Please, Mary, can I have one o' them biscuits you made?'

'That's better. Dora dear, can you reach up for the biscuit barrel off that shelf?'

'Good heavens, Mum! How often does *this* happen?' asked Dora, though she reached for the barrel and offered it to him, making sure that he took only one.

'Pam usually takes a rest while Derek has his afternoon nap, and this young man usually finds his way to the kitchen.'

'Good grief! And he's allowed to come pestering you for biscuits at a time like *this*?'

Dora was astounded at such thoughtlessness. 'All right, young man, you've had your biscuit, now clear off and leave my mother alone. Go on, scram!' She opened the door and waved him through it, closing it firmly behind him.

'You've been far too soft with the Yeomanses, Mum, and it'll have to stop,' she said, handing Mary a cup of tea. 'And what about Granddad? Has he been told yet?'

'Billy said he'd phone him after he sent the telegram for you.'

'Well, if he'd been told, he'd have been over straight away. I'll tell him. Where's the telephone?'

'In the hall, but it's for farm use only, Dora. He charges Sidney for using it, though he hardly ever does.'

'Well, sod that. I'll phone Granddad now.'

When Dora heard Eddie Cooper's cheery 'Hello!' she suddenly wanted to cry.

'Granddad, it's Dora.'

'What? Dora, my dear, where have you been? Your mum and dad have missed you so much. Are you speaking from London?'

'No, Granddad. I'm at Yeomans' Farm.'

'Why, what's up? Is my Mary all right? Is she ill? For God's sake, tell me.'

'Mum's all right, but – oh, Granddad, my dad – my dad passed away in the night,'

'*What?* Bloody hell, why wasn't I told till now?'

'Mum thought Billy had told you – oh, please come and see her, Granddad!'

'I'll be right over.' He hung up. Twenty minutes later, he strode into the kitchen from the back door, and gathered Mary into his arms.

'Mary, my poor girl, you've lost a good 'un,' he said simply.

She clung to him and murmured through her sobs. 'Oh, Dad, he was so good . . . he took me on . . . he's been a good father to Dora, and I couldn't have asked for a better husband.'

'Sssh, Mary, it's all right, I'm here now.'

At that moment Billy Yeomans came in at the back door. 'I saw you coming,' he said to Eddie. 'I tried to phone you earlier, but there was no reply. It's a bad business for Mary, and I've now got seventeen piglets to rear. Still, Mary doesn't need to worry, she's welcome to stay on here with no charge for bed and board. By the way, has anybody been upstairs to see my mother?'

There was no answer. Eddie stared at Yeomans as if unable to believe his ears.

'Then I'll have to go up and see to the poor old lady myself.' Frowning, Billy left the kitchen. They heard his footsteps on the stairs, and after a few minutes he came down.

'That poor old soul!' he said indignantly. 'Nobody's been up to see her – she's had nothing to eat, and had to get herself to the commode. She said she didn't want to bother Mary. Better put the kettle on, and do her a couple of eggs on toast. It's too bad that she's been left without attention.'

Dora guessed that this outburst of indignation was to cover his own lack of care, his failure to send for Eddie Cooper, and his annoyance at having to attend to the litter of piglets, which would have been Sidney's job for several days. There was a moment of dead silence, and then Eddie spoke.

'I always knew you were a selfish bastard, Yeomans,' he said levelly. 'You've treated my daughter and Sidney as slaves for years, and poor old Sidney didn't have the guts to stand up to you. Well, now he's gone, and I haven't got to watch you and your wife working them both to death, not any longer. You can look after the farm and the house yourselves from now on, starting with eggs on toast for your mother, and giving her all the care that Mary's given to her. You'd better let your wife know.'

'Are you threatening me in my own home?' blustered Billy, red in the face with a mixture of rage and embarrassment.

'I'm not threatening anything, I'm telling you straight. My daughter's coming home with me, *now*. Get your hat and coat, Mary, I'll come back for your belongings later. No

224

more skivvying for the Yeomanses. You come as well, Dora.'

The door opened and Pam Yeomans appeared. 'What on earth's going on?' she asked. 'All this noise has woken Derek, and Sammy says he was turned out of the kitchen and had the door slammed on him. There's no need to take it out on a little boy, even if there *has* been a death in the house.'

It was Dora's moment. 'Your husband's lost Sidney Goddard, and you've lost my mother, so from now on you're in charge of the house and poor old Mrs Yeomans. She won't get the care from you that she's had these years from my mother. Come on, Mum, let's get out of here. I'll fetch your hat and coat from the hall.'

Pam Yeomans looked worried as she took this in. 'Look here, you can't just walk out on me like this, Mary! Billy's willing for you to stay here, free bed and board – Sidney's death won't make any difference, and it wouldn't be fair of you just to walk out. We *do* appreciate you, Mary, really we do—'

Billy frowned at her. 'All right, all right, Pam, no need to grovel. We can manage just as well without them. She'll be back soon, I shouldn't wonder.'

'Oh, no, she won't,' said Dora, coming into the kitchen with Mary's coat, hat, gloves and handbag. 'Here you are, Mum, let's be on our way.'

With her father on one side and her daughter on the other, Mary Goddard left by the kitchen door of the house she had lived in for the last quarter of a century. Billy and Pam Yeomans stood watching them go, and neither said a word. It was slowly dawning on them that they were going to feel a cold east wind blowing through Yeomans' farm and farmhouse without the Goddards.

The news of Sidney's death spread quickly around North Camp, followed by the dramatic aftermath. People sympathised with Mary, though at the same time they silently applauded her 'great escape', as the Nevilles of Hassett Manor called her move from Yeomans' Farm to her childhood home, to live with her twice-widowed father.

'Can't remember when I last felt so good,' Eddie told Tom Munday and everybody else in the public bar of the Tradesmen's Arms. 'Since my poor Annie died and our boy moved away up north, I've kept the house on, though people asked me why I didn't move to a nice little bungalow. I kept putting it off, and now I know why! I've watched my Mary being treated like a skivvy all those years at that farm, but now that she's got away, I can keep my eye on her, and she can have a good rest.'

'How did Billy and his missus take it?' they all wanted to know. Eddie grinned.

'Hah! I'll tell you! When I went round there with Rob Nuttall's van to pick up Mary's stuff, and there was a lot of it, blow me down if that slave-driver didn't come crawling to me, slippery as a snake, to say that Mary had been a treasure and they'd never wanted her to go – the oily blighter even said they were missing her, and if she'd please come back, he'd pay her decent wages – and get a charwoman in daily to do the rough housework and the washing!'

'So what did you say to that, Eddie?' they wanted to know.

'I told him it had taken him twenty years to appreciate Mary, which was twenty years too late. He'd killed Sidney with overwork, and he wasn't going to do the same with my girl. Sent him away with a flea in his ear!'

Tom Munday joined in the general laughter that greeted this, but his own situation was far from amusing. There was no news from the Mother and Baby Home, though Doreen had gone past her estimated date of delivery. Grace continued to walk around in a daze of phenobarbitone, but Joan Kennard had visited Doreen, leaving the children in Miss Temple's care. She reported that Doreen looked pale and subdued, but that her general health was satisfactory, and she'd twice repeated to Mrs Kennard that the baby was to be adopted. There were several other girls in the same predicament in the Home, and almost all were there due to servicemen who had gone to the war, British and Canadian as well as the GIs.

It was arranged that Dora would return to her London base, and would be granted forty-eight hours' compassionate leave to attend the funeral at St Peter's.

'I haven't been in a church for ages,' Dora confessed to her mother. 'I suppose that gloomy rector and his wife are still there?'

Mary looked grave. 'I haven't been to church either, but I've heard that the Allinghams have been crushed by the death of their son, especially Mrs Allingham. She says she'll never set foot in—'

'*What?* Lost a son? Oh, my God, Mum, which one?' Dora broke in, putting a hand to her face and holding her breath.

'Howard, the elder one,' said Mary, alarmed at this reaction.

'*Howard?* But Mum, why didn't you tell me?'

'You didn't seem interested when I wrote that he was back from Dunkirk,' said Mary in some bewilderment. 'You've never said a word about Howard Allingham before. Why, Dora, what's the matter?'

For Dora had covered her face and was shaking with sobs.

'Oh, Howard, poor Howard, I was so cruel to him, so horrible!' she cried. 'I wouldn't kiss him, not even when he was going to the Front. He didn't want to go, and if he'd only had a kind word from me – but I thought I'd better not raise his hopes – oh, if *only* I'd kissed him and made him happy before he went! If only I could have another chance – but I was a bitch, a cold-hearted *bitch*!'

Mary put her arms around her and held her while she sobbed her heart out; but there was nothing she could say that would be of comfort. It was too late.

The news spread around North Camp that Doreen Nuttall had given birth to a little girl, and would be staying in the Home for six weeks, so that she could breast-feed her baby to give her 'a good start in life', as was the policy at the Home, until the babies were adopted. Rob Nuttall and Tom Munday went to visit Doreen and found her cuddling the baby who was 'the sweetest thing I ever saw,' reported Tom. Jack Nuttall also took a day off from the air base to see his sister and niece. He wore tinted glasses, but people still stared at his face or pointedly looked away. Jack was learning to shrug off these encounters, and quite forgot about his scars when he thought about Doreen having to part with her child, her own flesh and blood, never to see her again. Talking about the visit to his grandfather, they both had serious doubts about Doreen being discharged home.

'The poor girl's going to need a lot of care and support,

and your mother's in no state to give it,' sighed Tom. 'She wanders from room to room in this doped state, and might even be worse if Doreen came home. What we need is a suitably quiet home where Doreen could recover from all that she's been through. I'll go and see Isabel – she meets all sorts in the Women's Voluntary Service, and might be able to think of somebody.'

The following day was warm and sunny, with all the beauty of May blossom and new foliage. When Tom reached Hassett Manor he found Isabel and Sally Tanner taking tea on the terrace, with the sound of a piano being played in the room behind them. Accepting a cup of tea and one of Sally's home-baked biscuits, he came to the point of his visit, and asked if Isabel could think of anybody who could take Doreen as a lodger for a few weeks.

'I see what you mean, Dad,' said Isabel thoughtfully. 'I'd willingly have my niece here at the Manor, only that Grace would accuse me of stealing another daughter from her.'

'What about Ernest and Devora?'

'Oh, no, Dad, they've got a houseful already, and Ayesha gets these asthma attacks. Doreen needs somewhere more restful.' They sat thinking in silence, and Sally Tanner spoke.

'What about Philip's aunt, Miss Temple?'

'Oh, we couldn't burden Enid Temple,' said Isabel. 'She's got Nick to look after, and people are forever asking for her help – like Joan Kennard wanting her children minded while she goes to visit a parishioner.'

'Yes, but it would be worth asking her,' said Tom.

Exactly,' said Sally. 'Don't forget she's one of the thousands of spinsters left over from the Great War because all the men were dead. I suppose I shouldn't say it, but the war has been

229

a blessing to her. It's changed her life – turned her into a universal aunt – and she looks younger. Try her.'

'I'll speak to Philip when he's finished the piano lesson,' said Isabel, 'just to ask his opinion.'

Philip never turned down a chance to do Lady Isabel a favour, and said he thought it a good idea; his Aunt Enid would be glad to help the Nuttall family. Nick was a quiet boy, he said, and the upshot of this exchange was that two days later Enid Temple willingly opened her door to sad, bewildered Doreen Nuttall as a paying guest. Within days their growing household rejoiced together with the whole nation at the news of a triumphant achievement by a squadron of specially trained RAF airmen who had successfully bombed two vast dams in Germany, causing an unstoppable flood and drowning the industrial heartland of the Ruhr.

In the Tradesmen's Arms the bombing of the dams gave rise to jubilation as the first good news since El Alamein.

'It was done with a newly invented bomb that ricocheted across the water until it reached the wall of the dam and exploded against it,' said the man from the dairy, exhibiting his scientific knowledge.

'Did you hear Tommy Handley on ITMA say that ol' 'Itler's gone on his holidays, to paddle in the Ruhr?' asked the barman amidst guffaws of laughter.

'Pretty bad luck for the people, though,' commented Tom Munday. 'Thousands killed, houses smashed, farms all under water, cows, sheep, horses and all.'

'Oh, I don't shed any tears over 'em,' said Eddie Cooper. 'A lot of our boys on that raid got killed in it.' He lowered his voice. 'And judging by what's going on in Warsaw – Jewish families, kids and all, being rounded up to be taken God knows where – I wouldn't show the Jerries any mercy, not if we bombed Berlin to rubble.'

His sentiments found agreement among the punters, and Tom changed the subject.

'How's Mary?' he asked, and Eddie's face softened.

'Better than I've seen her for years. She was holed up in that bloody farmhouse, and after Dora left she got more depressed, and never went out anywhere. Sidney was a good bloke, but he could never stand up to Billy the bully. Now Mary's going to the Ladies' Circle at the Rectory, and knitting for the children of the forces. She's got the time now, you see!'

Tom said nothing. The mention of children reminded him of the little great-granddaughter he would never see, and the anxiety about Grace's state of mind. Dr Stringer had again hinted that she was suffering from a mental illness, and ought really to be in hospital.

As if reading his thoughts, the barman asked how Doreen was getting on with Miss Temple.

'Very well, thank God,' answered Tom. 'Miss Temple's such a good sort. She takes Doreen to the Ladies' Circle, and they're nice to the poor kid – no raised eyebrows about the baby. Like Eddie's girl Mary, she's much better off where she is.'

There was a murmur of approbation, but nobody asked about Grace, or enquired about Tom and Rob's life at 47 Rectory Road.

Captain Storey and Sergeant Richardson had returned to the army, and their destination was a closely guarded secret. Isabel

Neville hoped and prayed that Paul would not be sent to the Far East where the Japs had surprised the Americans with their cold efficiency, and had taken a number of prisoners. Heaven forbid that Paul would fall into their hands.

Scarcely two months after the bombing of the dams, there came important news from the Mediterranean.

'Have you heard? Eisenhower's invaded Italy!'

First the wireless and then the newspaper headlines announced the landing of American troops in Sicily, from the sea, and in a rapid advance had taken the capital, Palermo; by August Sicily was in Allied hands. A brief message came from Paul, saying that he was with the British and Canadian forces supporting the US invasion. The Allies' continued advance into the 'toe' of Italy was eagerly followed, and within days the seaport town of Messina was wrested from the German occupation; the fighting had been fierce, and the town was said to be in ruins. The general consensus of opinion was that the end of the war was getting nearer, though at Hassett Manor there were certain reservations. A telephone call from Father Flanagan informed Rebecca of the very low morale in the POW's camp where the men were desperately anxious for their families and friends, and she took an early opportunity to visit them, avoiding the Yeomans' farmhouse. Paolo and Stefano came to greet her, and the others waited around to hear what she had to say.

'The invasion is good news for your people at home,' she told Paolo, whose English was very much improved. 'They'll be freed from the enemy occupation of your country.'

'But they are caught in the crossfire between two armies,' he replied on behalf of the whole camp. 'We have a man here whose mother and father live in Messina, and his fear for them is so bad that he cannot eat or sleep. How can we comfort him, when we are all afraid for our loved ones?'

'Then you are all in it together, so you must comfort one another,' she said, but Paolo had other trouble to report.

'People stop being friends with us – they shout "bloody wops!" when they see us in the field, and Signor Yeomans call us lazy bastards and say we must not go to the kitchen door again. The kind Signora who gave us food, she not there, and the young Signora tell us to go away or she will call the Signor. We may not play more with the children – oh, Signorina, we have become your enemy!'

'You are no enemy of mine,' she replied firmly, 'and I'm sorry to hear how some North Camp people treat you. You are still welcome to share our table at Hassett Manor, and if you two' – she indicated Paolo and Stefano – 'walk back to the Manor with me, we'll ask Mrs Tanner what she can find in the pantry.'

There were eggs from the hen-house, and cold pork with bread and home-made pickle to make sandwiches; they thanked Sally warmly, and said they would carve a wooden love-spoon, just for her. To Rebecca Stefano whispered that, 'I make for you a Cross with the Body of Christ upon it, forgiving his enemies.'

By early September Italy was in desperate straits. The country had been largely overrun by the Allies, and there remained only Monte Cassino, on which an ancient Benedictine monastery stood. The monks had been turned out, and German soldiers now occupied it, a seemingly impregnable fortress that defied all attempts to storm it. Anybody or company approaching it from any direction would be seen and shot at.

'For heaven's sake, Becky, don't let the men see this newspaper,' warned Isabel, showing her the front page photograph of weeping Italian women, some with children, thin and listless from all the horror they had seen. 'Destroy it when you've read it.'

But there were others in North Camp who were not as kind to the 'Eye-ties'. The men were thrown copies of the newspaper and *Picture Post* weekly magazine which had the same photograph enlarged on the cover.

Inevitably there were consequences. Lady Neville found herself the butt of ridicule from a group of older children on their way home from school at Everham.

'Look, there goes Lady Mussolini! *Buon giorno, Signora!* She has the Eye-ties up for dinner at the Manor, and her daughter goes with—' whisper, whisper, followed by giggling.

Isabel was somewhat shaken, but ignored them, and continued to offer invitations to the POWs to join her and Cedric for Sunday dinner. He privately wondered what would happen if Paul suffered death or injury in the Italian campaign.

Rebecca's experience of mockery came from two land girls she overheard talking, quietly but just audible enough for her to hear.

'Yes, she's been seen carrying on with a couple of them! Honestly, you'd never have thought it of *her*, of all people!'

Unlike her mother, Rebecca had an almost irresistible urge to shout a reply, 'What's so surprising? What did you expect of the bastard daughter of a prostitute and a brute?'

She managed to keep her mouth closed, but the effort made her tremble all over.

* * *

One morning Mario and Stefano caught a glimpse of Rebecca cycling past their field on her way to visit a neighbouring farm. Mario laughed softly and murmured, *'Mi piacerebbe fare l'amore con lei nel campo d'orzo!'*

To his amazement, Stefano rounded on him in fury. *'Zitto!* You will not speak with disrespect of her, or you'll regret it!'

Mario assumed a blank expression and said no more. After all, he'd only been joking about making love in the barley field . . .

By Christmas the monastery of Monte Cassino was still held by Germans; fog and relentless rain hampered the Allies, so Storey and Richardson endured a seemingly endless stalemate. Prayers were said for them at St Peter's, also for Wing Commander Lester Allingham, lying wounded in an RAF Hospital in Buckinghamshire. The Allinghams went to visit him just before Christmas, and came back with the news that he had a suppurating wound which gave him a high temperature, and he was very weak. His parents insisted that he was too ill to receive any visitors other than themselves, and Mrs Allingham told God that if her remaining son recovered, she would start going to church again. Meanwhile the parish was exhorted to pray for his full recovery.

CHAPTER TWELVE

1944

The new year dawned on a cold, grey world, and Nurse Pearson was not sorry to be back at The Limes after a short break for Christmas which had been more frugal than festive. Mrs Pearson had coughed and sneezed with a streaming cold, and Valerie feared that she might catch it and pass it on to the children, though her mother said she thought it had been brought from The Limes. They had attended church on Christmas morning, though Mrs Pearson hadn't wanted to speak to anybody afterwards, only to get back home to the roast shoulder of lamb, then to settle down in her favourite armchair with a hot water bottle at her back, and listen to the King's speech. Valerie had gone out for a brisk walk, to fill her lungs with fresh, cold, untainted air, hoping to escape the infection; but on her return to The Limes she found that half the children had coughs and colds, needing to be dosed up with Gee's Linctus and a honey and lemon mixture that soothed sore throats and was kept in the medicine cupboard.

During her brief lunch break she dashed out to buy a birthday card for one of the children who was three years old that day. As she searched among the small selection, she heard a pleasant male voice behind her.

'Miss Pearson – Valerie – I'm very pleased to run into you!'

She turned to see Philip Saville with a bundle of official notices from the council offices to be posted. 'Did you have a good Christmas?'

'Hello, Mr Saville – yes, it was rather quiet, but quite nice. How was yours?'

'Splendid. Lady Neville invited us – my aunt and Nick and myself – to coffee and mince pies at the Manor. She was looking for you after church, but you disappeared into thin air!'

'Yes, my mother wanted to go straight home as she had a streaming cold, and shouldn't really have come out.' She turned down the corners of her mouth in a little grimace. 'And it didn't seem appropriate to wish everybody a merry Christmas, did it?'

He gave a wry chuckle. 'I'll wish you a happy New Year, then, you and your mother. But I still want to see you, Valerie. I've been talking to Lady Isabel, and she suggested that we take the children to the pantomime at the old Everham Hippodrome. I think it's *Aladdin* this year, but they're all the same, aren't they? Plus jokes about old Hitler and his henchmen – he's taken the place of the Demon King these days. Anyway, Lady Isabel said would you like to come with me to lend a hand, as we did for *Pinocchio*. I told her I was willing if you were. I couldn't cope with them on my own! So what do you think, Valerie?'

She felt a pleasant little tingle run down her spine. 'Well, yes, of course, I'd love to – only it would have to be a Saturday matinee when I'm not on duty at The Limes.'

'That's what she suggested. Which Saturday would suit you best – this coming one, or the following week? If I let her know, she'll order the tickets.'

'I think the following one would be best,' she said. 'Who will be coming?'

'Same as last time, Lily and Jimmy, plus Kenny and Danny from the Rectory – the Perrin boys and my Nick – remember they'll be three years older, so hopefully not too difficult to manage. So, shall I let her know?'

'I'd love to go, Philip – it's very kind of Lady Isabel.'

'Well done! We'll be Auntie and Uncle again!' He laughed. 'Oh, and I've just had a thought – you know my aunt has got poor Doreen Nuttall staying with us while her mother's not able to – er – keep her at home?'

'Yes, it's a sad business,' Valerie said.

'Well, wouldn't it be rather nice to ask her to come too? It would be a real treat for her, making her feel she was helping with the kiddies. Shall I ask her if she'll join us?'

'Yes, of course,' said Valerie at once, though a faint, inexplicable twinge of disappointment accompanied the words. 'Yes, that's a very good idea!'

The Allinghams looked tired after the long train journey to and from the RAF hospital in Buckinghamshire, but Mrs Allingham was a little more inclined to talk to the curate's wife on the following day.

'He's clearly very ill, that's obvious, with a temperature that goes up to one hundred and four or even five degrees,' she said. 'He has to have the wound cleaned and redressed every day, and his poor bottom is black and blue from these injections they're giving him. He's got a long way to go before he's better, but at least he's not going out on those terrible air raids. The death rate among those poor, brave young men is appalling. Roland and I can at least sleep in our beds while Lester's in hospital.'

Joan Kennard smiled and agreed.

'Roland says he's going back to full-time service as rector,' his wife continued. 'So your husband will be able to spend more time with his children. I must admit it's reassuring to know that Mr Kennard is here to take over the parish visiting.'

And a good deal more parish business than that, thought Joan. 'Alan will visit Lester one day next week,' she said.

'Oh, no, Mrs Kennard, you must tell your husband not to visit for the time being,' the rector's wife said hurriedly. 'Above all Lester needs peace and quiet, and we don't want his progress held up by well-meaning intrusions.'

Alan found this rather puzzling when he was asked to call at Hassett Manor where Lady Isabel handed him a sealed envelope addressed to himself and marked '*Private*'.

'Lester Allingham enclosed it in an envelope addressed to me, and asked me to pass it on to you, Alan,' she said. He thanked her and did not open the envelope until he was in his study.

'Dear Mr Kennard,' he read. 'Will you please come to see me in this place, as I need to have a confidential talk. Do not let my parents or anybody else know I have sent for you, and I've told Lady Isabel I need to see a clergyman for personal reasons. My brother Howard told me that you helped him before he went away, and I'm hoping you will also be able to help me. Best wishes, L.R. Allingham.'

Alan wondered if Lester wanted spiritual counselling and perhaps to make a confession: he made the visit a priority, and went by train to Halton the next day, telling Joan that he was going to see somebody in hospital, and would need to take the whole day. He regretted withholding the identity of that somebody from her, but knew she would guess.

Picking up a newspaper at the station, he read that in Russia there was rejoicing over the lifting of the two-year siege of Leningrad, although many of its citizens had died of starvation. With Stalingrad and Leningrad liberated, the Red Army was advancing towards the Crimea. It really did seem as if the tide was turning in favour of the Allies, though at home there was no let-up on rationing, and sporadic air raids still occurred. The siege of Monte Cassino continued, showing no signs of surrender by the Germans occupying the Benedictine monastery.

As soon as he set eyes on Lester sitting in a sunny verandah in dressing gown and slippers, certain suspicions deepened. The young man had lost weight and looked haggard.

As soon as he saw the curate, he got up and shook his hand.

'Thanks for coming, Kennard, you're a life-saver. Like to take a seat?' He indicated a wicker armchair next to his own. 'We're on our own in here – I told the other chaps to give me a chance to speak with the Reverend Kennard undisturbed.'

'I've come a long way to see you in confidence, Lester, and have told my wife a downright lie, so fire away,' said Alan briskly.

'You're a brick, Kennard. Look, it's like this. The powers

that be have said I can go home, but I have to attend a clinic each week for a check-up. The nearest clinic to North Camp is at Aldershot, an army hospital out-patients.'

'Go on, Lester, I'm listening.'

'Well, the fact is I don't want to go back to North Camp, to be fussed over by my mother. There's a small hotel a few minutes' bus ride from this clinic, and I'd rather stay there.' He looked at Alan with a question in his eyes, as if to test his reaction. Alan's expression was blank as he waited to hear more.

'The fact is that I don't want the old dears to be unduly worried, so I'll have to write to them as from this hospital, and they'll write back to me here.'

'I'm still listening, Lester.'

'It's like this, you see, Kennard, if I could use you as a sort of, er, go-between, I'd write a letter to them, stick it in an envelope and post it to you – and you could post it on to them. Then when they reply to this hospital, I'll have asked for all my mail to be redirected to this small hotel. Do you follow?'

'What about the postmark?'

'I doubt the old dears will spend much time poring over that.' Lester's face was flushed, and strands of hair stuck to his moist forehead. 'Then it would be reversed, Kennard. They'd write an answer, it would come here, and be redirected to the hotel. I'll tell them that I don't want visitors, *any* visitors, until I'm better able to face them. It shouldn't be that difficult, and I'd pay you, of course, starting with your train fare today.'

'How long do you reckon this would go on?'

'I don't know quite how long, and perhaps we might have to think it through again at some point. You'll do it for me, won't you, Kennard?'

He stopped speaking, and his eyes pleaded with the curate. Then Alan spoke.

'Whereabouts is this wound of yours, Lester?'

'At the top of my left thigh – not a place where people would look.'

'Your mother told my wife that you've been on a course of painful injections. Do you know what they are?'

'Oh, these women and their tittle-tattle! Some new treatment they're trying out, made from a mould, they say. Anyway, Kennard, can I rely on you?'

Alan looked into his eyes. 'Is it syphilis or gonorrhoea, Lester?'

'Bloody hell, you've been talking to the staff. Both. Oh, for God's sake, help me, Kennard. It would kill my mother if she knew.'

'So you want me to help you deceive the old dears, as you call your parents, by telling yet more lies? In my capacity as a clergyman, you expect me to practise deceit? And in any case, what you suggest would be bound to fail. Some official notice might arrive, from your bank, say, and your father might telephone this hospital. The idea is full of holes, and I'll have no part in it.'

Lester swore and tears came to his eyes. 'I just don't know what to do, Kennard.'

Alan drew a deep breath. 'Here's my best advice, Lester. I agree that this knowledge would be a fearful shock to your mother, and might well break her heart, so I'd agree to letting her remain ignorant. But your father should know, and you'll be better for telling him.'

'Oh, no, *no*! I couldn't bear it! Oh, God, help me!' Lester was now openly sobbing, and Alan rose to put a hand on his shoulder.

'All right, old chap, all right. You've got a few choices. You could tell your father alone, face-to-face, or I would be willing to be present when you tell him, or I would tell him first, to pave the way for you. Failing all of those, you could write it to him in a letter. Once he's been told, he can work out a way of keeping it from your mother. Come on, Lester, these things are seldom as bad as we think, not if we're honest and ready to take the blame for our own misdoings. Think about it. I shan't tell a soul, and I'm sure the rector won't either!'

Lester looked stricken. 'I couldn't face the old man – he'd go mad.'

'I doubt that. Anyway, it's time I left. Would you like me to say a prayer for you here before I go?'

'No, thanks. If you won't help me, there's not much use in praying.'

'Very well, I'll pray for you and your parents in my private prayer times. Goodbye, Lester, and think about what I've said.'

The outing to the pantomime went well, and Doreen Nuttall felt very important as she helped to shepherd the children on and off the train, walked them along to the Hippodrome, and assisted Miss Pearson in taking the girls to the lavatory during the interval.

'It was a good idea to bring her, Valerie,' remarked Philip Saville while Doreen was on one of these necessary visits. 'It's doing her a world of good to recover a sense of self-esteem, and to feel she's doing something useful, don't you think so?'

'Yes, and she's enjoying the pantomime,' agreed Valerie. 'It's good, isn't it?'

She had noted the *double-entendre* when the princess leant

out of the palace window and looking to the left and right, wailed, 'Three months gone, and still no sign of Aladdin!' There were some knowing chuckles among the audience, but Valerie had kept a straight face, wondering if Philip had noted it.

When they arrived back at North Camp station, Lady Neville met them in the pony-trap, and took all the children except Nick back to their homes. Philip, Doreen and Nick saw Valerie home, then went off into the dark winter evening, Doreen hanging on to Philip's arm, and chattering happily about the pantomime. Valerie told her mother it had been a great success – the children had all enjoyed it, and so had Doreen Nuttall.

'How kind of Mr Saville to take her with you,' said Mrs Pearson. 'She seems to have settled very well with Miss Temple and that nice boy. You never know, it might prove to be the beginning of a new life for both of them! He's a lot older than her, of course, but maybe that's just what she needs, in the circumstances.'

But is it what *he* needs? thought Valerie, feeling strangely flat.

The stalemate at Monte Cassino had dragged on for week after cold and comfortless week. With the Germans commanding an all-round view from the summit, it was impossible to attack it without being seen, and lives had been lost in attempts to do so. Lady Neville was again plagued with fear for Paul, and Rebecca knew that the Italian POWs were anxious for their relatives and for the ancient beauty of the Benedictine monastery, now desecrated by enemy occupation; when Paolo, Mario, Stefano and other POWs came to Sunday dinner at Hassett Manor, the subject was firmly excluded from the table-talk. By mid-February a decision was made by the generals and approved by the British Prime Minister Churchill, and the American President Roosevelt, and orders were given for bombs to be dropped directly on the monastery.

There followed the total destruction of an architectural treasure that had been turned into an enemy fortress.

'There was a series of huge explosions, and a pillar of smoke rose hundreds of feet up into the air,' Paul Storey wrote home later. 'We were all awestruck. It hid the building from sight, and when it finally cleared there was nothing but a heap of smoking rubble and body parts spread for miles around. It was a breath-taking sight with a kind of sinister beauty. None of us who saw will ever forget it, and the mixed feelings we had afterwards.'

When Rebecca went down to the prison camp, she found many of the POWs sorrowing over this utter obliteration of the monastery.

'The ghosts of the holy Benedictines from centuries past must surely weep at the sight,' sobbed young Guiseppe, and Rebecca had no words to answer him.

But Stefano had. 'We are friends, not enemies, to you and your family, Signorina Neville,' he said quietly. 'We pray for our families and countrymen, and I pray also that your brother Paul be not lost in all this waste of life.'

Rebecca's heart leapt, and not only for his sincerity in caring for her family at a time like this. Trembling, she held out her hand in friendship, but he took it and held it to his lips in a fervent kiss. 'May God return him safely to his family, Rebecca.'

She could only whisper 'thank you,' and no other words were exchanged.

* * *

From then on there was new hope in the air. British and American troops, Paul Storey and John Richardson among them, were being withdrawn from the war in Europe, and coming to bases along the south coast of England, giving rise to speculation of a forthcoming invasion of Europe; the Germans were spreading their defences along miles of Normandy coastline. When news came that American bombers were pounding Jap forces caught between two lines of fire, there was fierce jubilation.

'Give it to 'em, the little yellow bastards!' was the consensus of opinion at the Tradesmen's Arms, but then came news that Jonathan Pascoe, fighting in the Far East, had been taken prisoner, and elation turned to fear for the young man. There were terrible stories about the treatment of prisoners of war in Burma, and a shadow fell across the Mundays of Everham, waiting every day for news that they dreaded. Added to which David Munday had turned eighteen, so he too had been called up and posted to an army training centre near to Aldershot, and expressly forbidden to share any details with his family, who at least could give thanks that he was not with his cousin.

Mrs Pearson was taking an afternoon rest, so Valerie was able to spend a sunny Sunday afternoon walking beside the river Blackwater, an idyllic spot at a time when the earth was awakening to another spring. She recalled how six years ago she had spent her Wednesday lunchtimes here, dreaming of a romance with John Richardson, imagining them exchanging confidences, sharing their mutual interests in poetry and music – and kisses, shy and gentle at first, then becoming more fervent – and talk of marriage. How naïve she had been! The man she had yearned over had never existed, and the real John Richardson had turned out to be very different from her secret dreams, and held no appeal for her.

Her thoughts were interrupted by the sight of a man and a woman some way ahead of her, walking in the same direction, and she slowed her steps, having no wish to intrude on their privacy. She stared at the man's back: surely she knew that slight limp and the once golden, now greying hair? Yes, of course, he was Philip Saville! And the young woman holding on to his arm was Doreen Nuttall who now shared Miss Temple's cottage with him and Nick, the nice evacuee. She hesitated, then walked no further; the sight of the two of them was unexpectedly disturbing. Philip Saville, veteran of the Great War, now in his forties, was known to have a hopeless infatuation for Lady Neville – in fact it was a joke in North Camp. Poor Philip, they said, whose experiences of trench warfare had turned him into a one-legged semi-recluse living with a maiden aunt – that is, until Lady Neville had asked him to play the piano for the Ladies' Circle, and then to give piano lessons to her groom's twin boys; and yes, it had been Lady Neville who had arranged for him to take five children, two of them cheeky evacuees, on an outing to the cinema, to see *Pinocchio*. He and Valerie had laughed together over the children, and agreed how thankful they were *not* to be their parents, yet Valerie had wondered what having a real family would be like, with herself as a wife and mother. The outing to the pantomime *Aladdin* had not been quite so much fun with Doreen there to help. And now Doreen was living under the same roof – a sweet, simple girl less than half Philip's age, who had given birth to an illegitimate daughter and given her up for adoption. Could it be that Philip had at last got over his hopeless longing for a happily married woman, and chosen instead to offer a protective, almost fatherly, love to a girl like Doreen? And had Lady Neville actually encouraged him in this?

Valerie stood very still, watching the pair walk further along the bank until they disappeared from sight round a bend in the slowly flowing river. She could imagine them kissing, gently and shyly . . .

She turned to retrace her steps, giving herself a little shake. She had to be sensible and face up to the reality of life. She had benefitted enormously from her work at The Limes with children who trusted her, and little Georgie Tonks who unashamedly declared, 'I loves 'oo, Val!'

She was no longer the silly, romantic girl who had dreamt about John Richardson, and would not make the same mistake with Philip Saville.

The news from the Russian front, often scanty, now continued to be good: the Red Army had recaptured the Crimea, and were making headway in eastern Europe, practically unopposed. Reading this account in the daily newspaper, Tom Munday could have wished that his domestic situation was as hopeful. Grace continued to be unpredictable, and he had been woken in the small hours of the night by the sound of furious argument and a smell of burning; he had leapt out of bed to find Rob trying to restrain Grace.

'She's going mad, Tom!' he shouted. 'Only trying to set the bed alight and burn the house down! We can't go on like this. She'll have to be put away, no alternative!'

Dr Lupton shook his head when sent for. 'The trouble is that there aren't many mental hospital beds available these days – they've been taken over by the military for the wounded. There's the old workhouse at Winchfield – that's used for mental defectives – and the private place at Hollingbridge would be expensive. I'll have a word with Dr Stringer. Meanwhile I've given her a sedative by injection, and she'll rest for the next few hours.' He shook his head sympathetically. 'I'll be back, Nuttall.'

When he returned, he brought better news. Dr Stringer the senior partner had said that there were a few empty beds at Everham General Hospital, and Grace need go no further than there for the time being for rest and observation. Tom advised Rob not to tell Jack or Doreen as yet, as it would only worry them and there was nothing they could do.

There was trouble at Yeomans' Farm where Billy and Pam were having daily rows, realising more and more how much they missed Mary Goddard. Pam said she couldn't be expected to look after their two young boys and cook for farmworkers and land girls, as well as looking after the 'old girl upstairs'. It was when Billy went up to see his mother one evening, and found that she had been forgotten all day, with no food or assistance with going to the lavatory, that he had realised how urgently they needed extra help. Nobody who knew Billy and Pam wanted to work for them, and it was Miss Neville as Regional Officer for the Women's Land Army who made an arrangement, strictly hush-hush, that one of the land girls would help out in the farmhouse for three days a week, for which of course she had to be paid a fair wage. Rebecca also suggested that old Mrs Yeomans be brought downstairs, and the farmhouse parlour, seldom used, made into a bedroom for her. A threatening letter from the Inland

Revenue revealed that the farm accounts were in a hopeless mess, and Billy had to admit that he needed an accountant. Munday and Pascoe at Everham were recommended by a neighbouring farmer, but they too had to be paid. The events in Europe and Southeast Asia made little impression on Billy Yeomans' fury.

At the Rectory Lester Allingham had come home, white-faced and irritable. His mother told Joan Kennard that he was having to attend a special clinic at Aldershot each week, and needed rest and 'building up'. On the first occasion that Lester came face-to-face with Alan Kennard he muttered angrily, 'I made a mistake in confiding in you, Kennard. I suppose you'll be threatening me that you'll tell what you know.'

'Which shows how little *you* know about ordained clergy in the Church of England or any other Christian church,' replied Alan. 'It's up to you whether you tell your father or not.'

The incident led to another question of confidentiality for Alan, when Joan told him that Grace Nuttall was in Everham General 'for rest and observation'. Rumours had abounded that she had gone completely insane and tried to kill herself and her husband.

'Will you visit her, Alan? She's obviously very troubled.'

'Only if Rob agrees,' he replied cautiously. 'And then she might refuse to see me. At present I can only pray for her and all of them.'

Rob Nuttall and Tom Munday instantly agreed that he should visit, so the next day he called at Everham General and was led by the ward sister to where Grace lay in a single room. He sat down beside the bed and smiled.

'I must first ask you if you're feeling better, Grace.'

'They must have sent you to question me.'

'Not at all. I've come as your parish priest to see if I can be of any help to you, Grace. You haven't been well for a long time, have you?'

She sighed. 'No, I haven't. I wish I was dead.'

'Why? You can tell me anything, my dear. It will never go any further, I promise you. I don't even tell my wife what people confide in me.'

She sat up and stared at him. 'Well, you must know what's happened to me – everybody else does. My daughter Rebecca was taken from me as a baby and brought up by my sister. My son's face is burnt beyond recognition, and he doesn't want me near him – he's gone back to the RAF and never comes to see me. My daughter Doreen is simple, and got herself pregnant by an American soldier, and had the baby adopted. I just can't face having her at home, not with all the scandal.'

Alan smiled and shook his head slightly. 'Yes, Grace, I know all the facts you've just told me, but I want to hear *your* feelings about them. It isn't what happens to us, it's the way we face up to our problems that counts. And I know you have been greatly tried.'

'Yes, and you're the first person who's admitted that, Mr Kennard. I *have* been tried, tried beyond endurance, and it's driven me crazy.'

'And so have Rob and your father been tried, haven't they?'

'Oh, I suppose they'd say they had.'

'And in addition to all the trials you've mentioned, they've been worried about you.'

She shrugged. 'Now for the lecture. You might as well get on with it.'

'No, I've stayed quite long enough for today.' He stood up and held out his hand.

'I'll visit you again soon, Grace. We've got a lot more talking to do. Think about what you've told me, and I'll be praying for you.' He took her hand. 'God bless you, dear.'

As he left the room, she stared after him, and realised that she wanted him to visit again soon. He seemed to be her only friend.

After two months of rumour and speculation as to when the invasion of Europe would take place, the news came suddenly on Tuesday the sixth of June that a seaborne force of thousands of British and American troops under the joint command of Generals Eisenhower and Montgomery had landed at several points along the Normandy coast, where German batteries had already been pounded by RAF bombers. It was D-Day! The long awaited liberation of Europe had begun. Wireless broadcasts updated the progress from day to day, and families again waited with hope and fear for their menfolk; Paul Storey and John Richardson were known to be somewhere among the invading forces.

'Rebecca dear, I've had a letter.'

'Something important, then, or you wouldn't look so solemn.' Rebecca grinned at her mother.

'Yes, it *is* important, or could be. Just sit down for a minute.'

'What is it? Who's it from?' Rebecca was intrigued.

'It's from Shaftesbury – from Geoffrey Bannister.'

Rebecca gasped. 'Oh, my God, is it really? It's been so long since—' She broke off and bit her lip. 'How is he? I've long had a guilty conscience about him.'

'He sounds fine, walking around with his artificial leg, and assisting his father with constituency business. He's sent a photo of himself and his parents outside the Conservative party headquarters in Shaftesbury – look, here it is.' She handed a snapshot to Rebecca, who was clearly somewhat shaken.

'He certainly looks well, and, er, happy. But what does he say? Why has he written after – what, four years since Dunkirk? Oh, let me see, do!'

She held out her hand and her mother passed her the short, friendly note which Rebecca took with hands that trembled slightly. She read it, and put a hand to her mouth.

'He wants to *visit* us, Mother? After this long silence? After the way I – oh, Mother, poor Geoffrey! It seems like a distant memory - ages ago, another life.'

'Actually, Becky, he's kept in touch with Paul, so perhaps it doesn't seem as long ago to him as it does to us. Anyway, he says he would like to visit us – just a call, a couple of hours, as you see. Daddy and I agree that he would be most welcome here as Paul's friend, but we also agree that the decision must rest with you. *You're* the one he obviously wants to see again, and it's not hard to guess why. He's restored to health, proved by that photo, which also shows his interest in following his father into politics, maybe even becoming an MP himself in due course. So, Becky, you must tell us how to answer him.'

'Oh, Mother, what can I say? It was he who broke off our unofficial engagement.'

'Yes, and for the best of reasons, to set you free from the helpless cripple as he then saw himself; it was a truly noble action.'

Rebecca got up and paced around the room, clasping and unclasping her hands in agitation. 'But I didn't love him *then*, Mother – it was a release to me, as you know.'

'But you're four years older now, and a lot has happened since. The war has changed us all.'

'I simply don't know what to say, Mother. It would be wrong to invite him to call on us, even if only for a day, if I was not – was not—'

'Not as eager as he is to renew an acquaintance that could – and probably would – lead on to marriage, Becky. Let's speak plainly – you owe it to him to give an honest answer. *Would* you like to see him again, knowing what it would imply?'

'I don't know, Mother, I don't *know*!' Rebecca was on the verge of tears, and Isabel gave her time to continue, but she only repeated, 'I don't know,' shaking her head in real distress. A long silence followed, and then Isabel spoke again.

'My dear Rebecca, you know and I know that there has been idle gossip in North Camp about you and the Italian prisoners of war – and one in particular, Stefano Ghiberti.'

Rebecca sat down and burst into tears. Isabel looked on, without rising to comfort her.

'You realise, dear, that Stefano will go back to his home in Milan, where he tells us he was doing well in the car industry. If he took you with him, to spend the rest of your life in a foreign country, speaking a foreign language, your children would be Italian by birth.'

Rebecca continued to weep, but managed to sob out, 'I know.'

'You're twenty-seven, dear, and able to make up your own mind, so I will not advise you about your choice of husband. I'll just remind you that marriage to a politician, perhaps a Member of Parliament and in comfortable circumstances, would be an easier option, and not too far from us at Hassett Manor. Daddy and I could see our grandchildren, but don't let that influence you; it's not important when weighed against your happiness.'

'I know, Mother, I know.'

'I'll give you three days to think it over, Becky, and if you haven't given me a firm answer after the weekend, I'll write to Geoffrey and say that we feel a meeting would not be advisable. It will hurt him, of course, but it would be a much greater hurt to allow him to call on us and be disappointed. So, Becky dear, I'll leave it there. Let me know by Monday.'

She rose and went over to her daughter, putting her arms around her. Rebecca gradually calmed, surprised at her mother's perception.

When the excitement over D-Day and the progress of the liberation of Western Europe had settled into a daily eagerness for news and a confident expectation that the end of the war was in sight, there came 'a bombshell from Hitler', as many called it – a new terror to Britain, just ten days after D-Day.

'They call it his "miracle weapon", and he's unleashed it on us in retaliation for D-Day!' said Mrs Pearson in dismay. 'A horrible aeroplane with no pilot – it just comes over and explodes wherever it lands!'

'One of them's already destroyed a church and a hospital in south London,' Miss Temple told Philip when he and Doreen came in at teatime. 'It was on the wireless at five o'clock, and heaven knows how many more of these pilotless planes will be coming over.'

The pilotless plane, which Hitler called his V1, soon became known as the 'buzz-bomb', and then the 'doodlebug'.

'It comes over with a throbbing engine noise, and when it's used up all its fuel it cuts out and down it comes,' said the barman of the Tradesmen's Arms. 'It looks just like a plane with an orange flame coming out of its tail. You can see it at night.'

'He just wants to frighten us now that he's being invaded,' said Tom Munday. 'He knows the game's up, and it's his last throw.'

'It's easy to say that, but if he calls it his V1, there must be a V2 and a V3 coming up, and God knows how many more,' said the dairyman who had dropped in for a pint on his way home. 'They say they've landed in Bromley and Kingston, even as far as Southampton, and the ground shook as if it was an earthquake. It's like another Blitz, with doodlebugs coming down on shopping centres in broad daylight. Don't underestimate 'em'.

'If you see one of 'em buzzing overhead, you take cover and pray that it'll pass on to some other poor buggers,' said Eddie. 'I heard on the wireless that the RAF's bombing the launching sites of the doodlebugs in France and Holland.'

On the twenty-fifth of August came the wonderful news that Paris had been liberated amid scenes of wild rejoicing, though collaborators were dragged through the streets and beaten.

Rebecca echoed her grandfather's belief that the doodlebugs were not so much a miracle weapon as a parting shot from Hitler at the approaching end of Nazi tyranny, and, in a brief exchange with Stefano, they had speculated on how long it would be before the swastika was hauled down and burnt in every capital city, and what the future of Europe might be; no words passed between them regarding their own future, but their thoughts were in their faces, their hope of a time when he would no longer be a prisoner. Lady Neville had written to Geoffrey Bannister saying that much as she and Sir Cedric would welcome him at Hassett Manor, such a visit would be best left until after the war. She knew, as did Rebecca, that he would read between the lines, and be disappointed; but she had added that the end of the war seemed not so far off, thus giving him a tiny glimmer of a hope . . .

And then, a week into September, Hitler's second miracle weapon was unleashed on London and southern England, a deadly, silent, long-range rocket, the V2, able to drop vertically from a great height without warning. The first one landed on Chiswick with an explosion that brought death and destruction, and more quickly followed.

'See, the old bugger hasn't given up yet,' remarked Eddie Cooper in the public bar.

'It doesn't seem right to celebrate the Allies' marching to victory after victory over there while these bloody things are coming over here and nobody knows where they'll land, or what time.'

His listeners could hardly disagree, and shook their heads.

Sir Cedric Neville was tired. His duties as a JP took up ever more time, and running the Hassett Manor estate with a greatly diminished staff meant that he often had to don working clothes, roll up his sleeves, and get down to basic farming. He had to share his historic eighteenth-century home with Lily and Jimmy, now better behaved but noisy and demanding. Thank heaven for Sally Tanner, he sighed – she looked after them while Isabel was sorting out problems in the WVS while constantly worrying over her son Paul and nephew David Munday in the thick of the invasion and liberation of Europe. And now there were these damned doodlebugs and rockets, random killers that lowered Britain's morale just as victory seemed nearer.

'You looked whacked, my love,' said Isabel as they sat at supper.

'So do you, dear. Have you had a busy day?'

It was a routine question, but it got an unexpected answer.

'Well, yes, there's a problem that I can't do anything about,' she said.

'Why, what's up? What do you mean, Isabel?' he asked, instantly alerted.

'There's been an influx of wounded at Everham General, and my sister Grace has been sent home. Enid Temple tells me that she's much better, and seems to be in her rightful mind, thanks to Alan Kennard's visits.'

'But that's excellent!' cried Cedric. 'It means that Doreen will be able to return, doesn't it?'

'But Doreen doesn't want to return, so Enid said. Everybody says how happy she's looking. She's grown very attached to Enid and Nick – and Philip.'

'And the sooner *that* stops, the better,' said Cedric firmly. 'I'm surprised at Saville, letting a girl like Doreen get too fond of him, a man more than twice her age. Miss Temple should pack her off home as soon as possible.'

'You're probably right, dear, but there's nothing that *I* can do about it in the circumstances, seeing how much Grace resents me.' Isabel sighed wearily.

'I can see there's *one* thing you'll be called upon to do, my dear, and that's to talk some sense into Saville when he comes prowling round here again.'

Isabel looked up in surprise. 'But you've never minded that, have you, Cedric?'

'No, dear, I haven't said anything,' he replied, thinking how Saville had got on his nerves with his ridiculous adoration of Isabel. It was almost as bad as the business of Rebecca and the Italian prisoner of war; Ghiberti had said he was planning a future in cars, which could mean anything from owning a chain of garages to scratching a living as a used car salesman – not that there'd be many cars to sell in post-war Italy.

CHAPTER THIRTEEN

1944

From the moment she set foot over the threshold of 47 Rectory Road, Grace Nuttall asked to see Doreen; she now felt able to deal lovingly and sensibly with her daughter, longed to put her arms around her, setting the past aside, and to be all that a mother should be. Jack came over from the RAF base to see her, and she now treated him as an adult who had suffered serious injuries but had overcome the emotional effects of them, just as she had overcome a mental breakdown.

'The Reverend Alan Kennard did me so much good, Rob,' she said. '*He* didn't blame me for anything, he just asked me to tell him all about myself, and then left it to me to face up to my mistakes, see how selfish I'd been – and now I want to make amends to *all* of you – you, Dad and dear Jack and Doreen.'

'That's right, Grace,' said her husband, 'it's all over now, water under the bridge. Our Doreen'll be here just as soon as you've got yourself settled. We'll be a family again, and no looking back, eh?' He kissed her, and she responded eagerly. 'It's like old times!'

Doreen cried bitterly on hearing that she was to return home.

'Please, *please*, Enid, let me stay! I'm so happy here with you and Philip and Nick! I don't want to go back there.'

Enid Temple saw that she would have to be firm. She knew the real reason for Doreen's reluctance to return to her parents; it had been such a pleasure to see the girl's shining eyes and listen to her happy chatter when Philip was nearby, and he had not discouraged her – on the contrary they had gone on walks together, and he had remarked on how much better she was looking; the unfortunate business over the birth and adoption of her baby daughter no longer seemed to trouble her. Even so, Enid reproached herself for allowing Doreen to become so involved with a man old enough to be her father, yet wondered if in fact they might be right for each other.

'Doreen will be going home on Friday, Philip,' she told her nephew, watching for his reaction. 'She's not very happy about it, but it's probably for the best.'

He nodded, and decided to be frank with his aunt. 'It's true that she and I have enjoyed each other's company, Aunt Enid,' he said awkwardly. 'I have felt rather like a father to her, and because she's so sweet and childlike, the thought *has* occurred to me that one day – er, I might offer her—'

'I've wondered the same, Philip, but the best way of finding out is to let her go back to her family and see where her best interests lie. You'll have to stand back and wait.'

He promised to follow her advice, but neither of them anticipated Doreen's near-hysterical behaviour on the day her father came to collect her.

'Let me say goodbye to Philip!' she cried. 'Where is he, Miss Temple? Why isn't he here to say goodbye to me?'

Enid could not hide her embarrassment when Philip suddenly appeared, against her considered advice, and Doreen clung to him as if she were drowning. Only when he quietly promised to visit her soon did she relax her grip on his arm. Rob Nuttall glared at him, and quickly led Doreen out to the pony-trap he had brought for her and her belongings.

'Now, Doreen my dear, you're not to upset your mother and make her ill again,' he warned. 'She wants you at home with her, and you're to be the good girl you used to be.'

Doreen let her mother kiss and hug her, and kissed her grandfather. Rob had heard Saville's whispered promise to visit Doreen, and prepared himself for it. On a morning two days later, when Doreen and her mother had gone shopping, there was a ring at the doorbell. Rob caught Tom Munday's eye, and went to answer it. Philip found himself faced by Munday and Nuttall who stood at the doorway, and did not invite him in.

'Oh, good morning, Mr Nuttall – Mr Munday,' he said with determined good humour. 'If you have no objection, I'd like to see Miss Nuttall for a few minutes.'

'Well, you can't,' replied Rob very definitely. 'I'm not having my daughter pestered by a man more than twice her age, taking advantage of her – her *vulnerability*.' He had been practising the word, which came out correctly and full of disapproval.

'I can assure you, Mr Nuttall, I have no intention of

taking advantage of Miss Nuttall in any way,' said Philip, reddening.

'And we have no intention of taking that risk,' said Tom Munday sternly. 'We don't want you coming round here again, d'you understand?'

'I – I'm sorry, Believe me, I have every respect for her,' stammered Philip, dismayed by their united anger.

'Yes, stay away from this house, Saville,' said Rob Nuttall, coldly contemptuous. 'Go back and make an ass of yourself with Lady Neville!'

The door was slammed in his face, and Philip winced at the insult. Was this how North Camp regarded him – a fool infatuated by Lady Neville? He had no choice but to retrace his steps, burning with a shame he had not felt until this encounter with the men in Doreen Nuttall's blameless life.

At the rectory there was sudden consternation. Joan Kennard was getting the children ready for church when there came the sound of voices overhead, coming from the Allinghams' parlour. Alan was ready to leave for Morning Service, and wondered if he should venture upstairs. Lester was shouting, and Mrs Allingham was crying, though few words could be distinguished. While Alan hesitated, the rector came halfway down the stairs.

'Kennard, are you there? Look, we've got a bit of trouble, I'm afraid. I shan't be able to attend this morning, so you'll have to go ahead and take the service without me.'

'Very well, Mr Allingham.' The two families had never got round to using Christian names. 'Can I be of any help?'

'Only to take Divine Service, nothing else. No need to make a great fuss about it,' said the older man, as if his curate was being deliberately irritating. 'And keep the children away.'

Alan did not reply, seeing that the four children were always kept away from the Allinghams. He nodded and turned back, wondering if Lester had made a confession to his parents.

'I shall have to make some sort of excuse to the congregation,' he said to Joan. 'No doubt we shall hear all in due course.'

There was a certain amount of murmuring in church when Alan explained that the rector was unable to conduct the service, and as he stood at the church door while the people filed out, he was pleased to greet the Nuttalls; Grace and Doreen were holding hands, and Grace smiled up at him.

'I'm so happy to have her home again, Mr Kennard,' she said.

'It's a joy to see you both,' he replied, noting that she looked warily towards the Nevilles, as if hoping for a reconciliation there soon. He also noticed Doreen's eyes looking round for the organist, but knew that Philip had hastily escaped by a small, ancient door behind the organ. Philip had not confided in him, but he guessed there must be a connection with Doreen Nuttall. Miss Temple's polite 'Good morning, Mr Kennard' gave nothing away.

Later in the day Alan was told by the rector that Lester had gone back to the RAF.

'He missed the activity of service life, Kennard,' he said. 'Not much going on in North Camp for a young man of his nature. It has upset Mrs Allingham, naturally, but we've had to let him go.'

No details were given of the furious row that had erupted between Lester and his parents, and the verbal shaft he had hurled at them – that if he had to spend one more day in bloody North Camp, he'd go nuts – nor that he had referred to Alan Kennard as a pompous Holy Joe who got on his nerves.

The events taking place across the Channel continued to bring hope and fear: every family with a son, husband, brother or any relative or friend involved in the liberation of Europe dreaded the news as much as they eagerly awaited it. One morning Valerie Pearson received a letter from Mr Richardson of Thomas and Gibson's, informing her that his son had been sent home with a bullet in his left shoulder, and that he had been transferred to Everham General from a military hospital in Aldershot. Mr Richardson asked her – almost begged her – to visit John whose morale was very low, his father said. Valerie was of course sorry to hear this, and although she was disinclined to revive a relationship with John, she felt that a bedside chat with a man in a hospital bed could hardly be thought of as compromising, and only involved a short walk from The Limes.

'Hello, John.'

'Valerie! Oh, Valerie, how good of you to come! It's wonderful to see you – sit down, sit down, tell me how you are – and your mother. It seems such ages since—'

'Your father told me you were in here, John,' she said, careful to show that she had come as a friend rather than a girlfriend. He looked tired, and had lost weight. His left shoulder was swathed in a bandage that went around his chest and upper arm, and he wore a sling.

'I've brought you some flowers from the garden,' she said, putting down a bunch of chrysanthemums. 'I'll go and find a vase to put them in.'

'I shall look at them and think of you and your kindness, Valerie,' he said with a break in his voice. 'It's been a hard slog all day and every day in France, and then I got this' – he indicated his bandaged shoulder – 'and now I'm washed up here, missing all the fun!' He grimaced, and she realised he spoke ironically.

'Your father's very thankful to know that you're out of the danger zone, John,' she said, taking hold of his outstretched left hand. 'And so am I.'

'You're so sweet, Valerie,' he muttered hoarsely, 'and I haven't appreciated you as I should – as I do now.'

'All right, John, all right,' she said gently, and passed him a handkerchief from her handbag. 'You've just got to be patient, and give yourself time to recover.'

After a short silence he asked her how she was, and she gave him a lively description of The Limes and her young charges there.

John Richardson decided that if he wanted to keep her visiting him, he would have to assume an interest in the children who had obviously become central to her life. Fair enough – he could happily listen. It was better after all than having to hear about some new Romeo on the scene. She needed no encouragement, and he joined in her chuckles over the little daily dramas at The Limes, and the comical sayings of the children.

'You've done me so much good, Valerie, I can't thank you enough,' he told her when she got up to leave. 'You will come again, won't you?'

And unable to think of a reason why she shouldn't, she smiled and assured him that she would.

* * *

The news of the death of old Mrs Yeomans at Yeomans' Farm caused far more reaction in North Camp than her son had expected; he forgot that she had lived longer than most of her neighbours, and many of them remembered her as a busy farmhouse wife and mother, a countrywoman through and through. Mary Goddard was genuinely upset that she had not visited the old lady since leaving the farm, unwilling to confront Billy or Pam; she and her father attended the funeral at St Peter's, and were amazed to find the church packed to capacity. Billy hoped that they would not all expect to come back to the farmhouse afterwards to scoff the thick bacon sandwiches and economy fruit cake that Pam had grudgingly prepared; when he saw Eddie Cooper and Mary enter, he wondered if this might be a good time to approach Mary and offer her a generous wage in return for some help in the house, but on catching Eddie's unfriendly look he decided that it would not.

The funeral service was conducted by the Reverend Alan Kennard who asked Sir Cedric Neville to read the eulogy he had written, as Billy was unwilling to do so; Philip Saville played the organ to accompany the two hymns, and most of the congregation followed the coffin to the graveside where the earthly remains of the old lady were lowered to lie close to those of her husband. Billy Yeomans dabbed at his eyes, and Pam stared down at the ground to hide her satisfaction at the removal of a burden. At the conclusion of the burial, many bystanders came forward to shake Billy's hand and offer condolences, and Mary Goddard alone shed real tears at this farewell to the old lady she had looked after until Sidney's death freed her to return to her father's house.

No sooner had North Camp mourned the death of Billy's

elderly mother than another source of gossip spread from house to house.

'The old lady left 'em a nine-day wonder,' declared Eddie Cooper to the patrons of the Tradesmen's Arms, chuckling quietly at their astonished faces.

'Yeah, she got old Mr Jamieson the solicitor to come and see her when Billy and Pam were out of the way,' he said. 'My Mary was there, but they didn't want her in the bedroom, and now we can see why! Jamieson brought along a clerk and a secretary from his office to witness the new Will, and wouldn't I have liked to see Billy and Pam's faces when they went to his office in Everham yesterday and heard it! Hah! What a slap in the eye, eh?'

There were gasps and jaw-droppings as he told his story.

'Go on, go on, what did they hear, Eddie?' they chorused.

'They got the shock o' their lives – his mother had left the farmhouse and the farm to her grandsons – to the young nippers, Samuel and Derek – with a couple of thousand for Billy to work the farm until they come of age and can make a decision whether to keep it or sell it.'

'Strewth! I bet that shook 'im!' marvelled the barman.

'Ah, but that isn't all,' said Eddie, putting down his glass. Tom Munday, sitting beside him, nodded and prompted him. 'Go on, Eddie, you'll have to tell 'em.'

'She left the capital – *thousands* of pounds in war bonds and investments – to her granddaughter,' said Eddie. 'Her granddaughter and mine, young Dora Goddard!'

The older men among his listeners began to nod and understand, remembering Mary's hasty wedding to Sidney, following the news that the elder Yeomans boy, Dick, had been killed at the battle of the Somme. Sidney Goddard had not been called up because of his short sight, and had been persuaded to marry Mary Cooper and call her baby his own. Billy had been a late arrival in the family, born to Mrs Yeomans when she was forty, and Dick had been her firstborn, some twenty years earlier.

'Sidney was a kind husband to Mary, but he could never stand up to a tyrant like Billy, and after Billy married, it was even worse,' went on Eddie grimly. 'Sidney was worked to death on that bloody farm, and my Mary did all the housework and cooking, and then had the old lady to look after. Hah! Little did they *all* know what the old girl was planning for 'em!'

'Good for her!' was the unanimous verdict of the listeners and the families who passed the news from house to house.

'The old bitch! After all I did for her, the scheming, ungrateful old *bitch*!' stormed Mrs Pam Yeomans, but Billy remained silent as his wife ranted in fury, and shook his head when Pam demanded that the Will be contested.

'Jamieson said it would mean huge legal fees, and very little chance o' changing it,' he muttered, his thoughts on the brother he had never known, whose death had changed the course of his life.

As the skies became clear from the menace of the V1s and the V2s, all of which had apparently been used up in one final assault by a defeated enemy, Dora Goddard knew that the ATS would be disbanded after the end of the war, and that at twenty-seven she would have to consider where her future lay. She had gone out with GIs and Canadian soldiers, and her friend Gwen had married a GI and confidently looked forward to making a new life with her husband in the USA after the war. It was a comfort to Dora to know that her mother was happily settled with her grandfather in North Camp, but she had no wish to return to that narrow rural life; her world had grown bigger, and with her skills in wireless telegraphy she hoped to get work in London after the war; she might even travel to New York, a self-sufficient career woman, without forfeiting her independence by marrying a GI!

And then she was sent for to return to North Camp, and heard the news of her legacy. She saw her mother's tears, and when her grandfather began hesitantly to tell her that old Mrs Yeomans had been her grandmother, and the reason why she had inherited the money, it seemed to her as if she had always known. Her first thought was to go to her mother's side and kiss her.

'Sidney always treated you as his daughter, dear,' whispered Mary.

'Yes, Mum, and as far as I'm concerned he *was* my father, and I loved him, the only dad I ever knew,' Dora answered gently, tears coming to her own eyes as she spoke. 'Don't worry about it, Mum – you suffered years of bullying from Billy, and now it serves him right. I'll see you get your share of this money—'

'Oh, no, dear, it's yours!'

'It's *ours*, Mum, ours and Granddad's,' insisted Dora. 'I only wish that dear old Dad was here to share it!'

Towards the end of the year the lights gradually began to go on again in London and major cities, not as brightly as before the war, but sufficient to raise the people's spirits after the enforced darkness of the last five years.

It was Mr Richardson who saw the short news item on an inner page of the *Daily Mail*, and showed his son John, now home for Christmas.

John gasped. 'The silly bugger,' he said, shaking his head. In a few short lines it was reported that a certain Group Captain Lester Wilberforce Allingham, a decorated war hero now invalided out of the RAF, had been arrested following a drunken brawl outside a Soho night club, when he had punched a youth of seventeen and kicked a woman bystander, both of whom had needed hospital treatment. Allingham had resisted arrest, but was now released on bail, to appear before a magistrate's court in the New Year. This information was soon pointed out to other North Camp readers, and led to a selling-out of the *Daily Mail* that day, but a generally sympathetic attitude to a local war hero and his parents.

Alan Kennard was much disturbed by it, as it seemed to indicate that Lester was probably not leading a celibate life as he would have been advised by the army clinic, and wondered if he should write to him, reminding him that syphilis should still be regarded as infectious for two years, even with treatment, so could be passed on to any woman with whom he had sexual intercourse. After much inward debating with himself, and praying for guidance, he decided not to act in a matter that was not his business and might do more harm than good; he was already thoroughly disliked by the Allinghams' remaining son.

Unfortunately the weekly *Everham News* picked up the story and gave it full coverage, having been refused an interview with the rector and his wife. Mrs Allingham flew into a hysterical rage at the newsagent's in North Camp, and before a gaping group of bystanders loudly denounced the editor as a rotten coward for reporting a trivial incident involving her heroic son, shell-shocked after being wounded in the service of his country. This time Alan Kennard had no hesitation in writing to the editor on behalf of the Allinghams. Without mentioning Lester by name, he protested at such cruel treatment of a clergyman and his wife, and pointed out that they had already lost a son earlier in the war. He called for an apology, and his letter was printed in the following issue of the newspaper, together with an apology to the Reverend and Mrs Allingham, and like the curate's letter, there was no mention of Lester Allingham by name.

'I'll carry the lantern, Mr Kennard!' offered Nick Grant who had come with Philip Saville to join the carol singers, now congregated in the hallway of Hassett Manor, where Isabel Neville and Sally Tanner were handing round mince pies. Sir Cedric was ladling out the Christmas punch he had made.

'No worries, Alan, it's just our own home-brewed cider warmed with a few cloves and a dash of Mrs Tanner's sloe gin,' he said with a grin. 'You'll all be singing your heads off after this!'

Alan Kennard smiled and accepted a small half glass. The Christmas Eve service had been moved from midnight to eight o'clock for the benefit of tired families on a frosty night, and would follow on from the carol singing, scheduled to reach the church in good time for the service. He reckoned he would probably have to take all the Christmas services, as the rector had to stay to comfort Mrs Allingham; Lester had phoned briefly to say he was not coming home for Christmas, but was staying in London, and his mother was heartbroken, blaming the newspapers for causing him such embarrassment.

Looking round at the singers in their winter coats, scarves and gloves, he smiled gratefully at Rebecca who was in charge of the children – Lily and Jimmy from the Manor and Kenny and Danny from the Rectory. Their ages now ranged from seven to ten, and young Nick would be fourteen this year. All except Nick would be going home when the singing ended, meanwhile they were overjoyed at being allowed to join the carol singers. Alan noticed that Dora Goddard, now home on Christmas leave, had come to join them, and was hearing all the latest news from Barbara Seabrook.

'Look over there, Dora,' she whispered, 'at those three Italian prisoners of war. I wonder who gave *them* permission to attend. It'll start tongues wagging again, and my Dad says he wonders why Sir Cedric allows it.'

'The children all seem pleased to see them,' observed Dora. 'They all want to hold their hands! And they look like really nice fellows.'

'Yes, that dark one uses the children to worm his way into Hassett Manor and flirt with Rebecca Neville!'

'Good heavens! And does she – er – respond?'

'People have seen them walking close together, deep in conversation,' said Barbara, lowering her voice. 'You know she gave up a very nice chap who was Paul Storey's friend at university and lost a leg after Dunkirk. He adored her, and the Nevilles must have been so disappointed – and if she marries a *prisoner of war*, just think of the scandal!'

'Not really our business, though, is it?' said Dora. 'Who's the chap with the soulful eyes, talking to her ladyship?'

'Oh, you must remember Philip Saville, the organist – he

was another casualty of the first war, and became a semi-recluse, living with his aunt. He's opened up a lot since the war started, and the boy carrying the lantern is an evacuee who's billeted on them – a nice boy.'

Dora reflected that she too had benefitted from the war, in that her life had been changed by joining the ATS and discovering a wider world, but she thought it better not to tell Barbara who had stayed in North Camp and served in her father's butcher's shop.

'Right, then – are we ready?' called Alan. 'We'll make for the High Street first, and start with "God Rest Ye Merry, Gentlemen" and everybody's to sing up!' Dora and Barbara joined them, Dora remarking that the rector was not present.

Barbara did not answer, and when Dora repeated her remark, she replied with a shrug, 'You know that they lost their son Howard, and now I believe the younger son is giving them trouble of some sort.'

'Wait a minute, Mum was telling me about some rumpus he got into in London, and it was in the papers – of course, he's a great war hero, and it must have upset the old people,' went on Dora as a memory came to mind. 'You used to go out with him, didn't you, Barbara? I seem to remember you two as the stars of the tennis courts! You didn't keep in touch, then?'

'That was a long time ago, and it petered out when he joined the RAF,' said Barbara quickly. 'Oh, look, there's Valerie Pearson – with John Richardson, another wounded hero! Hello, Valerie – and John! Did your mother let you out?' she asked with a broad wink.

'I called to ask if she'd come with me to sing carols, and I have a way with dear old ladies,' laughed John. 'I persuaded her to let Val off the chain for one evening!'

'That's just not true, don't listen to him – my mother *told* me to join the carol singing,' said Valerie, frowning. 'She wanted to listen to the carols from King's College on the wireless, and so did I—'

'Until you got a better offer,' chuckled Dora. 'My oh my, things have changed in North Camp since I left!'

Philip Saville, seeing Valerie walking with Richardson, felt a sense of disappointment, regretted that he had not followed up Isabel Neville's subtle praise of Valerie, bringing them together at the children's outings to Everham, when he had so admired the girl's kindness to the evacuees. Then had come Doreen Nuttall's open adoration of him, and his stupidity at not discouraging her firmly from the start. He had got over his hopeless infatuation for Isabel Neville, but had failed to recognise Valerie's sweet nature, and now she had been taken up by Richardson, the latest war hero. He sighed over his own folly.

Apart from the children, the carol singers attended the Christmas Eve service and Holy Communion, and to Alan's fervent prayer that this would be the last Christmas of the war, they responded with a heartfelt 'Amen!'

Isabel Neville bowed her head and prayed that when victory came at last, her son would be safely returned to her, while at the Rectory Agnes Allingham wept for the son she had lost in the war, and the son who had chosen to desert his parents at Christmas.

CHAPTER FOURTEEN

1945

'Cry – God for Harry! England! And Saint George!' roared Laurence Olivier, charging full-tilt into the battle of Agincourt, the sky black with the arrows shot by the English longbowmen. John Richardson tightened his grip on Valerie's hand which he'd been holding since the film began.

'All right, darling?' he asked, his lips touching the tendril of hair at her temple.

'It's *brilliant*,' she whispered back. 'He really *is* King Henry V, isn't he?'

He let go of her hand, so that he could put his arm around her shoulders, drawing her closer to him.

'If you say so, sweetheart.' He kissed the side of her face. 'I'd watch anything with you, even Shakespeare. Mmm . . . you're so sweet, Valerie.'

'Let's just concentrate on watching the film, John.'

'Sssh!' said a male voice in the dark. 'If you can't shut up, get out!'

Valerie was embarrassed. 'Yes, John, be quiet,' she whispered. 'It's not fair on other people.'

'Sorry, dear,' he whispered back, though she could hear his amusement in the words. 'It's just that you're so lovely, and I want to make love to you.'

She shrugged her shoulders and determinedly gave all her attention to the film, finding a parallel between Henry V inspiring his troops at Agincourt with Mr Churchill's leadership of Britons through the war towards victory at the present time. Six or seven years ago she had adored this man, dreaming of a passionate love affair; and now here he was, returning her love beyond all her dreams. His wartime experience had clearly changed him for the better, and he had eyes for no other woman. He'd been totally honest with her, admitting his earlier infatuation for Rebecca Neville, now completely evaporated.

'And by what I hear, she's found consolation in a very different quarter – but don't let's talk about her now – *you're* the only one I'm interested in,' he'd told her, proving his point with a long kiss on her lips, closing his eyes. And Valerie had responded as he'd wished: what woman could possibly resist such adoration? Times have changed, she thought, and I've had to change too. The whole world's changed.

The war was coming to an end. There was an air of expectancy as the British and US armies advanced across Europe from the west, and the Russians from the east; it was clearly only a matter of time before they met in Berlin. But it was not all good news: what had been vague and terrible rumours over the past few years began to emerge as horrifying reality.

'Here, what d'you make of this business in Poland?' asked one of the regulars at the Tradesmen's Arms. The question met with head-shakings.

'Haven't you heard about it? The Russians have come across this place called – er – can't pronounce it, sounds like Ostrich. They say thousands of Jews were put into gas-chambers there, and killed – piles of bodies, they say, chucked into mass graves or left to rot in heaps.'

'Watch what you're saying, mate,' said the barman, looking round to check if there were any women present. 'I don't take too much notice of it. You always get propaganda in wartime, and I reckon the Russians have exaggerated it, to show up the Jerries in an even worse light.'

'It'll all come out at the end of the war, that and a lot else, I dare say,' said Tom Munday who had come in with his son-in-law Rob. Eddie Cooper was not such a frequent visitor since his daughter Mary had come to live with him, making his life much easier.

'We all know old Adolf's a villain, and a mad villain at that, but I can't believe even *he'd* order something as hellish as that,' said the barman, drawing a pint of bitter. 'And if he did, surely nobody would obey.'

February brought more news of the wickedness of war, but this time it was the British who were the perpetrators. It caused a heated discussion at the Ladies' Circle.

'It seems a bit late to go on a bombing spree like that,' said Mrs Tomlinson. 'I mean, Dresden is a historic town, full of treasures and—'

'And full of innocent civilians,' Joan Kennard broke in. 'Sixty thousand killed in one night, four hundred injured.

Just think of the children – imagine little souls trapped under wreckage, crying for their mothers who'd been killed. That "Bomber Harris", as they call him, must have a lot on his conscience – and just as the war looks like coming to an end. I wonder that Mr Churchill agreed to it, I really do.'

'For all we know, Dresden may have been at the centre of a secret network of information, just because it had no heavy industry,' said Mrs Pearson. 'But if that story of the gas chambers at Auschwitz is only half true, it shames the whole of Germany.'

Mrs Tomlinson shrugged. 'Even so, such devastation at this late stage of the war does seem ill-advised, to say the least.'

'The same thing happened to Coventry, don't forget,' said Mary Goddard, now a regular member of the Circle. 'Not to mention the blitz on London and all the other towns and cities that suffered the same as Dresden.'

Her sentiments were entirely echoed at the Tradesmen's Arms.

Ernest Munday, senior partner in the Everham family firm of chartered accountants still called Munday and Pascoe, was not expecting a visit from a client, but when he looked up and saw that Isabel Neville had come into the office, he at once rose and held out his arms to her.

'Isabel! Oh, my dear, how are you?'

'I just had to see you, Ernest,' his sister replied as they embraced. 'I just had to. Ever since we heard about that dreadful place in Poland – such wickedness – I've thought about you and Devora. How is she? How are you all?'

He experienced a rush of affection for his sister whose

son Paul had been away in the army for the past six years, and was now with the liberating army in Europe, as was his son David. Without giving him time to answer, she went on asking questions.

'And your nephew Jonathan, have you had any news of him?' she asked.

'No. They don't have post-boxes in Japanese prison camps. We worry about him all the time. And by the way, Isabel, we call Jonny and Ayesha our own children now, seeing that they lost their parents to God knows what fate.' He gave a shudder. 'One good thing is that Miriam and Ayesha have grown very close as sisters, both having brothers away, and Ayesha's asthma seems to be getting better – well, at least no worse.'

'That's good. But oh, Ernest, this dreadful war. We both lost our dearest loved ones in the last war, and here we are going through it all over again. I pray for Paul every day, and of course I can't expect Cedric to feel the same – Paul isn't his son.' Her voice faltered, and he drew her head against his shoulder. For a minute they silently clung together, and then he spoke again, deliberately changing the subject.

'Is there – has there been any reconciliation between you and Grace?'

'I'm afraid not, Ernest. I'd be very glad to be sisters again, but any overture would have to come from Grace. She owes Rebecca a full apology, but to date Becky's still too shocked at what Grace said to her in front of half the congregation. Everybody heard it – so unnecessary, so spiteful. I'm not going to urge Becky to forgive and forget. Grace must wait until she's ready. She's got over her nervous breakdown, which is good news for Dad and Rob, and Doreen's gone back to Thomas and Gibson's, which is good for her. But if Grace wants forgiveness from Rebecca, she'll have to come and ask for it. Oh, Ernest, how petty these family feuds seem, with so much cruelty and suffering in the world!'

He patted her shoulder. 'It will come in time, Isabel. Now, let's go and find Devora who'll make us a cup of tea. Come on!'

Isabel was taken aback at how Devora had aged, but reckoned that her sister-in-law probably thought the same about herself. They exchanged news about their evacuees, the two little Jewish girls, Ruth and Sara, much the same age as Lily and Jimmy at the Manor, and all four doing well at their schools.

'They've been a blessing to us, Isabel,' said her brother. 'They've given us something to occupy our minds, and we're quite proud of them – aren't we, Devora?'

'Yes, indeed we are,' replied his wife emphatically. 'Our children have saved me from losing my sanity over our sons, David in Europe and Jonny in a Japanese prison camp.'

'Well, Isabel's Paul survived Dunkirk, El Alamein, Monte Cassino and now like our David, fighting their way across Europe,' said Ernest.

'Yes, the end of the war really does seem to be in sight at last,' said Isabel.

'Not in Japan,' said Devora quickly.

'The Japs will probably give up soon after the Germans,' Isabel said seriously. 'There was a tremendous air raid by the US air force on Tokyo the other night – they said on the news that it destroyed the centre of the town, and thousands of civilians were killed and injured. The suffering there now must be frightful.'

'The American air force can flatten Tokyo – bomb it off the planet as far as I'm concerned,' returned Devora in a coldly matter-of-fact tone. 'Until we've got our dear sons safely home again, alive and undamaged, don't ask me to weep for the Japs.'

Ernest and Isabel exchanged a glance, both silently reflecting that the cruelty of war, though sometimes inspiring heroism in ordinary people, also brought out the worst in humankind.

As April turned into May, those who had doubted that Auschwitz, known as the death camp, had really been as bad as described by the Russians, now had to face the truth of a whole series of concentration camps in Europe, with names like Belsen, Buchenwald, Dachau and Ravensbruch, discovered by British and American armies in their progress through Germany. Their reality was proved by newsreel films shown at the cinemas by Gaumont British News and Pathé News. Audiences gasped and then fell silent as the dreadful truth was unfolded. Instead of gas chambers as at Auschwitz, these prisoners had simply been left to perish of starvation and disease. Horrified troops discovered the dead and the dying, skeletal bodies lying in heaps, and it was said that the overwhelming stench could be smelt for miles around. The weekly magazine *Picture Post* devoted a whole issue to this dreadful discovery, and Ernest and Devora Munday could only imagine the last days of Jonny and Ayesha's parents and their baby brother Benjamin, lost in this indescribable hell. Having no words, they wept together, and the dreadful facts could not be kept from Miriam and Ayesha; newspapers were hidden from Ruth and Sarah, and their teachers at school also tried with partial success to shield them from the mass annihilations of their race; Ernest wondered if the facts would be pushed down into their subconscious minds, to re-emerge as neuroses later in life.

On a mild Saturday evening in late April, Rebecca arrived home in her uniform, wearied after trying to sort out the problems at Yeomans' Farm. She found her mother holding a letter.

'I've received this today, Becky.'

Rebecca sank down on the sofa. 'Oh, yes? Who's it from, and what's it about?' she asked, stretching herself and yawning. Her mother answered with a question.

'Will you be coming to church tomorrow, Becky?'

'Yes, unless there's more skirmishing at Yeomans' Farm. Billy's threatening to give it up altogether, but he can't; it belongs to the two little boys – and as for Pamela—'

'You're always having trouble with that man – but listen, Becky, this is important.' She spread the short letter on her lap.

'Oh, my God, it's not from Geoffrey Bannister, is it?'

'No, it's from my sister Grace.'

Rebecca sat up sharply. 'Oh? What does she want?'

'She wants us to be reconciled, Becky. She says she'll never make any claim on you, other than as an aunt.'

'I should hope not!' Rebecca's pretty mouth had hardened.

'She'll be at church tomorrow morning, and she begs for us to talk to her afterwards. She longs to be forgiven, and all you'd have to do is touch her hand and smile, Becky. It's ridiculous to go on like this, when there's so much real suffering in the world.'

'I'm sorry, Mother, the very thought of touching that woman repels me, and I shall never forgive her. She's lucky to have Doreen as her daughter after the way she treated the poor girl. No, Mother, I can't, and please don't ask me.'

'But Becky dear, when we say the Lord's Prayer we ask for our trespasses – our sins to be forgiven, as we forgive those who sin against us,' said Isabel seriously, saddened to see her daughter's face so closed and unyielding. At that moment they heard the front door bang, and Sir Cedric's steps approaching rapidly. He strode into the room.

'Haven't you had the wireless on? Don't tell me you haven't heard the news! Italy has surrendered to the Allies, and Mussolini's been executed by his own countrymen!'

'Thanks be to God!' cried Isabel, getting up to exchange a kiss with him. 'We shall have a full church tomorrow, then, to give thanks!'

'Shall we celebrate with a bottle of Beaujolais?' he asked, beaming. 'I'll fetch one up from the cellar!'

But Rebecca had stood up, clasping her hands together. 'Stefano – I must go to him. This changes everything. I must go to him now!'

'Not at this hour, Becky, it's gone six, and they'll be at supper—' Isabel began, but Rebecca had speedily left the manor and was on her way to Yeomans' Farm; skirting the farmhouse, she took the lane that ran beside the field where the POW's hut stood, and climbed over the familiar stile to get to it. No one was in sight, and as she approached the hut she heard a low murmuring of men's voices in unison. Of course! It was Saturday evening, and Father Orlando would be celebrating Mass with them. She waited in silence until the Mass was ended, and the priest left, accompanied by Paolo to his car. As soon as Paolo caught sight of her, he called to Stefano, who hurried towards her, holding out his hand and silently beckoning her to a sheltered corner in an adjoining barley field, protected by a thick hawthorn hedge, where they had sometimes met to talk. Stefano had been much teased about this, but today the others agreed to look away, and as soon as they were out of sight, she threw her arms around his neck.

'Stefano! Have you not heard? We're not enemies any more – that's official!'

He gently drew back from her a little, and she saw that there were tears in his dark eyes. She slowly withdrew her arms, and stared into his face.

'What's the matter, Stefano? This changes everything, don't you see?'

'Yes, and this changes for us, *cara mia*, when I and these friends of mine will return to Italy when a troopship is available,' he said almost sorrowfully. 'We must soon part, and I cannot offer you anything, nor can I ask you to make a promise. It would not be right.'

'But Stefano, I love you – don't you love me, too?' she asked in dismay. 'And now you're *free*, so we don't need to hide it any more. Why does that make you sad?'

'We must wait, Rebecca. The war with Germany is not yet over, and all Europe is in turmoil. We must keep – we must hold our wishes until the time is right, and until that day comes I must say nothing.'

'But you do love me, don't you, Stefano?' she persisted, suddenly afraid that his interest in her had been just a game on his part, to relieve the boredom and helplessness of being a prisoner of war. 'Tell me the truth, for God's sake!'

'This is not a time to make promises, we must wait and see what happens when Germany yields, *cara mia*. Now is too early, we must wait and see,' he repeated. 'Do not make it difficult for me, I beg of you. You must go now.'

Silent and bewildered, she let him take her arm and lead her back to the stile, helping her to climb over it. He kissed her cheek, and whispered, '*Addio, Rebecca mia*', then stood watching her as she walked away, her eyes bright with unshed tears and unaware of the conflict raging within his heart.

Ten days later Germany capitulated, and surrendered to the Allies unconditionally. This was no Armistice as in 1918: this was *victory* – the end of the Second World War in Europe, and Hitler was reported to have committed suicide. Tuesday the eighth of May was announced as VE-Day, and great were the thanksgiving and celebrations. The war was truly over! In London the King and Queen with the two princesses appeared on the balcony of Buckingham Palace with Winston Churchill, and people roared themselves hoarse with cheering. There was dancing in the streets, and in Everham free beer flowed from two barrels in public houses competing with each other, which proved not to be a good idea.

Only at the offices of Munday and Pascoe, chartered accountants of Everham, was there silence.

'Victory in Europe is only half a victory,' Devora Munday told the children. 'We'll have our party when both David and Jonny are home.'

At the home of the Nuttalls in Rectory Road a visitor knocked on the door at mid-morning, and Doreen came to answer. Standing on the doorstep was Rebecca Neville, tall and graceful in a summery dress. Doreen stared in surprise; her cousin had not visited this house for as long as she could remember. She smiled and drew back the door to let Rebecca in.

'Thank you, Doreen. Can you take me to your mother?'

'Oh, yes, er, Rebecca, she's in the kitchen. Just come this way.'

When Grace Nuttall looked up from the kitchen sink where she was peeling potatoes, her face drained of all colour. She opened her mouth but no words would come. It was left to Rebecca to say the greeting.

'The war's over, Aunt Grace.' She held out her hand, and Grace seized it and kissed it.

'Oh, Rebecca, my – my dear, you've come after all.' She began to tremble like a leaf. 'Forgive me, please forgive me for everything.'

'I forgive you, Aunt Grace, and so does my mother,' said Rebecca, gathering the woman into her arms, for she looked likely to faint. 'The war's over, and – and we must be at peace, too.'

When Tom and Rob came into the kitchen in answer to Doreen's excited call, they shared in the reconciliation. Tom Munday, wiping away a tear, said that this was what he had hoped and prayed for, and there were smiles, tears and kisses all round.

'And where's Isabel?' asked Tom. 'Why hasn't she come too?'

'Mother doesn't know I've come here,' Rebecca confessed. 'It was something I had to do on my own – but she'll be so happy when I tell her – and then we must all celebrate VE-Day together!'

* * *

That evening the celebrations in Everham drew crowds of people from surrounding villages, and John Richardson called on Valerie Pearson to invite her to join him there.

'Come on, darling, we can't get to London, but there'll be a rare knees-up in Everham,' he'd told her. 'Get your glad-rags on, and we'll go and paint the town red, white and blue!'

Mrs Pearson was at first dubious, but Richardson persuaded her that this was a very special occasion, and that it was positively Valerie's duty to celebrate it with him. He then kissed the old lady respectfully on her cheek, and whispered, 'You can't deny your future son-in-law – *Mother*,' at which she smiled and told him not to keep Valerie out too late.

At six o'clock that evening the pair got on a noisy, crowded train to Everham, where the market place was thronging with revellers, singing, dancing and indulging in kisses as free as the beer. John eagerly downed a pint of it, and handed her one which she drank, grimacing at the bitterness – but she was determined to be part of this historic occasion, so when John handed her a large glass of port wine, she smiled and drank it all, thinking how delicious it was, and what a wonderful place this was to be on such a great day.

'All right, darling?' John asked, and she nodded.

'We'll remember Victory Night, won't we, John?'

'We most certainly will, darling – my little sweetheart.' He downed another glass, and leant against her, kissing her on the mouth. She felt his hand slide down her back to rest on her bottom, which he squeezed.

'My little Valerie – thought about you all the time I was over there – every moment I was dreaming of being this close.' She could feel his hard erection through their clothes, which she disliked and tried to discourage.

'You mustn't – you must let go of me, John!'

'Know what I want to do, darling, up against a wall!' he said thickly, and she felt herself being pushed back hard against the bricked entrance to a wood yard, now locked.

Her head was spinning, and she tried to struggle. 'Let me go, John – *now*!'

But his hand was up the skirt of her dress, pushing her thighs apart, trying to pull at her knickers and thrusting his exposed and swollen member against her flesh.

'No! Y-you let me go, g-get me go!' The beer and wine she had drunk was blurring her speech, and she was powerless to help herself.

'C'mon, li'l darling, they're all doing it, up against a wall!' he panted, and then groaned aloud: she felt a warm stickiness running down her right leg. The market square seemed to be reeling around her, and she made an ineffectual effort to push him away.

'Good – that was good,' he said, grinning stupidly, and hiccuped. 'Look at 'em, they're all up against a wall!'

To her utter dismay, she saw a circle of cheering spectators gathered around them.

'That was a good one, mate, give 'er another!' shouted a man's hoarse voice, and a woman giggled. John slumped against her, and the crowd jeered, singing, 'Up against a wall,' swaying to the obscene, tuneless rhythm. Near to them a man was pushing a drunken girl against the wall and openly violating her. Valerie moaned and closed her eyes, falling into the blackness of a nightmare. Until from far away she heard a voice calling to her.

'Miss Pearson! Miss Pearson, are you all right?' She opened her eyes and out of the blurred sea of faces saw one that she thought she recognised. It was Nick Grant, Miss Temple's evacuee, now a serious-faced boy looking older than his thirteen years.

'Is that you, N-Nick?' Her voice was weak. 'I can't get away!'

He called over his shoulder, and there followed a shout and a scuffle, then a firm arm encircled her, and Richardson howled with pain as a punch landed on his injured shoulder.

'All right, Valerie, I'm here.' It was Philip Saville's voice and Philip Saville's hand quickly readjusting her dress. He took her right arm in his. 'You take her other arm, Nick, and we'll get her out of this lot! I suppose the Perrin boys had better pick *him* up. If there's a train or a bus going, we'll get on it, otherwise we'll have to walk.'

'Oh, *no*, we don't want to go home, Mr Saville,' protested Charlie and Joe who had come with Philip and Nick to join the Victory celebrations in Everham. Philip now realised his mistake.

'This is no fit place for you boys, too much drunken behaviour,' he said firmly. 'What you can do is to help – er – this man come to his senses, and walk him along with us, if he's not too heavy for you. Pretend you're policemen!'

The boys eagerly accepted the idea of being police constables, and hauled Richardson up between them, placing his arms over their shoulders. He gave another howl of pain.

'Careful, he's got a bad shoulder where he was shot,' warned Philip. 'Steady as you go – he's going to feel sorry in the morning.' And for more reasons than one, he added silently.

There was no transport available, so the little party set out to walk the four miles to North Camp. Halfway along they came to a bench seat where Philip said they should rest for a few minutes. He sat Valerie down between himself and Nick, with Richardson on the other side of Nick, but the man was so helplessly drunk that he had to be supported by the boys to sit upright, much to their amusement, as well as the fact that he had copiously wet himself.

The exercise and fresh air had cleared Valerie's head a little, and she was beginning to realise where she was, and what had happened: it was too awful to contemplate.

'Are you feeling a little better now, Valerie?' Philip whispered.

She gave a moan, and held up her head to answer sensibly – but all she could say was, 'I can't marry him, Philip, I can't, I *can't*! I can't marry him!' Her voice rose with each word, and when Richardson gave a loud hiccup, the boys could not help laughing. Philip gently drew her head down onto his shoulder and whispered, 'All right, Valerie, all right, my dear, you don't have to. Sssh, don't cry, you're safe now.'

These were comforting words, but never in her life had Valerie Pearson experienced such shame and humiliation.

Arriving at North Camp in the twilight, Saville directed the Perrin boys to the house adjoining Thomas and Gibson's, to deliver John to his father. He and Nick led Valerie to Miss Temple's cottage where she drank two glasses of water, went to the outdoor lavatory, and was helped to wash her face.

'What on earth has happened, Philip?' asked his aunt.

'I'm sorry about this, Enid, but it wasn't her fault. I'll take her home now and think of a story to tell Mrs Pearson. Wish me luck!'

His bewildered aunt stared after him as he set off with Valerie, to confront her horrified mother.

291

'I'm sorry, Mrs Pearson, but she was taken ill, and almost fainted – and there was no bus or train, so I've walked her home. She needs to go to bed straight away, and get a good night's sleep,' he said, trying to show sympathy while making light of the situation. As he returned to the cottage, he thought he'd better send an apology to Perrin and his wife, for taking their sons to see such a spectacle.

And that was how Valerie Pearson and John Richardson returned from the celebrations of Victory Night at Everham.

Dora Goddard and her friends were waiting to be demobbed from the ATS. As well as the euphoria at the ending of the war, there was a certain regret at the loss of the camaraderie they had shared through the adventures of those dangerous years, and they vowed to keep in touch on their return to civilian life. Her friend Gwen had married a GI, so looked forward to sharing a new life with him in the USA. Dora had heard that there might be opportunities for women with her qualifications at the British Broadcasting Corporation. It would be a first step towards saving up to travel to the USA, but for the time being she said nothing about this to her mother and grandfather.

At Hassett Manor Rebecca's joy at the end of the war in Europe was somewhat dampened by Stefano's strange reaction, and on visiting the camp again, he said they were all making plans to see their families as soon as they could be repatriated; Allied troops returning home were given priority over POWs when a ship became available, and Stefano did not give her an opportunity to speak with him in private, only in the company of the other men.

'I expect he's concerned about his family in Milan, and anxious to see how they are after all this time,' her mother said, 'and it's quite natural that he feels he can't make any plans for the future.' But Rebecca could not fail to discern her parents' satisfaction at Ghiberti's attitude, and decided that when the time came for the POWs to leave North Camp for Southampton and the ship that was to take them home, she would insist on speaking to him, in front of her parents if necessary, to declare her intention to join him in Milan as soon as she was demobbed from the Women's Land Army. Meanwhile she carried out her duties towards the land girls in her region, many of whom wanted to stay where they were, having become part of the families on whose farms they worked. Farmers who had been slave drivers and treated the girls unfairly were soon left without their labour; Billy Yeomans was one such, and Rebecca had the pleasure of telling him that the Women's Land Army was to be disbanded, and he was no longer entitled to a land girl's assistance.

Valerie's hand shook as her mother handed her the envelope that had come in today's post, addressed to her in Philip Saville's writing. Mrs Pearson had said very little about her daughter's early return from Everham on Victory night, in the company of Mr Saville instead of John Richardson; she only remarked that Valerie looked pale the next morning.

'Mr Saville said you were taken ill,' she said. 'Are you feeling better after a night's sleep?'

Valerie, who felt dreadful, both physically and emotionally, answered that she felt fine; it was just that there had been too much drinking and bad behaviour in the town square, and

Mr Saville had offered to bring her home, for which she was grateful.

'And what about John?' asked Mrs Pearson about her future son-in-law, or so he had described himself.

'I think he came home, too, though I can't be sure, there was such a crowd of people drinking and dancing and – oh, Mother, I was just so thankful when Mr Saville – he was there with Nick and the Perrin boys – when he came and said he'd take me home,' said Valerie, not wanting to open the letter in front of her mother. She ate no breakfast, and as soon as she could get to her room, sat down on the bed, tore the envelope open, and read it in fear.

'Dear Valerie,' he had written. *'I hope that you are now recovered from the fainting attack on Tuesday night, and whether there is any service I could do for you or your mother. With your permission I would like to call on you as soon as you are feeling better.*
With my very best wishes,
Philip Saville.'

Valerie could have wept with relief. Dear Philip – he was clearly not intending to tell the truth about their encounter in Everham on that terrible night, but he sounded truly concerned about her. She told her mother of his wish to call on them, and when she went out to buy a loaf of bread, she deliberately left the letter on the table for Mrs Pearson to read. She waited two days before replying, thanking him for his kindness, and saying that she had recovered and was back at work at The Limes.

The following day he was at the door when she returned

from work. She blushed crimson and could hardly meet his eyes. Her mother invited him in, smiling.

'Come in, Mr Saville. I'm pleased to have a chance to thank you for your care of Valerie when she was taken ill on Tuesday night. It sounds as if there was a lot of rowdiness – such a pity to spoil the thanksgiving for Victory.'

'I agree, Mrs Pearson,' he said seriously. 'I'd taken Nick and the Perrin boys to join in the celebrations, but we all had to leave – the place wasn't fit for children.'

'You can guess how I felt when I saw you on the doorstep instead of John. What happened to him?'

Philip shook his head regretfully. 'I'm afraid he was in no fit state to look after a lady. There was just too much free alcohol.'

'You mean he was – intoxicated?'

'Yes. The poor chap must have been very sorry that he let himself down as he did.'

'How utterly disgusting!' she said indignantly. 'What on earth would Valerie have done if you hadn't been there?'

Philip noted Valerie's acute embarrassment, and shrugged. 'We must remember that he was wounded in the D-Day invasion. I believe he got home all right.'

Turning to Valerie, he smiled. 'I wonder if you and your mother would like to come to tea with my aunt this weekend? Enid would be delighted, and it would be a treat for her as well. Would you be able to come on Saturday?'

Valerie's eyes were still downcast, but her mother answered, 'How very kind of Miss Temple, yes, we'd love to come, wouldn't we, Valerie?' Mrs Pearson beamed, secretly relieved to hear Mr Saville's corroboration of what

Valerie had said; her own awful suspicions were therefore unfounded.

Valerie nodded and managed a smile. 'Thank you,' she murmured, briefly raising her head to meet his eyes. How good he was, she thought. How courteous and kind!

Mr Richardson senior was so ashamed on behalf of his son that he said nothing when John woke from a stupor on the Wednesday morning, and realised how disastrous the evening had been.

'I made a fool of myself, Dad, and I blame it on all the free beer,' he muttered, his eyes glazed and his head throbbing. The very sight of food made him feel sick, and his clothes and bedclothes needed to be washed.

'You must see to that yourself,' said his father coldly. 'I shan't ask Mrs McNab to do it.' He was referring to the charwoman who came in to do the house cleaning and washing.

'I'm sorry, Dad,' John repeated wretchedly. 'I'll apologise to Valerie and her mother.'

'You'll get the door slammed in your face, I shouldn't wonder.' Mr Richardson turned away and went into the shop to speak to Doreen, leaving poor John to his painful remorse.

As Philip had planned, his aunt and Mrs Pearson settled down to chat happily with each other after a tea and scones with last year's blackberry jam. They were full of praise for Mr Churchill who would win the coming General Election. After second cups of tea, Enid Temple knew her duty.

'Philip dear, there's a couple of notices to go in the parish magazine. Would you be kind enough to take them over to the Rectory for me? They should be in by today.'

'No problem, Enid,' he answered, getting up. 'Would you like to come too, Valerie? It's a lovely afternoon, just right for a stroll.'

Of course she would, and their walk to the Rectory and back achieved all that Philip Saville had hoped. If Tuesday evening had been the worst in Valerie's life, that Saturday afternoon was the very best.

He began by telling her that he was grateful to Lady Neville for bringing them together for the children's outings to *Pinocchio* and the pantomime. She nodded, and said she'd thought he was more interested in Doreen Nuttall. He assured her that poor Doreen had got the wrong idea about him, for which he blamed himself entirely, and spoke of his disappointment when he saw Valerie in the company of John Richardson.

'He wasn't worthy of you, Valerie,' he said, taking her hand. 'And neither am I, but at least I'm wiser now than I was. The war has changed us all.'

She was hardly able to believe what she was hearing, and making an effort to overcome her shyness, she replied softly, 'Yes, it has, Philip, and it's changed me, too.'

'If I may be allowed another chance, Valerie—' He stood still, and turned to face her as they stood outside the Rectory gate beneath an oak tree misted with the tender new foliage of May. Still holding her hand, he said, 'If I'm bold enough, if I dare to – to—' his words gave way to an unspoken question, and she answered it with a look and one word, 'Philip.'

And then he kissed her, and she responded, brimming over with happiness, all misunderstandings at an end. They were a man and a woman in love, destined to be husband and wife, father and mother.

CHAPTER FIFTEEN

1945

'Is that you, Becky? Come into the garden room – Sally's made tea and just taken her scones out of the oven!'

'Sounds lovely, Mother, I'll be with you as soon as I can. There's something I've got to do first.'

'What, Becky? What comes before tea and scones?'

'Sorry, Mother, but I have to go down to Yeomans' Farm and see Stefano. I just can't go on as we are, with him refusing to talk to me in private and acting so unlike himself – I'm going to insist that we lay our cards on the table!'

'No, Becky, no, no – wait.' Isabel looked at Sally in dismay. 'There's a letter for you, and you must read it first.'

'A letter? What letter? I'm not expecting one.'

'But you've got one, Becky, and you must come here and read it before you go anywhere.'

Rebecca came into the room where her mother and Sally sat. She frowned. 'You look glum – what's up?'

'Sit down, dear. It's no use going to see the POWs, because Stefano isn't there. He's left the camp with Mario.'

'*What*? Where have they gone? They can't be repatriated yet.'

'Do sit down, Becky, and here's the letter he left for you.'

'Oh, my God!' Rebecca's voice rose as she took the envelope from her mother.

'Listen, dear, do as your mother says – just sit down and take a cup of tea, and read the letter,' said Sally. Rebecca looked from one to the other with growing apprehension. Isabel longed to comfort her daughter, but first the truth had to be faced.

'Stefano came to see us this morning – your father and I. We so admired his honesty, his responsibilities to his parents. We didn't try to persuade him in any way, because we agreed with him. He's left the camp, and is on his way to Southampton to get on any boat that will cross the Channel – to Calais, to Amsterdam, any European port. Mario's with him, and they'll find their way overland by one means or another.'

Rebecca had torn open the letter and was reading Stefano's words; her hand went to her mouth. 'You forced him to write this! You sent him away without saying goodbye!'

'No, dear, it was his decision entirely,' said Isabel sadly. She called to her husband. 'Cedric, will you come, please?'

Sir Cedric, who had been waiting outside the door, now entered the room. 'My dear girl, what that young man says in the letter is true. Italy's at a low ebb, exhausted after the war, with poor prospects for employment. The car industry will be non-existent, and as he says, he can't offer you a home other than the one he lives in with his parents.'

Rebecca sat still as a statue, her face pale. 'I'd face all that and more.'

'There would indeed be a lot more to face, my dear,' Cedric went on, kindly but firmly. 'You'd have to forfeit your British nationality or be classed as an alien with no rights. You'd have to speak Italian for the rest of your life, and your children would be Italian by birth – and Roman Catholics. He's written it all down there – we didn't try to influence him, and he came to us of his own accord, we didn't send for him. As your mother says, we had to admire him.'

'How can he and Mario travel all that way without a penny to his name? And what about a passport?' demanded Rebecca, angry tears in her eyes as she questioned her parents.

'He and Mario have enough money for the journey, including bribes if needed,' said Cedric. 'The only advice we gave him was to take a friend for company. He's been very brave, my dear, and you must be brave too.'

'You gave him money.'

'Yes, Becky, we did.'

'And let him go without saying goodbye.'

'It was his wish, dear,' said Isabel. 'Please sit down now and have a cup of tea.'

'No, thank you. I'll go to my room.' And without another word, she left them.

The news of Philip Saville's engagement to Valerie Pearson took North Camp by surprise, and was generally approved. Mrs Pearson needed a little time to get used to the idea, and then became enthusiastic on her daughter's behalf. There were congratulations all round, especially from Lady Neville who told Philip it was what she had hoped for when she had put them both in charge of the children's visit to *Pinocchio* and the pantomime. One young woman who wept when she heard of it was Doreen Nuttall; her mother comforted her as well as she could, knowing that the disappointment would soon be forgotten. Rob and his father-in-law kept quiet about their brush with Saville when he'd come to visit Doreen, and thought his choice of Valerie was a good move. There was not much sympathy for John Richardson whose drunkenness on Victory night was talked about in North Camp, shocking the women and amusing the men. It became known that Philip, who had saved his money for years, was to purchase a house in North Camp, and that he and Valerie would share their home with Nick, to the boy's great joy, having no wish to return to his life of abuse in London.

Rebecca Neville managed to find out Stefano's address in Milan from one of the POWs, though he had told them not to disclose it. She wrote him a letter saying that she would wait indefinitely for him to send for her when he had picked up the threads of his life in his own country. A month passed with no reply, and she began to think that her letter had not reached him in the post-war chaos; she was about to write again when a letter arrived for her. With trembling fingers and racing heartbeat she opened it in her WLA office at Everham. He thanked her for her letter, which had reached him after a long and difficult journey with Mario across France and the Swiss Alps. He was reunited with his parents who had aged a great deal, but were looking better since his arrival. And he also wrote:

'There is a girl, Emilia, who said she would wait for me when I left, and so she has for these long years,

comforting my parents, especially when my father was
very ill with pneumonia. You will understand that I
have a duty towards her, and I shall be happy to marry
her as soon as things are more settled here. I shall
always remember you, Rebecca, and wish you great
happiness in the future with an English husband who
can provide for you as I cannot. May God bless you
and all your loved ones.

    S. Ghiberti'

She folded the letter and stared out of the window for several minutes. His message was clear and unequivocal, and she would not write to him again, though she would never know whether the loyal Emilia was a real person, or just a story he had made up to help her to forget the Italian prisoner-of-war that she had loved. Towards her parents she still felt resentment at the way they had interfered in her private life, as she saw it, and she resolved not to confide in them; let them go on thinking I'm waiting for him, damn them, she thought bitterly.

Close on the heels of the VE–Day celebrations came a general election, to elect a government to replace the coalition of the war years. Most of the ladies at the Circle were confident of an easy win for the Conservatives over the Labour Party. In the Tradesmen's Arms there was less certainty.

'It'll be the forces' vote that'll decide the outcome,' said Tom Munday, 'and maybe it's time for a change. The men coming home from the war after risking their lives and seeing their comrades killed – they won't want to go back to the old class system, neither will the industrial towns up north. Same with the young girls – they won't go back into service as housemaids and skivvies – not after taking over men's jobs at home during the war.'

'Maybe so, but old Churchill can't fail to win after all he's done,' said Eddie Cooper, and most of the regulars agreed.

The outcome was a Labour landslide. Winston Churchill retained his seat in the government, but he was no longer Prime Minister. His place was taken by a Mr Clement Attlee whom nobody in North Camp had heard of, and the indignation on Churchill's behalf was vociferous. At Hassett Manor, Cedric and Isabel foresaw the end of the pre-war inequality, and Isabel, a carpenter's daughter, was less surprised than her husband, a descendant of the old nobility that had bequeathed him his title. Besides, Isabel had something far more important on her mind: the return of her son Paul Storey, within days of her nephew David Munday. She and Sally and Rebecca took turns at holding him in a close, tearful embrace, and Cedric expressed his pleasure in having a son, though adopted, who would inherit Hassett Manor and its estate.

But Paul shook his head, and exchanged a smile with his mother as he replied, 'No, sir, I shall inherit something else. My father lost his life as a result of his experiences in that other war, and he also lost his faith. As a result of *my* experiences in this war, I have *found* faith, and I shall train for ordination in the Church of England, to carry on where he left off.'

Sir Cedric could not begrudge his wife her joy on hearing this, nor did he doubt that Paul's decision was a right one. To himself he argued that a clergyman had as much right to inherit an estate as any other man.

At Munday and Pascoe, chartered accountants, there was a joyful reunion as David Munday returned home, though Devora insisted that the war was not over, and there could be no partying until Jonathan also returned. She and Ernest tried not to dwell on what life must be like in a Japanese labour camp where prisoners were being forced to work on building a railway in pitiless heat, with only a handful of rice a day.

On the sixth day of August something happened which was finally to end the war and usher in a new age. All over the country and the civilised world people listened with awe to the wireless announcement that a new and terrible bomb had been dropped on the Japanese city of Hiroshima. It took time for the realisation to sink in that this weapon of destruction was like no other; while scientists spoke of splitting atomic particles, the listeners pondered on the devastation it had caused – a whole city obliterated and thousands of citizens killed by the deadly radiation. There was no refuge, no air raid shelter that could protect anybody from this instrument of death.

'The Japs have been left with no choice now,' was the consensus of opinion of all who looked upon the photographs of an enormous cloud, like a giant mushroom over the doomed city, the wide area of total devastation. 'They'll have to surrender now – they won't risk another one of *those*.'

But a day passed, and then another day, with no sign of a Japanese capitulation, no overture to the Allies from the Emperor, Hirohito. On the third day came news of a second atomic bomb dropped on the island town of Nagasaki, with the same terrible results, including radiation of the sea around the island. It brought about the surrender of Japan to the Allies. Victory over Japan! It was VJ-Day, celebrated in Britain with parties and bonfires.

There were a few voices, Sir Cedric Neville and the Reverend Alan Kennard among them, who expressed reservations about the mighty bomb which had caused hundreds of thousands of civilian deaths, but they were drowned out in the rejoicing that the war in Japan was over, and it meant the return of those prisoners of war, British, American and Australian, those of them who had survived the experience. Devora Munday still refused to rejoice until she saw the nephew who was as dear to her as a son – in fact she feared that the Japanese guards might kill their victims in revenge for the atom bomb; but mid-September brought news that Jonathan Pascoe had arrived home and was now in a Southampton hospital with severe malnutrition. Ernest and Devora went to see him as soon as they heard, and Devora wept at the sight of her once good-looking adopted son, now twenty-one years old, a living skeleton with decayed teeth and almost bald. They were warned to be very gentle as they embraced him because of the fragile state of his bones – yet he was *alive* and smiling at them in recognition! A doctor told them that he would recover, put flesh on his bones and grow some more hair, but that he would need to wear dentures. He was even able to joke with his parents.

'Being a Jew was no worse than being anybody else out there – they got us *all* building that bloody railway! We said it was the three aitches, Heat, Hunger and Hate, and it was the Hate that got us through – we wouldn't give in to the buggers!'

Now the war was truly over for Devora Munday, and

she held belated parties to which all their neighbours were invited. The little girls, Ruth and Sarah, now nine and seven years, had been returned to their Jewish parents in London; likewise Lily and Jim had tearfully left Hassett Manor. Ken and Dan, sturdy lads of ten and eight years, had no home or family, so were kept at the Rectory with the Kennards' two young daughters, and became their sons. Alan became rector when Roland Allingham took early retirement to look after his wife, whose mind was failing. Having lost their elder son at El Alamein, their younger never contacted them, though his name sometimes came up in the newspapers, as when cited in a society divorce, and being drunk and disorderly in the street – stories his mother resolutely ignored as malicious lies, for to her he was always their gallant war hero, the much-decorated Wing Commander Lester Allingham.

When the doorbell rang at the Nuttalls' home on a chilly October day, Grace did not at first recognise the tall, smiling man in the uniform of an American serviceman.

'Hi, Mrs Nuttall, pleased to see ya! Remember me? Gus Rohmer, alive and kicking and at your service. Here I am again to find the lovely Doreen if she hasn't been whirled away by some other lucky son of a gun!'

Grace's heart sank, for although the whole family had liked the young GI from Maine, she had no wish to lose Doreen to him or any other man.

'She's not in at this moment, she's at work, er, Gus.' Reluctantly she directed him to Thomas and Gibson's in the High Street.

'Thanks, Ma'am!' He touched his cap and set out to

find Doreen, while Grace went to tell Rob who was in his workshop.

'He's come back to claim her – to marry her – and I couldn't bear to lose her, Rob, not after all we've been through together,' she said, her eyes reflecting her anxiety.

'Don't worry, Gracie – he won't be so keen when he knows what happened.'

'Does he have to be told, Rob?'

'Well, yes – knowing our Doreen, she'd tell him herself sooner or later, forgetting all about that Saville man. No, our problem will be how to console her when he goes back to the USA, which I suppose is any day now – that's why he's came back to see if she's still here. Look, Grace, I'll tell him myself, and get it over with. He's a decent chap, and deserves the truth.'

And then he won't want her, thought Grace, secretly clinging to that hope.

Doreen greeted her long-absent GI with joy.

'*Gus!* Oh, Gus, I never thought you'd come back! Never thought I'd see you again!'

'Well, here I am, little girl, and you're as sweet as ever – sweeter, you look great! Missed me?'

'Oh, Gus, *how* I've missed you!' She held out her arms, and he enfolded her in a bear-hug which she eagerly returned.

'Mum and Dad thought you'd gone back to America, or that you'd been – oh, Gus, they thought you might have been killed!'

'No way, little Doreen, you were my sweet guardian angel when I was in the thick of it, and I was always dreaming about you. Ah, Doreen, baby – now the dream's come true!'

When Mr Richardson came into the shop as he often did, to help Doreen with an impatient customer, he found his lady assistant exchanging a passionate kiss with a happy GI.

'Oh, Mr Richardson, Gus is going to make me his GI bride!'

'Is he? Well, congratulations, Gus!' Wonder if he knows what she's been up to while he was away, thought Richardson. Somebody should tell him before she lets it slip out, poor kid. And I'll have to find another shop assistant.

Returning to the Nuttalls, the happy couple informed Doreen's parents that they were to be married, and that she would accompany Gus to a new life in the USA. Rob shot a glance at his wife.

'Your mother's getting dinner ready, Doreen, so you'd better go and help her. We'll give the women time to talk, Gus, while we go for a quick one at the Tradesmen's Arms.'

As they walked, Rob came straight to the point. 'If you want to marry our girl, there's something you have to know, Gus.' Rob forced the words out of his dry mouth. 'Since you were last here, she's given birth to a baby, and had it adopted.'

Gus stood still, his face registering his shock. 'For Christ's sake, who did it to her?'

'Another GI, I'm afraid – said he was a pal of yours, known as Chuck. It was only the one time he took her out. Her mother nearly went out of her mind when we realised what had happened.'

Having said what he had to say, Rob stood dreading the American's reaction.

Gus put an arm around Rob's shoulder. 'The unbelievable bastard,' he said quietly. 'I should have warned her about that sort of guy. My God, what you've all been through.'

'Yes, my wife had to go into hospital over it.' Rob did not add that they had sent Doreen away to a Mother and Baby Home, a fact about which he now felt ashamed.

Gus kept his arm on Rob's shoulder as he continued to speak in slow, measured tones.

'Thanks for telling me, Rob. It makes me even more determined to marry her. Look, I understand how it is with your Doreen. Her mind's like an innocent, trusting child's, and it makes her easy prey for reptiles like Chuck. I'd rather marry her and look after her than any of these smart girls who'd show me up for the dunce that I am. I want that sweet angel for my own, Rob, and you can trust me.'

Rob's throat tightened, and he could not speak.

'Come on, Rob, let's get that beer, or we'll be late for dinner.'

And so Doreen Nuttall's future was settled.

Lady Isabel Neville was unable to make up her mind what to do: how should she advise Geoffrey Bannister who had written to her again, asking if he might visit Hassett Manor before Christmas. It was already November in this year of victory, a time when autumnal mists thicken to fog, and the last of the leaves had fallen, blown by chill winds from the north-east. The war was over, Paul had returned and had applied to theological college, but the hardships of the home front remained: food and fuel rationing had become even more stringent. The Women's Land Army was being disbanded, though many of the girls wanted to remain where they were for the time being, and Rebecca's services as Regional Officer continued, though she knew that she must look for useful and challenging work to occupy herself in peace time. Isabel longed for an honest talk with her daughter, the sort they had shared in the past; but Rebecca was now an independent woman of nearly twenty-nine, and resisted confidences. When Isabel took a deep breath and made herself ask a question, the answer was brief and unemotional.

'Have you had any word from Stefano, Becky – since he went away?'

'Only that he's back in Milan.' Her tone forbade any further questioning, and her face was as expressionless as flint. Isabel's heart ached for her, but she dared not show any pity. Was Rebecca clinging to a hope that Stefano might return one day? Or did she intend to devote her life to a career – like training for the nursing profession or the Civil Service? Isabel had no way of knowing, and had no idea of how to answer Bannister. At last she turned to her faithful friend and confidante, Sally Tanner, who had been silently waiting to be consulted. Now she looked thoughtful, and smiled at the woman who had rescued her from despair and the temptations of alcohol in that other war, thirty years ago.

'I think you should be frank with him, Isabel, seeing that he's asking you straight out what you think of his chances with our Becky.'

'Yes, and I don't want to take away his last hope, Sally – he's so *right* for her in so many ways. On the other hand, I don't want to build up his hopes if she's not interested in him – and if she were to suspect that I'd invited him without telling her, it could make matters so much worse.'

'Yes, and that's why I think you should be honest with him, tell him that her heart's been broken by another man – you needn't say he was a prisoner of war who's gone back to his own country, just that he's left her for good, and she's not interested in any other.'

'That's very drastic, Sally, I don't want to hurt him, and to tell him *that* would hurt him badly,' said Isabel dubiously.

'Maybe so, but this is a case when you have to be cruel to be kind in the long run,' answered Sally firmly. 'Tell him to stay away for the sake of his own happiness!'

'But that sounds so unkind, Sally, I couldn't say that!'

'All right, then, tell him to come over and spoil her Christmas and his,' said Sally, not usually given to sarcasm. 'Spoil it for all of us with a big row!'

Isabel sighed at the sadness of the world, even after victory, and set about writing the letter, apologising for its contents. When she told her husband what she had done, and on Sally's advice, he agreed that it had been the right thing. And kept his own counsel.

Isabel Neville would rather have stayed at home. The two aspirin tablets she had swallowed had only partially relieved the throbbing headache behind her eyes, but she put on a determined smile at the last meeting of the Ladies' Circle before Christmas. At least a dozen had turned up on this damp, cold December afternoon at the Rectory where Mrs Kennard the rector's wife greeted them pleasantly.

'Today we're going to talk about Christmas preparations in the kitchen—'

'What, on our miserable rations?' an anonymous voice cut in.

'—and the theme is Christmas cheer unrationed! We're going to pool our ideas and suggestions for making the best use of what's available, and our first speaker is our friend Mrs Pearson, the future mother-in-law of our pianist!'

There was a burst of laughter and applause when Mr Saville rose from the piano stool and bowed low before them as Mrs Pearson came fussily forward, recipe book in hand. He's a very different Philip Saville to the one who first played for us, thought Isabel – and Mrs Pearson's another one whose life has been changed by the war. Her Valerie's going to be happily married, whereas my Rebecca – but no, such thoughts were futile.

Mrs Pearson's economy mincemeat was followed by Mrs Goddard's honey biscuits (Ernie Cooper kept bees), and Mrs Kennard's festive uses for local chestnuts.

'And now for a special treat, ladies – our own Lady Isabel is going to sing for us "The Holly and the Ivy", and we'll all join in with the refrain!'

Isabel stood by the piano and sang the old carol, each verse followed by the surprisingly sweet voices singing, *'Oh, the rising of the sun, and the running of the deer—'*

Isabel's eyes suddenly filled with tears, and she only just avoided faltering on the last verse. After the applause there was a break for tea and economy scones, accompanied by the usual buzz of talk, which turned to the subject of North Camp girls soon to leave home.

'My Doreen and her Gus will be with us for Christmas,' said Grace Nuttall. 'He should've sailed for the States a month ago, and Doreen should've followed in the New Year with a shipload of GI brides—'

'Babies and all,' added a voice, but Grace continued, 'but of course Gus wouldn't dream of leaving her behind, so they'll go out together as soon as he can book a cabin for them as paying passengers. Rob and I will miss her terribly, but at least we know she's got a devoted husband, so we don't have to worry about her – er – the future.'

There were significant nods and unspoken sympathy. Eyes turned to Isabel Neville as if they expected her to say something about Rebecca, now reconciled to Grace, but she was silent, and nobody dared question her. They all knew that romance had blossomed between Rebecca and an Italian POW who had left England, but there had been no recent news, and there was a whisper that she was waiting for him to send for her.

'And what about your Dora?' somebody asked Mrs Goddard.

'Oh, she's another one bound for America,' said Mary with deliberate cheerfulness. 'I mean, she hasn't lived at home since before the war, and the ATS gave her a taste for travel and adventure. She's got very good qualifications, and says she wants to work in New York, to start with.'

The ladies exchanged doubtful glances, clearly wondering why Dora could not settle with her mother and grandfather, and marry some nice local boy. Mary did not tell them that Dora would be spending Christmas at home, and was bringing a friend with her – someone called Pip Seagrave who, as an army sergeant, had taught Dora to drive at her first posting at Inchcombe, and had taken her out before she was posted to the anti-aircraft unit in London. Now it seemed that he had come in search of her again, so he must be serious. It might not come to anything, but Mary and her father had decided not to say anything now, but to wait and see.

'And how's your Rebecca, Lady Neville?' asked old Mrs Tomlinson, now retired from the district council, and losing her former quick discernment. The ladies listened eagerly for the reply, but Isabel was brief.

'She's still needed in the Land Army. Quite a lot of the

girls are staying put.' She turned to Philip. 'And what about that nice boy Nick, how is he?'

'He's fine, Lady Neville, thank you. Valerie and I are going to apply to change his name to Saville when we're married.'

This brought a chorus of delighted approval, and no further mention was made of Rebecca, at least not openly.

'Surprise, darling!' called Cedric as Isabel returned to the Manor where Sally greeted her with tea and biscuits. 'Our son, the future Bishop of North Camp has arrived!'

'Oh, *Paul*, how lovely! We weren't expecting you until the end of the week!' She held out her arms to her son, at the same time giving her husband a grateful look for his little joke and the way he had said *our* son. She sat down with him on the sofa. 'Now we shall all be home for Christmas, and Rebecca will be so thrilled. Now, we want to know all about theological college. Do they teach you how to deal with awkward parishioners?'

'Yes, they do, Mother,' he replied, popping a biscuit into his mouth. 'Mostly it's done by listening to them and telling them how valuable they are to the parish – and if they're in any sort of doubt or uncertainty—'

'I know, you tell them to pray about it,' said Isabel with a smile.

'Yes, pray by all means, and then let *love* show them the way.'

'Really? You say that to tiresome old ladies, Paul? Go away with you, you're pulling my leg!'

'Yes, that's right, Mother – and to tiresome young ones as well.'

She did not see the glance exchanged between Sir Cedric and Sally Tanner. Sally got up to refill the teapot.

'You're hiding something, Paul,' said his mother. 'And by what you say, I suspect there's a young lady in the picture – am I right?'

'You might be, Mother, you might be,' he said with infuriating calm. 'Be patient, and all will be revealed in time.'

Isabel shrugged in bewilderment. Paul put down his cup, brushed a crumb from his jacket, and said casually, 'By the way, I'm expecting a friend over this evening. He should be here round about now, actually.' He got up and went to the window. 'Oh, look, here he comes, right on cue!'

Isabel jumped up and rushed to the window. And saw Geoffrey Bannister coming up the drive, his arm linked with Rebecca's. They caught sight of the faces at the window, and smiled and waved.

'But Sally, you told me to warn him off – to tell him not to come!' protested Isabel, happy as she was at seeing her daughter and Geoffrey together, talking easily, laughing at Paul's cheeky jokes.

'Yes, Isabel dear, that's what I told you, and I thought to myself if he's half the man I take him for, he'll come right over.'

'*Sally!* And there I was thinking how harsh you were. And yet how right!'

But in fact Geoffrey had not come over straight away when he received the unwelcome letter, but had contacted his old university friend Paul who had been away fighting for most of the war. The two of them had met, and Paul confirmed that his sister's heart had indeed been broken.

'Cedric did tell me on the quiet that it had been an Italian prisoner-of-war, so you can imagine the talk. He was a decent fellow, and did the decent thing when the war was over, but

Becky was bereft, and never said another word about it to the parents. Look, you'd better hear all about it from her.'

'But if she's so upset – and her mother's told me to keep away—'

'Hang on, I'll give her a ring at her Everham office, and ask if I can come over and speak to her – and you'd better come over as well, old son!'

When Rebecca saw her brother and Geoffrey Bannister come into the WLA office in the fading December light, it was as if a pent-up dam was released in her heart, and she burst into tears. Paul held her in his arms and gently pacified her, then released her to Bannister. She learnt that there was no need to tell him about Stefano, whose last letter had mentioned his forthcoming marriage to Emilia.

'I knew he wouldn't write again, but I was angry with my parents, and didn't tell them,' she confessed. 'I know I should have done, and I know Stefano was right, but it was just that – oh, Geoffrey—' Her tears gushed forth again, and he tenderly drew her head down onto his shoulder. Paul gave him a thumbs-up sign, and quietly left the office.

'I know, Rebecca, I know, it was very hard losing such a splendid man – an honourable man. It's been a long, long time since I first loved you before the war, and it's changed us all – but I love you still, and I'll wait for as long as it takes for you to recover. Don't worry, my love, don't worry.' He stroked her hair as he spoke, and she gradually quietened. Paul came in to say briefly that he was returning to the Manor, and told them to follow in about an hour's time. 'To give me a chance to prepare the ground and get the red carpet out,' he said with a wink, though privately he sent up a heartfelt prayer of thanks.

EPILOGUE

Christmas 1945

On Christmas Eve at Hassett Manor the Nevilles welcomed Mr and Mrs Bannister and their son Geoffrey from Shaftesbury, to share their festivities. It was decided that only Paul would attend the midnight Holy Communion service, but that they would all go to St Peter's on Christmas morning, as a family.

Sally provided a good supper – her own vegetable and lentil soup, a cottage loaf baked that morning, cold ham with apple chutney and pickled onions. The talk was lively, for people were still rejoicing that the war no longer hung over the country. Mr Bannister was no longer a member of Parliament, having lost his seat at the July election, and he was playing a more active role on the board of directors of a shoe manufacturing firm, drawing up new regulations to protect the interests of the workers.

'But you'll be much occupied with constituency business,

'no doubt,' observed Cedric, and was surprised at Bannister's wry smile.

'Actually, I'm going to leave politics to Geoffrey in the future. He'll be standing at the next election, whenever that will be.'

'Yes, as a Labour candidate,' explained Geoffrey, at which there was a gasp of surprise, followed by silence until Isabel spoke.

'Yes, it looks as if it's going to be a socialist world in the future, Geoffrey. The whole world's been changed by the past six years. May you have a good career!'

Geoffrey gave her a grateful smile, though no other comments were made by the parents, for their opinions had all been well expressed already; but the topic of change continued to dominate.

'Some say there won't be any more wars because the atom bomb will be the great deterrent,' said Paul. 'And I've heard others who think that it will bring about the end of the world and humanity with it. Where do we all stand on this apocryphal issue?'

Sally Tanner spoke up. 'Same as where we stood before, Paul. None of us can see into the future, so we must go on as we are, doing the best we can.'

'Good old Sally, that's as wise a saying as any I've heard in a sermon!' Paul said admiringly. 'I wonder if Alan Kennard will say anything about it tomorrow.'

But the rector's sermon was one of thanksgiving, though the darker side of the war was acknowledged in a personal and compassionate way.

'Our thoughts go out to all families who've suffered the loss of friends and families in the bombing, and to those whose sons, husbands and fathers have not returned from the fighting; some of you are here with us on this Christmas morning.' He looked around at the congregation that filled St Peter's, and continued, 'And there are those who have welcomed their servicemen home but have had re-adjustments to make. There are the men who came home maimed or scarred in some way.' He did not look at Jack Nuttall, but his hearers knew his meaning. 'And there have been fine young men broken in health by starvation and ill treatment in prison camps.' He paused, and Isabel knew that he was thinking of her brother Ernest's adopted son Jonny, who would be worshipping with the family in a synagogue. 'And there have been men of extraordinary courage in defending our shores who have succumbed to temptations in peacetime, and drifted away from their sorrowing parents.' They all knew that he spoke of the Allinghams who had moved away from North Camp. 'We must pray for them all, my friends, as we give thanks for our own blessings. Let us kneel now, here in the Lord's presence.'

On her knees Isabel Neville rejoiced from her heart that this first post-war Christmas at Hassett Manor was surely the happiest ever.